THE CALL OF THE VOID

ALSO BY S. M. GAITHER

The Shadows & Crowns series:

The Song of the Marked
A Twist of the Blade
A Crown of the Gods
The Queen of the Dawn

The Serpents & Kings series

The Shift Chronicles

The Drowning Empire series

SHADOWS & CROWNS
BOOK THREE

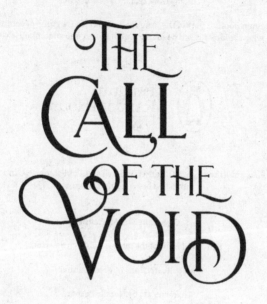

THE CALL OF THE VOID

S. M. GAITHER

PENGUIN BOOKS

PENGUIN BOOKS

UK | USA | Canada | Ireland | Australia
India | New Zealand | South Africa

Penguin Books is part of the Penguin Random House group of companies
whose addresses can be found at global.penguinrandomhouse.com

Penguin
Random House
UK

First published by S. M. Gaither/Yellow Door Publishing, INC in 2021
Published in Penguin Books 2023
001

Map illustrations by S. M. Gaither

Character art by Natalie Bernard

Printed and bound in Great Britain by Clays Ltd, Elcograf S.p.A.

The authorised representative in the EEA is Penguin Random House Ireland,
Morrison Chambers, 32 Nassau Street, Dublin D02 YH68

A CIP catalogue record for this book is available from the British Library

ISBN: 978–1–804–94584–1

www.greenpenguin.co.uk

MIX
Paper | Supporting
responsible forestry
FSC® C018179

Penguin Random House is committed to a
sustainable future for our business, our readers
and our planet. This book is made from Forest
Stewardship Council® certified paper.

For all of the broken but still bright lights

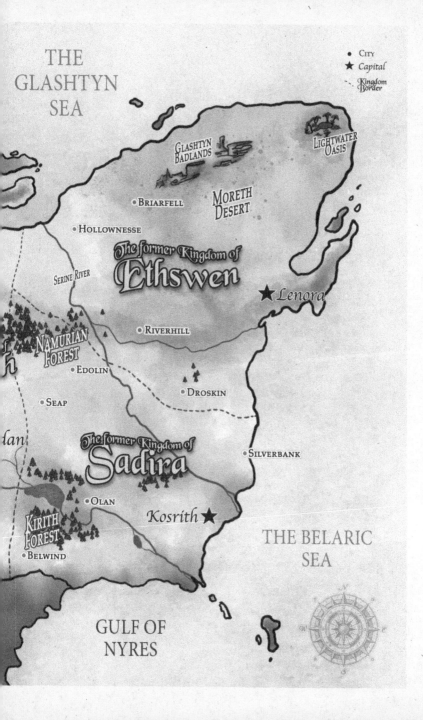

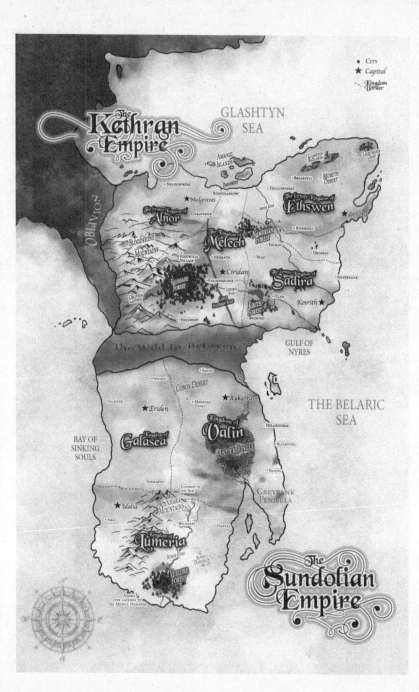

THE HIERARCHY OF GODS

Rook · Ice · Bone · Serpent · Fire

Sun · Star · Moon · Sky · Storm

Stone · Oak · Mtn. · Sand · Ocean

CHAPTER 1

GONE.

The door to the haven of the Moon Goddess was dark. Empty. Closed.

Casia was gone.

She was safe.

And that was the one thing—the *only* thing—that mattered to Elander. It was all he wanted to think about.

But as he turned away from the doors that led to the other godhavens, he came face-to-face with the divine beast he had once served: Malaphar. The Dark God. The Rook God. Chaoswalker, Nightbringer... A hundred different names existed for this towering beast.

None completely captured the terrifying reality of him.

The upper-god stepped closer, adjusting his grip on

his glowing white sword, and Elander could no longer dwell on what had become of Casia.

Rage twisted Malaphar's expression into something monstrous—something far less human-looking than the mask he had donned at the beginning of this meeting. The rest of his body was also changing as he moved. The black wings upon his back unfurled, the tip of one grazing the wall to his right, knocking an ornamental sconce to the ground and extinguishing the flame it held. A deeper darkness sank over the room, and Malaphar's eyes seemed to glow within that darkness, burning as bright and as terrible as his sword.

He lifted his hand, and a swirl of black feathers encircled his weapon.

When the feathers fell away, the sword he held had transformed into two separate blades, each pulsing with silvery-black energy.

He attacked.

Elander dove forward, slipping underneath the sweeping swords and narrowly edging past the upper-god's leg. He rolled across the marble floor of the Oblivion Tower that had once been his haven. Fought his way back to his feet—

Just in time to twist wildly and avoid a second strike.

Bits of that silvery-black energy fell from the Rook God's blades as he swung them, filling the space with swirling threads of magic that burned Elander's skin whenever he wasn't quick enough to avoid them.

He sprinted to the other side of the room, seeking cleaner air. There wasn't far to go in the circular space before he met a wall. He braced a hand against it and tried to catch his breath. Tried to think calmly. His gaze darted back to the last place he'd seen Casia; his eyes always seemed to seek her whenever he needed calm here lately.

But she was no longer there to find, of course.

Only the portal she'd disappeared through.

Even as Malaphar closed in, something about the portal caught his gaze—a pinprick of light in the center of it. He focused his senses, felt the distinctive energy still radiating from it...and with it came a creeping sense of dread.

The doorway was not as closed as he'd thought.

If he could do nothing else, he needed to *fully* close off that doorway. Destroy it, if that was what it took to give Casia a greater head start—to make it more difficult to follow her.

The only problem was that the Rook God now stood between him and that doorway.

He knew what he needed to do. But the question was *how* to fight his way past that monstrous god—and it was one he had been grappling with for weeks now. Because this fight went against the very laws of their world. Against the hierarchy that had built that world and filled it with life and death and everything between.

He had agreed to serve this upper-god, not challenge him.

He couldn't overpower the upper-god's magic—his own magic *derived* from Malaphar, and thus it was more limited by design. This was a battle Elander was not meant to win. He would be a fool to even fight it, honestly.

He foolishly scanned the room for a weapon all the same.

There was a sword on the floor a short distance away. *Caden's*. It had been knocked from the lesser-spirit's hand when Malaphar had attacked him, right before...

No.

Elander couldn't think about the things that had happened before. Only the present. Only the sword.

He raced toward it, grabbed it, and swiped it upward just as the Rook God descended with his dual blades falling in furious arcs.

Sparks of magic flew in all directions as the three blades collided.

The force of Malaphar's attack would have sent a normal human through the floor, but some of Elander's once-divine strength still remained—and this particular sword of Caden's was Elven-made, which helped it withstand the dark energy of Malaphar's blades better than most weapons would—so Elander managed to stay on his feet, and to push back.

Gripping Caden's sword more tightly, he pushed until that sword was locked against the crossed blades of the Rook God's. For several painfully long moments they remained in this stalemate, until Elander's arms began to shake and his balance threatened to slip against the slick marble floor.

He rolled abruptly away, throwing the upper-god off-balance, and then he backed up, catching his breath and getting a more proper grip on his weapon as he went.

The upper-god strode after him with calm, unhurried movements.

They circled each other, swords at ready, and Elander tried to spot any weaknesses he might manage to strike.

He'd seen Malaphar take this form before, but not often. His face was vaguely human, but had too-sharp edges wrapped in unsettlingly thin, mottled grey skin. The upper-god's armor was black as night, and the entirety of him was surrounded by the swirling shadows of his magic, making it difficult to tell where the armor ended and the physical body began.

But at least he was currently in a physical form... which meant he *could* be struck, if only Elander could figure out where.

Malaphar slashed one of his swords at Elander's chest.

Elander knocked it aside, sidestepped, and swung

forward in one fluid motion—only to have his blade parried away just as quickly.

Again and again they clashed this way, the metallic cries of steel echoing around them, the air growing chokingly thick with the Rook God's magic. Angry ribbons of Dark power siphoned off the god's hulking figure after every strike that Elander managed to defend against. Every successful parry only angered the god and his magic further, and soon the same desperate thought from before wound its way through Elander's mind.

You can't win this battle.

They both knew it.

The Rook God was toying with him.

But Elander pressed on, spinning and swinging until finally he noticed a flash of pallid skin amongst the dark shadows and armor—

He ducked to avoid a vicious swing, rose with a sweeping cut of his own, and the tip of his sword brushed the exposed skin of Malaphar's wrist. A hiss of pain escaped the upper-god. The pained noise quickly turned to laughter, but it didn't matter.

It had already betrayed a weakness.

Elander darted forward again without hesitation, aiming this time for the opposite wrist.

His blade cut deeply into that wrist. What looked like shadows spilled in lieu of blood, and one of the swords fell from Malaphar's grip as the upper-god jerked his hand away.

6

The sound of the weapon clattering against the floor was a small victory, one that sent renewed strength and determination surging through Elander's blood. He briefly considered knocking the second blade from Malaphar's other hand, but he settled for kicking the first sword across the room.

The Rook God bared his teeth as he watched it spin away. He moved toward it with the same unhurried, almost mocking stride as before.

Distracted.

Elander sprinted for the doorway Casia had disappeared through.

All of the doorways were constructed in a similar fashion. They were framed in *jobas* wood—a material that could withstand the magic that created the paths between the godhavens. Different symbols were carved in the wood, heralding the different deities that each door led to, and a jewel that served as an ever-renewing source of the pathway magic was affixed to the highest point of that wooden frame.

Like the portal beneath it, the jewel surrounded by the Moon Goddess's symbols had turned almost completely dark, all save for a tiny spot of light in its center.

With several quick, expert strokes of his sword, Elander carved the door frame into pieces. The jewel shifted loose and fell. As it bounced across the floor, he reached for the small knife at his boot.

He caught the gem and stabbed its center.

Cracks slowly spiderwebbed across its face. Ghostly wisps of pale green and silvery white magic drifted up, startlingly bright in the shadow-drenched room.

One more powerful stab shattered the gem completely.

As the pieces scattered away from him, Elander focused on them for an instant too long—he sensed the sword falling toward him, but not quickly enough to avoid it.

Steel pierced his shoulder.

He twisted instinctively away, and he was met with claws as they slammed upward into his stomach. The Rook God smiled as he lifted his once-servant into the air and hurled him into the closest wall.

The pain was dizzying. Paralyzing. Elander slumped down against the wall. His vision dimmed. The room twisted and shifted around him.

But he didn't care.

The door was destroyed.

The Rook God fixed his gaze upon the pieces, the tiny bits of the shattered jewel. More of his dark, humorless laughter echoed through the room. His voice was quiet, cold and calm as a snow-draped morning, as he turned back to Elander.

"You have turned out to be incredibly annoying."

Elander didn't reply. He tried to move, but the floor

beneath him was too slick to find purchase against. *Slick with blood*, he realized faintly. He was not exactly mortal, but he was no longer a true god, either. He was something in-between.

Something that was losing far too much blood.

He closed his eyes and settled back against the wall. He could feel the space growing colder. Heavier. It was the Rook God's anger made ever more tangible—more of those threads of magic reaching out, tightening around Elander's body. Already, Elander could scarcely breathe within their dark embrace.

"I imagine it will be sheer agony," said Malaphar. "Being truly human again, that is, after having tasted divinity—not that you'll last longer than a few minutes in that mortal form. Humans are such...*fragile* things, after all."

Elander kept his eyes closed, focusing on breathing through the pain, but he could sense the god moving closer. He pressed a hand against his stomach. Within seconds, warm blood had coated his fingers. The threads of the Rook God's magic tightened around him, and they caused more than just pain...it felt like they were pulling, clawing away all the most vital parts of him.

Like they were *draining* him.

A strange combination of horror and palpable relief washed over him—because he was being drained of his divine power, but now he could *also* feel the connection between himself and the upper-god severing even further, fraying like a rope stretched too low over a burning candle.

There was at least some small solace in the fact that he would die more freely than he'd been living.

He opened his eyes, but he didn't look at the god looming over him. Something else caught his attention, drawing it as though by magic—a small, unassuming medallion with a jeweled face rested amongst the rubble of the doorway.

For a moment, panic gripped him. His weary mind thought it was the jewel that had been connected to the portal he'd destroyed, that he hadn't truly managed to shatter it.

But no... this was a different kind of magical object.

The Heart of the Sun.

Casia must have dropped it when Caden swept her away to safety.

As Elander stared at it, all of the memories of the past days rushed through his mind: The realization of who Casia was; the battle they'd fought against her brother and his army; the betrayal they'd faced when they'd arrived in Oblivion; the fear that had gripped him when he'd spotted the Rook God's brand upon her face, and the fear of losing her all over again.

And now came another realization.

She isn't safe.

He exhaled a slow, painful breath.

No matter how many doors he destroyed, she could still be found. The bargain she had foolishly started to strike with the Rook God made certain of that—and the upper-god was not the only enemy hunting her, besides. Her battles were not over yet. *Not even close*.

Which meant his weren't either.

The upper-god was moving again, a storm of shadows and feathers descending, and then a shining blade extended from the dark, thrusting toward him—

Elander somehow found the strength to roll aside.

The sword struck the wall behind him, cutting more cleanly through it than any mortal-made blade could have. When the blade was withdrawn, a series of cracks broke violently out from the point of impact, sending pieces of plaster and wood clattering to the floor.

Elander rose up from the dust and destruction, pushing through the oppressive weight of the Dark God's magic. Caden's sword was still in his hand. The same warning still snaked through his thoughts.

You are not meant to win this.

And even if he survived today, what then? What if he found his way back to Casia? Where would they go? How did they ultimately win this war and all the others they faced?

He wasn't sure.

He only knew that he could not end here.

He had set his gaze upon the medallion that Casia

had dropped, and nothing was going to keep him from reaching it.

He darted across the room, snatched it up, and pressed it against his blood-soaked shirt.

'Heart' was an accurate name; he could have sworn he felt it pulsing in his fist, growing stronger and stronger. Almost as if it was coming to life at his touch. The energy it radiated was warm. Powerful. Familiar.

It felt like...*her*.

As the seconds passed, it seemed as if that energy was filling and fortifying all of the spaces that had been emptied by the Rook God's draining power.

He turned back to that god and saw something he had never seen upon Malaphar's face—not in any of the various forms the upper-god had taken over the past centuries.

Concern.

Elander looked down at the medallion in his hand and realized he hadn't imagined it coming to life; it was truly glowing, the jewels upon its face flashing bright for one beat, dark the next. Strength surged into him with each bright beat. And soon Elander felt—of all things— a reckless smile spreading across his face.

"Put it down," the upper-god commanded.

Elander closed it in his fist, lifting his gaze to meet the furious eyes of the towering god.

"You serve *me*," the Rook God snarled.

Elander shifted the sword in his other hand, rebalancing it. "Not anymore."

The god opened his mouth to reply, and with every bit of strength and speed he could summon, Elander brought his sword up and hurled it into the god's throat, cutting him off.

The god staggered back, taking the embedded sword with him. He didn't cry out in pain. Didn't flinch, even as the sword bounced gruesomely about with his movements. He ran his hand along the weapon protruding from his throat, as if he was more curious than concerned by it.

Elander clenched the Heart more tightly in his fist.

Malaphar ripped the sword out and threw it to the ground. Dark shadows rose on either side of him, swelling into a wave that he sent crashing forward with a flick of his wrist.

Elander didn't think. He only reacted. As the wave of magic descended, the hand clutching the Heart lifted.

Bright light met the falling shadows, the powers colliding as viciously as the two of them had been colliding for weeks now—master and servant, Moraki and Marr, a high-god of darkness and a fallen one clinging desperately to light.

The light waned as the Rook God's magic washed over it, and for a long, terrible moment everything was suspended and silent—black and endless, devoid of all reason and hope.

Then came a flicker of white.

Then another, brighter than the first. And another and another, until the collective shimmer of them became so blinding that Elander had to close his eyes and shield them with his arm.

When his surroundings finally dimmed enough that he could look up again, the Rook God was gone.

He dropped to one knee, heaving for breath. His wounded shoulder burned, as did his stomach, and despite the strength the Heart of the Sun had given him, his bleeding had not stopped. How much could he afford to lose?

How human was he at this point?

He crawled toward the wall. Braced himself against it. Dropping the Heart onto the floor, he studied it through tired, half-closed eyes.

Had it truly driven the Rook God away?

There were far too many things he didn't know about himself *and* this mysterious little object, it seemed.

Bright white light still illuminated the room, making it look more like a haven for the Sun goddess than the place his darker-self had once considered something like *home*. It was strangely quiet. Peaceful. The energy humming around him still felt like Casia—maybe that was why it brought him peace. And maybe that was why, after a moment, he thought he heard her voice.

He bowed his head to listen, but he heard nothing

else except the very faint beat of his own not-quite-human heart.

He leaned against the wall, closed his eyes, and drifted away among the silence and the blood and the brightness.

CHAPTER 2

CAS DID NOT REMEMBER HITTING THE GROUND.

But she opened her eyes, and there she was—sprawled across cold stone, her face warm with blood, her body aching.

And suddenly she remembered falling.

She remembered numbness tingling through her. She remembered approaching a bright light, a portal sucking her in, the very air tightening around her, and then...darkness. She had plummeted through a darkness that felt like it might last forever.

It was still dark, and she still felt off-balance, but she was no longer numb. Something had nudged her back into awareness—a powerful twist in her stomach, a pulling that reminded her of the uncomfortable feeling that summoning magic sometimes caused. Only she hadn't used any magic.

Had she?

Now that she was awake, she also became aware of a terrible scraping sound. She lifted her head, searching for a long, confusing moment, until she finally spotted the source of the noise—*Caden*.

The lesser-spirit had sprouted claws from his fingertips, and he was using them to destroy the frame of a crude doorway. There were several other doorways surrounding them.

The scene felt familiar, though Cas was certain she'd never been here before.

Her head pounded. She squinted and tried to make sense of where she was, to remember more of what had happened. And then it struck her.

Caden was destroying the path back to Oblivion.

With a startled cry, she stumbled to her feet and lunged for him.

She didn't have claws, but she dug her fingers into his arm just the same, digging and digging with all her might, until finally he was forced to abandon his destruction and deal with her. He caught her by the front of her shirt, and with inhuman speed and strength, he unceremoniously lifted her and flung her away.

She slammed against the floor hard enough that it dazed her.

And so she was back to where she'd started, sprawled across the cold ground, fresh blood trickling down from a scrape on her forehead.

She hadn't even put up a fight. She hadn't been *able* to put up a fight, and now the very thought of lifting her head was agonizing.

Why was she so weak?

More memories flashed through her mind: Elander's eyes meeting hers; the awful, gut-wrenching pain in those eyes; his magic hitting her, draining her energy and making it impossible for her to fight as Caden picked her up and whisked her away from Oblivion...

That draining Death magic still lingered, wrapped around her like a cold embrace that was both comforting and infuriating.

"Stop," she cried. "*Stop*. We have to go back!"

Caden ignored her.

"You can't just leave him alone on the other side!"

The lesser-spirit kept up his methodical movements, reaching now for the shimmering black jewel suspended above what was left of the door.

Cas fought her way back to her feet. Her knees threatened to buckle, but she refused to let them. "I want to go back."

"No."

"Yes!"

"You've made a big enough mess of things already," he growled, spinning around to face her. "So just sit down and shut the hell up for a moment so I can *think*."

There's nothing to think about, she wanted to scream. *I just need to get back to him.*

But she didn't scream.

It wouldn't do any good.

The doorway was nearly gone. It had been reduced to nothing but a rapidly-fading, spinning vortex of white light against a frameless black void, and she was too weak to fight off the partially-divine being standing between her and that void.

"Sit down and shut up," Caden repeated.

She glared at him. "You're incredibly lucky that I am not at my full strength right now, because otherwise I would make you regret talking to me like that."

"Yes," he muttered, "I feel so *lucky* to be trapped here with your weakened and useless self."

She kept glaring.

He went back to ignoring her.

Standing required too much effort, so she furiously plopped down on the stone floor instead. She didn't want to cry, but she was too tired to keep the tears from falling. They slid down her cheeks, winding around the sticky trails the blood had already made. She wiped them away with the heels of her hands several times, but just the simple motion of that was exhausting, too.

She felt like giving up.

She drew her legs toward her, buried her face against her knees, and let the tears fall.

Minutes later, the sounds of Caden destroying the way back to Oblivion finally ceased. She felt him turn to her. Felt the uncertainty stretching between them, heavy and ominous as a sky bristling with storm clouds.

Caden sighed. "I don't believe he's dead, for what it's worth."

She lifted her burning eyes to his.

"Not yet, anyway."

She swallowed, trying to open the tightness in her throat. "You can sense him, can't you?"

"Faintly."

"The magic that binds you to him... Elander mentioned something about how it helped him know where you and his other servants were. I guess it works both ways?"

Caden nodded. "To an extent."

"And it's the same magic that makes it impossible for you and Elander to entirely escape the Rook God, right?" She touched the mark that upper-god had left upon her own skin. He'd struck her in Oblivion, drawn blood as part of the bargain she had almost finished making with him.

Almost.

Elander had interrupted, so she wasn't certain how deep her connection to Malaphar was, or what would become of that impulsive decision she'd made.

Caden only nodded again in answer to her question, averting his eyes from that mark.

One crisis at time, Cas supposed.

She managed a deep breath. *Not dead*, she reminded

herself. It was not as good as *here beside her*, but she could handle that. She could keep moving. They would find each other again. They always did.

In the meantime, she needed to focus on staying *not dead* herself. And there were others whose fates she was equally concerned with. The past days had brought one devastating challenge after another, and not everyone had made it out unscathed.

What had become of the rest of her friends and allies?

As far as she knew, Laurent was in Sadira, along with the young ruler of that fallen kingdom. They were still recovering, picking up the pieces and counting the dead from the latest battle they'd fought against the King-Emperor of the Kethran Empire.

Meanwhile, Rhea and Nessa were in the southern empire, refugees hiding within the palace of the High King and Queen of Sundolia.

And Zev...

Not dead, Cas thought as furiously as she could—as if that would somehow guarantee it remained true. In her heart, she *felt* it was true enough. None of her friends were dead. But they were all scattered, stretched ragged and thin, and she had to fix it somehow, to keep moving until they were all back together and whole again.

On to the other side of this disaster.

She swept a glance around the room. In the darkness, she could make out little beyond the freestanding doorways encircling her and the gritty stone floor she sat upon. "Where are we, precisely?"

"In the mortal-realm haven of *Yosu*—or Inya, as I believe most humans call her."

"The Moon Goddess?"

"Yes."

The doors resembled the ones she'd seen in Oblivion. Maybe that was why this place felt familiar. Were all the godhavens connected to one another? If so...

She looked closer at the frames of those doors until she spotted one embedded with several small carvings of trees with intricately twisting roots. "That's the symbol of Namu, the Goddess of Healing, isn't it?"

Caden nodded.

"Elander carried my friend to her." Cas rose shakily to her feet once more. She took one last look at all that was left of the portal to Oblivion. Her chest ached at the thought of turning away from it, but she had no choice but to change direction if she wanted to keep moving.

"I need to go see her," she said.

"Her door won't open without the magic of *this* realm's keeper," Caden informed her.

Cas clenched her fists. "Then I will find the Moon Goddess and make her open it for me."

"Assuming she's actually here, and that she would grant you an audience..."

She ignored Caden's pessimism and started to walk —one foot after the other through the darkness, searching for moonlight and the goddess that dwelled within it.

She found neither.

But she did eventually find a hallway, and as she moved deeper into it, a cool breeze stirred from behind her, lifting the strands of her hair and her clothing and pulling these things in front of her, pulling her onward.

Guiding her?

After a moment she heard Caden following. Reluctantly, she assumed. They walked in silence for several minutes, until the hallway ended. Suddenly, there were no walls, no ceiling, and the ground beneath them was softer, spongier. Like they had stepped outside. It was colder and darker than the doorway room—almost too dark to see.

But high in the distance there was a faint glimmer of pale blue light.

Cas moved toward it.

The ground sloped steeply upward. Her legs burned in protest as she climbed, but she kept going and kept her eyes on that orb of light. It disappeared as she reached the top. A brief despair threatened, but it was forgotten the instant she peered down at the sight awaiting her on the other side of the hill.

A soft gasp escaped her.

Everything looked like it had been dipped in moonlight: A forest of willow trees that stretched farther than she could see, a river that wound through it, the stone walls that crisscrossed the landscape—all of it glowed with the same pale blue, lunar-esque light, even though the sky above was empty of both the moon and its stars.

There was a field of flowers to the right of the forest, a carpet of blooms in all imaginable shades of blue and purple and white. Cas started toward it, pulled by the same cool breeze that had guided her in the hallway. She made her way over and knelt beside a patch of shimmering, silvery-violet flowers. She curiously touched her fingers to the petals closest to her, and she pulled them away to find them coated in a dewy, silver-tinged substance.

A rustling sound made her lift her head.

A creature was weaving its way through the field, walking toward her with slow, graceful movements. It was deer-like, but with strangely glowing eyes and massive antlers with more prongs than Cas could easily count. Suspended between those antlers was a slowly-spinning object shaped like two crescent moons entangled with one another.

"The goddess is here after all."

Cas jumped a bit at Caden's voice; he moved so quietly she'd almost forgotten he was following her.

"Try not to offend her," Caden muttered. "I know you've made a habit of offending the gods, but it won't do us any good for you to keep that up."

"I haven't made a *habit* of offending the gods. I've

been more polite toward them than I should have been in most cases."

Except for that one time I called the Goddess of Storms a bitch, a quiet voice in the back of her mind reminded her.

But in her defense, she'd been a touch hungover at the time, and the goddess had been acting like a bitch.

"When in doubt, just hold your tongue. That's all I ask."

We'll see, thought Cas—though she did hold her tongue for the moment. A deep sense of awe had overtaken her and rendered her speechless as the deer-like creature stopped before them, and that awe numbed her completely as the creature lifted onto its hind legs and began to change.

Ribbons of white light encircled its body, cocooning tighter and tighter until no trace of the deer remained visible. When the ribbons unraveled, a woman stood before them, wearing a dress that shimmered between shades of blue and silver when she moved. Her skin was a rich, dark brown, swirling with odd symbols and splashed with freckle-like specks of diamond-white, and her irises were a blue so pale they were nearly lost in the whites of her eyes. She folded her arms across her chest, lifted her hand, and rested her chin upon her long, elegant fingers.

"Hello, travelers." Her voice was all silk, with a soft echoing quality to it, and it made Cas feel as though she

25

was floating on her back in the middle of a calm sea. "You look weary," she said.

"Hello, Yosu," said Caden, his gaze lowered in respect.

"Where is the fallen god you serve?" She tilted her head curiously toward the lesser-spirit. "It has been some time since I've spoken with him."

"He's otherwise occupied, I'm afraid."

Cas felt her throat threatening to tighten up again. She nearly choked with the effort of trying to keep her breathing normal, and the sound drew the goddess's gaze to her.

"And who are you, traveler?"

She hesitated, uncertain of how to reply. The answer to that question had changed so often over the past weeks that it made her head spin.

"Have you no name?" asked the goddess.

"It's just that I...I've had many. I've walked so many different paths, and I'm still not sure which ones were right and which ones were wrong."

The goddess smiled. "I know a few things about different paths."

"You...yes, of course." Cas lowered her eyes slightly, overtaken by awe once more at this reminder of who she was talking to.

Inya was the Goddess of the Crossroads, of reflection and decision. When people came to a fork in the woods, they prayed to the Moon Goddess for the clarity to know which direction to take, and it was said that nothing was ever truly lost to those who carried her mark.

Cas touched her hand to her jawline, below the brand the Rook God had clawed into her. There was a much older mark located there—a scar that was vaguely shaped like a curved moon. As a child, she used to pretend it was truly a sign she was blessed with Moon-kind magic, because such magic meant that she could never be as lost as she had often felt.

"My identity keeps changing is all I meant," she said.

"The only constant in life is change," the goddess commented. "And right and wrong are not words that I would use to describe all of life's different paths, different decisions…"

"Some of my decisions have certainly *felt* wrong," Cas couldn't help but say.

"But now you bear interesting scars, as most of the well-traveled souls do." Inya's startlingly pale eyes flicked to the fingers Cas held against the crescent scar, and then up to the one the Rook God had left.

Cas tried to subtly angle her face so that neither of those 'interesting' scars were visible.

"That one on your cheek there…it festers with powerfully dark magic, doesn't it?"

Cas didn't reply.

"And yet I also sense a very different sort of magic dwelling deep within you." The goddess hesitated a moment, as if giving Cas a chance to deny that magic.

Then her gaze moved on to the lightning-shaped mark on Cas's wrist. "And you also carry the mark of the Tempest, I see. But you are not truly Storm-kind, are you?"

"No. I'm not. The Goddess of Storms gave me her blessing a short time ago, in hopes that it would help me."

"Help you?"

"With that *very different* sort of magic you sense." Cas took a deep breath. "That magic you sense...I wasn't blessed with it in the usual way," she began, slowly. "I have it because I was exposed to a stolen piece of the Sun Goddess's magic, first in, um, in a past life." It sounded absurd, even as she said it, but she kept going. "And that upper-goddess decided to bring me back into this world, in a different body, for reasons I still don't understand. I've carried this magic of hers for all of my current life, I suppose, but it's only recently been waking up in earnest."

"I see," Inya said, sounding as though she had already seen it all very long ago. Perhaps she had. She *served* that Sun Goddess after all. And the middle-goddess of Storms was within this same divine court as well, along with the Marr who carried the symbols of Sky and Star. So it wasn't too far-fetched to think they might have spoken about these matters amongst themselves...though it did feel bizarre to Cas, imagining these divine beings swapping stories about her.

"And did you come here hoping I might help you as well?" asked the goddess.

I came here mostly because someone dragged me through the doorway.

The thought made Cas want to wither all over again.

But she caught herself. There were too many things —too many people—that were counting on her staying on her feet. So she dug deep down into herself and managed to find a tattered scrap of courage. She was here now, and she would make the most of it.

"Yes," she said, more boldly. "I need you to open a path for me—to open the door to the Oak Goddess's haven, specifically. A very close friend of mine was taken to her realm, and so that is where I am going next."

The goddess arched a silver brow over her pale eyes. "It's rare that a human informs *me* of the path they intend to take. Usually they come asking me for answers about where to go." Her tone had a hint of a gentle challenge in it.

But Cas had already decided on her next move, and she wouldn't waver. "I already know where I am going," she said. "And I will get there with or without your help." Caden coughed, pointedly, so she lowered her gaze and quickly added, "I mean that respectfully, of course."

A long silence stretched between them. She thought for a moment that she really had offended the goddess

—perhaps she *was* developing a dangerous habit of doing that.

"Very well, then," Inya finally said. "Though I should warn you that the Goddess of Healing is not as fond of wayward travelers as I am. She's very...hm...let's say *impatient*." She lifted her left hand in front of her and traced circles across the center of it—as if designing a spell of some sort— before beckoning Cas to come closer.

Cas obeyed. Inya reached out and dragged one of her elegant fingers over Cas's jaw, directly across the crescent-shaped scar, and suddenly Cas felt the same as she had when this goddess had first spoken to her—as though she was floating in a quiet sea, moonlight sparkling around her and an endless expanse of possibility above and below her.

Such a simple touch, but the power it transferred was unmistakable. Cas's entire body shivered with it. Her eyes fluttered shut for a moment, and when she opened them again, the goddess was watching her with a dreamy half-smile on her lips.

The crescent-shaped scar felt cold, but in a relieving way. Like ice applied to an aching bruise. The dark brand the Rook God had left, in comparison, had started to burn, as if in protest to whatever magic the goddess had left. Cas fought to keep herself from trembling under the combined weight of these warring powers, but she wasn't entirely successful.

"Come," said the goddess, her gaze lingering for just a moment on the darker of Cas's marks. "You can open the paths yourself now, but I will escort you anyways. Just to be certain."

Certain of what? Cas wanted to ask.

But now a reverent silence had fallen, and something made her feel like she shouldn't interrupt it...as if she *couldn't* interrupt it. Even with this latest powerful blessing tingling over her skin, she still felt small and insignificant in the goddess's wake—like a small child trying to keep up with her mother's much longer strides.

As she followed that goddess and left the world of glass and moonlight behind, a sudden and fierce sorrow overtook her. She couldn't explain it really; she just knew she wanted to stay among the moonlit flowers and trees. Among safer things. Every step she took away from those things caused the knot in the pit of her stomach to tighten.

The ominous feeling settling over her grew more intense as they walked back into the dark hallway, guided by the soft glow that surrounded the goddess.

As they approached the room full of doorways, the feeling became so intense that Cas slowed without meaning to. The goddess walked on, but Caden turned and gave her an impatient look.

"What are you doing?" he demanded.

"I just...I have a bad feeling suddenly."

He swept a look around them—the casual surveying

glance of a long-serving soldier. He started to reply, but then frowned, closed his mouth, and kept walking.

It took Cas a moment to keep walking herself. She caught up to Caden quickly enough, but only because he had stopped again at the end of the hallway. Something in the room beyond had caught his attention.

Fire.

One of the doorways below was surrounded by white and red flames.

It was not ordinary fire; the heat and power it radiated were too intense. All of the air in the room seemed to be funneling toward the flames, making it difficult to breathe.

"He always has to make a dramatic entrance," Caden mumbled.

"He?" Cas coughed out.

Caden didn't reply. He had already turned to the Moon Goddess, and he was speaking to her in some ancient tongue Cas didn't recognize.

The goddess watched the doorway out of the corner of her gaze as they spoke. She didn't seem surprised by the fire.

Was this why she had insisted on escorting them?

Cas took a few steps forward, studying the doorway more closely. The flames were contained for the moment, swirling and striking against an invisible barrier of magic that was apparently stretched across the doorway. She thought she saw a creature writhing

32

amongst them—an occasional glimpse of ash-colored feathers and beady black eyes. An eagle.

An eagle with fire-tipped wings...

She had seen pictures of a similar creature in books, she realized.

"That's *Moto,* isn't it?" she whispered in horror.

Moto. The middle-god of Fire and Forging, one of the twelve Marr who had shaped their world. Who else could it have been? Who else could have sent such a terrible sensation washing over her, if not one of the powerful middle-gods? She knew Moto had a reputation for bloodlust and violence, that he was the deity most often worshipped by soldiers marching to war.

And she knew he served the Rook God.

Which meant there was a very good chance he was here in search of *her.*

Cas took a deep breath to steady herself. She wiggled her fingers and tried to will electricity to spring from them.

Only a few sparks appeared—and she was surprised she even managed that. She still hadn't recovered from her last battle or from Elander's attack against her, and the oppressive weight of the Fire God's magic did little to help her concentrate on her power.

She reached into the pocket of her coat, searching for the smooth, familiar medallion she'd been carrying with her over the past few weeks. The Heart of the Sun had always brought her strength and clarity in the past, even before she realized what it truly was, but now...

"It's gone."

Caden snapped his head toward her. "What's gone?"

"The Heart of the Sun, I had it in my pocket when we arrived in Oblivion, but now—"

"If you dropped it in Oblivion, Elander will find it."

She had felt a powerful surge of magic earlier; that was what had woken her up, what had pulled her out of the darkness. Was it because he'd already found the Heart? Because it had reacted to his touch, same as their first meeting had caused her magic to react?

A sudden flash of light and heat shook the room, jerking Cas from her thoughts.

"It doesn't matter either way," Caden continued, sharply. "We need to go. *Now.*"

Cas nodded, but hesitated as she realized that the door they needed to go through was directly beside the Fire God's building inferno.

Of course.

The Moon Goddess calmly stepped in front of them and stretched out a hand. Moonlight unrolled like gossamer threads from her fingertips, and with a few twists of her wrist, those threads tangled together and then stretched into the shape of a long bow. In her opposite hand, she used the same trick to create a shimmering silver arrow.

The arrow was whistling through the air a moment later.

It struck the invisible barrier over the fiery door and made it visible, feeding more magic into it until it turned opaque and shimmering and powerful enough to push the flames back, to fold them into the darkness on the other side.

But a flicker of orange still remained in the center, and within seconds, it was already building its way back into a tumbling, roaring wall of fire.

"There are many different paths twisting out before us now," the goddess said. "Sides are being chosen. And some of my fellow gods are making unfortunate choices."

The words sent a chill down Cas's spine. Terrible images of destruction—of that beautiful moonlit forest gone up in flames—flooded her mind. "The Fire God is here for me," she said, breathlessly. "And he will be furious if I disappear. If he gets in..."

"He will get in eventually. Moto is known for his stubbornness."

"Yes, and he's *also* known for his love of violence and destruction."

The goddess readied another arrow. "Perhaps. But this is not your fight. Not today. Not like this. Go and regain your strength for the battles ahead."

Cas wanted to protest further, but Caden cut her off. "Can we be followed?"

Inya eyed the pieces of the door Caden had destroyed. "The Goddess of the Sands built these doorways and infused them with her temporal magic to make them functional, but it is *my* magic that shaped the actual paths between them. I can rearrange them as necessary." Her gaze, full of serenity and resolve, met Cas's.

For the second time since arriving here, Cas was struck with an intense desire to *stay*.

But she was not a fool.

This had become a battlefield for gods. And whatever power and potential lay within her, Cas was currently so drained that she scarcely felt like a human, much less one that might fight alongside, or against, the divine.

"Go," the goddess commanded.

Cas went.

Fresh flames licked out from the Firehaven doorway, reaching ever more deeply into the room. Arrows of moonlight flew to meet them, setting off tiny explosions whenever they collided.

Cas kept her head down and kept running until she reached the portal that would carry her away. But as she finally reached it and braced a hand against it, she couldn't help pausing one last time to glance back.

All traces of the goddess and her silvery light were gone, engulfed in a blaze that was swiftly expanding. The heat was becoming unbearable. Cas squinted, trying to find figures amongst the smoke. Her eyes watered too intensely to see anything at first, until finally...

There.

The Goddess of the Crossroads was kneeling in the center of the room, her bow braced against the ground in front of her. A dome of fire had settled over her, but she was holding it at a distance with her reflective magic. Her head was bowed, her features as tranquil as ever.

The fiery dome pushed closer. The shimmering reflection magic trembled under the weight of that fire, shaking more and more violently, until finally—

It shattered.

The goddess drowned beneath the flames.

Cas felt a scream rising in her throat.

But before that scream could escape her, she was being pulled through the doorway and falling once more into darkness.

CHAPTER 3

Elander's eyes blinked open.

Darkness.

He lifted a hand, clenched it into a fist. Then the other. Then he bent his knees, one at a time, and he curled himself upright. Everything seemed to be functional. Weak and covered in blood, but functional. He wasn't sure how he kept managing it, but he was still breathing. His heart was still beating.

His vision adjusted to the near pitch-black room, and a different sort of Heart came into view—that unassuming medallion he'd long ago stolen from the Sun Goddess was still on the ground next to him. Its power seemed to have been drained; its light was so faint he had almost overlooked it.

As he stared at it, a voice floated over to him. "That was strange magic."

The voice was familiar, but it still took him a moment to place it.

Tara.

He had forgotten she was there. But now it all came flooding back: How she had been struck, paralyzed by the Rook God's magic.

Right after she'd betrayed them.

She was the reason the Rook God had been in Oblivion, prepared for an ambush. She had told him who Casia truly was. After an age worth of servitude, she had betrayed Elander, and now Casia carried a new, terrible mark, and the complicated messes they'd already been facing had gotten even *more* complicated.

He spotted her as she emerged from the shadows on the other side of the room, and he no longer felt weak, suddenly.

He felt like killing someone.

His rage carried him across the space in seconds. That fiery wrath was stronger than the pain radiating through his stomach and shoulder. It made the blood staining him seem insignificant.

Tara tripped as she tried to stumble out of his path. He caught her by the arm and wrenched her upright.

He was very aware of the new limits of his power after the last draining attack the Rook God had used against him, but he would use every ounce of strength and magic he had left if it meant making Tara answer for the things she had done.

39

Her body shook in his grasp. If he hadn't been holding her so tightly she likely would have collapsed.

"*Traitor*," he snarled.

She lifted her chin. "I only did what you could not."

His hand moved from her arm to her throat, and he shoved her against the wall.

She choked under his grip but somehow kept talking. "You were blinded by your love for that woman—"

"I was not *blind*."

"I did what had to be done to spare myself from the Rook God's punishments."

His grip tightened.

"And I..." She coughed several times before managing to gasp out more words, "*I'd hoped he would spare you too.*"

His heartbeat thundered in his ears.

He kept seeing that mark on Casia's face. The blood running over her skin. Kept hearing the sound of her scream as she was pulled through the doorway.

A quiet, rational voice in the back of his mind told him these disasters were not entirely Tara's fault.

A much louder voice told him that it had to be *somebody's* fault. That somebody needed to answer for these things—somebody needed to die—and that it would be therapeutic, killing that somebody with his bare hands. If he could control nothing else, he could control the grip of his hand on Tara's throat. Bit by bit, he could squeeze her life away. She was still partially divine, as was he, but he could still kill her. He *should*.

The mark.

The blood.

The screaming.

"I should kill you," he said, his voice low and bristling with barely-suppressed rage.

She didn't reply. Her eyes had closed. Her body was slumped against the wall, as if she had resigned herself to her fate.

He wasn't entirely sure why he decided to let go.

But one by one, his fingers uncurled from her neck. And then he jerked his hand completely away. She crumpled to the floor, massaging her throat, and kept her gaze downcast as he turned away and walked back to the Heart.

It took him a moment to find it, even with his inhuman vision, because the faint light in its center no longer pulsed.

"It's gone completely dark," he muttered, more to himself than Tara, as he knelt to pick it up.

Tara still answered him. "Strange that it ever lit up in the first place, as I was saying."

He cut her a sidelong glare.

"It's just...why were *you* able to activate any of its magic—and enough to drive an upper-god away, at that? Your magic should be in opposition to that of the Sun Goddess's." He turned to face her more fully. The full weight of his glare seemed to startle her into silence. Finally, she visibly braced herself and continued, her voice strained and quiet. "Do you know what else is strange?"

"I don't care," he snapped. "Say one more word about the matter and I will finish what I started a moment ago."

He already had enough questions to deal with, and he was tired of listening to her traitorous mouth.

He stepped back to the circle of doorways, pausing at the one he'd destroyed. He had no regrets about destroying it, but he'd done so with the belief that he would not be leaving this room alive. And yet here he was...alive. So now he needed to figure out the fastest way to find Casia and Caden again.

"Are you going to go after her?" Tara asked.

Of course I am, he thought.

But he said nothing.

"I suppose you're done telling me your plans." She huffed out a bitter laugh. "Afraid that I'll tell them to someone?"

"You'll find out my plans soon enough." He lifted a hand toward her. The Death mark on it flickered—entirely too faintly. An annoying reminder that he didn't carry the same power he once had. But hopefully it would still be enough to do what he needed to do. It might take too much of what little energy he had to spare, but he would not risk letting Tara run to the Rook God again.

Her body tensed as he stepped toward her. He thought she might try to run. He moved quickly, cutting off the path to the stairs that led down the tower, and in the end she simply sank back against the wall again, once more resigned to her fate.

He dug deeper into his magic. He felt the invisible threads of her life as they twisted around her. There was a distinctive energy that was different from most living things. She was alive, but not purely of either the human or divine realms. Strange and caught in the middle, just as he was.

A shudder rippled through her body as his magic overtook those threads and bound them. She fell in slow motion, dropping to her knees and then tumbling face first onto the marble. Unconscious.

She wouldn't stay that way indefinitely—not once he and his magic went away from her—but he knew of a place where he could imprison the traitor. And the same place *also* contained an old ally that might be able to help him find his way back to Casia.

He only hoped the Storm Goddess was feeling benevolent today.

A SHORT TIME LATER, after gathering his strength and enough magic to open the proper portal, Elander made his way into Stormhaven. After a brief conversation with the women guarding the portal, he took a deep, bracing breath, and he set off toward the sprawling room in the center of the haven.

Even if the guards hadn't informed him that he would find Nephele in her sitting room, he would have guessed it himself; she spent more time in this mortal-world haven, drinking wine and feasting on sweets, than she did in any of the divine places most of the Marr passed their time in.

It was a long, winding walk to reach his destination. He carried Caden's sword in one hand, and Tara's lifeless body was draped over the shoulder on the opposite side. He hadn't bothered cleaning the blood from his clothing or skin.

Perhaps it was the combination of all of these things that caused Nephele to heave a visible, dramatic sigh when she saw him coming.

She didn't get up from the throne-like chair she was lounging in, but with a wave of her hand—one that sent tiny sparks crackling through the air—she dismissed all but one of the women gathered around her. Once they were gone, she fixed Elander with a deadpan look.

He unceremoniously dropped Tara's body at the goddess's feet.

She barely glanced at that body. "And here you are again, invading my humble, peaceful abode."

"Did you miss me?"

Her expression didn't change. "I didn't miss the trouble you tend to bring. And from the looks of the body you've just dragged in here, and all of the blood..." she wrinkled her nose as she looked him over, "...*trouble* is precisely what you've brought this time, as well." She sounded annoyed about that trouble.

But he knew better.

The only thing Nephele loved more than creating storms was being in the center of the most interesting patch of conflict she could find at any given moment. She was second only to the God of Fire when it came to warmongering—though she tended to be more logical about the battles she chose to start.

"The blood is an unfortunate side effect of dueling with upper-gods, as it were."

Nephele's eyes flashed to a brighter shade of indigo, unable to feign annoyed disinterest anymore. "Oh, you *are* in trouble this time, aren't you?" She settled back in her chair and folded her arms across her chest. "I'm going to take a wild guess here and say that your little girlfriend is somehow involved."

He hesitated.

"Out with it. The world is changing, and it seems we may not have the eternity we once did to take our time with these things."

He settled down in a chair across from her, ignoring the scowl that she shot his direction as his blood-stained clothing touched the velvety cushions. The one servant who had remained in the room tentatively approached and offered him a glass of wine. He took it with a gruff *thank you*.

"Well?" prompted the goddess.

"Casia started to make a bargain with Malaphar."

"Of course she did." Nephele lifted her own glass of wine from the table beside her and took a long sip. "I had a feeling she'd turn out to be an idiot."

His eyes narrowed.

"Ah. You don't like it when I insult her. Sorry." She looked as unapologetic as a being could possibly look. "But what are you going to do about it, anyway? Bleed on the rest of my furniture and ruin that too?"

"She isn't an idiot. She did it to save her kingdom. And to save...me."

"That last part makes her an even *bigger* idiot."

"This is not the help I came here for."

"Oh, it's my help that you want, is it? Well, why didn't you say so?"

He lifted the glass to his lips and drained most of it. Closing his eyes, briefly, he lamented that the liquid burning down his throat wasn't something stronger. "I need two things from you."

"Do tell." She yawned. "I'm waiting on pins and needles over here."

"Firstly, I need somewhere to hold *her*." He jerked his head toward Tara. "She betrayed me once. I'll deal with that more thoroughly at some point, but in the mean-

46

time, I need her guarded and secure. And secondly, I need to use your portal to Moonhaven."

"And why should I help you with either of these things?"

"Because despite the mistakes I've made, we were allies once. Friends, really—even in spite of the feuding gods above us. And that upper-goddess you serve has clearly marked Casia for some reason. You helped her before because of this, didn't you? So don't think of it as helping me. You're helping her."

The goddess summoned a tiny ball of lightning as he spoke, bouncing it back and forth between her hands and avoiding his impatient stare.

"Also? You look bored. I know you don't want to be left out of this chaos."

She snorted. "I feel like I should be insulted by that comment."

"But we both know it's true."

She stopped bouncing the electric sphere. It hovered in the air beside her head, drawing the strands of her pale blue hair toward it. "Fine. I'll lock up your little traitor." She glanced at the wine-bearing servant with a meaningful look.

That servant bowed and left the room, but she returned within moments, flanked by four more women who all wore the insignia of the Storm Goddess. Together, they picked up Tara and carried her off.

"And I'll escort you to Moonhaven," Nephele

continued after they'd gone. "But only because I need to go there myself. I sent a messenger to Inya earlier and they have yet to return."

An uneasy feeling crept along Elander's spine as he wondered what might have been keeping the messenger. He shook it off, finished his wine, and stood. "Whatever your reasons, let's just get moving, please."

She still didn't get up. "Shouldn't you rest for a moment first? You're still bleeding, if you hadn't noticed."

"I'll rest once I've found her again."

"Or once you pass out from blood loss."

"Whichever comes first," he muttered, already heading for the room's exit. He could practically sense the goddess rolling her eyes at his retreating back, but she didn't voice any further objections.

She eventually caught up with him and led the way to Stormhaven's room of doorways.

The middle-gods could travel with ease to any part of the mortal world, and they could also transport themselves to their own havens from anywhere, but to enter a haven that was steeped in another's magic required taking the proper pathways. The path between the Storm and Moon havens was a well-traveled one, Elander knew. The two goddesses were close, and not simply because they served the same upper-goddess; Inya—or *Yosu*, her true name—was far older than Nephele, and she had become the Storm Goddess's mentor and confidante soon after Nephele ascended. Even though Nephele's sister had ascended as well—becoming the reclusive Sky Goddess—she was closer to Inya.

Nephele activated the portal with her magic, frowned one last time at the wounds on Elander's body, and then waved him through the doorway. "After you."

They stepped into the darkness. Elander closed his eyes and meditated his way through the uncomfortable magic as it pulled them along. Traveling these paths hadn't always been uncomfortable, but between his fading divinity and his injuries, the power that enveloped him now was irritating at best.

He finally managed to catch his breath and his sense of balance, and he opened his eyes to see the silvery glow of Inya's haven coming into view.

Something was wrong.

Along with the light and pressure that usually accompanied approaching a gateway, there was also an intense, unnatural heat. The scent of smoke and singed flesh washed over them as they stepped into the Moon Goddess's domain, and they found the messenger Nephele had sent within moments of searching for her.

She was lying on the ground, dead, her face nearly burned beyond recognition.

CHAPTER 4

"FUCK," ELANDER MUTTERED.

"Indeed," Nephele concurred, frowning as she knelt beside her dead messenger and swept a cautious gaze over the room.

A soft growl sounded from behind them.

Elander spun toward the sound, sword at ready.

Nephele summoned a ball of electricity and tossed it into the air. It exploded a moment later, sending a dome of light over the room and illuminating a lanky, dog-like beast with pinned back ears.

It leapt for Elander.

Elander twisted aside, but the beast's claws scraped his injured shoulder. He felt the wound that had started to heal reopening, fresh blood soaking his clothing. His entire arm started to feel numb.

The beast shook off its unsuccessful attack and

circled back, fangs bared and eyes burning bright red. Flames quickly ignited and extinguished wherever it stepped, leaving a trail of scorch marks as it stalked toward Elander.

When it leapt for him again, Elander caught it by the throat. He lifted it with one hand and brought his sword up with the other, impaling the creature in its stomach. It yelped and writhed about, trying to break free of his hold, before finally going limp.

As Elander shook it from his sword and tossed it to the ground, a second beast tore out of the shadows, flames erupting around its entire body as it came.

The rest of the pack followed swiftly after it. A third beast, a fourth, a fifth—Elander lost count as he fended them off, caught up in a whirlwind of fire and blood and magic and the gruesome, unpleasant sounds of his blade stabbing in and out of muscular flesh.

A second group of hounds emerged from the other side of the room, encircling the Storm Goddess as she moved to help. The air was soon filled with static—with bolts of lightning that singed flesh and sent a chorus of yelps echoing through the space.

They were not particularly strong creatures...more of a nuisance than anything. If Elander had been at his full strength—or even half of it—he would have finished them all in an instant.

It took considerably more effort in his current condition, but he still managed to vanquish all of the ones that attacked him, one by one, until none remained.

Nephele did the same, and within minutes, the seemingly never-ending stream of beasts had ended. The room turned quiet once more and, without the fire the hounds had been giving off, it also grew eerily dark.

Elander knelt for a moment to catch his breath, wincing as he pressed a hand to his bleeding shoulder.

Nephele summoned another orb of electricity for light. As the space brightened, it revealed signs of another, far-more fiery battle that must have raged soon before they arrived. Black scorch marks covered the walls. The railings of a nearby staircase appeared to have partially melted. A fine coat of ash covered most surfaces.

Nephele cleared her throat, interrupting the quiet that was quickly becoming uncomfortable. "Have you bled to death over there?"

"Not yet," Elander said, staggering upright and walking back to her side.

"These are Moto's beasts," she muttered, nudging one of the dead animals with her slippered foot. "And that bastard was obviously here too; the fire-hounds could not have caused this much damage on their own. This is..." Her usually confident, nonchalant voice trailed into worried silence.

Elander knew what she was thinking. The Marr often squabbled—rarely did a month go by without some kind of dramatic flare-up—but this was more than a petty quarrel. The Fire God descending into another's realm in such a destructive fashion was...concerning. To say the least.

At the moment, however, he was more concerned with *when* that god had arrived, and when he'd left.

He had ordered Caden to sweep Casia into this realm because he'd thought she would be safe here.

But what if he had sent them both to a fiery grave?

He was suddenly consumed by a single-minded desperation that made it impossible to speak or think or do anything except start searching again.

The Storm Goddess watched in confused silence for a moment before darting toward him and grabbing hold of his arm.

He started to jerk out of her grasp, but she held tight.

"I can't help you if you don't explain what's going on," she said testily.

"The reason I needed to come here was because I sent *her* here," Elander snapped. "But Malaphar knew that as well. I destroyed the doorway in Oblivion so that he couldn't follow her, but it seems he sent another to do his bidding...and without a single damn second of hesitation."

Nephele let go of his arm. Her lips pressed into a thin, disapproving line. She was preparing to tell him what a fool he was for thinking the upper-god would not be ruthless in his pursuit, most likely—as if that hadn't already occurred to him.

But in a rare show of restraint, she refrained from chastising. "She could have escaped before Moto arrived."

"Not without the Moon Goddess's help, and we can't be certain that goddess was even here when Casia arrived. She doesn't spend much time in this mortal-side realm, does she?"

Nephele hesitated, as if she wished she had a different answer to give. She shook her head. "She tends to head for the higher realms whenever there's any sign of unrest amongst the mortals. So...no, she hasn't spent much time here as of late."

He went back to searching—for the goddess, for Casia, for Caden. Every minute that passed without any sign of them made his heart beat a little faster. He kept expecting to stumble over another body that had been burned like that messenger. A body that could be...

No.

He wouldn't think of it.

Nephele joined in the search after a moment, continuing to cast her magic to illuminate every nook and corner.

The room ultimately appeared empty, and Elander was moving toward the melted staircase when he caught something strange out of the corner of his eye— one of Nephele's spheres of electricity seemed to hit an invisible wall. He paused, and he watched as it bounced waywardly away from this wall, burning more brightly as it went.

"Aim your magic at that corner again," he said.

"What?"

"Just do it, please."

She did, and the same thing happened. Her sphere clearly struck something invisible, turned a brighter shade of blueish-white, and then bounced away. Amplified and redirected...

Moon magic at work.

With a curious frown, Nephele concentrated more than just a tiny sphere toward the corner. Threads of electricity spiraled from her hands and twisted into a net, which she draped over what appeared to be empty space.

The web of Storm magic molded into the shape of a dome—and then was instantly bounced away.

She channeled even brighter, more powerful bolts. Powerful enough to overcome the reflective magic—to cut through it. After a few cuts, the dome began to falter. And in the exposed places, Elander saw what he'd expected he might: The Moon Goddess.

She stirred into motion as Nephele's magic sparked closer to her. Her bowed head lifted, and her gaze followed a trail of that Storm magic for a moment before finding its way to Nephele.

As the two goddesses made eye contact, Inya made a

small motion with her hand. Her protective cage began to dissolve, little pieces of silver light peeling away into the darkness.

Elander almost heaved a sigh of relief—the Fire God hadn't annihilated everything after all—but he stopped short of doing so. Because although the goddess was safe, she was also alone.

There was no sign of Casia or Caden within her reflective cage.

The goddess held a bow that looked to have been fashioned out of moonlight. She caught sight of Elander, and an instant later, an arrow appeared in her other hand. She nocked it and pointed it at his chest.

"Another member of the Dark God's court here to start a fight with me?" she challenged as the rest of her protective dome fell away.

Elander moved toward her, thinking only of demanding answers from her—whether it meant starting a fight or not, he didn't care.

The goddess kept the bow lifted and pointed at him.

"Inya, wait," said Nephele, stepping between them. "He doesn't really belong to that court any longer, and you know this."

"What do any of us really know?" asked Inya, her voice an odd mixture of soft and seething. "For example, I *thought* I knew the laws and principles that the Fire God held to. But apparently not."

Nephele darted a worried look between her and

Elander, but she could hardly refute the other goddess's point, given the destruction they were surrounded by.

Elander dropped Caden's sword to the ground and lifted his palms to the Moon Goddess. "Shoot me if you want to. I don't care. But tell me something before you do."

Inya's softly furious gaze swept down to the dropped blade, then back up, calculating.

"I sent one of my servants to this realm so he could escape the Rook God's wrath," Elander continued. "And there was a woman with him."

"The grey-haired one?"

His breath caught. "Yes."

The goddess studied him for a moment longer before finally lowering her bow—though not completely. "She's safe. They both are."

The space around him felt like it was shifting, as if the walls were expanding outward and finally giving him enough room to breathe again.

"They went to Oakhaven. The woman said the Healing Goddess was taking care of a friend of hers."

Elander glanced behind him, looking to the row of portals there and searching for the one that would take him to that haven.

"I used my magic to temporarily close all of the paths leading into that forested realm, much to the Fire God's displeasure," Inya informed him. "And I don't think it would be wise to reopen them again with so much turmoil going on."

His heart fell at the thought of not being able to find Casia as soon as he'd hoped, but he still nodded. "You're right. They should stay closed."

She would be safe in Namu's forest with both Caden and that middle-goddess for protection.

Wouldn't she?

"We have other problems, anyway," Nephele insisted. Her gaze traveled over the room, catching on the dead fire-beast closest to them. "Because how *dare* the Dark God send one of his servants to attack this realm? Solatis will hear about this." She turned her gaze to Inya, clearly looking for someone to share in her righteous fury.

But Inya only frowned. "Tell me...does our goddess respond when you seek an audience with her lately?"

For the second time since arriving in this realm, Nephele's usually confident demeanor faltered for a moment. She remained silent, which was enough of an answer for the Moon Goddess.

"I believe she sleeps in spite of the disasters befalling us," said Inya. "She *must* be sleeping, or else how could the Rook God be moving about so freely? So violently? She has always kept him under control in the past."

"There seems to be an ever-growing list of things I don't understand," muttered Nephele.

"Could you try to summon her somehow?" Elander

wondered aloud. "Perhaps the other two of your order could help."

"A meeting of the Sun Court..." mused Inya.

"It's past due, perhaps," said Nephele.

They fell into a quiet discussion about the matter, while Elander found a scrap of cloth—what appeared to be a part of a fallen, burned tapestry—and used it to wipe the blood from his sword. He knelt among the ashes and destruction and absently cleaned that blade while he considered his next move.

Minutes later, the goddesses ceased their chatter, and Inya turned to Elander. "We can focus on trying to summon and appeal to Solatis for help with these matters, but what will you do, fallen one? Where will you go?"

Fallen.

The word was starting to lose its meaning. It had once been like a knife to his gut every time someone threw it at him. Now it was a mere discomfort, like a pair of boots not yet worn into comfortable shape.

He had accepted that he was more human than god at this point. But as for where one *went* after such a fall...

He had no idea.

But he knew that Casia would likely try to make her way back to the kingdom of Sadira where her allies would be awaiting her return. And if he could not follow her into Oakhaven, then he could at least be waiting for her when she returned. He had previously created a gate of sorts—a concentration of his power—in the capital city of Kosrith. With any luck, his magic would still be able to draw him toward that gate.

"I'm going back to the mortal realm," he said, standing. "To the last place I fought alongside the woman I mentioned earlier. There are more battles set to come in the Kethran Empire. I intend to help her fight them."

"Getting caught up in the wars of mortals is an exercise in futility," said the Moon Goddess.

"And you're in no condition to transport yourself back to the mortal world, anyway," Nephele pointed out. "You might not make it there in one piece."

"Was I not clear before," he asked, "when I told you that I would not rest until I found her again?"

Both of the goddesses fixed him with disapproving looks.

He ignored them.

It would certainly be agonizing, transporting himself to the gate in the shape he was in. Agonizing and dangerous. But he would still do it. He would do whatever it took to get back to her.

"Why do you care so much? Surely you haven't fallen for yet *another* human woman so completely? Even you could not be that much of a fool."

He started to turn away without answering, but Nephele's challenging gaze caught his and held it. And he owed her the truth, perhaps, given that she'd agreed to help him.

"Casia isn't *another* woman," he said quietly. "She's the same woman."

Nephele looked at him as if he had lost his mind.

"And I don't know if this will help get the upper-goddess's attention," he said as he reached into his pocket and retrieved the Heart of the Sun, "but it can't hurt for you to have it. Consider it a show of faith between us, if nothing else."

He wasn't certain what the future held, but he had a feeling that having these two as allies would prove useful. So he offered the Heart to Inya, who stood closer to him, and he waited patiently while she studied it and then took it with a hesitant hand.

Nephele's confused expression mirrored the one the Moon Goddess wore. Then it quickly turned to disbelief. "That...I've seen that before. That's the treasure you stole from Solatis."

"The same."

"Were you carrying that with you when you came to my realm earlier?"

He nodded.

"Why did I not sense it? It should be drenched with her magic. You shouldn't even be able to *touch* it without suffering. You...you..."

Elander thought of the enormous light that had driven the Rook God away, and of how weakly that light had pulsed afterward...before extinguishing completely. "There's a small chance I might have broken it," he said.

61

Nephele exhaled a slow breath, and the air around her briefly filled with sparks. "Of course you did."

"It's certainly not what it once was. Most of its power seems to have transferred to Casia a long time ago—that played a part in bringing her soul back to the mortal realm, is my theory."

Nephele's brow furrowed. Disbelief and irritation shimmered in her eyes.

"A fluke?" Inya guessed. "Or did our upper-goddess intend for it to happen?"

"I'm not sure." Elander frowned. "Add that to the list of things to ask if you manage to summon her."

A long silence stretched between them, until Nephele narrowed her gaze on Elander and said, "This woman that has repeatedly driven you to foolishness... what *bargain* did she start to make with the Dark god?"

He couldn't bring himself to answer right away.

"Tell me." The air around her filled once more with electricity. "Now."

He fixed his gaze on the Heart in Inya's hand as he finally said, "She agreed to serve him. And she didn't specify in what capacity." He looked to Nephele, saw the silent horror spreading across her face, and shook his head. "The ritual wasn't finished, at least. I stopped it."

"If it *is* finished, if he manages to draw her to his side and fully into his command, and if she *does* have Solatis's power buried inside of her—"

"It won't be finished. He won't take her." The words

62

had rushed so fervently from him that he had to pause and catch his breath. Calm himself down. "But I will deal with keeping her safe, if you two deal with finding Solatis and asking for her help."

Nephele continued to seethe while the Moon Goddess regarded them both with a quiet curiosity. "A used-up, broken show of faith..." she said, daintily lifting the Heart from her palm and twisting it back and forth. The faint silver light surrounding her seemed to bend toward it. "How lovely."

"It's symbolic, obviously," Elander said, "but that still counts for something, doesn't it?"

"Not really," was Nephele's flat reply. "You absolute idiot."

He flashed her a charming smile that, as per usual, she didn't appear charmed by. "Either way, I suspect you two have a better chance of figuring out its secrets than I do. So I'll leave it in your care for the time being. Just let me know what you and your court manage to accomplish as soon as you can."

"I will," Nephele agreed, somewhat stiffly. "*If* you don't perish somewhere in the abyss while stupidly trying to transport your weak and wounded self."

"Exactly. Anyways—thank you for your help."

She sniffed.

"I'll take that as a *you're welcome*."

She had already turned away from him and started to more closely inspect the Heart.

Elander left them to it and braced himself for the travel ahead. He could picture his destination clearly in his mind—the gate he'd created in Kosrith, tucked away in the room he'd been sharing with Casia, shimmering with the threads of his Death magic. He closed his eyes and reached out with his magic, trying to visualize himself stepping through the gate once more.

Finally, he felt the telltale pulling on his skin that told him he had connected to that gate. He opened his eyes and took one last look at the haven around him. It disappeared quickly, blurred away by the growing energy of his impending travel, but the images of ash and destruction stayed in his mind even as he was pulled away from it.

And he couldn't help thinking it looked like the start of a war.

CHAPTER 5

CAS WAS ENVELOPED IN A STRANGE WARMTH THAT REACHED down into her very bones. Comforting, and yet her entire body still ached. Her eyes stayed tightly shut as she tried to breathe through the pain.

"Why does traveling through those pathways have to *hurt* so much?" she mumbled.

She expected silence to be her answer, or perhaps Caden's smug voice telling her she deserved that hurt.

Instead, a rough-edged, female voice replied, "Because you are a mortal. And it is almost as if we would prefer that mortals like you *didn't* make a habit of crashing unexpectedly into our realms."

Cas opened her eyes.

A woman stood over her. She was tall—a giantess, really—with a ruddy complexion and piercing green eyes. It looked as if she had attempted to tame her billowing nest of auburn hair only to give up partway through the job; there were several neat braids framing her face, but the rest was a tangled mess threaded with clips and pins and at least two moth-like insects that Cas thought might have been real.

"Namu?" Cas breathed.

"One of my mortal-given names. Probably my least favorite—not that it matters." She turned and walked away.

Cas sat up and glanced around. Canvas walls surrounded her, and sunlight bled through them—a tent of sorts. The floor was an uneven patchwork of planks. She heard birds singing in the distance, and a warm breeze made the cloth door rustle. Namu was sorting through a large woven basket beside that door.

"I don't remember arriving here," Cas thought aloud.

"I daresay that's because you were unconscious. Your lesser-spirit companion carried you in here and insisted I see to you." The moths in her hair *were* real; they fluttered around the goddess's head as she spoke, and they took flight as she turned and walked back to Cas. She carried a small bottle in her hand.

"I have a friend here," Cas told her, "one that was injured, which is why I—"

"Yes."

"Is he...?"

"He'll live." She took the stopper from that bottle and dumped its contents into her palm—a trio of feathers, a pinch of insect wings, two tiny pebbles. All of it was coated in a shimmery golden dust. Her hand closed over the random assortment of items.

When it unfolded a moment later, the only thing in her palm was a small red berry.

Cas was momentarily mesmerized by this. Before she could ask any more questions, the goddess held out the berry to her. "I have other things to go tend to at the moment, but you should take this for your headache."

Cas hadn't mentioned a headache, but almost as if on cue, her right temple was suddenly throbbing. She tentatively took the tiny fruit—or whatever it truly was—and studied it more closely.

"Come speak with me later."

Cas nodded. It didn't occur to her to ask what the goddess meant by *later*. Her head felt as if it had been stuffed with cotton, her thoughts muddled and buried, and time suddenly felt irrelevant. She'd experienced similar feelings in the other godhavens she'd been to, and she wondered—not for the first time—if time truly did pass differently in these places.

At some point after the goddess left, Cas finally remembered that she needed to keep moving. After a brief debate with herself, she ate the berry. Every story she had ever heard of Namu painted her as a benevolent force, and a goddess of healing wouldn't poison her, she reasoned.

Nothing seemed to happen because of that berry anyway. Her body still ached, and she still felt as if she was moving through a slightly-too-warm, entirely-too-hazy dreamworld as she pulled on her boots and stepped out of the tent.

She found herself in the middle of a forest. Her tent, and several others like it, were perched high among the tree-tops—so high that, when she cautiously knelt and peered over the side of the wooden platform she was on, she couldn't see the ground. There were only thick clouds of fog. Maybe there *was* no ground. Each of these godhavens seemed stranger than the last, so it was not so odd to think she might have been floating high out of reach of the mortal world.

She backed carefully away from the edge and continued surveying her surroundings. An intricate network of swinging bridges connected the larger trees and the platforms built around them. Dozens of people moved over these bridges, chatting and laughing. Others lounged in hammocks stretched between the ample supply of sturdy branches. Mortals—Cas was fairly certain—like the countless ones she'd seen serving in Stormhaven. Nephele's servants were Storm-marked humans who had spent their lives studying in her various temples, perfecting their magic until they'd proven worthy of walking in her haven.

She wondered if the people here had a similar backstory.

There were birds perched in nearly every tree, most of them with long, sweeping tails and elaborate crests of silver, green, and blue feathers. Cas was staring at a particularly colorful specimen when she heard someone approaching her.

Caden's voice reached her. "You're awake."

She glanced back at the tent she'd left behind. "How long was I unconscious for?"

He shrugged. "Two days, give or take."

Uneasiness curled into a heavy weight in her stomach. She was all too aware of how quickly disasters could occur—how things could go from bad to worse in less than a day.

What had become of the world while she slept?

She met Caden's cold brown eyes, trying not to think of all the possible disasters that might be occurring outside of this divine realm. "You stayed."

"I was given an order to protect you. So that's what I'm doing."

Elander's orders.

Of course.

She hesitated, steeling herself before she asked, "Can you still sense him?"

He averted his gaze. An obvious enough answer, and that uneasiness in her stomach shifted and threatened to make her sick.

"Your friend is in the tent across the bridge over there, if you wanted to see him," Caden told her.

It was a clear attempt to change the subject, but Cas was grateful for it. She didn't want to dwell on what had become of Elander. All that mattered at the moment—all that she could currently act upon—was the fact that Zev was close by.

Alive.

She repeated the word over and over to herself as she hurried in the direction Caden had indicated.

She hastily introduced herself to the two women keeping watch outside of Zev's tent, and then she pushed her way inside, past another woman, until she finally saw him.

Alive.

He was whole and breathing and resting peacefully, and for the first time in what felt like ages, Cas felt light cracking through the dark clouds that had gathered around her heart.

She restrained from sprinting and crashing excitedly into him—she didn't want to wake him. She tried to move quietly across the space. She had almost made it to his bedside when her boot fell upon a plank that creaked so loudly the mortal world likely heard it.

Zev stirred and popped one eye open. "You're late," he yawned. "As usual."

The sound of his voice, weak as it was, nearly made

her burst into tears. "I'm worth the wait," she informed him.

"Debatable."

She rushed forward and embraced him, burying her face in his shoulder and trying to choke down the sob rising in her throat.

"Nice of you to stop by and visit my deathbed, either way," Zev said, the words muffled under her crushing embrace.

"Deathbed?"

"Mm-hm. I'm a hopeless case, I'm afraid."

Cas leaned back, grinning. "The goddess already told me you're going to live, so you can drop the dramatic act."

"That's no fun, though." He settled back against the pillows and closed his eyes again. The exhaustion was evident in his features, but the smile never left his face.

Her gaze went to the hand he had against his stomach. Terrible images of the battle at Kosrith flashed in her mind, and suddenly she was back on her knees beside the roaring Belaric Sea, crawling to Zev's side, her face buried in his blood-stained coat, her throat hoarse from crying and begging Elander to do something...*anything*.

And Elander had.

He'd saved Zev by bringing him here, but it had set off a chain of terrible events, and now...

"You know I'm not dying," said Zev, "and yet you're

still crying. So tell me again who the *dramatic* one is?" His eyes had opened again, and they were studying her with a combination of amusement and concern.

Her eyes had misted over without her realizing it. She wiped them with the heels of her hands and settled down on the edge of the bed. "In my defense, you look terrible," she told him. "And it's partly just the air in this realm. It's too warm. Or too flowery. Or too...something."

The amusement faded from his expression, and the concern deepened, pulled the corners of his smile downward. But then he simply nodded. "It *is* warm, isn't it?"

They were quiet for a long moment—or a long moment by Zev's standards, anyhow; he was almost always the first one to break silences, and this time was no different.

"You really *are* late." He was staring at her face, at the mark the Rook God had clawed into it.

"I took the scenic route."

"And that mark on your face is...new."

"Yes."

"Another complication?"

"Perhaps the biggest one yet." She sighed, picking at a loose thread on the blanket she sat upon. "But one we can deal with later. What about you? How do you feel, honestly?"

"I've been better. Also worse. The goddess was quick

to heal me...bedside manner could use some work, though. She isn't particularly nice."

Cas gave him a wry smile. She doubted the goddess cared what he thought about her bedside manner. "That seems to be a trend with all these deities," she said. "Although the Moon Goddess seemed nice enough."

"What? You met her?"

Cas braced her arms against the edge of the bed and swung her feet back and forth across the floor. "Briefly."

Zev shook his head, a quiet, disbelieving laugh bubbling out of him. After another unusually long pause he said, "Did you ever think we would end up in a place like this?"

"Conversing with gods? Battling with kings? Taking refuge in havens like this?" She mirrored his laughter. "No, none of this ever occurred to me as a possibility."

"Me either. I miss the simple missions. The tracking, the spying, the relieving people of their wallets and their burdensome extra coin..."

"We were above petty theft," Cas reminded him.

"Yeah, Asra always said that. But *she* stole plenty. Especially when we were younger and couldn't help support ourselves. Also? I never agreed to be above petty theft. Why do none of you ever remember that?"

Cas huffed out another laugh as she stretched out beside him.

"Speaking of when we were younger, you know what I *really* miss?"

"What's that?"

"That old house in Faircliff. Do you even remember it? You were younger than me, so maybe you don't." He chuckled softly. "Practically everything in that place was stolen."

"I still remember that. Vividly, actually."

Asra used to work a side job cleaning homes for the elite families of Faircliff. Her real reason for doing so was to gain access to the gossip and information that pointed her and her associates toward other, more questionable—but also far more lucrative—jobs. And yes, occasionally she also came home with a few bonus items in addition to that information. Cas didn't realize until much later that those *bonuses* had not been given, but taken.

Nothing wrong with a little redistribution of wealth, Zev had told her when she found out.

Faircliff was the place Cas thought of most clearly whenever any conversation turned to talk of childhood homes. She had lived in other places before then. Some she remembered, some she didn't. Her earliest memories were faulty at best, ravaged and rearranged by trauma and—apparently—by the wild magic that had accompanied her rebirth into this world. There had been her first adoptive parents, the Lord and Lady Tessur, and an orphanage before that...

But the rickety old house in Faircliff, with Asra sitting by its brick fireplace, chatting with Rhea while

Zev constantly found new ways to make messes and blame her for them... Those were the memories that remained among her most vivid.

Maybe because staying in that house was the first time she had ever felt like she was *home*.

Zev was quiet again. She thought he had fallen asleep, wrapped up in the cozy embrace of nostalgia, when suddenly the bed shook once more with his quiet laughter.

"What's so funny?"

"I was just thinking about the old treehouse that Asra built us."

It had been a lookout perch, technically. But Zev had declared it a treehouse instead, and then he'd promptly made up arbitrary rules as to why Cas was not allowed in it.

It had been annoying at the time. Now, the memory filled Cas with warmth, and suddenly she was laughing too. "It hardly qualified as a treehouse. It was missing most of the walls and the roof, as I recall."

"True. But being in the treetops here still made me think of it."

She nodded, and then she cut her eyes toward him. "You know what else I remember? You pushing me off the ladder leading up to that treehouse."

He shrugged. "You deserved it. You stole my favorite knife. And besides, you only fell like...seven feet. At most."

"I cut my head on a rock when I landed."

"Yes, but you survived, didn't you?"

She pushed her hair away from her forehead, absently massaging the place where that cut had been. Her head was no longer throbbing after the remedy Namu had given her, she realized. And there was no scar upon it from her long-ago fall, either; only the memory of it remained, tucked safely alongside all the others they'd made at that house.

"Gods, you were such a pain in the ass," she said.

"You're *still* a pain in the ass."

She punched him softly in the arm.

"Punching the fatally wounded? That's low, even for you."

"You aren't *fatally* wounded."

"Keep hitting me like that and I might be. Who taught you to punch, anyway?"

"You did."

"Ah. Right. I did a damn good job, didn't I?"

She shrugged. "You did okay."

"I did the best I could, considering my incompetent pupil."

"Do you want me to punch you again and show you how competent I can be?"

"Or you could use a knife," he suggested. "I think there's one among my things in the corner over there, if you wanted to steal that one too."

"Are you going to push me out of this treehouse if I do?"

"I might."

She laughed again. She had done more of that in the past five minutes than she had in days. Weeks, maybe. She felt as if she were ten years old again, side by side with her best friend, hiding in their treehouse to avoid the chores and all the uncertain, darker things that awaited them outside.

Their laughter trailed into comfortable silence. Despite the goddess's healing, she could tell Zev was tired, so she kept quiet and minutes later, he was snoring. Loudly and obnoxiously, as per usual.

With a slight smile, she curled up beside him and closed her eyes. She tried not to think about all of those darker things outside, and she found it surprisingly easy to do. Maybe it was the berry the goddess had given her. Whatever the reason, she had soon dozed off herself...

Only to wake up a short time later to the feel of Zev's hand against her face.

"What are you doing?" she asked, groggily, as she swatted him away.

"I swear that mark on your face looked like it was darkening."

She tried to cover her alarm with a laugh. "So your first instinct was to *poke* it?"

"Asks the woman who was punching my injured body earlier like some kind of sadist."

She sat up, gingerly touching that mark and avoiding Zev's worried gaze.

"What happened to you, Cas?"

The laughter of earlier was now a distant memory; it didn't even feel like it had been real.

She clasped her hands in front of her and kept her eyes on them as she spoke. "Before I came here through the Moon Goddess's haven, Elander and I tried to go through Oblivion first. The Rook God was waiting for us there. We fought, and I tried to strike a bargain with him to make the fighting stop. Elander interrupted our deal-making, but not before...well, *this*." She gestured toward her face.

"So what are you then? Half-marked? Half-cursed? What does that mean?"

"I'm not sure."

"Well, what about Elander? Where is he now?"

"I don't know that either." Her voice broke a bit toward the end. The Rook God's mark had started to ache slightly. It might have been her imagination, but whether it was real or not, she could sense a panic attack building in response.

She wanted to be alone when that attack struck, so she got to her feet. "There's a lot to figure out," she said. "We can talk about it later, though. You should get some more rest while you can. I suspect the Oak Goddess is going to kick us out soon."

"...Good chance of it," he agreed.

"I'm going to go speak with her—maybe she'll be able to answer some of these questions."

He looked reluctant to let her go on such an unfinished note, but she forced a smile and an unwavering voice as she said, "I'm so glad you're okay, by the way."

And then she was gone before he had a chance to argue against it.

CHAPTER 6

THE ACHE IN HER NEW MARK DID NOT ABATE ONCE CAS WAS outside.

She hurried out of Zev's hearing range before he could call her back, tapping her fingers against her palm as she went, counting each solid connection she made and trying to keep herself calm.

There were more beings outside than before. Some looked entirely human, like those servants in Stormhaven. But others, she now realized, were slightly...different—though they might have passed for humans, if not for things like the strange glowing patterns swirled upon their skin, or their too-fluid movements, or their oddly bright eyes.

She walked by a woman with long, silver-blue feathers instead of hair, and Cas couldn't help staring at her, thinking of those elegant birds she'd spotted earlier and wondering if they could have been the same creature in different forms.

Her anxiety ultimately kept its distance—enough that she was able to stay on her feet, at least. She suspected it might have been that berry the goddess had given her, creating a sort of shield around her thoughts. The waves of panic rolled toward her only to strike a wall too high for them to wash over; they battered against her mind and then receded, and she steadied herself after every hit and kept moving.

She found a secluded bridge and paused in the center of it. Gripping the railing, she willed her fingers to keep still and her lungs to breathe normally as she surveyed her surroundings, searching for a clue as to where the goddess might be, or for a friendly face that seemed eager to help point her in the right direction. But most of the beings she made eye contact with mirrored that middle-goddess they served—stern and mildly disappointed in her being here. At best.

She was safe here, but clearly not *welcome*.

She started to move again—she would find the goddess on her own if she had to—but she didn't make it far before she heard Caden approaching her once more.

"The goddess sent me to fetch you." He frowned as he looked her over. "Are you all right? You look as though you're seconds away from fainting."

Cas nodded without hesitation. "I'll be fine. But let's take the long way to that goddess."

He arched a brow.

"I just need more...air."

And more time to finish pulling myself together.

He didn't object. They walked silently for several minutes, climbing higher and higher into the trees. The swirling fog below dissipated completely as they reached what she guessed was the highest level of the realm. Everything here was bathed in golden light instead of mist.

"Have you been able to sense him yet?" The question escaped Cas before she could stop it. She wished she could take it back, but Caden had already heard her; he was shaking his head.

"Do you...do you think he survived Oblivion?" she asked, quieter.

Caden took longer to reply this time, and Cas's heart sank a little deeper with every passing second.

"Yes," he finally said.

He didn't elaborate. Cas didn't pressure him to. The *yes* had not sounded convincing, and she was afraid it might change to a *no* if she challenged it.

But she couldn't help talking about Elander now that she'd started; it made her feel closer to him—as if he couldn't be gone as long as they kept speaking of him. "You've served him for a long time, haven't you?"

"I have."

"How did you meet? How did you become a divine spirit in his court?"

"The same way that all divine beings, aside from the Moraki themselves, ascended."

"Which is how, precisely?"

That seemingly permanent scowl of his deepened, and he picked up his pace.

She briefly considered turning and marching the other direction, finding her own way to that goddess just so she wouldn't have to spend another second in Caden's disagreeable presence.

But she had no idea where she was going. There were a dozen different tents and rounded huts on this level of the haven—that she could *see*. So she begrudgingly caught up with him once more.

He said nothing for several paces. She sighed, and he cut an unimpressed glance in her direction. But after a moment he said, "It's not a subject I particularly like talking about. I don't like to think about what I was before."

"Mortal, you mean?"

"Yes. A mortal closing in on death, suffering from a sickness the doctors could neither name nor fix. When Elander encountered me, I was a soldier in the service of a king who is long gone now, marching off to a war I didn't intend to return from. I had plans to die on the battlefield—go out on my own terms, I guess. The Death God met me on one of those battlefields. There were a lot of souls passing on and needing guidance during those bloody days."

"But you didn't pass on, obviously."

"No."

"Because he turned you into a servant spirit instead?"

Caden nodded, hesitated, and then said, "I've asked him *why* multiple times over the centuries, but he's never really told me."

She wondered about it herself while they walked. "Perhaps it was because of how you walked onto the battlefield, unafraid of death?"

He seemed to consider this for a moment, rather than outright dismissing her—which was surprising.

"Perhaps," he said.

"So a middle-god chooses a mortal, marks them, and passes enough of certain facets of their power into their body to allow them to ascend..."

"Essentially."

"And lesser-spirits can mark humans and give them magic at birth, too, right?" Cas pictured Nessa and the Feather-spirit mark she carried. Her heart clenched, wondering when she might see her again.

"Yes," Caden told her. "Though not enough to create another divine being. The hierarchy of the divine ends with the lesser-spirits. And there are limits, too, for both the spirits and middle-gods—we can't just create an infinite number of servants, divine or otherwise."

It was essentially the explanation she'd worked out on her own, but it was different to hear it all spoken of so plainly, and from such a direct source.

"So he chose you, for whatever reason," she said. "He saved you. You're more than master and servant."

"Always have been."

Elander had told her something similar—several times, actually. She'd gotten the impression that Tara and Caden were his makeshift family, same as Zev and the others were hers.

But then Tara had betrayed him.

The thought triggered a visceral reaction on his behalf. She couldn't imagine one of her friends betraying her in such a way, or how sick Elander must have felt about it all...

"So though I am not thrilled about how you've complicated things," Caden continued, "I suppose the alternative would have been worse."

"The alternative?"

"Him not finding you again."

She slowed to a stop, unsure of what to say. Elander not finding her again seemed precisely like the sort of alternative that Caden should have been thrilled about.

Was he being honest with her?

Caden stopped walking as well, just long enough to tilt his face back toward her. "I still remember what it was like the day he lost you. I had never seen any being, divine or otherwise, so devastated."

He continued along the path, and she hugged her arms against herself and trailed after him, thinking, wishing she knew what to say.

"And I would not be a particularly good servant *or* friend if I hadn't hoped that there might be a way to fix it," Caden said, almost more to himself than her. "Though I'm still not convinced it *is* fixable. Obviously. Given the current mess we're in..."

She caught up to him, but she kept her eyes on the wooden path before her, not wanting him to see the uncertainty that was likely shimmering in her gaze as she said, "I'm going to find a way to fix it."

He didn't reply.

They had arrived at the door of a large, circular building that rose high above all the other structures around them. Five separate bridges converged toward it. They were alone; there were no servants—or any other living creatures—in sight. It was strangely silent, as if the warmer-than-ever air had suffocated even the sounds of rustling leaves and birdsong.

Caden nodded toward the door, giving her a meaningful look.

She took a deep breath and stepped inside.

It was similar to the tent she had woken up in, only bigger. Sturdier. The Oak Goddess was hunched over a table on the far side of the space. The center of the ceiling was open, revealing a patch of peach-colored sky and bathing the space in the same golden hues as outside. Moths fluttered and shimmery dust sparkled through air that smelled of honey and smoke.

"Sit," the goddess commanded without looking at her.

Cas did as she was told, settling down on one of the colorful cushions that lined the wall. She waited for the goddess to speak.

Several minutes passed.

"I never properly introduced myself," Cas finally blurted out. "I suppose I should tell you—"

"I know who you are." She kept her back to Cas even as she spoke. "And I know who you *were*. Because we've met once before." She plucked a small knife from a block upon the table, went to the row of plants spread along a nearby shelf, and started to harvest their leaves with tiny, jerking cuts. "The Death God brought you to me in the last hours of your previous life. He begged me over and over to save you. On his knees, in this very hut."

Cas tried to picture Elander begging for anything.

She couldn't do it.

The confident, bordering-on-arrogant Captain of the King's army was still the personality she most associated with him. Even now, she was still trying to wrap her mind around the fact that he had always been someone and something else altogether—that *they* had once been something else altogether. And that he had apparently loved her enough to fall to his knees and beg for her life.

It was terribly frustrating, not being able to remember that other life they'd lived together.

Was there a way to get those memories back?

"And before that," the goddess continued, sweeping the cut leaves into her palm, "he tried to convince me to help your ailing sister."

"But you didn't help either one of us."

"If I helped everyone who came and begged me to spare someone, the cycle of life and death would be irrevocably ruined." She dropped her collected leaves into a small bowl and moved on to another shelf of plants.

Her hands were forever busy, Cas was noticing, and there were smudges of what looked like soil on one of her cheeks. It seemed strange that a goddess with powerful magic would bother to collect herbs and berries and such to infuse with her power. Perhaps she just liked the feel of her hands in the dirt.

"Your sister in that past life was meant to die," said Namu. "Your friend in the tent down below would have healed on his own, eventually—I simply sped up the process of that healing. There is a difference. I don't *overturn* death. Neither did the Death God, even before his fall from grace. That power is beyond the Marr—it is beyond all but Solatis, the creator of life. And he has always known that. Even when he came to me in desperation, deep down he surely knew that I couldn't, *wouldn't*, save anyone that wasn't meant to live."

Cas considered her words. Elander had told her before that his powers allowed him to both cause death and temporarily stall it, but not reverse it. For the majority of his existence as the Rook God's servant, he had mostly been in the business of guiding souls and maintaining the paths between the mortal realm and the afterworlds.

"What about the past me?" she asked. "Was I meant to die as well?"

"Perhaps not." The middle-goddess dropped more leaves into her bowl, placed the knife on the shelf, and gently examined one of the plants she hadn't harvested from. "But that was a special case. I did not help that past you because of the circumstances surrounding your demise. I had no desire to get involved in a feud between Malaphar and Solatis. I still have no desire to get involved, just so we're clear."

"You serve neither of those upper-gods..."

"Correct."

She served Belegor, the Stone God, the one who had given the world shape, formed its mountains and valleys and seas...and then, according to most legends, had promptly removed himself from the affairs of mortals.

Neutrality is worse than outright animosity, Cas thought, bristling.

She remembered Caden's warning about offending the divine, but she couldn't help the challenge that rose out of her. "You're aware that *I* am currently involved in a feud with Malaphar, correct? I assume Elander told you as much when he brought my friend here? Or that you've heard it from one of your fellow Marr?" Most of her encounters with the divine thus far had led her to believe they were a dramatic, gossipy bunch.

The goddess finally turned to face her.

"But you helped my friend, anyway," said Cas as she rose to her feet. "So I don't think you're as neutral as you claim."

She fought the urge to brace a hand against the wall as the giant goddess took a step toward her. The golden light in the hut seemed to dim, while the insects and shimmering trails of dust moved more sluggishly through the air.

"When he brought that young man to me," said the goddess, her green eyes boring into Cas's, "he told me who you were, trying to convince me that you were worth helping. He seemed to think that it was imperative that you were able to keep fighting, that it would be for the betterment of the mortal world—and our divine realms—if you did. And that you would find it easier to fight with your friend beside you, healed and in one piece."

"And he convinced you to think the same things, apparently."

She turned away again, took a ceramic mortar and pestle from a drawer tucked under the table, and started to drop ingredients into that mortar. "The Death God has a persuasiveness about him," she finally admitted. "A skill that has caused all of us a lot of trouble, honestly." She glanced back, and her gaze softened for a fraction of a moment as it caught on Cas's face. "He didn't mention that mark on your cheek during our conversation, however."

"It's a more recent addition."

"I see." She closed the space between them and examined Cas's cheek, just like the Moon Goddess had. Her fingertips gently glided over the skin, same as they'd done with her plants a moment ago. Diagnosing her, apparently, because after a moment she drew her hand away with a disgusted hiss. "The Dark God's magic. Of course."

Cas was about to reply when she realized that the ache in her cheek had subsided, just from a mere touch of Namu's hand, and she was stunned into silence.

"You're lucky the magic doesn't run as deep as it could. *Yet.*" The goddess wiped her fingers on the folds of the emerald dress she wore, as if trying to rid them of that magic's invisible residue. "He didn't finish his curse."

Cas was still marveling at the lack of pain she felt, and now she couldn't help but ask: "Can you take it away?"

"The mark itself? Yes. And any topical pain it's causing."

Cas touched her fingers to that blemish. It was so

smooth—not at all like the ragged-edged scar she had been expecting to form there. It seemed more like a birth mark, like something that had always been a part of her. She cringed inwardly at the thought. "But there is a cost for that, I assume?"

The goddess stared at the ceiling, at the small patch of sky it revealed, as she replied. "Pain rarely goes away entirely. It simply changes form."

With that, she went back to the mortar and pestle and sprinkled a few more leaves into the bowl, along with an assortment of other ingredients. She brought her fingertips together, scrunched her face in concentration until ribbons of light swirled around her hand, and then directed those ribbons into the concoction she was mixing.

Cas silently watched her work.

The ribbons of light she'd summoned would not be contained in the small bowl; they overflowed and encircled the goddess, lifting the strands of her hair. The air grew smokier, warmer, heavier—so heavy and warm that Cas's eyes had started to close when the loud *thud* of a drawer being shut made her jump.

The goddess walked back to her with a small jar in her hand. "If you get desperate enough, you can take this to ease your pain."

Cas took the jar and inspected the plum-colored salve within. It was glowing faintly. "And it will erase the mark?"

"It will cause it to fade, at least in appearance. But what it represents—the burden it's given you—is too powerful for my magic to erase. If it were to leave you— if you somehow found a way to expel it—it would simply find another host. Bargains like that do not come undone so easily."

"Another host...like another person, you mean?"

"Yes."

Cas recoiled. "I don't want it expelled then."

The goddess canted her head. "You wouldn't even consider it? Even if it meant that you could free yourself of the Dark God's curse and command?"

"Not at the expense of forcing someone else into his command."

"Interesting."

"Aren't you a goddess of Healing? How could you think I *should* want to curse someone else?"

The goddess bared her teeth at this. "I have a better question for you."

"And what is that?"

"Who do you heal first," she asked, "when the whole world seems to be aching? And have you considered that your life might be worth sparing because of the weight it carries? Do not be so eager to martyr yourself, child. The Death God was not wrong when he spoke of the importance of your fight. You carry a heavy purpose—a heavy magic. And now you carry a heavy curse, and all of these things together might mean disaster for your world if

93

you do not tread carefully. Or they could mean healing. So what next? What will you make of the things that have been given to you, both the good and the bad? Never mind the mark the Dark God left; what mark do *you* plan to leave behind?"

Cas inhaled deeply. She didn't know the right answer. Not yet. She wasn't certain there *was* a right answer.

"Whatever you decide, you cannot stay here." Namu's voice was firm. "The Sand Goddess and her attendants belong to the same divine court as myself," she continued. "I have sent for Cardea, the Air spirit that serves that other goddess. This spirit can transport you to wherever you wish within the mortal realm. So decide where it is you plan to go next, and do it quickly. You will be taking your friend and leaving as soon as that spirit arrives." Her orders given, she went back to the table and started to clean and organize her supplies.

"Tell me one more thing before I leave," Cas said, once she found her voice again. The goddess did not object, so she kept talking: "This curse...you easily recognized it for what it was."

"I did."

"So do you know what it will ultimately do to me if it isn't removed?"

Her hands stilled in the middle of reaching for something.

94

"Tell me the truth." Cas's voice shook, but she still forced the words out. "Please."

She went back to arranging her supplies. "As your beloved Death God loses his divine power," she said, "it must go somewhere else. Someone else must ascend in his place. In this case, the transfer of that power is happening a bit more strangely, and more slowly, than usual, but the end result will be the same, I suspect."

"Another will ascend...?"

"Yes. And it seems the Dark God has found his new host." She tilted her face back toward Cas. "You."

CHAPTER 7

SIDE-BY-SIDE, CAS AND ZEV STEPPED OUT OF THE PORTAL THE Air spirit had created for them.

After the unnatural warmth of Oakhaven, the frigid air of the fallen kingdom of Sadira seemed even more brutal than usual.

They'd requested a gateway that opened into a secluded stretch of forest north of the capital city of Kosrith, and Caden had gone through it before them, scouting the path and making certain there were no ambushes or other dangerous surprises awaiting them. He was on a distant hilltop now, awaiting their arrival. When he caught sight of them, he signaled that it was clear to move forward.

Shivering, Cas glanced back one last time at the lesser-spirit, who lingered at the edge of her created portal. She was a tiny slip of a creature with milky skin and iridescent wings. She had not spoken a word while carrying out her duty, and she did not speak one now. Her large eyes met Cas's. Blinked.

"Thank you," Cas said.

The spirit bowed her head. And then she was gone, turning to smoke before twisting into nothingness along with that portal she'd made.

"Ready?" Zev asked, giving Cas a little nudge.

Cas nodded. She was not eager to return to the wars awaiting her in this place, but she *was* eager to see her friends and allies, and to be back among the familiar air of the mortal world.

The trek back to the city—and to the former-temple-turned-war-base where they expected to find those allies—was not a short one, but the time in the Healing Goddess's realm had been rejuvenating; Cas felt as if she was back at her full strength for the first time in weeks, as did Zev, and so they made good time. The crumbling face of the old temple was in view within a half hour, just as the sun rose over the distant hills and started to warm away the grey gloom of the morning.

Once they were safely within the yard of that temple, Caden left to go tend to other things within the city. He didn't elaborate on those things. Cas suspected he simply wanted a bit of freedom, to escape his protection duties now that his ward was relatively safe. But perhaps that wasn't the *only* reason; he still didn't sense Elander's presence, he'd told her.

What was going through his head, now that he was back among mortals and without the rest of his divine court?

She thanked him for his help and watched him leave —wondering where he might end up, and if he'd bother to come back—until Zev eagerly snatched her hand and pulled her toward the temple.

The guards at the front door recognized her after a moment of staring. With respectful nods, she and Zev were admitted inside, and they had started to make their way down a long hallway when a sudden squeal rang out. Cas recognized it immediately. She took a step back, glanced into the room she'd just passed, and her heart swelled so fast she thought it might burst from her chest.

Nessa.

The young Feather-kind woman was out in the hallway in the next instant, throwing herself at Cas and knocking her back against the wall.

Rhea was not far behind her, Silverfoot draped in his customary place over her shoulder, his green eyes shining with magic as they swept over the scene and relayed it to his master.

Rhea went for her brother instead of Cas. After a quick, crushing embrace, she leaned back and roughly took hold of Zev's face. The fox on her shoulder tipped forward, his eyes narrowed, looking as stern as a small, fluffy creature could possibly look.

"I heard you were being reckless on the battlefield," Rhea snapped, her grip tightening as she gave her brother a furious little shake.

Cas found herself fighting laughter at the chastened look on Zev's face.

"And that you nearly got yourself killed trying to be a hero," Rhea continued, before Zev could edge in a response. "What did I say to you before we parted ways in Rykarra? Didn't I tell you not to do anything rash? You *idiotic*—"

"Did you also hear that, due my rash actions, I'm horribly injured?" Zev asked. "Because I am. So maybe stop shaking me like that, you crazy woman."

"He's not *that* horribly injured," Cas interjected, still hugging Nessa. "The Healing Goddess is very good at what she does, it turns out."

"I'm still in pain," Zev insisted. "Awful, terrible pain. Don't listen to Cas. She's a sadist who enjoys my suffering."

Rhea took a deep breath. Let one hand fall away from her brother's face, scratched Silverfoot's chin, and collected herself.

"So much pain," Zev insisted.

His sister turned her attention to Cas. "Well, someday this pain will be useful to you, I'm sure," she muttered as she went.

"Yes, but that day is not *today*," Zev muttered back,

rubbing the spot where his sister's fingers had pinched so tightly.

Nessa grinned, and she finally let go of Cas so Rhea could embrace her.

"We arrived just this morning from Sundolia," Rhea told Cas. "And Soryn told us you'd survived the battle with Varen only to disappear without a trace. We've been anxiously trying to figure out where on earth you'd gone ever since. Laurent mentioned that Elander took Zev to Oakhaven..."

Cas started to explain her chaotic travels from the past days, but before she could find the words to do so, Soryn herself rounded the corner ahead of them. The exiled queen was flanked on one side by Laurent and by Sade—the emissary of the High King and Queen of the southern empire—on the other.

Soryn exhaled a slow, relieved breath as she caught sight of Cas and Zev. "You had us worried," she said, extending a hand as she approached.

"No need to worry," Zev said, taking it. He offered his hand to Sade next, but the Sundolian woman simply nodded in greeting, keeping her arms folded across her chest.

"You managed not to die," she said. "Well done."

"I'm a professional at not dying," Zev informed her with a smile. "Nearly impossible to kill."

"Much like a cockroach," Nessa put in, grinning again. "In so many ways, really."

Zev shot her a cross look, while Sade mirrored her smile, her normally icy expression briefly melting.

Laurent wrapped Cas in a quick, one-armed squeeze. "Are you all right then?"

She nodded. But as he let her go, Cas surveyed the room, and the elation that had ballooned in her heart slowly began to deflate.

She kept smiling, kept focusing on the faces of her friends. Zev and Nessa teasing one another. Rhea sighing and shaking her head at the two of them. Laurent falling back into a quiet, serious conversation with Soryn and Sade. Everyone was back in one place. Everyone was safe...

Almost everyone.

Caden had told her Elander wouldn't be here. But she had still hoped, by some miracle, that she'd find him here waiting for her. She didn't realize how desperately she'd been hoping it until now, when she realized that it hadn't come true.

"Casia?"

She turned at the sound of Soryn's voice, and she found the Queen watching her with a grim expression.

"The rest of our catching up will have to wait," said Soryn.

"Why's that?"

"Because you're just in time for another reunion. One that won't be as happy as this one, I'm afraid... Varen is close by. He's waiting at the port, at the old dockmaster's house. He wants an audience with you."

"And did you tell him to go fuck himself when he requested it?" Zev asked.

"I would have," Soryn said gravely, "if he and his soldiers were not holding several dozen of *our* soldiers hostage."

Cas's heart finished deflating. It felt like it had sunk down and created a cavernous pit in the bottom of her stomach.

"They gathered them up after the battle at the cliffs, it turns out," Soryn said. "We've been making up excuses and finding ways to stall him while we awaited your return, but his patience grows thin. And we suspect he's going to start taking his impatience out on those hostages soon...if he hasn't already."

Cas nodded, understanding what had to be done, even though she desperately did not want to do it.

"I will see him once I've changed and collected my sword," she said. "I'm assuming my things are still in the room I was staying in before?"

"Yes," Soryn confirmed.

"We could surely come up with some other plan, couldn't we?" Rhea asked, her voice soft with worry. "Something that doesn't involve sending Cas straight into the jaws of the enemy?"

Murmurs of agreement and arguments started among the rest of the group, but Cas didn't reply; she had already started for her room, moving with slow but determined steps, while the words of the Oak Goddess floated through her mind—

What will you make of the things that have been given to you, both the good and the bad?

What mark do you plan to leave behind?

A SHORT TIME LATER, Laurent and Nessa accompanied Cas as she made her way toward the edge of the sea.

A small army of Sadiran soldiers trailed closely behind them as well—just in case. Rhea had stayed behind at their base, and she'd insisted on Zev staying and resting more as well. He'd been smart enough not to argue with her for once.

The air had warmed considerably as the day pressed on, and it had grown damp with the promise of rain. The sky was darkening, the winds shifting. Waves were rolling, slamming with increasingly violent tempers against the shore.

Memories of the battle that had recently been fought upon this shore crashed just as violently in Cas's head, trying to break into her thoughts. She kept catching glimpses of rocks and driftwood stained with what she thought might have been blood. There had been so many bodies scattered across this beach, so much blood spilled...too much for even the sea and Sadira's frequent storms to wash away.

It wasn't difficult to find the spot Varen had taken up residence in—dozens of his soldiers lined a rickety wooden ramp, leading up to a ramshackle building that overlooked the expansive Port of Kosrith.

Like the temple that served as Soryn's base, this building looked as though it had been grand at some point—back when this port was the busiest in the Kethran Empire, and the dockmaster had overseen a massive exchanging of goods between Kethra and Sundolia. But decades ago, trade with that southern empire had ground to a halt as a result of sanctions imposed by Kethra's increasingly anti-magic rulers. Anything imported from Sundolia was considered dangerous, tainted by the magic-drenched air of the south, and thus had to be highly regulated.

To this day, Kosrith was nowhere near the bustling port it had once been. Most of the buildings around them were boarded up. The pier stretching out to their right had been reduced to patchy scraps of sun-bleached wood, like of the skeletal remains of a long-dead beast.

Her brother was standing beside the dockmaster's house, staring out at the choppy sea. As she approached, he calmly turned toward her. Their gazes met. He smiled.

Cas slowed to a stop.

Nessa grabbed her arm. "Are you sure about this?"

"I'll be okay," Cas replied, pulling free. "He doesn't frighten me."

She'd mostly been trying to reassure Nessa, but she was surprised at how true the words sounded. Perhaps it was the Rook God's curse upon her skin—whatever tendrils of his power had seeped from his claws when he struck her—but she felt...angry. Full of a dark, powerful fury that gave her a terrible kind of confidence.

One of Varen's demands had been that she speak with him alone.

It should have frightened her.

It didn't.

She wasn't afraid to fight her brother, if it came down to it. Because part of her, she suddenly realized, was *hoping* for that fight.

"We'll be close by," Laurent said. It was a threat as much as a reassurance. His eyes were on Varen as he said it, and his voice was loud enough to carry up to the King-Emperor, even over the noise of the rising wind and crashing surf.

Varen turned and walked into the house.

Cas followed without looking back.

It was dark inside, the windows shuttered, the only slice of stormy daylight coming from the front door that Cas left partially open.

She went deeper into the house, until she reached a shallow nook that looked as though it might have served as a kitchen at some point.

Varen stood in this room, behind an old wooden table that had all manner of crude words and images carved into it—by bored dockworkers, she assumed. Rather than opening the windows, Varen was busy adjusting the light of a lantern in the center of that table.

Cas strode toward him. She yanked one of the table's chairs out and sank down into it, making herself comfortable, refusing to let the darkness or the quiet bother her as she glared at her brother.

"At last, we meet again," Varen said. He finally lifted his gaze to her. "It feels like it's been a lifetime since our last chat, doesn't it?"

"And yet in other ways it feels like it hasn't been nearly long enough."

He went back to adjusting the lantern's light.

"What do you want, Varen?"

"To talk. Isn't that what you wanted before?"

"Yes. *Before* being the most important word there. *Before* you attacked this kingdom."

Before Zev nearly died. Before I was cursed by an angry upper-god. Before I lost Elander...

That desire she felt to fight Varen nearly overwhelmed her. Her hand shook from the effort of not reaching for her sword. She gripped the arm of the chair. Tightly.

Varen's gaze drifted toward her clenched hand. She thought she saw the corners of his mouth lift a bit. She tried harder to relax her hand.

"But now we're in the after," she continued. "And I'm afraid that I am not feeling very *talkative* today."

"I see. Then just listen, perhaps?"

She scowled.

He continued all the same: "I wanted to talk, because that magic you used against me during our last little scuffle...I found it very *curious.*"

The Storm-kind magic.

She had used it against him during that last battle, and in doing so she had finally managed to shatter the shield of divine power that protected him. A shield that she herself had inadvertently placed on him when they were children.

It had almost slipped her mind, amidst all the other distractions. But now that he mentioned it, she inhaled deeply and focused, trying to feel for any trace of that shield that remained.

There was nothing there.

She held back a smug smile.

"And I am not the only one who found it curious," he went on. "Many of my most trusted sources and advisors have been trying to make sense of you for weeks now. They tell me that you have been experimenting with magic unlike anything they've seen in this empire. Or other empires, for that matter."

She picked at a bit of dirt under one of her nails, *listening.*

"I suppose I should have expected you would push the boundaries of magic, given the company you keep."

She lifted her eyes to him but still said nothing.

"Speaking of disgraceful company, where is that rogue companion of yours, anyway? My former captain?"

The reminder of her loss shot an ache into her belly and fire into her blood, and though she tried, she couldn't hold her tongue any longer. "Why do you care? Are you thinking of switching sides now that you've seen what I—and my *rogue companion*—can do? Reconsidering my offer to work with me instead of against me, are you?"

He seemed to be turning the question over and around in his mind. And then, to her surprise, he said, "What if I am?"

She somehow managed to keep her expression blank and her reply flat. "That offer is now void, I'm afraid."

"Pity. Because you're right—I think I might have underestimated your magic. I am not above admitting that I made a mistake."

A sudden realization struck Cas. "You know, don't you?"

His smile turned pressed and thin.

"You know what that former captain of yours is."

"I have spies everywhere, dear. There isn't much I *don't* know, and there is nothing I can't find out. So yes —I have reason to believe that Captain Elander was not as human as he appeared during his time in my palace. And, as I said before, I now know that *you* are even stranger than you first seemed as well."

It made her sick to her stomach, thinking of how often his spies might have been close to her and her friends without her realizing it.

"And you've been seeking out more divine beings, haven't you? I was told you crossed the Cobos Desert, mere weeks ago, in search of one." Varen's voice trailed off toward the end, as though he didn't quite believe this particular piece of information.

It was a rare show of uncertainty from him, and Cas couldn't help sneering at it. "What was it you said the last time we met this way?" she asked. "That the gods don't frighten you, I believe? So why do you care if I've visited any of their mortal-side havens?"

"I never said I was frightened." He took a step away from the table, away from the lantern's light. With his face half-hidden by shadows, he continued, "Just curious, as I said. I want to know precisely what you've been tangling yourself up in, and what magic you truly possess."

"So that you can get the details correct on my execution order, I presume?"

He casually slipped his hands into the pockets of his coat. The golden trim of that coat glistened, and it was perfectly fitted to his lean figure, in perfect condition— no stains, no wrinkles. Even here in this dilapidated building, among the ghosts of the once-lively port and the shadows of their previous battle, he looked as if he was preparing to host an elegant dinner at his palace.

"If embracing that magic is the path to ending this silly feud between us before irreversible damage is done," he said while gazing up at the ceiling, "then I was thinking perhaps we could negotiate a deal."

Cas folded her arms across her chest and sank deeper into her chair. "Says the little boy king who, just weeks ago, claimed he wanted to eradicate the ones who carried *any* sort of magic."

"Weeks ago, I told you that I longed for peace above all else. But perhaps you weren't listening to that part?"

"I was listening. I simply assumed it was a lie, considering the majority of what you say is a lie."

"At the time," he went on, as though she hadn't spoken, "our peace appeared to be threatened by your out-of-control magic. My people feared you and that magic, so I reacted swiftly to prove I could keep them safe from it. But now it seems you've managed to control it—our last battle proved that well enough. The dust has settled, and so it makes more sense to ask: How do we make peace between us?"

"You aren't interested in *peace*. You're interested in power. I am not an idiot, Varen. You sense the power shifting, and you want to be on the winning side. You are nothing more than a rat caught in a flood, scrambling in search of higher ground."

"Such nasty words," he tutted.

She didn't reply.

"And what if I am interested in power?" He stepped to her side of the table, his hands still in his pockets. "Do you know what I have had to endure since our parents died? For nearly my entire life, people have been trying to claw my power away from me, the *little boy king* who was thrown on the throne far too early. Call me a rat if you like—but those creatures are adept at surviving in the most horrid of conditions, you know."

"I'll start a petition to have the family crest changed from a tiger to a rat then, shall I?"

He smiled in that cold, unsettling way of his. "More nastiness. What's gotten into you, sister?" His gaze lowered slowly to her face, and then narrowed in on her cheek. On the Rook God's mark.

She should have used the salve the Oak Goddess had given her to make it disappear. But she'd been hesitant to do so, because she didn't want to hide that mark from her friends. Her plan had been to tell them—and show them—as much of the truth as possible, and perhaps then she might have concealed it...

She hadn't counted on being immediately thrown into this encounter with her brother.

She kept perfectly still as he leaned back against the table, mirrored her folded arms, and canted his head.

"What is that ugly thing on your face?" he asked.

"None of your concern."

"It *looks* concerning," he said, reaching for it.

Her skin crawled, and her grip closed around the handle of one of the knives secured to her belt. "Unless you want to lose your hand, I suggest you don't touch me."

A slow smirk stretched across his face, but he drew his fingers back into a closed fist and left the mark alone. "Oh, how I wish things were *different*," he said, walking to one of the shuttered windows, unlatching it, and squinting into the grey daylight as he pulled it open. "I wish we could help one another."

"You can help me by releasing the Sadiran soldiers you took captive."

"Done."

"Liar," Cas snarled.

He turned his gaze on her once more, and he kept it there as he shouted for one of his guards.

A man with dark eyes and a battle-worn face stepped into the room a moment later.

"Release our captives," Varen told him, his eyes never leaving Cas. "And give the order to start travel preparations. We'll move out under the cover of night and make for Ciridan with haste. I've been away from my throne long enough, I believe."

The guard hesitated. "All of our captives, Sir?"

"Yes. Because Lady Valori and I have reached an understanding," he said.

Except they hadn't.

More of his mind games, of course. But she kept her lips pressed tightly together, and she stayed in her seat, perfectly still. If it meant those captives would be safely released, then she could pretend she and Varen *understood* each other for the moment.

The guard hesitated a moment more, but then he bowed his head and left.

Varen waited until the sounds of the guard's steps faded away before he continued. "The magic in this empire is growing more restless. Despite my father's—and my own—efforts to eradicate it, it grows ever more dangerous." He paused and massaged the space between his eyes. "You may think me a monster, Valori—"

"Casia."

He arched a brow.

"My name is not Valori de Solasen, and it never will be."

A strange expression crossed his face. There one instant, gone the next. It could have passed for sadness, almost—as if he had just been told that a distant relative had died. It was nothing more than an act. But it was a convincing one, she had to admit.

"Of course," he said, placing a hand upon his chest and dipping his head. "My mistake."

"But you were right about the other part," Cas muttered. "I *do* think of you as a monster."

When he lifted his head again, his eyes were shining

with such ambition—such *hunger*—that it made her entire body tense.

"Sometimes it takes a monstrous person to defeat monstrous things," he said. "And regardless of what you may believe, we are very much at the mercy of monstrous gods." He stepped closer to her, and his voice grew quieter, as though she was the only person in the world he could speak his next words to. "I only want to protect our world. And I want your help to do it. It's all I *ever* wanted. But you had to go and complicate things, didn't you?"

Monstrous gods.

The words encircled her like a cage she couldn't break free of.

She didn't know the full extent of the Rook God's plans, or what his servants might do. She only knew that he wanted revenge against the rulers who had not fulfilled their part of a struck bargain, and against the humans who had been forsaking divine magic for too long. And what was it the Moon Goddess had said?

Sides were being chosen.

And some of her fellow gods were making unfortunate choices.

Monstrous choices, maybe.

Varen walked back and settled down in the chair across the table from her. He studied her in silence for a long moment, one ankle propped upon his opposite knee, his elbow on the armrest, his face leaning casually against his fist. "You've had intimate encounters with the divine," he finally said. "That is no secret anymore. So do your empire a favor and *tell me what you know*."

Only a short time ago, Cas would have.

She would have explained her fears to him, would have reached out her hand and hoped that he might reach back. She would have dared to hope that they could have worked together instead of against one another. Even now, she wasn't sure how she could fight a war against her brother *and* the gods. It was tempting to believe that they might unite against those gods; it was the only way they could stand a chance, wasn't it?

But she couldn't bring herself to believe in the possibility of that partnership.

Not anymore.

The past weeks had changed her. Fear had twisted her heart into an unrecognizable shape. Grief had hardened it. The trust that had once come so easily to her was finally slipping away—turning into a distant memory she wasn't certain she wanted to recall. She'd held onto it for as long as she could.

Things were different, now.

And the fury that had carried her into this building was still rattling in between her bones. Whether because of the Dark God's curse, or her grief—or some combination of the two—it was eating away at her, hollowing out her once-soft places like wind eroding stone.

That cold wind pushed her to her feet. She braced her arms against the table, leaned over it, looked her brother directly in the eyes and quietly said, "You want to know what I *know*?"

He opened his mouth, but she continued before he could reply—

"I know that you are a tyrant. And a fool. That your soul is black and beyond repair. I know that you are afraid of me and my magic—and you *should* be afraid— because I have walked among gods and goddesses and lived, and I have already gained power that you could only dream of, and I intend to gain *more* power. So, leaving this place is precisely what you need to do. Run back to your throne and sit there quietly. Stay out of my way. I have other things to deal with, and I don't want your crown. But I *also* know that you have used that crown to do far more harm than good, and if you do not stop doing harm, I will make it a priority to come back to Ciridan and rip it from your head myself. And then it will be your *own* blood that stains your kingdom's soil for once."

The wind picked up outside, rattling the building's loose boards.

Varen stared at her, his face disturbingly devoid of emotion.

"Is there anything else you'd like to *know* while I'm here?" asked Cas.

A particularly loud howl of wind shook the walls,

and Varen's gaze slid momentarily to the window before returning to her. "No. I believe that will suffice for the moment."

"Good." She pushed away from the table and straightened to her full height. "This meeting is over."

With that, she turned and started for the door. Her heart thundered. She placed a hand on the pommel of her sword and squeezed it with every step, trying to keep herself grounded and calm enough to make her movements appear smooth and confident.

"Farewell, Casia."

The dark tone of his voice sent a chill down her spine. She shouldn't have turned around, but she did— just one last quick glance.

He was smiling at her again.

"Let's talk again soon, my dear sister," he said.

She kept walking.

CHAPTER 8

HOURS LATER, CAS SAT WITH HER FRIENDS IN THE COURTYARD of their temple base, trying to decide what to do next.

Varen had kept his word. All of the ones he'd taken captive had been released. Most were intact, though two of them had sustained injuries—tortured because of Varen's *impatience*, as Soryn had feared.

One of these two was being tended to in a room that Cas and her party could see from the table they had gathered around. Cas was making a concentrated effort not to look toward that room. She was afraid that she would see a black cloth being fixed over the window—a custom shared by the kingdoms of both Sadira and Melech when it came to the deceased.

But even as she tried not to see what was happening in that room, she would have sworn she could still *sense* it. And what she sensed was a fading energy, a fluttering like a second heartbeat in her chest that was getting weaker and weaker.

So she wasn't surprised when Soryn returned from checking on that wounded soldier with an exhausted, grim look on her normally alert face.

The young Queen raked her fingers through her dark hair. Her odd, teal-colored eyes appeared dull, the creases beneath them more pronounced.

"How is she?" Nessa asked softly.

"It... doesn't look good."

As Soryn continued to explain the woman's poor condition, Cas felt it again—a mass of energy slipping away, beat by beat by beat.

She could sense the woman dying.

She was almost certain of it. She was feeling the approaching hand of death, just as she had sensed the Fire God approaching Moonhaven. She was already connecting to such things because of the Dark God's mark upon her—she could think of no other explanation.

And it terrified her.

Her hand numbly reached for that mark. She had told everyone present about her encounter with the Rook God, the reason for that mark, and much of the aftermath—or a condensed version of it, at least. The only part she'd fully left out was what the curse might ultimately do to her if it wasn't removed.

She hadn't told them of the Oak Goddess's ominous

prediction, because she was not going to let it come true. She was not going to ascend to any divine court that served the Rook God.

She was going to find a way to erase that mark.

"Let's focus on the battles we can fight, shall we?" Laurent suggested.

"Yes—let's," Sade quickly agreed. "Varen has fully retreated, according to our scouts."

"And if he was telling the truth about wanting to negotiate," added Rhea, "it sounds like he's afraid of the magic Cas possesses."

Cas shook her head. She had seen nothing resembling *fear* in her brother's eyes. "Changing tactics doesn't make a person a coward."

"The fact that he's shown a willingness to change his plans, whether because of fear or otherwise, is actually more concerning than anything," said Soryn. "We can't underestimate him. He has no moral compass, perhaps, but he isn't a reckless fool."

"Which is a shame," Sade added, "because reckless fools are so much easier to fight."

"Agreed," Soryn said, frowning.

"Is there any chance that he was telling the truth when he said he would negotiate?" Nessa asked, a faint, stubborn hint of hope in her tone. "Perhaps if he knew more about the gods we've encountered, and the instability among the divine courts...maybe he would understand the need to unite in order to keep our world safe?"

"He might," said Cas. "At least until the power shifted back toward him. And then he would put a dagger in the back of anyone he no longer deemed useful."

Disappointment clouded Nessa's eyes, and Cas suspected it was not simply because of the answer she'd given, but because of the harsh, hopeless tone of her voice—because she had once been the other optimist in their group, alongside Nessa.

But now she felt like a fool for ever believing that she could reunite with her brother. Every time she thought of those moments when she had tried to reach out to him, the new, dark anger inside of her reared its head and threatened to swallow her whole.

"I was speaking with one of our generals earlier," Sade said, "and he informed me that there are encampments forming along the Fellbridge River to the north of us. Varen's minions have crept their way into Ethswen, it seems, and they're entirely too close to Sadira's northern border. Trying to pin us in, would be my guess."

"Are the leaders of Ethswen allies of yours these days?" Rhea asked. "Will they hold that northern border for you?"

"Ethswen has two queens, Caelia and Izora," Soryn answered, after a brief hesitation. "I've met Caelia several times; she and my mother were close friends as children. But to use the term *allies* now would be very... generous. I doubt they would align themselves with

Varen, but I wouldn't count on them aiding us, either. We've tried to secure their support in the past without much luck. And the plains between the Fellbridge River and our border are essentially no man's land—the queens won't go out of their way to secure this area. Especially since they've got other battles they're currently dealing with."

"They're entangled in conflicts with the elves of Moreth and Mistwilde, aren't they?" asked Cas. The High King of Sundolia had mentioned something about the matter during her recent stay in his palace.

Soryn nodded. "Something your friend and I have discussed at length over these past days." She looked toward Laurent, who suddenly appeared to be fighting the urge to get up and walk away.

Cas could only guess at the reasons why. He had left Moreth years ago, she knew, but he had always been reluctant to talk about the reasons for his departure—and he was not the type to be persuaded into speaking his thoughts.

"Laurent has informed me that he has connections with the King of Moreth," Soryn continued. "My advisors and I believe the elves could be of great assistance to us...*if* we could somehow effectively plead our case to them. Normally, Mistwilde and Moreth are both off-limits to humans, but these are unprecedented circumstances."

"I've agreed to do what I can," said Laurent,

sounding uncharacteristically unnerved by the idea. "And I can get us into that hidden realm, at the very least. But after that..."

"What?" asked Zev. "We hope and pray that the elves have somehow forgotten that they hate humans?" He gave the rest of them a dubious look. "I can't be the only that has heard the disturbing legends. You know, like the ones about the human heads on stakes that form fences around their territories?"

"He's right," said Sade, though she looked somewhat reluctant to admit her agreement. "The stories have traveled all the way to my empire as well; King Theren of Moreth is known to be particularly hostile."

Out of the corner of her eye, Cas watched Laurent, looking for some sign to either confirm or deny these things. But his face had turned back into its usual stoic mask.

"The other nobles of Moreth have shown flashes of kindness toward humans in the past," Soryn insisted, "and we have one of their kind within our midst, so we may be able to sway them to our favor. All of those stories you speak of are exaggerated, I believe—and either way, we have to try *something*. We need more allies. And not only would the elves be formidable partners in any battle against Varen, they also have knowledge of the upper-gods and their history that could likely be of great use to us."

"If you can pry it out of them, sure," said Sade.

"Their well of knowledge runs deep, but they aren't known to be forthcoming with it."

Cas nodded; she had thoroughly researched this very topic just recently, at the Black Feather Institute in Sundolia. The reason they possessed such knowledge—she now knew—was because the creatures known to most of the world as *elves* were actually the beings the Moraki had first given magic to. More magic than any human today possessed...too much magic, it had turned out, and eventually they were stripped of their gifts for various transgressions against the upper-gods.

But the descendants of those original beings were still altered because of that original magic, and they were neither truly human nor divine.

"We have to make a decision on our next move, one way or the other," said Soryn, her gaze sliding toward Cas.

The others' gazes followed.

They were divided, and they were looking to *her* for a decision, she realized.

She'd fooled them all earlier, when she'd marched so confidently to meet her brother. She'd fooled herself too. But perhaps that was the trick, she thought; if she simply kept pretending to be the leader they needed, eventually it would become a reality.

"...We'll head northwest toward Moreth," she said. "And we will see what kind of allies and information we can gain there. How quickly can we prepare for travel?"

"I can start gathering resources for you immediately," Soryn told her. "We can be ready by morning."

"Good." Cas swept her gaze over each of the faces looking to her for direction, and she tried hard to not think about the face that was missing. "We're leaving at first light."

LATER THAT AFTERNOON, Cas sat alone at the end of a weathered pier, staring out over a grey and churning, wind-swept sea.

The day was fading too fast.

Tomorrow was approaching too quickly.

First light, she'd said.

It had to happen. They couldn't stay here and hide within their temple and hope that their problems would sort themselves out. *She knew this.*

But she *also* knew that leaving meant letting go of the faint hope she'd had of a reunion with Elander. He had come back to her before—to this very city—even when he was wounded and weak and barely able to use the traveling gate he'd established in this place.

There is nowhere you can go that I can't find you, he'd once told her.

And she'd believed it. She still did. Even as all her other hopes and beliefs cracked and crumbled around her, she'd managed to hold on to this one. She knew he would have walked, would have crawled to her, if he had to.

So the fact that he wasn't here...it could mean nothing good.

She had sensed the Fire God. She had sensed that dying woman earlier. But no matter how hard she tried, she couldn't sense Elander, and now a new question was eating away at her. If her Death-related powers were growing stronger, did that mean his were already growing weaker?

How weak?

There couldn't be two gods of Death. So even if he *did* eventually find her again, what would become of them if...if she...

No.

She wasn't going to ascend, so it didn't matter.

She dug her fingers into the pier, indifferent to the splinters of old wood as they slid beneath her nails and pierced her skin. Dark clouds were gathering on the distant horizon, and her stomach twisted as she watched them shift and swirl with the wind. But at least there was no lightning or thunder yet.

She lifted her hand in front of her. She hadn't tried summoning her Storm magic since that moment in Moonhaven, when she'd proven too weak to manage it. But she tried it now. She wanted to feel in control of something, in charge of the storms both in and around her.

Sparks danced on her fingertips after a moment of concentration. They soon twisted into proper bolts that snaked up toward the sky, but they were faint, and it felt almost as if something inside of her was pulling them back. As if the source of them had been bound, tangled up and suffocated by the Rook God's Dark power.

It made her want to scream.

She had finally started to figure out her magic, her true identity...but now everything was all mixed up again.

"There you are," came a sudden, relieved-sounding voice—Rhea's. The *thumps* of her staff against the pier broke Cas's concentration, and she released the lightning magic she'd summoned.

Silverfoot bounded to the end of the pier. He surveyed the choppy sea for a moment before glancing back and yipping a sharp, extra warning about the dock's terminus.

Rhea stopped well short of it and placed her hand on Cas's shoulder, steadying herself.

"It isn't safe to be out here alone," she told Cas, giving that shoulder a little squeeze. "There are still Melechian soldiers lingering... not all of them agreed with the decision to retreat, I hear. There have been several skirmishes at the city borders. And it isn't just those enemy soldiers we have to worry about, either..."

"I'll be fine," Cas assured her. "I'm feeling better than I have in days."

"Physically, maybe."

"And that's the most important thing when it comes to taking down any of my would-be assassinators, right?"

Rhea was quiet for a long moment, and then she sat down beside her. "Even the Goddess of Healing herself can't mend everything, as I understand it. Some things, she can't even touch."

Cas drew her knees up and rested her chin on them.

"Broken hearts, for example. And such things can be terribly distracting when you're trying to survive assassins."

"I'd rather not talk about my heart," mumbled Cas. She didn't regret telling Rhea and the others about her encounters with that Healing Goddess and everything else. But she still felt raw from the telling, afraid that if she *kept* talking about it all, it might rip that rawness into something more bloody. Something more painful.

Rhea nodded, seeming—as she so often did—to understand the unspoken things between them. "Okay," she replied.

"Sorry."

"For what?"

Cas shrugged. "I don't mean to be difficult."

"Hush," said Rhea as she dug through the bag slung across her body. She pulled out a loaf of berry-flecked bread wrapped in a thin cloth and offered it to Cas.

"Here, I brought you this. I know you haven't eaten all day."

"I'm not hungry."

"Don't care. Eat it."

Cas took it, offering a quiet *thanks* as she picked at the fruit embedded in the fluffy bread. They were haggith berries, a perfect mixture of tart and sweet, and this region was known for adding them to practically every dish they cooked. "How did you know I haven't eaten?"

"Call it a bonus sense. I don't need my eyes to see you, love."

They sat in silence for several minutes, until, to her surprise, Cas found herself wanting to speak again. "I was warned, wasn't I?"

Rhea patted Silverfoot's head, and the fox shifted in her lap and turned his gaze so they could both see Cas's face.

"*It won't end happily,*" Cas recited. "The Storm Goddess said those exact words to me. And Zev, and Laurent, and all of you tried to tell me the same thing. So why did I think it *could* end happily?"

Rhea considered the question for a moment, and then she said, "Because it's perfectly human to hope. To believe in things despite evidence to the contrary."

Cas lowered her gaze, staring at a patch of grey water that was visible through a wormhole in the wood.

She didn't feel particularly human at the moment. She felt monstrous and messy, restless and churning, like that sea below her.

The dark clouds in the distance unleashed their first bolts of lightning. Thunder rumbled soon after, and Cas suppressed a shiver.

Rhea reached out her hand and said, "Show me the storm."

It was an old, familiar request, and Cas felt the corners of her lips lifting in spite of the raw ache in her heart.

She took Rhea's hand and pulled it closer. Tucked a windswept strand of her hair behind her ear and out of her eyes, and then she looked up, watched the lightning, and recreated the patterns it made by tracing her finger along Rhea's palm.

"I still remember the first night I told you to do this," Rhea said.

"That was a long time ago."

"Yes. Back when you were a mean, feral little thing, and we didn't get along particularly well. We were both dealing with our separate hurts in our own separate ways, you know? And it was usually Asra that comforted you when the storms came."

Cas's stomach clenched at the reminder of her old mentor. She paused, halfway through mapping out the latest web of lightning, and made a concentrated effort to block out the images of the night Asra had been killed.

"But I still remember the first night you cried out loud enough to wake me up," Rhea continued. "Asra and I both reached your door at the same time. *Go to her*, she said to me. So I did. And I didn't know what else to do, so I just gave you my hand. I was shocked when you actually took it." She trailed off, laughing quietly and shaking her head. "Back in those days, you were always drawing, doodling with sticks in the dirt, or with whatever parchment and pens you'd stolen from Asra's study. So I told you to draw the lightning in my hand as you saw it—to show it to me through touch, because I couldn't see it clearly. I really just wanted you to contain it in some way. Give your fear a shape and control it so that it wouldn't control you. I don't know if it helped."

The dark sea of anger inside of Cas stopped churning, if only for a moment. "It did," she said, quietly. "It does."

"Good."

She went back to absently tracing her lightning lines across Rhea's palm.

"It's moving away from us, I think," Rhea concluded after a moment. "Calmer skies are ahead."

"I hope so," said Cas, closing her hand over Rhea's and resting her head on her shoulder. They sat like this for a few more minutes, until Cas felt strong enough to let go and lift her head once more. "You should go back and prepare for tomorrow. I'll head there in a little while, I promise."

Rhea hesitated, but eventually she gave in and left Cas to her thoughts.

The storm did not retreat as Rhea had predicted.

Instead, it picked up in earnest shortly after she left. Sprinkles of rain turned abruptly to buckets, and Cas was thoroughly soaked before she came to her senses and pulled up her hood. As usual, the storm caused a tight feeling in her chest and a trembling in her bones that she couldn't stop.

But she was no longer a child cowering in her bed, awakened by thunder. She had controlled bigger storms thanks to the magic she'd been given, and now it was easier to remind herself that even storms had their uses. That she could survive them and come out stronger on the other side.

A wave slammed into the pier and made the entire structure shake. It would have been reckless to stay put, so she fought her way to her feet and trudged back to more solid ground.

She meandered through the broken streets of Kosrith, toward their base, passing people huddled beneath porches and awnings to get out of the rain. She felt the stares of those people following her.

More than once, she heard the quiet splash of footsteps and knew she was being followed, but whether by friends or foes, or simply curious onlookers, she didn't know. No one dared get close enough to her for her to find out. Perhaps because of the sword at her hip, or the sparks of Storm magic that she occasionally summoned to the hand hanging casually by her side.

The rain was nearly blinding by the time she reached the street the old temple was located on. She lowered her head against the stinging drops and walked on, until finally that temple came into view. She started to heave a sigh of relief, thinking of her dry room and its fireplace—

She sensed someone behind her.

How had they gotten so close?

Rhea's warning echoed in her head. She didn't trust her control over her Storm magic at the moment, and the heavy rain would make proper form with her sword tricky, so her hand instead moved subtly to the knife tucked into her belt. She withdrew it and held it against her body. Let her eyes flutter shut as she honed the rest of her senses, listening for footsteps. She had one chance to catch her attacker by surprise.

She spun and stabbed—

And missed.

She'd been quick. Her target was quicker. Quick enough to duck her swing and take her wrist in a powerful grip. She fought for balance but couldn't find it against the slippery, wet road, and before she could break free, her back was suddenly against a broad chest. Her knife hand was still immobilized by that powerful grip, and then an arm wrapped around her waist and pulled her closer.

"Drop the knife," came a man's voice, low and barely audible over the rain.

"Not a chance in any hell," she snarled back.

The man's chest rumbled with quiet laughter.

Cas was an instant away from taking her chances with her magic when the man's grip on her suddenly relaxed. He spun her away so they were facing each other. She wrenched herself entirely free of his hold and drew her weapon back, preparing to swipe.

He removed his hood.

And she dropped the knife after all.

She didn't bother to pick it back up. She couldn't. She was trembling too badly, and the world was spinning too fast for her to do anything but stare and try to keep breathing and try, try, *try* to remember how to speak.

But she couldn't speak.

Not a single word—not even his name—not even as her mind was shouting it in disbelief.

Elander.

He took her hand. Pulled her closer once more. "Thorn." The nickname was a whisper between them. "Why are you standing out here in the rain?"

She was still frozen, immobile, as he tipped his mouth toward hers, as he kissed the drops of rainwater from her lips with slow, savoring movements. He pulled away—too soon, it would always be too soon—and she finally found her voice.

"I was waiting for you, you fool," she told him, and then she was laughing to keep herself from sobbing, as she wrapped her arms around his neck and kissed him back.

CHAPTER 9

THE STORM MOVED OUT AS AFTERNOON EASED INTO EVENING, and as the last rays of hazy sunlight washed through the temple's windows, Cas found herself hesitating outside the door of the room Elander had been resting in.

She heard no sounds coming from within that room. The rest of the building was equally quiet; most of the planning and arguing had ceased by this point. More concrete plans had been made for their journey to Moreth—who would stay, who would go, and what methods they might use to appeal to King Theren and the rest of his realm—and now there was little else to do aside from resting until it was time to leave. Soryn had insisted that Cas do precisely this, assuring her that she had plenty of others who could take care of any last-minute preparations.

And Cas had tried to rest.

But it had quickly proved impossible.

She and Elander had been separated soon after they came back to the base—the small army of healers Soryn had summoned to tend to him had pushed her out of his room so they could do their job.

Cas had argued with the lead healer until Nessa intervened and pulled her away.

She'd spent the past two hours sitting with Nessa and nursing her irritation over a tankard of Sadiran ale. But even with that notoriously strong drink *and* Nessa's calming magic working through her, her anxious thoughts kept finding their way back to Elander.

She needed to see him.

There were things they needed to talk about—things more important than her own rest.

So here she was, standing outside his door.

She took a deep breath, quietly cracked that door open, and peered inside.

He was awake, standing with his arms braced against a dresser, his eyes partially closed. Meditating against pain, it looked like. He was shirtless, bandages crisscrossing over his stomach and one of his shoulders, loose pants hanging low on his hips

And maybe it was the way the setting sunlight fell upon the muscular lines of his back, or the way he still managed to appear powerful and poised in spite of his pain...but she couldn't speak right away. She couldn't stop staring. She briefly wondered how she had ever thought he was a mere mortal. Even in this fallen, battered state, he still looked...well, *godly*.

She pushed the door open a bit more. It let out a soft creak. Elander tilted his head toward her, and a slow, tired smile stretched across his face.

"Hi," he said.

"Hello." She took a few hesitant steps inside. "Sorry if I disturbed you. I just wanted to check on you."

He shook his head. "You don't need to apologize for coming to see me. Ever. I'm glad you're here."

I'm glad you're here.

Even after everything they'd been through together, the butterflies still came when he said things like that— fresh and fumbling around as if they had just emerged with their new wings.

She moved closer, but she stopped just short of his reach. "I overheard some of what those healers were saying earlier—before they pushed me out of here, I mean."

"And?"

"And they were saying your wounds were...awful. Too deep for an average human to survive."

"It's lucky I'm not an average human then, isn't it?"

"Yes." She frowned. "But still, it sounded like you were in much worse shape than you let on earlier."

He shrugged, and then flashed a crooked smile that she suspected had covered up a grimace of pain.

She didn't return that smile. She tried but couldn't

manage it. All of the anxiety she'd felt for him over the past days suddenly rose to the surface and left her too numb to do anything but stare.

When she finally managed to move her mouth again, the words that slipped out were only a whisper. "I thought I'd lost you, Elander. On top of everything else I...I..."

His smile faded as he reached out his hand to her.

She didn't take it. "I was so *mad*. What you did was—"

"I would do it again."

She pressed her lips together, firmly, trying to keep herself from saying something she would regret.

"If it comes down to risking my life, my power, my *everything I have* to protect you, I *will* do it again. I swear it."

"And what if I don't want you to do something so foolish?"

"It wasn't foolish. There is nothing foolish about keeping you alive. Nothing. And I need you to understand that." He reached for her again.

She thought about turning and running away. She just needed to step outside for a moment. To hide. To catch her breath. To...*gods,* she didn't know.

But in the end she took his hand.

She let him pull her toward the bed. He sat on the edge of it, but she remained standing, walled in by his thighs. He was tall enough that they were still nearly eye-to-eye, and she couldn't help staring into the blue depths of his gaze.

"What about the fact that I almost lost *you*?" he asked.

"I made my choice. I was prepared—"

"And I was supposed to just be okay with that choice?" He slipped his hand from hers and reached instead for the mark upon her face. Anger flashed in his eyes, and his fingers shook with the same barely-checked fury, as he touched that mark. After a moment of studying it, he lowered his head as if ashamed by the sight of it. Ashamed that he hadn't stopped it from happening, maybe.

"I was just trying to protect everyone," Cas said, quietly.

The moment stretched into a long, tense silence.

Finally, he lifted his head. The rage darkening his eyes had not lessened, and suddenly a cold wind was stirring inside of her, rising to meet that darkness. She pushed it back down. She didn't want to be angry at him.

She wanted to kiss him.

But she also wanted to hit him, and her bottom lip trembled with the effort of trying to hold back all her frustration and fear and uncertainty.

"Everyone but yourself," he said, tracing a thumb along that quivering lip. "And you *really* don't understand why I had a problem with that?"

She understood perfectly well. Too well, really. She hadn't forgotten what he'd said. *I love you, and I always have, in this lifetime and in every other.*

And it frightened her.

Because she had lost every home she'd had while growing up. She had lost Asra. Over these past weeks she had nearly lost all of her friends—one after the other it seemed—and so she had concluded that loving so deeply meant *hurting* deeply, too, and the thought was...terrifying.

The last time they'd talked about such things, she'd told Elander that she didn't regret loving, even if it ended in loss.

But now that the losses—and the almost-losses—were mounting, it was impossible not to ask how much a heart could take before its hurting turned into something darker. Before that new cold wind blowing inside her fully unleashed and carried her away.

"Is this what we're going to be, then?" she asked quietly, her hands trailing over his shoulder, lightly touching the bandages there. "Two fools trying to out-sacrifice the other one?"

"You can't ask me to stop trying to protect you." He caught her hand, stopped its wandering. "I won't do it."

She started to protest, but the way he was looking at her made her breath catch. Devotion shimmered in his gaze, and his grip on her hand was tight. Painfully tight, almost, as if he'd forgotten he was holding on to her. As if he'd forgotten everything else the instant he looked into her eyes.

No one had ever looked at her like that before.

Or maybe he had?

She felt that increasingly familiar frustration with herself for not being able to recall the lifetime they'd spent together before this one, and suddenly she was moving before she realized what she was doing, leaning in and bringing her lips to his.

He was slow to return the kiss, and she started to lean away, uncertain—but he stopped her. He gripped the back of her head, raking his fingers through her hair, and he pulled her mouth back to his.

They fell together against the bed. She was careful not to press against his wounds, but her kiss was far from gentle; she channeled all her frustrations and fears and all her other messy, angry emotions into it. Her knees pressed tightly against him, and she used all of her weight to straddle his body and keep it pinned firmly beneath her.

One of his hands stayed against her head, pulling her deeper and deeper into the kiss. The other roved along the small of her back, lifting her shirt and finding skin. His touch inched higher, lifting little bumps upon her flesh as it went. It swept between her shoulder blades and back down before trailing around to her stomach and up toward the swell of her breasts.

"Wait," she whispered against his mouth.

His fingers clenched more tightly in her hair, but he waited.

"We probably shouldn't. You're injured."

She braced an arm on either side of his body and stayed balanced over him as he stared up at her, his eyes shining with an emotion she couldn't readily name. Wonder, perhaps, mixed with something that made her stomach clench with desire.

"Suddenly I feel much better, actually," he said. "Like all of my wounds have miraculously healed."

She leaned in until her lips nearly brushed his once more. "Idiot," she murmured.

He laughed softly, and then he sat up, kissing her as he came, backing her into an upright position as he resumed one himself. His arms wrapped around her, strong and unyielding and holding her nearly flush against him. Little flares of heat ignited wherever their bodies touched together. She wanted to collapse into that heat, let it burn away all the things that frightened her.

He brushed the hair from her face, and she found herself breathless again, just from that simple touch.

She leaned her head against his chest. There had been more she needed to say, more they needed to talk about, but suddenly she didn't want to bring any of it up.

So all she said was, "I'm sorry, by the way. I was...reckless."

He mirrored the hushed tone of her voice as he replied, "I'm sorry, too."

"I meant what I said before though." She kept her head against his chest as she said it, let the strange beat of his inhuman heart lull her into a calmness that made it easier to keep speaking. "I don't want you to sacrifice yourself for me. I want you to stand beside me instead."

He didn't answer right away.

She lifted her head and met his eyes, and he finally nodded.

"I can do that," he said.

"Good."

He took her hand, lifted it, brushed his lips across her knuckles. "Stay in here tonight."

She gave the barest of nods. "I'll stay, but there's a chance those healers will come back and throw me out of here again if you aren't sleeping."

"I'm not sure what you're insinuating," he said, letting go of her hand and crawling toward the pillows. He tucked one hand behind his head as he stretched out and made a show of looking perfectly casual and innocent. "I plan to sleep—nothing else. I only want to rest with you beside me, that's all."

She gave him a properly skeptical look before excusing herself to her own room, promising to come right back after she'd cleaned up and changed into more comfortable clothes.

. . .

HE VERY NEARLY *WAS* ASLEEP when she returned a short time later.

More tired than he was acting, she thought with a pang of concern.

She quietly pulled the curtains closed, turned the lamp on the nightstand to its lowest setting, and then crawled into the bed.

Elander's eyes didn't open as the mattress shifted under her weight, but he soon rolled toward her, and he found her in the near-darkness; his arms wrapped around her and pulled her back against his chest.

She had changed into a simple night shift—one of the articles of clothing Soryn had loaned her. Her legs were bare, cold against the sheets. Elander radiated heat, so she moved closer to him, sank more completely into his embrace. She closed her eyes and focused on the way they fit together, the curves of her body and the soft fabric of her night dress against the firmness of his muscles.

The arm he had draped over her stomach slid lower.

One of his hands came to rest between her thighs, and suddenly she no longer had to worry about being cold, because her entire body flushed with heat.

Had he done it on purpose?

Was he truly asleep?

Her pulse raced as he moved against her, brought his mouth closer to her ear, and asked, "Are you okay?"

"Yes."

"You're not sleeping."

"I...I know."

That hand between her legs moved, clearly on purpose this time. It slipped beneath the hem of her night dress and found the thin undergarment there—the only thing separating his touch from her center that was pooling with heat. Her entire body shivered with a want she couldn't deny, and his fingers slid underneath that thin scrap of fabric and teased her with slow, light strokes.

"You're supposed to be resting," she said, breathily.

"I am," he murmured into the curve of her neck.

"Your hand isn't."

His lips were still pressed lightly against her skin, and she felt the smile curving them. "My hands don't need to rest," he told her.

"No?"

"You're underestimating their strength and stamina, I think."

"I..." she trailed off with a little gasp as one of his fingers slipped inside of her.

"And see, that sound..." he said, sliding his free hand under her hip and jerking her more firmly against him, "...gives me life. This is very therapeutic, in other words. Much better than sleeping."

"You're impossible."

"Are you complaining?" His finger slipped out, traced her soft, sensitive folds while he kissed a trail between her shoulder blades and up along the back of her neck. "You're not, are you?"

She was too focused on the pulsing warmth between her legs to reply. His touch hovered at her entrance, poised and waiting, teasing her until she answered him. She bit her lip, and she shook her head.

Two fingers demanded entry this time, caressing and stretching her, sinking deeper until her body twisted and turned with the pleasure of it.

And no, she definitely wasn't complaining.

"Then arch your back for me, Thorn."

She did, slowly, and it drew his fingers more deeply inside of her; angled them so they pressed against the most tender part of her inner walls and made her body tremble and her mind turn briefly, blissfully blank.

"I think I know why you weren't sleeping." His voice was low—wicked with intent—his breath warm as it spilled over the back of her neck.

"Do you?" she managed to gasp out.

"You were thinking of other things."

"Like?"

"Like this—" He pulled her tight against him once more, and she felt the hard, impressive length of his arousal against her backside. "Which explains why you were already so wet. Did it turn you on, seeing me here all wounded and such? I suppose you were thinking you could just have your way with me while I was injured."

"I could have my way with you even if you weren't injured," she replied.

He laughed, and he met the sultry challenge in her voice with a deeper thrust of his fingers. "I'm not against the idea of you being in control."

Her eyes fluttered shut as the words slid over her.

"But we'll have to save that fantasy for another night, I suppose," he said. "Because for the moment it seems the control belongs to me."

She could hardly argue with his assessment. He knew precisely what he was doing with his words—his touch—and her body was already beginning to feel separate from her mind, like an instrument that only he knew how to play. How to *command*.

The heel of his hand pressed into her throbbing center, and her back arched further in automatic response. Desire shivered through her; she needed to be against him, needed to press harder into his body. She was *desperate* with that need.

"I love the feel of you moving against me like that." He thrusted his fingers more deeply into her, making her move again—there was no fighting it. She was a slave to his touch, to that need that his fingers kept reigniting with every tap and stroke against her skin.

She rocked back against his erection, and her mind flashed back to all the times she had felt it throb inside of her. A low growl of pleasure rumbled through his chest as she pushed harder against him, and he seemed to lose himself in that pleasure for a moment, yanking her more tightly to him and holding her there while he buried his face in the curve of her neck.

His fingers continued to work toward her release. His ragged breathing was hot against the pulse of her throat, and then his mouth moved, nibbled her earlobe for a moment before he paused and whispered, "Roll over so I can see your face."

She hesitated, only because it meant pulling away from his fingers, but his teeth nipped her ear, hard and insistent, and she did as he asked.

Once they were facing each other, he gave the thin gown she wore an expectant little tug.

She kept her gaze on his as she sat up and pulled the garment off, tossed it aside.

He inhaled slowly at the sight of her laid bare before him. His eyes darkened, wild and wanting, as they roved over her figure and then back up to meet her gaze.

His hand slid between her legs once more as his lips crashed against hers. He was as skilled with his tongue as he was with his fingers, smoothly exploring the warmth of her mouth while his hand continued to caress her. After a moment he drew that hand away, and his fingertips swept up over her stomach, her breasts, across all the curves and dips of her body. Then he brought them up to his mouth. Licked them. "It tastes like you," he told her. "*Sweet*."

Her breath hitched. "I'm glad you approve."

His eyes danced again with dark amusement as he pressed his fingers to her lips, held them there and kissed them, sharing the taste.

"I could savor that taste all night," he murmured.

The sudden sound of voices outside their door threatened to ruin that plan.

Cas hesitated, her lips still against his fingers, but the amusement in Elander's eyes only brightened as his gaze tracked toward the door. "It sounds as though you might get in trouble for disturbing their patient," he said. "Just as you predicted."

She reluctantly started to reach for her discarded nightgown.

He grabbed her arm and pulled her back.

She ended up straddling him as she had earlier—except now there was barely any clothing between them.

"Not yet." His tone had taken on a rough edge. He cupped her jaw, guided her lips down to his. "Let them wait. This is therapeutic, remember?"

She started to reply, but then his fingers were inside of her again, slick from a combination of his mouth and her own arousal, and her words became a whimper of pleasure instead.

The hand on her jaw slipped away, moved to the small of her back. Then lower. It spread into a powerful grip that pushed her down, forcing his fingers more deeply inside of her.

She balanced herself over him, lowered her body closer to his. Her breasts settled near his mouth, and he mapped their curves with his lips before finding the velvety tip of first one, then the other, and sucking them both into stiff peaks.

Her head tipped back, and heat rushed through her, consuming whatever inhibitions she might have been clinging to.

He pulled his mouth away from her long enough to repeat, "Let them wait." A growl slipped into his voice as he added, "I want to feel your release."

The harshness in his tone was enough to send her crashing toward crescendo—to start a series of waves that were soon building, lifting her toward that release.

He *wanted* it.

And she wanted to give it to him.

She wanted to give him whatever he asked for in that moment, so long as it meant he would keep touching her, so long as he didn't let go of her.

She curled closer to him as the waves grew more powerful. His lips found the throbbing pulse in her throat once more.

Her weakness.

He knew it was, and this time, his tongue flicked relentlessly against it until she was completely at his mercy, her hands clutching the pillows, her senses indifferent to anyone or anything that might be lingering outside of the room.

He held her tightly as she shattered, a strong arm around her waist, his hand still working against her sex, coaxing every last bit of tension and need from her body.

Her face came to rest against his. She was dizzy. When she finally managed to lift her head, the first thing she noticed were the bandages across his shoulder, a section of them loosened and rumpled from their brief bit of fun.

The realities of what they'd endured over the past weeks came crashing back, and she rolled slowly, and somewhat sheepishly, off of him.

He rolled after her. Took her hand and kissed her knuckles first, and then a trail along her arm, her shoulder, up along the side of her neck before he stopped and leaned his forehead against her cheek.

He didn't say anything else.

He just kept still, softly and contentedly breathing her in.

Her gaze drifted toward the door, listening for a moment, before she moved, brushed the hair from Elander's slightly-dampened skin and said, "I feel like I should return the favor."

"It wasn't a favor," he said, voice little more than a whisper. "It was a pleasure."

She blushed, and another aftershock of her release trembled through her.

"But you can still return it later, if you like," he added. "We'll have time."

He planted a gentle kiss on her cheek before settling back into the pillow. His eyes fluttered shut. His hand was still lightly grasping hers. She wove her fingers between his and held more tightly as she watched him fall asleep.

Minutes passed. Little by little, she sank down from her high. Her shivers subsided. Her mind cleared. And without the distraction of his touch, her racing thoughts returned.

We'll have time, he'd said.

How could he sound so certain about that?

She tried to silence these thoughts. She just wanted to be present in this moment—not in the future, not in the past. *Just here.*

But her brain didn't work that way.

"You're still thinking of things other than sleep," Elander said, and suddenly he was looking at her just as he had earlier—with that same devotion and concern that both thrilled and overwhelmed her.

She averted her eyes, and she again tried to remember her lifetime before this one, searching for a memory of the two of them together, perhaps just like this, once upon a time...

Nothing came to her.

Her eyes blinked back into focus, and she quietly said, "Tell me who I was before. What was I like?"

His lips parted, but he didn't reply.

"You remember, don't you? The me in that past life."

"I...Yes. Of course I remember."

She stared at him expectantly.

He sighed, though the beginning of a smile lifted a corner of his lips. "Let's see," he began slowly. "Personality-wise? Much the same as now."

"Describe me."

He squinted, as if taking her in for the very first time. "Stubborn. Reckless. Impatient." She started to object, but he silenced her with a kiss. "Let me finish, you *impatient* woman," he whispered.

She blushed and held her tongue.

He cleared his throat. "As I was saying: Impatient and...kind. Brave. Smart. An optimist even when the situation didn't call for it." His eyes glazed over and his smile brightened, as if he was remembering a particularly fond moment. "*Especially* when the situation didn't call for it, actually."

She met his smile with her own. But her heart felt heavier, suddenly, because she knew she was moving farther and farther away from that optimistic woman that he'd once known—in this life and the other.

"You looked different, of course," Elander continued. He rolled over onto his back and stared up at the ceiling for a long moment, as if searching it for lost memories. "Darker eyes, darker hair.... But I didn't fall in love with the way you looked, so that doesn't matter, does it?"

"No, I suppose not." She rocked into a sitting position. Pulled her knees toward her and rested her chin on them as she turned his words over and over in her mind. After a moment she looked his direction again. "And you...?"

"As long as you've known me, I've always been this same unbearably handsome and stunningly brilliant being."

"And always this modest, too, I presume?"

"A patron saint of modesty, essentially."

"*Saint*." She huffed out a laugh. "Not a few minutes ago."

The gleam in his eyes was nothing short of sinful as he met her gaze. "My actions were saintly compared to some of the thoughts I was having," he said with a shrug.

She started to speak several times, but she couldn't seem to get anything out.

He smiled, leaned up, and kissed her speechless lips. "Anyway...no more questions tonight."

"I only have a thousand more to go," she protested.

"Sleep, Thorn. We'll have time to answer them later."

"Time enough to discuss those *thoughts* you were having, too?"

"Yes. Plenty of time."

She nodded, averting her eyes again—this time so he couldn't see the fear in them.

He must have read that fear all the same, because he took her hand, laced his fingers through hers, and whispered, "Side-by-side, as you said. From now on, whatever we face, we face it together. I'm not going anywhere." He pulled her toward him, guided her head to his chest.

She closed her eyes. Focused once more on his heartbeat, on trying to steady herself to the rhythm of it. But her voice still came out too small and too soft as she said, "Swear it?"

His arms tightened around her. "I swear it."

CHAPTER 10

She was walking through a barren field. Grey dust blew up and swirled around her with every step, until it was so thick she could no longer see. But something was pulling her —calling desperately to her—and so she walked on in spite of her blindness.

She walked all the way to the edge of a dark abyss—and then nearly into that abyss. Her body pitched forward and she kicked backward, scrambling wildly for balance. She found it. Barely. The grey pebbles she'd kicked free fell into the blackness, and that blackness rippled like water as they struck it.

Curious, she dropped to her knees and reached her hand downward.

It wasn't water she touched.

It was emptiness.

Cold and infinite emptiness.

And yet, as she drew back, it rippled again, and a watery reflection of herself appeared. She stared at herself. Normal at first—her skin unblemished, her grey hair floating around her despite the distinct heaviness in the air.

Then the mark of the Dark God appeared, spilling like black ink over her cheek.

Her right eye began to itch. She reached to touch it, and the black ink seeped from the mark into that eye. Then the other eye. She blinked, and black tears squeezed from her eyes and dripped down her chin. Onto her arms. Every drop sent lines of black spreading out from the point of impact, until finally—when she looked into that abyss beneath her, her reflection was gone.

Pain flared in the mark on her cheek, and Cas jolted awake, breathing heavily as she clutched her face.

It was morning. Warm sunlight made the curtains glow. She could hear the distant hum of voices and footsteps as people emerged from their rooms and started their days.

She was still in Elander's bed, and relief flooded her at the sight of him. Still beside her, still in one piece.

Focus on that, she commanded herself as her hands shook and her breaths turned shallow. Tangible things. She needed tangible things, needed to ground herself in them before this current of fear carried her away. She clenched the sheets in her fists and silently recited affirmations to herself: *It's going to pass. It always passes. You've survived every panic you've ever had before this one, and you'll survive this one, too.*

No matter how often she said these words, she never really believed them until she actually survived.

But after a few minutes the end did come, and she finally—finally—managed a normal breath. Her hands unclenched. She lifted her gaze back to Elander, still sleeping, oblivious to the battle she was fighting just inches away from him.

Good.

He would have held her through her battle, she knew. He'd done it before, as had the rest of her friends, but sometimes she just wanted to fight alone. To not burden anybody else, to claw herself back to the surface with her own strength just to prove to herself that she could.

He must have felt her staring at him, though, because after a moment his eyes slowly blinked open.

"Good morning," he mumbled. He yawned, and she managed a small smile in spite of the remnants of panic still spiking through her blood, because in that instant they felt so...normal.

"What are you smiling about?" he asked.

She started to shake her head, but then decided to tell him the truth: "I went to sleep with you beside me. I woke up with you beside me."

"And?"

"And I can't remember the last time we..." She trailed off, her cheeks warming at the sleepy, adoring look he was giving her. "It's a stupid, little thing, I know. But I just...I need these little things. They keep me from going to...to a dark place. Or from staying in that place, at least."

He slid his arm around her waist and pulled her closer. "I love you," he said. He kissed her forehead, and when he drew back, he was wearing that familiar, roguishly handsome smile. The one that unraveled her from the inside out. The one she so desperately did not want to lose.

"I love you too," she said, before pulling away from his embrace and moving to sit on the bed's edge. "Which is why... there's something else I needed to talk about last night. Something we need to discuss before we leave for Moreth."

"And what is that?"

"When I was in the Healing Goddess's realm..."

His smile fell as a slight tremble slipped into her voice.

She forced herself to continue. "I asked her what would ultimately happen if this mark—this link I have to the Rook God—wasn't dealt with." His face paled, and she could tell she didn't need to elaborate. "You know what this mark means too, don't you?"

He sat up, holding his injured shoulder and moving

a bit more stiffly than usual. He was on his feet in the next instant, slowly crossing to the window, opening the curtains, gazing out at the trees that were coated in raindrops and glistening in the sunlight.

"Elander?"

His head dipped and his eyes closed, just as they had last night—as though in atonement—weighed down by the guilt of not stopping the Rook God from inflicting that mark.

She wanted to go to him. Wrap her arms around him. Tell him it wasn't his fault.

But she couldn't make herself move.

The morning light felt unbearably bright, suddenly, illuminating all the pieces of that nightmare she'd tried to bury. She felt the claws of anxiety sinking in again, grabbing hold of those pieces, drawing them closer to the surface. No matter how hard she tried to push them back down, they resurfaced. It felt like her skin was too tight to contain them without breaking at the seams.

Finally, after what felt like another lifetime had passed between them, Elander looked back at her and said, "Nephele and the rest of her court are working to appeal to Solatis on our behalf. The elves may provide more help as well, and we..." He took a deep breath. Steadied himself. "We'll figure it out, somehow."

She couldn't bring herself to speak, so she just nodded.

But as she watched him moving silently through the

room, gathering his things for the journey ahead, she felt as if she was standing once more on the edge of that great black void from her nightmare.

And the darkness beneath was calling for her, trying to pull her down and swallow her whole.

CHAPTER 11

AFTER THREE DAYS OF HARD RIDING, THE NORTHWESTERN border of Sadira was finally within easy reach.

Casia's entire group of friends had come along for this journey, alongside Queen Soryn, the emissary of the Queen's southern cousin, and several dozen of Sadira's soldiers.

Caden had returned for the trip as well, and he rode beside Elander now, wearing a contemplative look. He'd been uncharacteristically quiet for much of the trip, but Elander didn't care. He was only glad to have one of his own court beside him once more—it brought another bit of normalcy to this otherwise strange turn his existence had taken.

Their group had numbered too many to travel by magic, or at least by the limited magic they possessed. So they were traveling in the safer, old-fashioned way—

by horseback. Or by dragonback, in the case of the Sundolian woman—Sade was her name, wasn't it?—who was currently flying high above them, searching their surroundings for threats.

They passed through an edge of the Namurian Forest and came upon a wide stretch of the Serine River. Soryn gave the order to halt, and while scouts rode out to determine the area's suitability as a campsite, Elander stayed between Casia and Caden, watching Sade and the dragon soar against an orange-streaked, sunset sky.

Before he'd encountered that dragon during his recent visit to the Sundolian Empire, it had been a long time since he'd seen one in the flesh.

The creature eventually swooped down and landed with delicate precision upon a patch of rock beside the river, flaring its leathery wings and sending ripples out across the relatively calm water. It lowered its serpentine body to the ground, and Sade leapt from its back and strode toward Soryn.

"There's a group of tents on the north side of the river, about five miles west of here, that could mean trouble," she said. "But otherwise, it's clear as far as I could see."

Soryn nodded, thanked her, and kicked her horse into a quick trot. The divine magic symbol on her wrist glowed to life as she headed for the outskirts of the potential campsite. She was Sky-kind, and magic such as hers could be used to create shields, among other things, that were similar to those created with Moon-related magic—both the Sky and Moon Goddesses had taken similar strands of this power from Solatis.

For the past two nights, Soryn had been using that Sky magic, creating an enclosure that had slowed down any thieves or vagabonds or other stray beasts that had happened upon them.

"The Queen has no shortage of other, perfectly able magic users to tend to that shield," Elander overheard Zev saying. "Wonder why she insists on doing it herself?"

"If you're going to ask your followers to do something, you should be willing to do it yourself too," said Casia, dismounting and starting to unfasten the bags her horse carried. "That's what she told me, anyway. I think it's admirable."

"Plus, those other magic users probably need to save their strength, since it will be on them after tonight," Nessa added.

Soryn had insisted on seeing them safely to the Sadiran border, but after tonight, both she and Sade, along with most of the soldiers they'd brought, would be heading back to Kosrith. That capital city still simmered with unrest, and it wouldn't be wise to leave it without its leaders for long. And aside from this, they could only march so many across the border—and eventually into Moreth—without giving the impression that they were there to cause trouble.

They wouldn't have far to go once they entered the kingdom of Ethswen, and Casia had assured the Queen that they could make do by themselves, with only a handful of her Sky-kind soldiers for support.

Elander hoped she was right.

The group of them continued their discussion about the Queen and her magic. He lingered on the edge of this conversation, his gaze still studying the dragon. It had folded one wing to its side, and it was currently using its teeth to remove a tangle of leafy branches that had caught on the tip of the other.

Eventually, Soryn returned and officially declared this their stopping point. The dragon took flight once more, heading into the forest, and Elander dismounted and tended to his horse.

As he finished brushing the mare down, his gaze wandered over the rest of the campsite as it came together. It caught briefly on Casia, and he wondered what she was thinking—if her head was still full of thoughts about what made an *admirable* queen.

She still didn't see herself as a queen of any sort, he was almost certain. But everyone else was beginning to. It was clear enough to anyone paying attention; she was the one directing people, the one everyone looked to for answers as often as—if not more often than—they looked to Soryn.

"I've been informed that we're on firewood duty," said Caden, coming up beside him.

"Casia informed you of this, I'm guessing?"

"Yes. And I was told, and I quote, to *not complain for once.*"

Elander grinned. "You probably shouldn't complain then."

"I think the power she's gained over these past weeks is going to her head," said Caden, tapping his own head for emphasis before bending down to pick up a thick tree limb. He headed deeper into the forest, and Elander laughed quietly as he turned to follow him.

"You know," Elander said after a few moments of walking, "you could leave if you wanted to. The bonds of our court are essentially severed now. I don't expect you to keep the oath you took. We're beyond that, I believe."

"Yes," said Caden drily. "We're certainly beyond that."

But he just kept collecting scraps of wood.

They gathered all they could carry, and as they turned back toward the camp, Caden asked, "Any news from the Storm Goddess?"

Elander shook his head. He'd been watching the skies for more than dragons during these past three days; Nephele often sent messages through tiny, white, birdlike creatures known as the *magari*.

"You think it was wise, trusting her and her cohorts with something so important? Even if the power of the Heart was completely drained, it still feels strange to not have it with us, doesn't it?"

Casia had asked him the same question when he'd explained the whereabouts of the divine-but-broken object.

And he told Caden precisely what he'd told her. "What other choice did we have? We're going to need more help when it comes to dealing with Malaphar. We need Solatis on our side, and somehow I don't think she would have answered if I'd been the one calling. At least Nephele and the others have a chance of reaching her—and I thought the Heart might help them do so."

Caden frowned, but he couldn't seem to come up with an argument against this plan. "Letting them deal with that is one less thing for us to worry about, I suppose," he said with a shrug.

"One battle at a time," said Elander in agreement.

"And hopefully the battle awaiting us in Moreth will prove easier to deal with."

"No divine beings will be interfering with us there."

Caden nodded. It was common knowledge that the gods and their monsters did not walk among the elves anymore.

After a moment, however, his brow furrowed in concern. "But is it just me, or does it seem like it's been too long since our last brush with monsters in *this* realm?"

Elander reached reflexively for the shoulder the Rook God had stabbed. His wounds from that battle had more or less healed, but the memory of the blade was still sharp.

And Caden was right; it had been unusually quiet these past days. It seemed strange that Malaphar hadn't sent any other beasts to attack them after he'd sent the Fire God to Moonhaven. He almost certainly knew Casia had escaped that last attack, and finding her again would be no trouble now that she carried his mark.

Maybe he wasn't in a hurry because he knew that mark would eventually overtake her, whether he sent one of his minions to harass them or not?

Elander hadn't worked out precisely how it was happening, or how to stop it, but even now he could sense the magic of that mark growing stronger, weaving more tightly around Casia with every passing moment. It was only a matter of time before she faced ascension.

If anybody could resist such a fate, it would be her.

But he'd never heard of a being rejecting ascension once an upper-god had destined them for it.

Then again, he'd *also* never heard of a middle-god ascending while the previous one still lived. And he was very much alive, despite the Rook God's best efforts, and he intended to stay that way. He and Casia were rewriting the very laws of their world, it seemed, creating a story unlike anything that world had ever seen.

If only he knew how it ended.

There will be more answers in Moreth, he kept telling

himself. The elves had knowledge that even the middle-gods didn't possess; they had existed before the Marr, during a time when the Moraki were more forthcoming with that knowledge—and with their magic.

Caden was still awaiting his reply, he realized.

"...Perhaps we should try to reach Nephele ourselves," Elander said, shaking his head to try and derail his racing thoughts, "and see what she's found out."

"I could take a quick trip to Stormhaven," Caden offered. "And then I can catch up with you toward Moreth."

"You'll have to travel through Oblivion." Elander frowned, trying to think of some way that could be avoided. But he couldn't. "It will be risky."

"Everything we're doing as of late is risky, isn't it?" Caden shrugged. "Besides, it will be more entertaining for me than *firewood duty*." They shared a wry smile.

"Very well," Elander said, "you can go in the morning if we don't receive some sign from the goddess before then. But let's give it a little more time."

Caden agreed to wait, and he dropped his gathered firewood and went to help a group of nearby soldiers who were struggling to raise the Queen's command tent.

Elander started toward the tent as well.

Then he sensed a powerful presence, along with the feeling that he was being watched. Curiosity got the better of him. He turned away from the camp and took a few steps back into the forest. He quickly came upon what he'd expected he might—two large eyes were peering out from a dense thicket.

The dragon was watching him.

It kept perfectly still even as he moved closer. Its scales had changed from their usual pale amethyst color, blending so closely into the foliage around it that Elander might not have noticed it at all if he hadn't sensed its life-force—an energy that had likely flared because the creature had used magic to conceal itself.

He stared back, unable to shake the feeling that the dragon's eyes saw more than most beings did.

They seemed to recognize him.

"You aren't truly human, as I understand it," came Sade's voice as she emerged from the trees and dropped her own collected wood into the pile behind him.

"...No," Elander said. "I'm not."

"She senses it."

He reached out his hand to the dragon.

The creature stretched out of the dense brush and gave that hand a long, curious sniff without taking its milky blue eyes off his face.

"She is not of this mortal realm, herself," said Elander.

"Correct," Sade said, looking pleased that she'd found someone who understood her dragon companion. Elander had gotten the impression, during his brief interactions with this woman, that she had little patience for people who *didn't* understand things. "Her name is Rue," she told him, wiping her hands to rid them of wood debris. "According to legend, she used to dwell in the middle-heavens, alongside the middle-goddess, Mairu."

Mairu.

The Goddess of Control.

She technically belonged to the same divine court that Elander once had—a servant of Malaphar.

"But according to that legend, Mairu herself was not fond of sticking to the divine dwellings," Sade said, walking over and placing a hand on the dragon's head. She stroked its feathery mane, and the creature made a noise that was remarkably similar to the purr of a cat. "She escaped those dwellings often—or parts of her did, at least, because she could create copies of herself that could walk the mortal world without restraint. Divine *shades*, the stories called them. One of those shades took a human lover even, and had a child with him." She let the words hang in the air, as if waiting for Elander to offer corrections.

He shrugged. "It's true, more or less."

Wayward one, many of the other Marr called her. It was no secret how often she strayed away from them and the divine realms, preferring instead to dabble and make mischief and love among mortals.

But it had been years—decades, maybe?—since he'd seen the goddess for himself. He wasn't sure what had become of her, whether she was hiding or had suffered some terrible fate; he'd been too preoccupied with his own potentially terrible fate to dig more deeply into hers. But he already knew this story Sade was telling him. He'd thought often of the ways it paralleled his own— another deity forsaking the rules because of love.

Maybe it was the greatest folly of the upper-gods, their belief that they could strip all of the humanity out of the ones they chose to give divinity to. Sometimes he wondered if *all* the middle-gods might eventually fall back into this mortal world and stay there, if given enough time.

"Our gods are a meddlesome, messy sort, aren't they?" Sade commented.

He didn't reply.

She continued just the same. "I used to not even believe in them."

"They're very real."

"Yes. I caught on soon after I came face to face with this beast," she said with a nod toward the dragon.

He smiled a bit at that. The beast *did* make it impossible to deny the gods; the reason he hadn't seen a dragon in the flesh in so long was because of its connection to those gods—it didn't belong in this world, but in theirs.

The bigger, more powerful creatures like this could not stay in the mortal realm without something divine tethering them to it. The hounds he'd fought alongside

Nephele had arrived in the mortal-side haven only after the Fire God had made a path for them. The beasts the Rook God had sent over the past weeks—the garmora in Belwind, the night-vanths in Rykarra—had been drawn, in part, by Elander himself.

And in this case, he presumed the tether was the High Queen of Sundolia—a daughter of Mairu's *shade* and one of her human lovers. That young Queen was not a divine being, but she was apparently close enough to one that this dragon was able to stay here and serve her, even in spite of the distance currently between them.

"You aren't in possession of any dragons we should know about, are you?" Sade asked, arching a brow.

He shook his head. But the more he thought about it, the less certain he was. Casia's question from the other night suddenly resurfaced in his mind—

Who was I before?

He was glad she hadn't asked for more details. He wasn't sure he could have given them to her. Because he was forgetting who *he* had been, too. Everything he'd done, every power he'd had, every beast that might have once answered to him...

It was all getting more blurry by the day.

With every shift in his power and divine status, more things seemed to go missing. And he suspected that this Sundolian woman wanted to interrogate him further regarding those blurry things. So before she could do that, he excused himself and wandered back toward the camp.

He felt the dragon's eyes following him as he went.

Soryn's command tent had been successfully erected by this point, but Caden was nowhere to be seen. Elander kept to himself, and he stayed busy by carrying their collected wood to a more central location and starting to build a fire.

Laurent soon joined his efforts, and he found that he didn't mind the company; out of all of Casia's friends, he found the half-elf the easiest to talk to. Perhaps because they were both half in one world and half in another. It gave them a common starting ground at least.

The fire was quickly built, and they settled around it and quietly observed the rest of the camp. After a few minutes, Elander peered through the flames and said, "You aren't looking forward to returning home, I've gathered."

Laurent kept his eyes on those flames. "I wouldn't say I'm overjoyed. And I wouldn't say it's home. Not even close."

"How long has it been since you lived there?"

Laurent dug through the leather pack at his feet, withdrew a canteen, and took a long sip. "I never lived there, actually. I tell people I'm from Moreth because it's true, in a way—and because fear and superstition usually stop them from inquiring more closely about the matter."

This was a surprise. "You kept this from Casia and the others?"

"I didn't think it mattered where I came from. They never acted like it did, anyway. I believe that's the reason I've stuck around with them for so long." He took another sip. "I suppose the truth is a relentless bastard, though. As is the past. Not much chance of escaping any of it."

"Not entirely, anyway," Elander agreed.

He had escaped much of his own past only by losing his divinity and being subjected, over and over, to the Rook God's draining, torturous magic. But it had still caught up in other ways. The sound of Casia's voice floated over to him in that instant, reminding him of this.

He still didn't know *how* or *why* they had caught up to one another again, but here they were.

"I wasn't born in the elven realm," Laurent continued. "My mother was human, and she was from River-hill—and she returned there when she realized she was pregnant. But we didn't stay there for very long after I was born, either. She couldn't hide what I was, and what I *was* didn't sit well with the folk of that village. Those people of the river have always been a god-fearing sort. To them, associating with elves meant bringing misfortune on their family, because of all the ways those elves had supposedly offended the upper-gods. But Moreth was not an option, as my elven father already had another person to tend to instead of my mother and me."

"Another?"

"The elven woman he was actually married to."

"Ah."

Laurent picked up a stray limb and started to break it into smaller pieces, his eyes glazed over in thought. "If the laws would have allowed it, my mother always said my father would have chosen her—would have chosen *us*. I suspect she only said that so I wouldn't feel like I was an accident. Who knows, though? I've never met my father, so I couldn't say what he wanted—one way or the other."

"So where did you go? Where did you live?"

He shrugged. "We got by in one small village or another. Never any particular one for very long."

"And your mother is now...?"

"Buried on a hilltop outside of Lenora, overlooking the sea. Where we would have lived forever, she once told me, if settling down ever became an option for us."

"I'm sorry."

Another shrug.

Elander shifted his weight from one side to the other. He should have known what to say. All the time he'd spent amongst the dead and dying, walking between this world's various heavens and hells...

Why didn't he know what to say?

"What about you?" asked Laurent. "I've been

curious ever since Casia told us who you really were. I know that all of the divine beings aside from the upper-gods were once mortal creatures. You must have had a family before you ascended, correct?"

Elander nodded, but once again, he wasn't sure what else to say. He'd had a mother and a father once. He must have.

But he couldn't picture them at all.

It was a common trend among the middle-gods—particularly the ones that were older and more powerful; most had little, if any, recollection of who they'd been before ascension. To rise as a divine being ultimately meant leaving one's human memories behind. Some of the lesser-spirits managed to hang onto theirs, but even that was rare.

And now that Elander was falling rather than rising, it seemed to be happening in reverse—the memories of his time as a divine being were beginning to slip away.

One or the other. God or human. The structure of their world did not seem to allow for being both. Which made his existence—and now Casia's, too—all the more complicated.

"I don't remember anything about them, honestly," he said quietly.

Laurent gave him a curious look, but he didn't pry. He didn't seem to be the type to pry.

Another reason Elander preferred his company to most of the others.

"I honestly don't think about the family I came from very often." Laurent tossed the broken limb into the fire, piece by piece, his eyes sliding out of focus again as he lost himself in thought. After a long pause, he said, "It doesn't matter where I came from as much as where I'm going, I always told myself. And it didn't matter at all before this little adventure we've found ourselves on."

A sudden concern struck Elander. "You believe you can get us into Moreth, despite your...*questionable* heritage?"

He sighed. "The gate to the realm will open for me because of my elvish blood—or my mother once told me it would, anyway. But what happens next is anybody's guess. Which is why I thought I should tell you all the truth before we go charging into Moreth. Soryn already knows."

"And the others?"

"I told Casia and Nessa as well, and I assume they've told most everyone else." His gaze shifted toward the river, to where the two in question were wading in the water, and a half-smile lifted one side of his mouth. "Nessa is convinced a happy family reunion awaits me there. I have my doubts. But I guess we'll see."

They trailed into silence.

Elander's gaze lingered for a moment on the river. The sun was setting, casting a warm glow that made the water sparkle. Casia was glowing within that orange sunlight, hair on fire, body a burning silhouette that kept drawing his gaze over and over again. He was thinking of getting to his feet and going to speak with her when Zev was suddenly standing in front of him, blocking his view.

"What are you looking at?" Zev asked. There was a faint hint of alcohol on his breath.

"The river," Elander answered, yawning.

"Liar," said Zev, and that was all he said for a long moment.

"Is there something else I can help you with?"

"I have a question for you," Zev began, plopping down on the ground across from him.

Another minute passed in silence, and finally Elander asked, "Well?"

Zev narrowed his eyes suspiciously. "Do you love her?"

Elander arched a brow. "I feel like I'm taking a test, suddenly."

"Nonsense," said Zev, leaning back against the log Laurent was sitting on. He pulled a knife from the sheath at his ankle, tossing it back and forth with impressive dexterity for someone who seemed well on their way to being drunk. Eventually, he caught it and stabbed it into the log behind him, all in one smooth motion. "You better not fail it, though."

"Knock it off," Laurent said, fixing him with a disapproving look. "How much have you had to drink, anyway?"

Zev inhaled deeply before jerking the knife out of the wood. "Not enough, my elfy friend," he replied, clapping a hand on Laurent's shoulder. Then he hoisted himself back to his feet, sheathed the knife, and waltzed away as quickly as he'd arrived.

"Did we really pack that much alcohol?" Elander asked as he watched him go.

"No. He disappeared when we were riding through Edolin, if you didn't notice. Then he reappeared with several new saddlebags...and now we know what was in those bags, it seems."

"Priorities," Elander mused.

Laurent huffed out a laugh. "He struggles with that." His eyes went back to the river. After a moment they narrowed, and he sighed. "And the two of them plus alcohol is usually trouble."

Elander followed his gaze once more, and he quickly understood his concern; Zev appeared to be trying to catch the river on fire. He had summoned fire to both of his hands and was sweeping it around him in a crazed sort of dance, while Sade and Nessa both stood on the bank, their arms folded across their chests, looking thoroughly unimpressed.

Casia was still knee-deep in the water, doing her best to aid her friend in his efforts. She was dumping something onto the surface of the water—something flammable, apparently. Another questionable thing Zev had picked up in Edolin, no doubt. It sizzled and smoked as embers of his magic fell upon it, until, finally, it ignited. Casia stumbled back with a shriek that soon turned into laughter.

It was becoming one of Elander's favorite sounds, that laugh. And there had been a moment, just days ago, when he'd thought he might never hear it again. When he'd been crumpled against the wall in Oblivion, blood pooling around him...

So to hear it now was a balm to his tired soul—even if those flames that were making her laugh *were* getting disturbingly high.

"I should go chaperone that," Laurent muttered.

Elander nodded. "Please don't let him accidentally set Casia on fire. I *do* love her, and I'd prefer it if she remained in a single, unburnt piece."

"I'll do my best," said Laurent, smiling briefly before heading off toward the river.

Elander stayed by the fire.

People came and went around him. Some chatted with him, but none stayed for very long. He was used to it. Even when he had commanded armies for Varen and the former King-Emperor—even when he lived in the palace in Ciridan, surrounded by people—rarely did anyone get too close to him. An aura of Death still clung to him even now, he supposed, and Death was treated similarly across almost every culture he'd witnessed—as an ever-present entity that people acknowledged and occasionally flirted with whenever they needed a rush, but one that they were afraid to stare at or sit with for too long.

Night crept in.

Soryn sent Sade and her dragon to fly the stretch of route that he and Casia and the others would be taking tomorrow, and then the Queen retired to her tent, most of her soldiers following her example.

Casia, Nessa, and Zev sat on the riverbank, but Laurent had confiscated their liquor, and Rhea had scolded them loudly enough that their ears were likely still ringing from it. Nothing was on fire, and they were safe for the moment.

Elander was becoming more and more restless, so he found Caden and volunteered them both for patrol duty —an excuse to wander without being questioned.

They spent nearly an hour combing the paths around their campsite. He ventured far enough away that he could no longer hear any of that camp's hushed conversations, and the night seemed to grow heavier as it grew quieter, wrapping around him like a comforting cloak.

His thoughts finally began to settle, and he was considering returning to camp and attempting sleep...

Until he caught sight of a group of trees in the distance, glistening strangely in the half-moon's light.

At first, he thought it might have been sap oozing from the trunk, and perhaps dew collecting on the leaves. But as he got closer to the trees, it became immediately obvious that their shimmering was from neither of these things.

The trees were covered in *ice*.

Despite the relatively warm, dry air, the casing of it was thick around several trunks.

"Is that what I think it is?" Caden asked, reaching out a hand and touching the ice for himself.

Elander backed away from the tree slowly, his gaze sweeping down the trunk and following the sparkling pathway that led away from it. "The Ice Goddess walked here. Briefly."

It was always *briefly* these days, as there wasn't enough magic circulating in Kethra to comfortably support a god or goddess walking about in their fully divine form for very long. But all it took was a brief visit to leave an anchor of magic—a tether like the one that kept that dragon in the mortal realm, serving the Sundo-lian Queen...

"Has she chosen the same side as the Fire God?" Caden wondered.

Elander didn't answer. He didn't know. That goddess had once been his friend, another one of his court. But she had ignored his latest attempts to reach out to her.

If he had to guess, he wouldn't count on her being on their side.

He continued to follow the trail of ice. It stretched

straight on for a half mile at least, and then it veered sharply to the right, toward...

"Something went toward the camp." Panic gripped him, and he was running before Caden could reply.

He didn't slow down until he hurtled out of the trees and into the middle of their camp.

A camp that was still there—still intact, still calm.

Nothing seemed amiss. Most of the soldiers were sleeping, but a few heads turned and stared curiously at him, and then at Caden as he broke just as urgently into sight.

Elander caught his breath and forced himself to move calmly. They were all safe—the barriers that Soryn had erected had done their job, apparently. And yet...

Something still didn't feel right.

With his hand resting lightly on the short sword at his hip, he strode deeper into the camp. He wanted to find Casia, to see for himself that she was safe.

And after a few minutes of searching, he finally spotted her standing waist-deep in the river once more.

The river that was suddenly, rapidly turning to ice.

CHAPTER 12

ELANDER COULD STILL MOVE WITH INHUMAN SPEED, FAST enough to outrun everyone else who had started toward the river.

He wasn't fast enough.

Casia saw the ice forming, stretching closer to her, and she started frantically backing toward the shore. She had nearly reached it when something caught her and yanked her to a stop. She struggled for a moment, trying to pull her leg from its grip, sinking a little deeper with every attempt—

And then she was gone—jerked beneath the water.

Ice swept over her head in the next instant, trapping her.

The camp had exploded into motion all around Elander, but he didn't take his eyes off the last spot he'd seen Casia. He hit the frozen river with a knife already in his hand, crouched to lower his center of gravity, and moved as swiftly as he could without losing his balance. He knew her energy. He could find it if he could just *concentrate* and not panic.

Seconds later, he felt it—the familiar pulse of *her*. It was somehow both frantic and fading, a rush of energy followed by a slow descent into terrifying stillness, over and over again.

He moved toward it. Caught a glimpse of grey hair in the dark water on the other side of the ice. Lost sight of her. Found her again, and this time he fell immediately to his knees, stabbing downward with his knife as he dropped.

This was not typical ice; it resisted even his partially divine strength at first. But he could still see Casia. He could still feel her fighting.

And he wasn't going to lose her.

Some powerful combination of fury and fear eventually drove his blade through the ice. It cracked away from the puncture he'd made, and now that he had a starting point, he tossed the knife aside and used his fist to finish the job. The ice shifted and caved dangerously around his knees, and his knuckles were soon bloody from scraping the jagged and broken edges of it, but he kept punching until he had an opening large enough to pull a body through.

He could still see Casia. She was still conscious,

fighting her way toward the opening he'd made, her hands feeling their way along the icy ceiling above her.

He reached into the river.

Her fingertips brushed his.

And then they fell away.

He kept his hand in the water, kept reaching out to her even after she'd drifted from his sight.

The water was chilling rapidly, magic teeming within it, and the unnatural cold bit at his skin, numbing a path up his arm. Diving in after Casia would be a foolish way to end them both. He *knew* this.

He was an instant away from doing it anyway when her hand finally closed over his wrist.

He held more tightly to her arm than he'd held to perhaps anything in his existence, and he hoisted her up out of the water, cradled her against his chest, and carried her to shore.

Frost clung to the tips of her hair and eyelashes. Her skin was pale, her lips blue, her eyes fluttering in and out of focus.

"Stay awake," he commanded, pulling off his coat and wrapping it around her. "*Stay awake.*"

She muttered something that sounded like an argument.

Good.

If she still wanted to argue with him, then her brain was apparently functioning normally.

The entire river had frozen over by this point, and

the ice was spreading onto land. Veins of it snaked up across the muddy bank and reached toward them. Lifting Casia into his arms once more, he sprinted away from the river as he shouted for Zev, who took one look in their direction and then was running toward them, summoning fire to his hands as he came.

Elander stopped once he'd made it to the top of a small hill. The ice followed, spreading over the ground, turning the grass to crystal daggers, encasing bushes and small trees, snapping limbs. Out of the corner of his vision he saw it catch at least one soldier who moved too slowly. The soldier stumbled as ice wrapped around and up his legs, turning to a frozen statue that made an unsettling cracking sound as he hit the ground.

Fire swept toward Elander a moment later. It encircled him, caught on the tall grass around him and lifted into a high, protective wall. He glimpsed Zev on the other side of the ring, controlling the flames and keeping them from spreading too close.

Within the circle of sweltering heat, Casia's skin flushed closer to its normal color. After a moment her eyes opened, and they finally *stayed* open.

"Can you stand?" he asked.

She met his gaze slowly, still somewhat dazed and shivering. She nodded. He placed her on her feet, but her balance swayed. She caught his arm, bracing herself against his strength.

"I'm fine," she said in response to the concerned look he gave her. "What is going on?"

Before he could reply, the heat around them shifted, drawing both their gazes toward a large section of the fiery ring that had started to dim.

Zev now stood back-to-back with his sister, who was wielding her fire-spitting staff. They were working together, attempting to free the soldiers the freezing magic had caught before that ice tightening around them could snap their bones. It was a delicate operation. One they were mostly failing at.

Soryn was racing from one end of the shore to the other, calling her fellow Sky magic users into action. Soon there was a wall of that Sky magic rising, wrapping around the horses, as well as the tents and the supplies within them.

Elander had started toward Zev and Rhea, intending to help them, when he heard Casia gasp.

She was pointing toward the river.

He twisted and saw a creature rising out of the water.

It didn't break through the ice, but rose *from* it, building its body out of frozen shards that crackled and glistened in the moonlight. A fine cloud of freezing mist shrouded it as it stretched taller and taller, and they watched as that mist swirled into the shape of two long arms—one of which clutched a sword made from yet more ice.

When the ice finally stopped shifting and forming, the beast stood as tall as the tallest of the trees surrounding their camp. Black eyes glinted in wide recesses of a helm-like skull. Its mouth was cavernous with teeth like jagged rock formations jutting haphazardly about.

It lifted its sword, and with speed that seemed impossible for such a large creature, it sliced that blade toward the wall of Sky magic Soryn was trying to establish.

The Sky magic withstood the initial blow, though the earth all around it trembled violently. The Queen fell to her hands and knees. Wisps of her magic floated around her, strands of pale turquoise peeling away from her body and slipping free of that shield she'd been weaving.

Elander turned back to Casia, but she was no longer there; she was running for the break in the fire that shielded them.

She stopped only long enough to strip a bow and quiver from a fallen soldier, and once armed, she was running again, jumping over patches of frozen ground and sliding precariously over others until she was at Soryn's side.

She pulled Soryn back to her feet. Stepping between the queen and the monster, she nocked an arrow and took aim.

The arrow struck the beast's shoulder.

A second arrow flew into the opposite shoulder a moment later—this one courtesy of Nessa, who was perched on a nearby hill, just above another shield of Sky magic.

Both arrows had the same effect, chipping a small section of the monster's body away and sending the shards of it spinning toward the ground. Two more arrows followed, each slicing away a larger chunk of shoulder.

But then came a cracking sound, and a tinging like a fork tapping glass—the sound of the beast growing more ice to replace what it had lost.

Elander caught up to Casia, and without taking her gaze off that beast, she asked, "What in the hells *is* this thing?"

Proof that the Ice Goddess is not on our side.

"Elander?"

"A servant of the Goddess of Winter, Taiga," he answered. "But beyond that, I don't know. I've never seen it before."

"So you don't know how to get rid of it, I'm guessing?"

As he shook his head, Soryn went back to shouting orders, directing more archers to fire. Dozens upon dozens of arrows volleyed over their heads and struck the creature, hacking its body off bit by bit. But even this barrage was not enough to drive it away; it simply kept regenerating itself.

"But we aren't getting rid of it like *that*, apparently," Elander said.

Casia muttered something under her breath, and then she turned to speak with Laurent and Zev as they approached.

While they argued over a plan, Elander focused on trying to feel the creature's life force. Whenever it regenerated, that force swelled, making it easier to pinpoint the spot where it flowed from—though it was still difficult to focus on it, between the argument beside him and the increasingly panicked shouts and scrambling throughout the camp.

"It has to have a weakness," he overheard Casia say. Desperation clung to her words, making her voice louder and sharper than normal, and an instant later that desperation turned her gaze back toward him.

He wasn't certain he'd found a true weakness, but...

"It has a distinct energy," he told her, "and it seems to be gathered in its lower stomach. There's an odd pulsing there."

"Like a heartbeat?" Laurent asked.

"Maybe."

Casia squinted at the spot in question. "The ice looks thick." Her gaze shot toward Zev. "You'll have to melt it."

"I don't have an unlimited supply of magic," Zev replied, frowning. "And it's moving too quickly for me to concentrate what magic I *do* have."

"Focus on its legs first then," said Elander, drawing

his sword as Laurent did the same. "They'll be a thinner, easier target. If you can weaken them enough for our weapons to have a chance, we'll be able to slow it down, and then you and your sister can both take aim at its stomach. And Casia can be ready to strike whatever vital organs you will—hopefully—uncover."

Casia nodded, her jaw set and her eyes shimmering with determination.

Zev appeared less certain. "This seems like it has the potential to go disastrously, and I'm still too drunk for this—"

"And neither of those things are new problems for us," Laurent interrupted, grabbing him by the arm and yanking him into a sprint.

Elander followed closely behind.

Within seconds, they were swallowed up by the monster's shadow. It noticed them approaching, and it drew its blade of ice back before sweeping it forward in a low arc.

Elander had to leap over a frozen, fallen body in order to narrowly avoid the serrated edge of that blade. And though it hadn't struck him, the air started to chill with the same unnatural freeze that had overtaken the river. It was disorienting. The cold gripped his head like a set of claws, squeezing more and more tightly until throbbing pain blurred his vision.

A flash of fire brought his focus back.

Soon it became more than a flash; a steady,

sustained inferno surrounded Zev. That tumbling mass of fire quickly flattened out—stretched into a kind of rope that obeyed every twist of his wrist and gesture of his hand.

Zev's expression was perfectly solemn. Focused. The complete opposite of how he normally looked. Elander couldn't help but be impressed—and to wonder what he might be capable of when he *hadn't* spent the evening drinking himself senseless.

That fiery rope lashed toward the beast's legs, at what might have been considered its ankles, and wrapped tightly around both simultaneously. Water dripped like blood from the places that rope burned into. The beast let out a terrible sound—like a harsh wind screaming through a mountain pass—and its head turned to follow Zev. But its attempts to give chase were hindered by its deteriorating legs.

Distracted and stumbling.

Now was their chance.

Elander went left.

Laurent went right.

It took all the strength Elander could muster to cut through the weakened and weeping ice. Several times he had to yank his blade out, spin back, and come at it from the other side, but he finally managed it, as did the half-elf a moment later. Melted ice gushed from the severed legs. The monster tottered dangerously for several seconds before tripping on the steep slope of the riverbank and crashing down, rumbling the earth as it hit.

It landed on its side, exposing its stomach to Rhea, who stood on top of that slope with her staff in hand and Silverfoot on her shoulder. Zev joined them, and they summoned flames that wove together in the air, creating a spear of fire that they drove deep into the beast's belly.

Elander felt the creature's life force skip faster, hammering harder and harder as the fire sank into its body. The organ that life flowed from was visible for a fraction of a second, just as they'd hoped it would be—a dark, fleshy blob that did indeed resemble a beating heart.

Casia aimed and released her arrow in that same fraction of a second.

But the ice started to reform as quickly as it had melted.

The arrow didn't break all the way through.

The beast's legs were taking shape once more, the ice on the frozen ground moving as if sentient, spreading up and around the broken appendages, sealing off their melting stubs and building them back taller than before.

It rocked itself back upright, settling into a crouch as it tested its weight on the newly-formed legs.

Casia was still standing before it, unfazed by its regeneration.

Move, Elander thought. *Move!*

But she wasn't moving; she was readying another arrow.

She managed to sink that second arrow right next to the first, but it still wasn't enough to reach the vital center. And the beast was smart enough to realize what she was trying to do; one of its arms wrapped protectively around its stomach. Slowly, smooth like a ribbon unfolding, it rose back to its full height. Its mouth opened in a furious display of teeth, and its gaze fixed on Casia.

"Its eyes, Nessa!" Elander shouted.

An arrow soared from the hilltop and struck the beast's right eye. Several more followed as Queen Soryn bellowed out an order to finish blinding it. The beast stumbled back, swiping at its face as projectile after projectile landed in its dark and shining sockets.

Casia scrambled away from it, avoiding wildly stomping feet as she sprinted toward higher ground.

The beast winked one eye open, briefly, just long enough to spot Casia again. One of its hands slammed down, trapping her within a cage of long, icy, fingers.

Elander raced toward her.

An explosion of frigid air hit him before he could reach her, stinging his eyes and knocking the breath from his lungs. He dropped to one knee. The air around him shimmered with frozen crystals of magic. Breathing it in felt like swallowing knives. Coughing, he lifted his head and saw that bodies were scattered all around him —all of them shining, all of them covered in the same thin coat of frost that also covered him.

No one else was moving.

And though he had fared better than most—he was still conscious and still upright—his legs felt useless, bound by invisible, bitterly cold chains.

He stared, horrified, as the beast's hand pressed down and crushed Casia out of sight.

Ignoring the pain radiating through his legs, Elander crawled forward, reached out a hand and tried to summon his magic. He could do this. How many had he killed before this moment? Beasts and mortals alike...stopping hearts had once been as easy as breathing to him. And even now he felt his magic rising, the tendrils of it reaching out in search of the life force he needed to suffocate.

But then—

Gone.

As if the wind had snatched it away. His power was simply...*gone*. And there was no sign of his magic impacting the beast at all, and yet he still felt drained, as if he'd just summoned five times the amount of magic he'd actually been trying for.

Suddenly the air grew colder with a chill that was different from Ice magic. Darkness settled over the riverside, deeper and more desperately hopeless than any natural night, and he realized...he knew this magic.

Because it was *his* magic.

Only, he was not the one controlling it.

He couldn't see much in the darkness. But the Ice beast's magic lit it from within, outlining parts of its body in a hazy white glow, and so Elander could see that the cage of fingers around Casia had lifted. The mark the Rook God had clawed into Casia's skin was shining brightly as well, a terrible beacon in the blackness.

Her expression turned eerily vacant as she stood and stepped toward that beast that had almost crushed her.

The cold and the dark deepened, and the beast clutched its stomach. Its heart. Elander could still sense that beating source of life—just barely.

And then it stopped.

The beast fell to its knees. As it hit the ground, cracks struck through its stomach, its chest, its head, little pieces of ice chipping off and falling, shattering against the dirt. Swirls of white and pale blue magic surrounded the creature, swept those shattered pieces of it up and carried them away, bit by bit, until nothing remained.

The air warmed.

The scene lightened, the moon and stars sluggishly blinking back into sight, as Casia knelt in the dirt, one of her arms wrapped around her stomach, the other braced against the ground, her head tucked toward her chest.

The frost coating the ground and seemingly every other surface began to melt, and the sound of trickling water filled the air. Soon the rush of a newly-freed river joined it, along with the noise of a camp slowly coming back to life—stunned and confused voices, people stumbling to their feet, the frantic neighing of horses.

Casia still hadn't moved.

Some of the people getting back to their feet were staring at her, at the large puddle in front of her, still shimmering with a few slivers of ice. And they were starting to whisper.

Elander didn't have to listen to know what they were whispering about. They knew who she was, what she had done, the places she'd been. Most didn't know her *entire* story, but they knew just enough to speculate about that mark on her face—and what they'd just witnessed would no doubt turn those speculations into something...*darker*. Something more complicated.

But Elander didn't want to think about any of that right now.

He rose in spite of the cold still shooting daggers of pain through his legs, walked over, and knelt before her.

"Casia," he said softly.

She slowly lifted her head and stared back at him, speechless and afraid, her breath coming in starts and stops, like it was no longer reflex but a concentrated effort.

He could sense more and more heads turning to stare at them. So instead of talking there in the middle of them all, he offered his hand. She let him pull her to her feet, and together they walked to the edge of the camp, away from prying eyes. A few tentatively followed them. Casia's gaze slid over every person that was watching her, not truly focusing on any of them.

But then she fixed her eyes on him—only him—and she said, "That was Death magic I just used."

Elander nodded.

She sank back against a nearby tree, her hand pressed to her cheek, as if the weight of the mark on it was suddenly too heavy to bear while standing up. "I wasn't even *trying* to use it," she whispered. "I was trying to summon Storm magic, but it wouldn't come. It feels as if the Dark magic he put in me is suffocating every...every other thing inside of me and I...I...."

"Death magic can neutralize other magic," he reminded her. "And there's something else—"

She buried her face in her hand.

He hesitated.

"Go on," she mumbled.

"When the gods of a particular court are together, they're stronger. The Ice Goddess answers to Malaphar, same as I once did. So our magic, though it appears vastly different, is actually comprised of at least some similar energies. Her magic played some role in drawing the Death magic out and above your Storm magic, I'm sure. Same with the Fire God when you were in Moonhaven; you told me you felt as if your Storm magic was being suffocated then too, didn't you?"

"So it wasn't the Fire God's magic that was suffocating it," she said. "It was simply his proximity that made it harder to summon a different sort of magic? That and whatever magic you'd used against me."

"Yes. And now that I think about it, I suspect sending his servants after us is probably less about trying to attack you, and more about trying to hasten your ascension by forcing you to use such magic."

She pushed away from the tree. Paced deeper into the woods, only to walk back to his side, and then back to the woods again.

Over and over she did this, until finally she shook her head, lifted her eyes to the dark sky and said, "Perhaps it was the Ice Goddess's magic that triggered it, but there was something strange about how it happened. Because I could have sworn I felt that magic coming from you at first. And then it was gone and I...I..."

He wanted to lie.

But she deserved the truth. Or what he suspected was the truth, at least. Mirroring her quiet tone, he said, "It seems like the transfer of power is happening more aggressively than I thought it would."

"And if this keeps happening..." Her eyes lowered and locked on his once more, and he could see the question simmering in them, though she didn't manage to ask it out loud—

How much time do we have left?

CHAPTER 13

THE CAMP WAS RELATIVELY CALM ONCE MORE, AND CAS WAS stretched out in her bedroll, pretending to be asleep. Nessa lay beside her, clutching the hem of her shirt. The Feather-kind woman had been using her magic to help keep Cas's thoughts from running away with her, and trying to warm her towards something like sleep. A thoughtful effort—one that Cas was grateful for.

But now Nessa was asleep herself, and that warmth her magic had created was slipping away.

They rested just outside the reach of firelight. Rhea, Laurent, and Soryn sat around the fire, talking in hushed voices. Zev was on the opposite side of their little circle, fast asleep; Cas could hear him snoring even with the distance between them. She focused on the sound of it, and it brought a wistful almost-smile to her face. Normally that sound drove her mad, but tonight it was a welcome, familiar note amongst the uncertainties surrounding them.

After an hour or so of pretending to sleep, she heard Caden approaching the group by the fire—or *sensed* him, rather, just as Elander was able to sense him—and she tucked her knees to her chest and tried to focus only on Zev's snoring.

But she couldn't help overhearing things.

It was no surprise when the topic immediately turned to her. To what she'd done. Elander had disappeared with Caden earlier to discuss these things, she knew. And she didn't know where Elander had gone now, but she assumed he'd sent Caden back to speak to this core group of their allies, to explain things...likely so that Cas wouldn't have to suffer through that conversation herself. He was protecting her. She scoffed at this last thought, telling herself she didn't *need* such protection.

And yet she also didn't bother to interrupt Caden.

For close to an hour, the group by the fire talked in circles, voices quiet and quick with a palpable, fearful urgency. Cas already knew much of what was being said, and that made it easier to not pay attention, until—

"So what happens as she gains more of the fallen god's power? All of it, perhaps?" Soryn's voice. She had an unapologetically loud way of speaking, even in the middle of the night, and Cas found herself drawn, unwillingly, back into the conversation. "Does he simply go back to being human?"

A pause, and then, "No. I don't think so. Or if he does, he won't last long in that form."

The volume of the conversation dropped lower. Low enough that Cas could have blocked out distinct words if she'd only buried her head a little deeper into her blankets. She wasn't sure why she kept listening.

"It's almost too cruel, isn't it?" she heard Rhea say. "Not only is she going to potentially replace Elander, but she's going to destroy him in the process."

Cas closed her eyes. Dug her fingers into the cold dirt beside her and squeezed. Her stomach ached. No matter what position she tried to curl into, she still felt as if she might vomit. After a few minutes of tossing and turning, she sat up. The chatter around the fire immediately stopped. Cas focused on taking her blanket and draping it over Nessa, who had started to shiver as soon as she moved away.

When she finally looked toward the fire, she found four identical, concerned gazes turned her direction. She said nothing. She only averted her eyes once more, pulled on her boots, and excused herself from their company.

AFTER TAKING A LONG, wandering walk through the campsite, she decided to search for Elander.

She spotted him quickly enough. He was walking along the river, an absent expression on his face as he massaged his wrist—the spot where the symbol of Death was branded into his skin.

He stopped and tilted his head toward her as she approached. Something in his gaze made her legs freeze up and refuse to carry her any closer.

"Are you okay?" he asked, frowning.

"Yes." She forced a nod. "But we didn't finish our conversation earlier."

"...No, I suppose we didn't."

She gestured toward the campfire she'd left behind. "And I overheard Caden talking to the others about some of the things we didn't get to discuss."

His eyes went back to the water, and he was silent.

She inhaled a deep breath. Took one slightly shaking step after the other, until only a short but steep, muddy incline separated them.

All the words came pouring out of her in the next moment, as if sliding down that slick hill before her, falling faster and faster as they crashed toward him. "Without your power, you can't exist. That's how Malaphar will ultimately finish you. That's why he agreed to my deal—he knew it wouldn't matter if he spared you in that moment, anyway. Because if I ascend and serve him, it means you no longer have your divine powers. And without them..."

She swallowed several times before she managed to get her next words out.

He didn't interrupt her.

"All the years catch up," she whispered. "You can't last as a mortal now."

He nodded without turning around. "I originally believed there was a chance that Malaphar might simply curse me to be human again if I failed him, but that was probably never a real possibility. And it certainly isn't now, as furious as he's become. He won't be stalling any death of mine."

"Which means that it's dangerous for me to even be near you if I can't control this Death magic. Since I'm apparently draining it from you without even *meaning* to."

He hesitated.

"That's what you said earlier, right? The transfer of magic is...aggressive."

He nodded again. The movement was slower this time—more stiff, more reluctant. It made her knees feel weak.

Was this really how they ended?

After everything they'd gone through together, in this lifetime and in every other?

She struggled to take a deep breath. All those lives felt very heavy, suddenly—so heavy that she needed to brace herself against something. Against him. She picked her way down the muddy slope and met him there at the riverside, wrapped her arms around him from behind, and buried her face against his back.

"What do we do now?" she heard herself ask.

His reply came slowly. Quietly. "I don't know."

His hand found hers, wrapped it up, pressed it more completely against his chest. Against his heartbeat. And she could read the promise in his touch, in the silences between his steady breaths, as clearly as if he'd whispered it into her ear. *I don't know, but I still love you, either way.*

"I'm sorry," she breathed. "I'm so sorry. I shouldn't have made that bargain, I just..."

He turned to face her, his gaze intense, his eyes a stunningly vivid blue in the moonlight. She was reminded of the day she'd met him in Oblivion, when those eyes had been the only bright thing in an ocean of darkness. She forgot what she had started to say for a moment. All her different powers raged in her veins, strong and unsettled and full of terrible and brilliant and frightening potential, and yet she couldn't remember the last time she'd felt so helpless.

"I'm sorry," she tried again. "I—"

He silenced her with a kiss, taking her face in his hands and holding it gently, keeping her still even after he'd pulled away. "Enough. You didn't know what would happen. *I* didn't know what would happen. We are..." His brow furrowed as he searched for the right word. "Unprecedented," he decided on, and her heartbeat fluttered at the way he said it. "And whatever happens now..."

"I'll keep fighting it off," she interrupted, a fresh surge of fear suffocating her voice, making it soft. "*That* is what is going to happen now. I'll figure out a way to make it stop. I'll work harder to only use the magic of the Sun. That magic was strong enough to bring me back into this world and guide me back to you, so it can be stronger than whatever curse or claim the Rook God has laid on me, right? It isn't over, I don't have to let this mark—this darkness—that *stupid* bargain I made claim me. I *won't* let it."

His hand lifted, brushing away a stray tear that had escaped her eye.

"I don't want you to go," she said, steadier now. "Don't go."

The moment stretched on. She found herself bracing for his response, expecting him to tell her that she was selfish and foolish, that it made more sense for them to be apart. She couldn't have argued against any of those things very convincingly.

But what he said was, "I told you I wasn't going anywhere. And I meant it." His lips quirked. "Also? I never doubted—not even for a second—that you would keep fighting. You've never known when to quit. Not for all the days I've known you."

In spite of the tears gathering in the corners of her eyes, she still smiled a bit at the droll tone of those last words, and she buried herself more deeply into his embrace.

The river behind him rumbled on. A soft, constant murmur that sent unpleasant images flooding back into Cas's mind. The ice overhead. The gleam of moonlight slipping away. The bubbles and the foam churning in the dark water as she struggled to keep swimming. More images to add to her ever-growing collection of nightmarish things.

But she had made it back to the surface, hadn't she?

Back to Elander's hand, which had never stopped reaching for her.

She kept her arms wrapped tightly around him, but after a moment she lifted her head and rested it on his shoulder—a feat that was only possible because the slope of the bank lifted her to his impressive height. Her hands clenched into the folds of his coat. The tears stopped. Her breathing settled. And as she stared at the black water before her, she swore a quiet promise to herself.

No matter what dark waters awaited them, she would keep fighting her way back to the surface.

CHAPTER 14

MORNING EVENTUALLY ARRIVED, THOUGH FOR A LONG TIME IT felt like it wouldn't.

Cas had not slept. Neither had Elander. They had passed the night sitting on the riverbank together, her head on his shoulder, his arm around her waist, with hardly any more words spoken between them.

Despite this, she was not tired. Not physically, at least. She had always had more stamina than an average human—because of that power of the Sun Goddess that had been buried within her, she now knew. It was more divine power than any human was meant to have, and the divine themselves had no real need to eat or sleep.

And now that the bargain she'd made was dragging her closer toward divinity, she found herself more or less indifferent to the lack of rest, and her stomach perfectly content with remaining empty for the time being.

Elander moved from their riverside spot first, nudging her out of her trance-like state as he did. "I'll see to your horse," he told her, stretching. "The Queen will want to speak with you again before we part ways with her, I'd imagine."

Cas nodded. She'd already been contemplating what she needed to say to Soryn before that parting of ways.

She got to her feet and dutifully headed into the heart of their camp, where she found the Queen already locked in a discussion with one of her soldiers. Her eyes cut toward Cas, and she regarded her with a smile, even as her brow furrowed in concern. She quickly finished her discussion with the soldier and headed toward Cas.

"After last night's excitement, I must say I'm more hesitant to carry out this plan of going our separate ways," she said as she approached.

Cas brushed the words aside. "It isn't the first time we've battled monsters. Won't be the last. We'll be fine."

Soryn's gaze drifted down the riverbank, to a spot where the ground sank in with evidence of that latest monster's visit. Her forehead was still creased with worry.

"I'll feel better knowing you're handling things in Kosrith," Cas insisted. "You've done enough, seeing us safely this far north. Your city needs you, and *we* need you to stay closer to our allies in the southern empire."

"You're right, of course." The Queen flagged down a woman and gave her a curt order in Sadiran. This woman nodded and hurried away, moving with a noticeable limp.

Cas wondered about the extent of her injury, and how many others had sustained similar—or worse—injuries last night.

Soryn turned and started to walk, beckoning her to follow. They strolled through the camp, talking one last time of plans and potential problems, while Cas subtly appraised the soldiers they passed. There were many more like that woman who were obviously bracing themselves through painful movements.

How many were nursing injuries?

Three were already dead, she knew for certain; before she'd collapsed into her bedroll by the fire last night, she'd stood with Soryn and watched as others performed an abbreviated version of the funeral rites that were common in Waterhall—the Sadiran realm those three hailed from. It had involved chants and offerings of salt and coin to the lesser-spirit of Luck, who was much revered by the fishermen in that realm of marshes and lakes.

Were there more funerals to come?

Others who would succumb to their injuries before they made it back to Kosrith?

All of these soldiers...they were following her as much as they were following Soryn, and Cas could no longer deny it. She had felt the weight of their expectations settling over her as they traveled, growing heavier with each day that passed.

It was so heavy in that moment that she was glad Soryn kept walking, because otherwise she was certain she would have started to sink.

Minutes later, the woman Soryn had given orders to caught up to them and handed the queen a small silk pouch, from which Soryn withdrew a simple, yet elegant, bracelet. She offered it to Cas.

"I wanted to give you this before we went our separate ways," she said. "Like the sword I carry, it has been passed through my family for generations. From one queen to another."

Cas took the bracelet and turned it around in her hands, admiring the beads of white and silver. Glashtyn silver. When the sunlight struck it just so, it glinted the same shade of turquoise as that vast sea that shared its name.

"It's elven-made," Soryn continued, "and it was originally a gift to my great-great-grandmother from one of the old Lords of Moreth during a brief period of peace and camaraderie that they shared with our kingdom. Maybe it will remind King Theren that such alliances are at least *possible*, hm?"

Cas thanked her profusely for it, though she was hesitant to put it on.

From one queen to another...

Soryn took the bracelet, slipped it onto Cas's wrist,

and tightened it herself. "Varen may deny any claim you have to the throne in Ciridan," she said, as if she could sense the doubts trying to rise in Cas's mind, "but you are more of a queen than he is a king, with or without a crown or throne. Don't let anybody tell you otherwise."

Cas lifted her gaze from the bracelet to the young ruler before her. The *Orphan Queen*, she had heard some people calling her—though only in hushed voices.

And some did not even call her a queen at all.

Until Sadira is no longer in shambles, they whispered, *what can she truly be the queen of?*

It was a bitter and thankless role—one that Soryn would not have been forced into if the world was fair and just—but one that she had embraced, nonetheless.

Her hand rested on the sword her mother had given her—*Indre's Grace,* she'd said it was called. The Shield-maker. It was glowing in the rising sunlight, as was the Queen herself.

And it was silly, perhaps, but the sight of that glow sent a warm, hopeful feeling twisting through Cas. She couldn't help herself; she threw her arms around Soryn and hugged her tightly, thanking her again for her gift.

Soryn seemed startled at first, but after a moment she relaxed into the embrace and patted Cas gingerly on the back. "I'll see you when you return. Safe, and in one piece, yes?"

It had sounded more like an order than a question—

as the young Queen's words often did—but Cas still nodded.

Safe and secure, and with new allies to stand beside Sadira.

She could do this.

Soryn was the first to break their embrace, and then she immediately went back to business. "Follow the river road north," she said, "until you come to the fork southwest of Hollownesse. The sign will only mention Hollownesse, and it will urge you northward; go east instead, and you'll eventually come to the edge of the Badlands of Glashtyn, and the start of the road that runs parallel to those barren lands. Follow this road, but don't speak to anyone you may pass on it. You'll know you're drawing close to the elven realm when the sky darkens and the trees start to whisper."

Cas was about to inquire further about these *whispering* trees when the shadow of Sade and her dragon suddenly overtook them.

The pair landed a moment later, rattling the earth and sending soldiers tripping over themselves to get out of the way. Sade hopped from the dragon's back, said something to the beast in Sundolian, and then turned her attention to Soryn and Cas.

"We flew as much of the route as we could overnight. There have been rumors of Varen supporters rising up near Rosefall and causing trouble, but we saw nothing to suggest this is true. I can't tell you if the

Badlands Road to the northeast of that region is clear, however." She turned her attention back to the dragon and scratched the space behind one of its horns, which caused the creature's throat to rumble with a purring sort of sound and its tail to thump in a slow, pleased rhythm. "Rue won't get that close to the Moreth Realm."

"The barriers the elven-kind have put up against such divine beasts are as intact as ever, it seems," Soryn explained.

Sade nodded, and her gaze slid to Cas. "Neither you nor Elander are fully divine, so I don't believe those barriers will actively *hurt* you...but your magic will certainly be suppressed. I'd prepare for the worst."

"But hope for the best," Soryn added.

"That's essentially what I've always done," said Cas. She shrugged and managed a reassuring smile.

The thought of not being able to fully access her magic was unsettling—but a relief, too. She hoped it would slow the dangerous transfer of power happening between her and Elander. And perhaps her conflicting magic would be easier to sort out while it was all subdued by elven power. Besides, it wasn't like she was helpless without magic; she'd gotten by without it for most of her life.

She would be fine. One way or another. There were answers and allies in Moreth, and she was not going to let her fears keep her from reaching them.

She said her goodbyes to Soryn and Sade, and then

she joined Elander and Laurent as they worked to ready the horses for the long day ahead. The task was automatic after three days of riding, and it passed in a blur. Before Cas knew it, she was sitting atop her horse and waving one last farewell to the Queen and the rest of her party.

Caden went a separate way as well, off on a mission to Stormhaven at Elander's orders. This was apparently where Tara was being held captive, and it was past time to go and check on her.

The goddess in command of that stormy realm was still missing too. Elander was hopeful that there would be servants at Stormhaven who could give Caden a means of reaching the middle-goddess—or at least some sign that the middle-goddess was still intact and on the move, still trying to do her part to help aid them. Elander hadn't spoken of the matter much before this morning, but Cas could tell the lack of communication from Nephele concerned him.

But what else could they do? They had enough to worry about here amongst the mortals.

Truth be told, she was actually *hoping* that the divine would stay tangled up with each other in their own realms for the time being. And the more she thought about it, the more she was looking forward to reaching the elven realm and its barriers. No more divine monsters, no more fiery gods trying to chase her down—at least for a few days. All these twisting threads would converge soon enough. But in the meantime...

One battle at a time.

Their group of nearly one hundred had become one of just over a dozen—Cas and her friends, Elander, and the handful of men and women Soryn had deemed most useful to the next leg of their journey. With fewer in their party, they traveled faster, following the Serine River as it wound its way north. The terrain was easier along this stretch as well, and they reached the fork in the path that Soryn had mentioned by late afternoon.

The farther they trekked from the river, the fewer signs of life they saw. The path never became a true road. It seemed to go on forever, until finally it led them to the edge of a cliff that overlooked what could only be the Glashtyn Badlands.

It was the first time Cas had ever seen it in person, though she'd heard plenty of stories about this place. She paused for a moment to study the landscape; it was impossible *not* to stare, to be both unsettled and awed by it. A jagged sea of stone and dust rolled as far as she could see, painted a hundred different shades by the early evening light. The most prevalent color was a dark, burnt shade of red. Like dried blood.

The common legend said that nothing grew in this place because of the things that had been buried here—the victims of an ancient battle between the upper-gods, supposedly. There had once been a prosperous, sprawling city in the center of this land, it was said, but it had been decimated by those gods who got so caught up in their battle that they didn't realize—or perhaps didn't care about—the destruction they were leaving in their wakes.

The only crime of those humans they destroyed was being in the wrong place at the wrong time; they were otherwise innocent. And the blood of innocents made nothing grow.

Cas rolled her shoulders out, trying to settle the shiver crawling along the back of her neck and scalp. She fought the urge to touch the Dark God's mark on her cheek.

It was only a legend, but staring out over these barren lands still made her think of all the horrifying things that could happen when the gods went to war.

They turned and made their way north, and they soon came to a more proper road—the infamous Badlands Road, one of Soryn's soldiers informed them.

After a few miles, Soryn's directions proved correct once more. The sky was darkening, but not in a natural, coming-of-night sort of way; it was more as if color was being leached from their surroundings by some strange magic. The leafless trees made no sounds yet, whispers or otherwise, but the wind picked up and created a low, mournful sound as it weaved in and out of their branches and bent their rickety trunks.

Along the edges of the road, shadows seemed to be

gathering and falling into what often resembled living creatures. People, even. Every time Cas looked closer, these figures were gone.

And yet it still felt as if someone...or some*thing*...was watching her.

The Queen's cryptic warning surfaced in Cas's thoughts. *Don't speak to any strangers along the road.*

"I heard a story once," she began, feeling the need to interrupt the wind's eerie song, "that this road was haunted. And I never really thought much about it, but before we left camp earlier, Soryn warned me about speaking to anyone while we were traveling along it."

Zev slowed his horse's pace to match hers, seemingly just so he could smirk at her while looking her in the eyes. "You scared?"

Cas bristled. "I'm vigilant."

He chuckled. "You're scared."

"Be quiet."

"Kind of strange to worry about *hauntings* when you're regularly fucking the former God of Death, isn't it?"

Elander laughed, and Cas blushed as she narrowed her eyes in his direction. "Don't encourage him."

"But he has a point." He gave her a crooked grin, and Cas looked away before he could see that she was unwillingly mirroring that grin.

Neither of them mentioned the fact that she might also be on her way to becoming the *Goddess* of Death.

The wind picked up even more, swirling the dust around her into a dance and making her horse's ears pin back, and despite all of those intimate encounters she'd shared with death in all of its different forms, she still found herself fighting off another shiver.

"I've heard the stories too, Cas," said Nessa supportively. Her eyes grew even wider than usual as she lifted her gaze to the trees bending over their route, to the silver branches flipping back and forth in the wind in a methodical rhythm. Those orderly movements almost made it seem as if the limbs were being twisted by invisible hands. "The legend I'm most familiar with said that the souls wandering this road are elvish ones...and that they're looking for new bodies to steal." Her voice lowered toward the end, as though she was concerned about offending those souls, and her gaze shifted toward Laurent.

He ignored her at first, his lips drawn in their usual serious line. But he eventually gave in, and he humored them with his first-hand knowledge. "That legend came about because elves supposedly can't enter any of the heavens or hells the upper-gods created," he said. "Part of their punishment for abusing the power given to them. But they are not truly immortal either; their bodies eventually decay, just at a slower rate than humans. So, some take their own lives once the decay gets too bad. *Noblesmor*, is the name they use for the ritual in Moreth, I believe. There are different...*under-standings* regarding what happens then."

"And one of them is that they go snatch themselves a new body, right?" pressed Nessa.

If it was anybody else asking the question, Cas had a feeling Laurent would have gone back to ignoring the conversation.

But he had always seemed to have a soft spot for Nessa, and perhaps because of this, he sighed and said, "The most far-fetched of those legends is this, yes."

"I'd like to see them try and steal my body," said Zev, bringing fire to his fingertips with a flick of his wrist. Maybe it was Cas's imagination, but the shadows at the roadside *did* seem to draw back as that flame flickered.

"I wonder...do they have to deal with the previous owner's thoughts whenever they take over a new body?" said Rhea, her head tilting toward her brother. "Because if so, they'd probably give your body back after about two days."

"*If* they lasted that long," Laurent added.

Nessa fell into a fit of quiet laughter.

Cas managed another smile, even though her thoughts had started to drift again to the past and all of its complications.

Another body, another lifetime...

But before she could drift too far, Nessa's laughter abruptly stopped. Cas glanced back and saw that her horse had stopped too, and she was squinting at something off the side of the road.

"What are you doing?" Cas asked.

"There's a person lying in the trees over there." Nessa leapt from the saddle and hurried to the spot she'd been staring at, the haunting stories of this road and whatever fear they'd caused her seemingly forgotten.

Cas frowned, drawing her own horse to a stop. "Don't talk to strangers on the Badlands Road, remember?"

"He looks injured," Nessa called back in protest. "Surely that matters more than superstition."

"It could be a trick," warned Laurent.

"It is *definitely* a trick," said Zev.

But Nessa was stubborn. She knelt beside the body, and in the gloom, Cas could see the Feather-shaped mark on her hand start to glow.

She was almost certain this was a terrible idea, but Cas still dismounted and walked over and knelt beside her. She fought the urge to gag as her gaze fell over this man that Nessa had insisted on helping.

His skin was a mottled purple and pale white, and it was shining with sweat. Foam had gathered in the corners of his mouth. There were signs of a crash all around him—broken tree limbs, the scattered contents of a saddle bag—as if he'd fallen off mid-gallop and his horse had left him for dead.

Cas could sense his life-force. It felt like he was hanging on to it by mere threads. She looked over her shoulder toward Elander, seeking confirmation, but his attention was elsewhere, eyes narrowed and searching the road for threats.

"I don't think there's anything we can do for this man," Cas said, placing her hand gently on Nessa's back. "We should keep moving."

Nessa's face fell. "At least...at least let me make him comfortable as he passes."

Cas heard several of their group moving, protests building in whispers between them. With a sigh, she turned and held up a hand, telling them to wait. This would only take a minute.

And now that she was here, there was something else she wanted to do.

She was suddenly thinking of a moment, weeks ago, when Elander had used his magic to bring the souls of her adoptive parents back into this realm, if only briefly. He had once been known as the *Death Speaker*, and part of his duty in Varen's command had been to pull secrets from the newly-deceased—or the soon-to-be deceased.

Could she do the same thing?

She was curious—both about the extent of her own powers and about what had happened to this man.

But then she remembered the promise she'd sworn to herself and Elander last night; she couldn't risk using those powers if it would hasten her ascension.

She had started to reach for the dying man, but her fingers curled back into a tight fist.

A low growl caught her attention; Silverfoot was on the ground, slinking back in the direction they'd just traveled from. His ears were flicking back and forth, as if trying to pinpoint where a sound was coming from.

Elander and Laurent were off their horses and heading toward her and Nessa a moment later, drawing their weapons as soon as they hit the ground.

"We need to move on," Laurent said, his gaze sweeping through the trees as he took Nessa's arm and pulled her, gently but firmly, away from the dead man.

Nessa started to jerk away from him—

Just as an arrow struck the ground at her feet.

CHAPTER 15

A SECOND ARROW HIT CAS'S HORSE AN INSTANT LATER.

The creature bolted, taking her weapons with it. Cas instinctively took a few steps after it, and the distraction proved a mistake, as a man—one dressed from head to toe in the same shade of silver as the trees—cut off her path, swinging a sword as he came.

She dropped low and sprang aside, dragging her foot and catching his ankle. He stumbled. She stayed crouched against the ground, eyes scanning for more threats and potential weapons.

A second attacker was already approaching from her left.

Elander appeared seemingly out of the air, knocking this second man's blade aside with his own. Before the man could recover, Elander grabbed him and threw him against the nearest tree. The man's arm slammed around the trunk with a loud *crack*, and the sword in his hand dropped. Elander grabbed it and tossed it to the ground beside Cas.

She snatched it and rose to meet the first man. He jabbed forward. She sidestepped, slipped around behind him, aimed a slicing blow at his back. He spun around to meet her, and the force of their blades colliding made her arms shake. She bounced away, readjusting her grip and her stance.

Thankfully, the blade she'd picked up was light, well-balanced, easy to move with. Her attacker was fast. She parried every hit, dodged every swing, but the swings kept coming. She heard Laurent and Elander engaged in battles of their own a short distance away, but she couldn't afford to look and see how they were faring; her own battle was demanding too much attention. She and her opponent were too evenly matched.

She needed a way to tip the scale in her favor. Sparks ignited around her hand at the thought. Her Storm magic could finish this more quickly than her sword, and such a feat would have been *easy* just days ago.

But now she felt that increasingly familiar sensation of Death magic rising in the same breath as her Storm power, trying to wrap around the sparks and suffocate them out of existence.

She could have let that Dark power keep rising.

She could sense the threads of her enemy's life weaving around him, and she didn't know exactly *how* to do it, but she knew Death magic could have severed those strands. Or weakened them enough for her sword to finish the job, at least.

And yet... she'd sworn she would choose the Sun Goddess's power over that of the Dark God.

So that was what she did.

Even though she was certain the Death magic would have been easier to summon, she focused on drawing forth the light.

And she managed it.

Somewhat.

Not enough to kill, but enough to distract her target, confuse him—and when his gaze lingered an instant too long on one of the bolts she had commanded to her side, she rushed forward and sliced her sword cleanly through his wrist.

Not *into* it.

Through it.

The strength that had surged through her swing had been inhuman, and the dark magic inside of her seemed to relish in that lack of humanity. As she wiped the spatters of her assailant's blood from her arm, that darkness swelled in strength once more, swallowing up the lingering sparks of her Storm magic. She tried in vain to make those sparks come back.

While her inner battle raged, her opponent stumbled away from her, his eyes widening in disbelief as he glanced from his bloody stump of a hand to the sword in

Cas's grip. He had clearly not been expecting her to prove a formidable opponent. The thought only further provoked that darkness inside of her, and it made her want to chop off his other hand.

She stifled this morbid thought. "Who are you? Why did you attack us?"

His eyes darted to the group on the road. Then back to her. His still-intact hand lifted. He snapped his fingers, summoning a gust of wind that made the tree branches around him clack together—

And then he was gone.

From her *sight*, at least; she still sensed his energy. It was growing fainter. He was invisible, and he was running away.

"Coward," Cas muttered.

Elander and Laurent had succeeded in chasing their opponents away as well. They were racing back to the road where Nessa was busy using her magic to try and calm their spooked horses.

Cas hurried back to them. One of the Sadiran soldiers had chased her horse down, and she was striding toward it when the distant sound of clopping hooves suddenly filled the air. She slowed to a stop.

What now?

"...Protect the supplies," she ordered, her eyes narrowing toward the sound.

There was no sign of what was actually *making* that sound. But her allies hurried to form a circle of protection around the packhorses, and Zev dismounted and paced around that circle, fire weaving through his fingers, preparing to make a wall if necessary.

They waited.

The clopping grew louder. The wind from earlier had vanished, but there was still the sound of rustling and rattling branches...even though those branches were not actually moving.

Was this the *whispering* Soryn had mentioned?

Finally, a large host of riders emerged from the trees.

Just like the men that had attacked Cas and Nessa, these riders were swathed entirely in grey. Every inch of skin was covered, save for the space around their eyes and noses. The horses they rode were also gray—all of them a nearly identical dappled pattern—making them easy to lose against the backdrop of silver tree trunks.

They stopped a short distance away. Their ranks stretched across the entire road, five deep, and Cas noted that each of the riders was heavily armed with swords hanging from their saddles and bows strapped across their backs.

She kept her own sword lowered at her side as she cautiously stepped forward to meet them, flanked by Elander on one side and Laurent on the other. She had just started to declare that they wanted no trouble when the group parted abruptly.

A solitary woman rode forward.

She was dressed just as the others, but the beastly

stallion she rode was black, and its saddle and headgear were adorned with sapphires. She stopped mere feet away from Cas and studied her for a moment while her mount snorted and stamped his massive hooves.

She unraveled the scarf around her head, revealing a sharp face, waves of black hair, and ears that tapered at the ends.

An elf.

Her eyes were contemplative and cold as they swept to the traveling party behind Cas. "So many riders upon our road tonight," she commented in a voice of ice and silk. "Bound for where, I wonder?"

Lying seemed pointless and likely to lead to more trouble, so Cas simply lowered her head in a slight bow and said, "For your fair realm, actually. If you would have us."

"Oh? Coming to collect your fellow vagabond, were you?" She nodded toward that man Nessa had been trying to help.

Cas shook her head. "That man was—"

"A spy and a thief," interrupted the elf woman, sounding almost bored. "He disguised himself with magic and somehow snuck into our *fair realm*. A cowardly act, and so he is now dying a coward's death." She lifted her hand, signaled, and the riders at the front of her group dismounted and drew their swords.

Cas's group started to answer by drawing weapons of their own, but she ordered them to be still.

"If you were trying to help that coward," continued the elven woman, "then you must *also* be thieves or spies who mistakenly believe we have things worth stealing in our sacred cities."

"Let's talk about that logic, can we—" Zev's protest was cut short by a blade to his throat, courtesy of one of the elves who moved too quickly for anyone to react.

"We didn't come to steal or spy," Cas said. "We came to speak with King Theren about a political matter."

The elven woman snorted. "I doubt he'll be interested in your politics."

An uneasy hush swept over Cas's party, until Laurent broke it with a simple question. "Why not?"

"Because he's dead."

Cas stared into the cold eyes of the elven woman, unsure of how to reply.

This had not been part of any of the countless plans she and Soryn had made.

"Take your hands off your weapons," Laurent said quietly.

It took Cas a moment to realize he was talking to her and the rest of their group.

"Just trust me," he pressed.

She chanced a quick glance behind her. The others were looking to her, waiting to see if she would do as he said. She looked back to Laurent, her heart pounding. She *did* trust his judgment, more than perhaps any of her other friends, but this...

The elves moved, forming a tighter circle around her allies.

Cas dropped her sword and lifted her palms in surrender.

Slowly, the others followed her example. The elven woman watched them surrender without comment, a curious gleam in her pale eyes and her hand still tightly gripping her own sword.

Laurent took a deep breath and said, "The King of Moreth had a son, did he not?"

The woman's face was perfectly expressionless as she gave a single nod.

"If he still lives," said Laurent, "then we request an audience with him instead of the deceased king."

Her reply was curt. "He lives."

The elven riders began to shuffle a bit uneasily, but their leader did not take her gaze off Laurent. She studied him almost as if trying to place his face. But if she *did* recognize him, she gave no outward sign of it beyond a confused frown.

Cas's fingers itched, preparing to reach again for her sword, certain she was going to need it.

"If they want to speak with the new king," said the elven woman, "then we shall grant their request. But they will not do it freely." Her eyes narrowed one last time on Laurent before she turned her attention to her followers. "Bind and disarm them," she ordered.

CHAPTER 16

"*Take your hands off your weapons*," said Zev in a mocking voice.

But Laurent could not respond to this mockery of his words—because Laurent was not locked in the same room.

Their group had been separated as soon as they came to this palace, which sat on a stretch of land between the two elven cities of Torath and Galizar. *Briarfell* was the official name of the massive building and all of its accompanying grounds—and it was the residence of the King and Queen of Moreth and their expansive court.

Cas had been tossed into this cramped room along with Rhea, Zev, and three of the soldiers traveling with them.

She didn't know where Nessa, Elander, or the other

soldiers had been taken. Laurent had been taken somewhere by himself, she believed. Her blindfold had started to slip by the time they reached Briarfell, and she had gotten one last glimpse of him before they were all pulled away from one another. She'd seen him being roughly marched away by two heavily armed guards. But as to *where*...

She had no idea.

"We should have fought," Zev muttered. "Should have at *least* let them know we don't intend to roll over and do as they say."

"We were outnumbered five to one," said Jeras, one of the Sadiran soldiers, wearily. He was studying the Sky mark on his hand, trying in vain to make it glow brightly. It would flash for a moment, but then it would fade away, taking whatever strands of Sky magic he had managed to summon with it.

"Well, we technically made it into Moreth, didn't we?" Rhea said. "And we were not coming here to fight, if you'll remember—we came to negotiate. We're just taking the scenic route to those negotiations."

"This scenery was absolutely not worth seeing," said Zev.

Cas had to admit he had a point.

They were surrounded by grey walls that hugged so close they barely left enough room for all of them to stretch their legs out. There were no windows. No light, save for that of a few candles in ornamental sconces. No rugs to warm the stone floors. The only thing that might pass for decor were the statues that lined recesses in the walls high above them.

Each of those statues was carved from white stone with a skilled hand and an eye for detail; even with all of the space between them, and even in the dim light, the solemn expressions on their faces were easy to make out, as were the tapered points of their ears. There was a small platform against the back wall too, the wood worn in a pattern that suggested it had been knelt upon many times. It seemed like a room designed for prayer to those solemn statues—to whatever elves they represented. And it felt like those beings were watching her.

It made her uneasy.

"They really need to consider adding some color to their lives," said Zev, following Cas's gaze as it took in the drab room. "Maybe it would make them less grumpy."

"You should submit a formal complaint," she said, her eyes still on one of the marble statues directly above her. "I'm sure they're interested in your opinion."

Zev muttered something indistinct before he leaned against the nearest wall, folded his arms across his chest, and closed his eyes.

Cas studied the statues for a moment more, and then her gaze fell back to her companions. To Rhea, who was now huddled in the corner, quiet, with her head bowed. Silverfoot was curled up in her lap, shivering.

The magic that linked them—that allowed the fox to lend Rhea his vision—was likely suppressed, along with all of the other divine magic, Cas realized.

She crawled over to Rhea's side and nudged her gently. "Are you all right?"

Rhea nodded, lifting her head. "I can still see well enough. The images are just coming a bit more faintly and more slowly than usual. And Silver doesn't like it here...it's like the air is suffocating him."

Zev and Jeras both agreed, as did the other Sky-kind soldiers. They *all* felt suffocated. Cas included. How completely subdued her magic was, she wasn't sure— and she was nervous about experimenting with it, given the small space.

She studied the mark the Storm Goddess had bestowed on her. She was a moment away from risking a small spark when the door suddenly opened and bright light rushed in, blinding her. When her sight adjusted, she saw the woman who had taken them captive standing in the doorway.

Her eyes fixed immediately on Cas. "You. Come with me."

Zev moved as if to stop her from complying, but Cas shot him a look.

It would do no good to try and fight. They were outnumbered, and though Cas didn't know where this woman intended to take her, she would have a better chance of figuring out their next move if she wasn't locked in this room.

She got to her feet without protest, mouthed *I'll be back soon* to her companions, and then followed the elf woman into the bright hallway.

Outside of her cell, and without a blindfold this time, she was finally able to get a feel for this dwelling where so few humans had walked.

The walls and floors were made of grey wood, and they seemed to curve around them; it made her feel as if she was walking through a petrified, hollowed-out tree trunk. At the end of the hall, they came to a large, rectangular room. She had heard stories of the sort of revelries that went on in this realm, and this room...it looked—and somehow *felt*—like the kind of space that would encourage the wildest of those parties.

The ceiling soared high above her, inset with panels of gold and skylights with patterned glass, which made for interesting shadows and shows of light across the polished floor. Plush couches and armchairs lined the edges of the space, some of which were occupied by elves who watched Cas with curiosity as she passed. The air was heavily perfumed, a mixture of heady spices and soft vanilla. Several long counters were affixed along the walls, each lined with golden goblets, decanters, and countless bottles of wine and other spirits. There was a long, gilded table in the center of the room, piled high with colorful fruits and breads, but no one appeared to be eating anything from it.

Sweeping balconies extended the space on both sides, flanked by ivory curtains that shimmered in a slight breeze. More couches awaited outside, and almost all of these were occupied by lounging couples. Cas's gaze was drawn to one of these laughing couples—just in time to see one half of that couple kneel beside the couch and bury his face between his companion's legs.

She quickly averted her eyes. Her escort kept her own gaze straight ahead, ignoring the peals of laughter and the moans of pleasure that suddenly seemed to be rising all around them. They walked on to the other side of the room, and then down another long hallway. At the end of this hall, she finally spoke again. "What is your name?"

"Casia Grey—"

"Your *real* name, you stupid girl."

She had a feeling this woman already knew the answer. She reached for the bracelet Soryn had given her, clenched one of the beads tightly between her thumb and forefinger, and said, "I am the first-born child of Cerin and Anric de Solasen. I was named Valori de Solasen at my birth, but I left that name behind a long time ago, and I chose my own: Casia Greythorne. And I am not a *stupid girl*, I am the true heir of the throne in the human kingdom of Melech, and to all of the power it holds."

"Yes. Your friend told us essentially the same story." She sounded thoroughly unimpressed. "You'll have to forgive us for not preparing our halls for you, *Your Majesty*."

"Where is my friend?" Cas demanded. "Laurent? Where did they drag him off to? And the rest of my group—"

"Patience." The word sounded like a threat.

Be patient, or else.

Cas took a deep breath through her nose and kept walking.

The elf woman—who still had not offered her own name—brought her to a narrow, spiraling staircase, which led up to what appeared to be an observatory of some kind. There were various telescoping instruments sticking out of the windows of this room, scraps of parchment with all manner of diagrams spread across various desks, and countless charts stretched across the walls, mapping out the sky and its stars.

A man stood before one of those charts, a golden goblet clutched in his hand. He tilted his face toward them as they approached.

Elegant was the only word Cas could think of at first. From his slender ears to his lithe figure, to the tailored shirt and pants he wore, to the layers of fine jewelry around his neck and wrists...all of it gave off an air of sophistication that made Cas suddenly self-conscious about her own travel-worn appearance. His light brown

241

hair was perfectly straight, secured neatly at the nape of his neck with a golden clasp. His eyes looked both red and brown in the lamp light, a strange color that made Cas think of the coppery peaks of the Bloodstone Mountains.

"My husband," said her escort. "Alder of Briarfell, the King of Moreth."

"That last part isn't official quite yet," said Alder, tipping his goblet into his mouth and letting out a loud, satisfied *ahh* after swallowing its contents.

"The rituals will make it so in seven days."

"My Lady Sarith." He spoke his wife's name and title like a firm caress, an attempt to be both commanding and amicable, it seemed. "Let's allow my father to go cold in the ground before we start talking of these things, shall we? I don't need to be reminded of those upcoming rituals."

Cas puzzled over this in silence. King Theren's death had been recent it seemed, so it made sense that word had not reached Soryn yet. Perhaps that also explained why she and her friends had been handled so roughly? So suspiciously? The passing of their king had apparently put Lady Sarith and her soldiers on edge.

She *hoped* that was the only reason for it, anyway.

She spoke her next words carefully. "My condolences for your loss. I had hoped to speak with King Theren, and it pains me to think I won't get the opportunity."

Prince Alder turned to face her more fully, his curiosity clearly piqued.

"Did he go suddenly?" she asked. "Peacefully, I hope?"

"Quiet, human," hissed Sarith. "Such matters don't concern you."

The prince shook his head. Whether at Cas's ignorance, or at his wife's harsh tone, Cas wasn't certain. He said something to his wife in the ancient language of their kind—not the heavily accented common tongue they'd both been using—and whatever it was, it made Sarith give a disgruntled nod.

"Not peacefully, unfortunately," he said, his gaze returning to Cas. "But thank you for your sympathy." He placed his goblet on the table before him, reached for a bottle of clear liquid, and uncorked that bottle. But he hesitated to pour, looking suddenly introspective. "Although, I didn't have you brought here to pay your respects and give your sympathies, of course."

Cas's gaze trailed over the room while she waited for him to continue, marveling at those star charts on the walls, at the elvish words that she didn't recognize, and some that she couldn't even pronounce. She'd heard a legend, once, that Belegor—the Stone God, who had shaped the world—had given the elves the honor of bestowing the stars with their true names. It had seemed like a fanciful story, nothing more. But now she wondered...

She could feel the prince studying her. When he didn't speak after a minute had passed, she pressed the conversation along herself. "May I ask why you did bring me here, then?"

"Because my brother insisted I speak with you."

She pulled her gaze back to him. "Brother?"

He responded to her confused tone with an amused look. "Your friend, isn't he? Laurent? We had a very long talk, he and I. He's told me all about you and your journey."

Cas kept her face impassive, though she was inwardly reeling. Laurent had never mentioned he had family in such an important position—and it seemed like a rather important detail to leave out. She felt foolish admitting it, but Alder was still looking at her curiously, so she said, "I didn't realize he had a brother."

"Half-brother," Sarith corrected. "And the proof he presented of even *that* was questionable."

It would have been smarter to keep her mouth shut, but Cas was liking this elven woman less and less. So she locked her gaze with Alder's and said, "I think I can see the family resemblance."

"It's obvious, isn't it?" The prince chuckled, and he angled his face toward the nearest window and studied his own reflection in the glass for several seconds past the point of vanity.

Cas could feel Sarith's eyes burning into her, but she kept her gaze on Alder. "And where is Laurent now?"

"Out of the way, as we agreed upon."

"Out of the..."

"Just in one of the rooms up above," he clarified with a wave toward that upper level. "Because as much as I would love to spend the evening chatting away with both of you, there are other things that I must see to this night. I wanted to apologize to you in person before I saw to those other things, however, and to tell you we only separated and confined you all out of utmost precaution. I hope you understand. We have no quarrel with you or your allies. So now that this is cleared up, you can be on your way, and I'll head off on mine."

"I can't go yet; I came here for a purpose—"

He cut her off with a sigh. "Yes, yes, I know what you seek. I've heard all about it, as I said."

"And?"

"And I'm afraid I can't help you. My hands are full at the moment."

Cas frowned, though this wasn't an unexpected response. "The rulers of Ethswen are giving you trouble, correct?"

He nodded. His eyes narrowed on that bottle he'd uncorked, but after a moment of consideration, he replaced the stopper without pouring himself another drink. He reached for a coat draped over a nearby chair as he said, "I actually have a meeting with some members of that fallen kingdom's court—or what remains of it, anyway. And I do believe I'm late for said meeting."

"You are," confirmed Sarith drily.

"See? There you have it. I really must be going."

"Maybe I could help you negotiate with them?" Cas suggested.

He laughed as he kept preparing to leave. Not a cruel laugh; it seemed more out of surprise than anything.

"*Negotiate* is not quite the word for where we are at, unfortunately," he said. "It is more like a sparring match. A trading of barbs in which my only real hope is to come out alive, and—if I'm lucky—relatively unscathed."

"We suspect they are the ones responsible for King Theren's death," said Sarith, her tone a flat, harsh contrast to her husband's blasé one. It sounded like she was attempting to frighten Cas into minding her own business.

She clearly had no idea what sort of frightening *business* Cas and her allies were already dealing with.

"Murder? What proof do you have of that?" Cas asked.

The elven lady sneered at the challenge, and it was her husband who ultimately answered Cas, as he shrugged into his coat. "We were not able to apprehend the culprit in that particular case—not yet, anyway. But we have had a few incidents with Ethswenian soldiers in the recent past." He smoothed the sleeves of his coat with a far-off look in his eyes. "And to think, our walls used to be impenetrable."

"Our walls could be impenetrable once more," said Sarith, almost to herself. "We could rebuild them, if only we were a bit more aggressive about these matters."

"Another topic for another day," said the prince offhandedly, his focus now on buttoning his coat. Once he'd finished, he started for the stairs without another word.

Cas felt her opportunity dangerously close to slipping away, so she blurted out, "Can I at least join you in this meeting?"

Lady Sarith bristled as her husband paused at the top of the stairs and gave Cas a look that seemed to say, *why in the world haven't you given up yet?*

"I won't even speak," Cas insisted. "I won't try to negotiate. I only want to listen. To shadow a seasoned noble in his work."

She didn't actually get the impression that he was a *seasoned* noble at all, but flattery had gotten her what she needed plenty of times in the past.

His face slowly broke into a bemused smile, as if he thought her a child who had come up with a very amusing game—one that he didn't quite understand. It was insulting, but Cas held her tongue. This was a chance to gain valuable insight, and to perhaps weave herself into the future king's good graces...

At any rate, she was not going to let him send her away from this realm so easily.

"I've often admired the legendary Court of Moreth from afar," she said. "And it would be an honor to bear witness to such nobility in action."

"Why not," he declared, after studying her a moment longer. "Maybe it will confuse them and give me an edge in this sparring match, hm?"

"She's covered in road dust and blood," Sarith protested.

"Then lend her one of your dresses, if you *really* think it's necessary."

"I—"

"But she looks no worse than the ones I'll be meeting with, I'm sure," he added with another yawn. "Knowing the court of Ethswen, half of them probably have blood staining their clothes too."

And then he was off, humming to himself as he wound his way down the staircase.

CHAPTER 17

CAS SCURRIED AFTER HIM WITHOUT LOOKING BACK.

She caught up in the hallway below and followed him as he walked in the opposite direction of the prison she'd been pulled from. They eventually came to another room with balconies on either side—though much smaller and more sparsely populated than the last one she'd walked through—and Alder wandered over to the larger of these balconies and indicated for her to gaze over the railing with him.

Down below, a small crowd of people had gathered around a stone table in the center of a garden. The crowd was nearly lost among the countless flowering plants that edged the space.

"A picturesque setting for a potentially bloody bit of politics," said the prince, wistfully, as he reached and plucked a silver-green leaf from a vine that had wound its way up and around the railing of the balcony. "The beauty almost makes the whole ordeal tolerable."

Cas's gaze swept over that setting, over white and pink trumpet-shaped flowers, over leaves as big as her body, and over something that gave off a musky scent that was overpowering. Her eyes eventually caught on one of the people down below—a young woman with the palest blonde hair she had ever seen. She was wrapped in grey and brown furs despite the relatively warm air. Her body was relaxed, slumped in her spindly wooden chair, but her face was alert and scanning the space with relentless focus.

"That woman at the head of the table...who is she?"

"The Princess of Ethswen, Sybell Amarok," he told her. "She has been the main emissary for her mothers since she came of age a few years ago. She's lovely, isn't she?"

Cas nodded. She *was* lovely...in a frightening sort of way. Like a distant, dark sea was lovely—beautiful but foreboding and, she suspected, full of potentially deadly things.

"The first time I met her, she offered me a glass of her kingdom's famous black currant mead. I thought she was flirting with me. But alas, the drink turned out to be poisoned." He sighed with his whole body, looking as though he was still genuinely crushed over the failed connection.

Cas frowned, and she jerked her head toward the crowd below, some of whom clearly looked like they were growing impatient. "Didn't you say you were late for the meeting?"

"Ah. So I am," he said, and she wondered if he might have forgotten about the entire thing if she hadn't mentioned it. "Come along. Casia, isn't it?" He didn't wait for her to reply either way; he was already off again.

Lady Sarith waited for them at the top of the stone steps that led down into the garden. Her gaze jumped over Cas as though she was empty space, which seemed an improvement over the death glares she'd been giving earlier, so Cas kept her gaze directly in front of her and did nothing to attract extra attention.

Most eyes focused on Prince Alder as he entered, but a few curious gazes took note of the grey-haired woman who had joined him. One man in particular let his bloodshot eyes linger in Cas's direction for longer than seemed necessary. He looked as if he was trying to place her.

She avoided looking at him, setting her gaze on the Princess instead.

"The King of Moreth finally makes his appearance," said Princess Sybell in an airy, unaffected voice. Her eyes darted between the two men to her left and right, and they sat up straighter at her unspoken command.

"Sybell. An honor as always." He took her hand and

kissed it, his mouth lingering against her skin until she pulled it away with a barely noticeable curl of her lips.

She reached into the bag beside her chair and drew out a handful of rolled and bound pieces of parchment. "I've brought our terms," she said, tossing them onto the table between them.

The elf Prince did not pick any of these terms up. His hands steepled together as he leaned back in his chair. "I could have sworn we had already agreed to terms—what was it, almost three months ago to the day, I believe?"

"We did agree to them. With your father."

"And your terms are different for me, are they?"

"Afraid so."

"I see."

"King Theren was more of a known entity. We knew he would hold up his end of our various deals. You are more of an...enigma. So we must protect our interests more securely."

Alder's eyes fell on the still-tied scrolls on the table before him. "And that protection involves more payment upfront, I assume."

"Defending both our own realm *and* yours requires an extraordinary number of resources," said the Princess, gritting her teeth into a smile.

"It does," said Alder with a noncommittal shrug.

"For nearly a century, our armies have kept this

realm safe from its surrounding enemies. And if you would like us to keep protecting you, we demand something more in return."

"Of course you do."

She continued with her demands as though he hadn't spoken. "Yield more of your claims to your so-called *sacred* lands and resources along the north shore, or we will stop digging into our own resources to save you. It's that simple."

"Simple?" He laughed.

The Princess did not share in that laughter. Silence stretched over the space for a long, uncomfortable moment, until she narrowed her gaze on him, and quietly said, "The armies of Sadira are growing again, you know. They mounted an attack against Varen and his followers just last week. They drove him back to Melech, expanded their holds in the west, and they will look toward the north next. The young, would-be Queen of that once-kingdom is as ruthless as her parents were. She will crush you without our help."

"That isn't true." Cas did not realize how loudly she'd said the words until nearly every set of eyes in the garden turned her direction.

She thought for a moment that Lady Sarith might leap out of her chair and choke her into silence.

But the elven woman only gripped the table before her, her long, gold-painted nails digging into the soft wood. And no one else moved or spoke, so Cas continued. "I know the young Queen of Sadira, and she has no desire to crush either of the elven realms. The opposite is true, really—she would prefer an alliance with them for the greater good of the empire."

Silence settled once more over the group, thicker and more tense than before.

"There is no *greater good* for the empire," the man to Sybell's left finally snarled, "because there is no true *empire*. And it is better that way. We strike deals when the need arises." He glanced at the rolled parchments on the table, looking for a moment like he was considering spitting on them, before concluding, "And otherwise, we mind our own business. Which is how it should be."

"Until you have a problem that requires cooperation from all of the different realms," Cas argued.

Such as an upper-god bent on the destruction of those realms.

Her stomach flipped at the thought, and panic nearly sent words spilling out of her—desperate pleas for them to consider cooperating with her and aligning with her cause. But she kept them to herself. This did not seem like the time to bring that particular problem up.

She wasn't even supposed to be *speaking*.

Sybell rose slowly to her feet. Her hand settled casually against the hilt of the knife at her hip as she strode closer, and Cas was suddenly very aware of her own lack of knives.

She had no weapons, no guarantee her magic would function in the strange airs of this place, and she was surrounded by people who *were* armed—and each of those people looked angrier than the one beside them.

But she had been surrounded by plenty of angry, unsavory groups in the past when questionable jobs had taken her into questionable locations. And the surest way to make oneself a target, she knew, was to look afraid.

So she kept her head up, and she met Sybell's quietly furious gaze with an equally angry gaze of her own.

"Who are you?" the Princess demanded.

Cas hesitated, trying to think of the smartest, safest way to answer. But she didn't have to, because someone else answered for her—that man who had been staring at her with his bloodshot eyes since she'd walked in.

"I know who she is," he said. "The Fade-marked appearance, the divine marks and curses upon her skin... This is the one that has been waging a war with Varen. Rumor is she's joined with the rebel Queen of Sadira to try and destabilize the southern parts of our lands, so that Sadira might rise up and take control of those lands for herself."

More lies.

Cas's skin burned with indignation, but it would be foolish to call them out on those lies. She could read a room well enough to see that they were all braced for a fight, and she sincerely doubted she would find any supporters amongst them. Not tonight, anyway.

"What is this, precisely?" asked Sybell, her eyes drifting back to the elf Prince. "Are you trying to go behind our backs? You'll ignore our pleas for cooperation while you align yourself with the wretched Orphan Queen, and for what? So that you can secretly wield the Sadiran army against us when you claim you want neutrality and peace?"

"I have no alliance with Sadira," said Alder. He sounded almost amused by the turn the conversation had taken. Cas was beginning to think he simply enjoyed chaos.

Was that the only reason he had agreed to let her tag along with him?

"If she is a spy for that Queen," snapped Sybell, "then she should be relieved of her head, just as the former King and Queen of that kingdom were."

Mumbles of agreement and even harsher suggestions followed.

Sybell walked back to her chair and shoved it under the table. "I will say no more in front of her, either way."

"A shame," the prince drawled, "as I was so enjoying all of the things you had to say." He rose to his feet and pushed in his own chair, his movements far calmer than Sybell's had been. He walked to Cas's side. "But I'm afraid this spy is my guest, and I will not treat her so rudely as that. Beheading her? Honestly. And *my* kind are supposedly the barbaric ones. You should be ashamed for even suggesting such a thing."

This brought most of his rival court to their feet. They spoke swiftly and angrily in the language of their kingdom, until Princess Sybell silenced them by lifting her hand and clenching it into a fist.

The man to her left moved in to whisper something in her ear. She nodded after a moment, looked back to the elf prince, and in the common tongue she said, "We will be back soon, Alder. And I expect you to have memorized those terms we've drawn up, and to be prepared to swear by them."

"I'll look forward to the visit." He gave a low bow, and Cas briefly wondered at the decision to expose his neck so completely while Sybell's hand still rested on her knife.

But the Princess made no move to attack as she started toward the staircase.

The man who had identified Cas followed closely behind her, his bloodshot eyes sweeping over Cas one last time before he let them trail toward the Prince of Moreth.

Then he lunged toward him.

Cas didn't think, she simply reacted—or her magic reacted *for* her, rather. Electricity surged forth and wrapped around the sword the man had withdrawn. The bolts were weak, but against the conductive metal of the sword, they grew wilder. He tried but failed to let the sword go; it stayed in his hand, stuck in his possession by the ropes of building lightning, as he writhed and fell against the ground. The scent of crisped flesh filled the air.

Panicked whispers echoed through the garden.

The Princess locked her gaze on Cas, and she did not move—did not flinch—even as the man at her feet let out a horrible, guttural cry of pain.

Finally, the magic dissipated with a crackle of power. The man's sword hit the stone path with a *clang,* and he curled against the ground, groaning.

No one moved to help him.

The Court of Ethswen joined their leader in staring at Cas. A mixture of awe and fear filled their eyes.

Sarith was on her feet, her hand clenched and slightly out in front of her, as if she'd started to grab for Cas but had stopped.

It had been a weaker display of magic—the only reason the Ethswen man was now stumbling to his feet instead of dead— but the fact that she had managed it at all seemed to have stunned Sarith and everyone else.

It had stunned her too, honestly.

Sybell's gaze slid to Alder, and then back to Cas. "Not allies," she said with a snort. "Good to know."

She hissed something at the electrified man in their language. An insult, it sounded like. He bowed his head and clutched his singed arm, and then joined the rest of their group as they filed up the staircase to where a heavily armed unit of elven escorts awaited them.

Once they were gone, the Prince slowly turned to Cas. "You're an interesting creature, aren't you?"

She should have been offended by his use of the word *creature*, maybe. And the way he was looking at her too, as though he saw her as more specimen than human. She sensed no real malice in that look, and yet she still didn't sense any trust or warmth, either.

She needed more time to figure him out. More time to try and sway him to her cause. "I have no shortage of interesting things I could tell you, if we were allies—and I know you're curious to hear them."

He didn't deny this. And his curiosity apparently won out, because after a moment of deliberation, he said, "I don't know about allies, but perhaps you *could* stay for a few days, and we could discuss some of those interesting things."

In the corner of her vision, Cas saw Sarith slowly move from her place beside the table. And for the second time since entering the garden, she thought she might have to fend off an attack from the elven lady.

But Prince Alder spoke before his wife could act on whatever violent thoughts she might have been having. "Sarith, my love, why don't we make our captives more comfortable?" He glanced toward her for only a fraction of a second before refocusing on Cas. "It's been some time since we've entertained guests. Perhaps it would be good to visit with these outsiders and enjoy their fresh perspectives on some matters."

Sarith looked as though she would rather light herself on fire. But as soon as his expectant gaze turned on her, she smiled. "Of course. I will see it done."

CHAPTER 18

After the orders were all given, the proper servants summoned, and the guest wing preparations truly underway, Alder led Cas back to his observatory.

He stared at the winding stairs they'd climbed to reach that space, as if he feared someone might be following them. When no one else showed, he poured himself a fresh drink and studied it for a long moment, shaking his head, before he started to sip it. "So now you've seen the problems I'm dealing with," he said. "Or a glimpse of them, at least. Sybell was quite tame today. You seemed to be a mitigating force, so thank you for that."

"She seemed adamant about securing your lands." Cas frowned, thinking of the knife the Princess had so tightly gripped. "I didn't realize the northern shore was so valuable."

"They claim they want our lands, the resources we supposedly hoard, but..."

"But it's more than just resources they're after?" she guessed.

"The prejudice against our kind runs deep." He shrugged. "They would see us destroyed whether or not we had tangible things to concede in our defeat. Both us and the elves of Mistwilde. We are the last of our kind in Kethra, you know. And if Ethswen's rulers succeed in tearing us down, then they will be able to claim that they purged this fallen empire of us." He *hmphd* into his glass before taking another long sip of its contents. "Quite the achievement *that* would be, eh?"

"Can they actually succeed? Against both yourself and that other realm? The stories of the elves and their prowess in battle must have some truth to them."

He considered the question, his eyes glazing over. He looked tired suddenly. "Our collective army remains impressive. More impressive than the Queens of fallen Ethswen and their allies know, although it's true enough that—much like their own army—ours isn't what it once was. Which is why I am trying to avoid a full-scale battle between us. We could likely win such a battle, yes, but it would be devastating for everyone involved."

"We could help each other," Cas tried. "What I said about Queen Soryn is true. She is no warmonger."

"No, I didn't suspect she was."

"And there are more important battles that need to be fought. If you and your army would stand with us, present an example, a united front to—"

He held up a hand. "No more talk of armies and battles tonight. Please."

Frustration twisted Cas's stomach into knots.

But pressing the matter didn't seem like it would lead anywhere. Not yet. She needed to find another angle. *Come at the target sideways*, as Asra used to say. It kept those targets from throwing up their hands and pushing you away.

She left the prince to his thoughts, until she came up with what she believed would be a less provocative question. "What makes those lands along the northern shore sacred to your kind?"

He settled down in a chair by one of the windows. "Much of what was truly known about that place has been lost to time and memory." He squinted into the moonlight streaming through the glass for a moment before continuing. "But they say there is a spot along those shores where Solatis—the Lightbringer—often used to dwell. A place that, to this very day, still teems with her magic. *Dawnskeep*, is the common tongue name for it."

"A place that teems with her magic...like the mortal godhavens of the Marr?"

"Yes, something like that. Though, unlike those havens, I don't believe any mortal has ever stepped foot there. The magic is too overpowering for most to even approach it. Supposedly, the most ancient of my kind were once able to visit it, back before our relationship with all of the Moraki truly soured. They even built a monument to Solatis there—one of her favorite places to rest in this world, allegedly. But I've never seen that monument, personally, and I don't know anyone that has."

"If mortals cannot step foot there, then why are the rulers of Ethswen so interested in it?"

"Dawnskeep and its monuments take up only a small section—the lands around it are rich beyond natural explanation. The waters are overflowing with fish, the crops that grow there are impossibly fertile... Some of the things that grow there possess different kinds of magic, even. Our entire livelihood is harvested from this relatively small area, and *these* are the resources that we've been accused of hoarding. Our belief is that the richness comes from the concentration of Solatis's power that still flows from the center of Dawnskeep. But who knows, really."

"A concentration of power?" The words sent a shiver of possibility rushing through her. Could such a place hold the key she needed to rid herself of the Dark God's curse? Elander had told her that Solatis was the only being who had ever managed to keep Malaphar under control. If she could somehow make her way into that place, or even get *close* to it...

Maybe there was something there that could help the Sun magic inside of her push down the darkness, once and for all?

"But never mind such stories," the Prince said.

"No, I'm very interested in hearing more."

"I'm sure. But I've probably said too much already." He splayed his hand out in the air in front of him, wiggling his fingers so that the many rings upon them flashed in the moonlight. It looked as though he was trying to see his reflection in the largest of the ring's polished stones. "Laurent assured me that you were a force for good...but as my wife rightly pointed out, I have no real reason to trust *him* other than my own gut feeling. You could all be here to assassinate me, for all I know."

"We're not."

"Well, you wouldn't be a great assassin if you told me otherwise, now would you?"

"I have enough wars on my hands; I've no desire to start one with your kind."

He pried his eyes from his own reflection and studied her instead. She thought he was going to challenge her, but he simply shook his head. "What a strange turn of events the day has taken. What a strange turn this *empire* has taken, with all its messy wars and divided hearts."

Cas wasn't sure how to respond. She moved to the window on the opposite side of the room. The glass in this one was a patchwork of colors and patterns—a tangle of light and dark that filled her with a sudden and fierce sadness that she didn't quite understand. As much to herself as the Prince, she said, "Yes, our empire is very fractured."

"I've come to the conclusion that you humans prefer it that way."

Cas understood *why* he had concluded that. She still couldn't help but say, "Not all of us."

"But then again, you aren't precisely human, are you?"

She glanced over and found him staring at the Rook God's mark. She swallowed to clear the dryness in her throat. "I'm...interesting, as you said."

He smiled. "Yes."

He reminded her a bit of Varen when he studied her the way he was doing now, which set every nerve in her body alight. She felt that cold darkness stirring in her heart, that newfound suspicion she had toward everyone and everything rising toward the surface. Opening up and trusting Varen and others had cost her dearly over these past months. She might end up regretting any information she shared with the elven Prince too.

But what else could she do? She couldn't win all her wars without more allies. She would have to trust again eventually. She would just tread more carefully than she had in the past.

Expect the worst, hope for the best.

He continued to study her, and she told herself that this was a good thing. It was better than being outright dismissed by him.

She kept quiet. She would let him speak again before she did—let him believe he was the one controlling the conversation. She could practically feel his curiosity burning in the space between them; it was only a matter of time before he gave into it once more.

She could still sense his gaze, bold and without shame, upon her face, as he said, "Tell me, where did that mark on your cheek come from?"

After a moment of hesitation, she settled on a condensed version. "It isn't only a war against Varen I'm waging, but one against the gods as well."

She had decided not to erase the mark of that war upon her face. The salve the Oak Goddess had given her was still tucked safely away in one of her bags. Let this elf Prince—and any other potential allies—see that she was marked, cursed, and that she had carried on in spite of it. Let them see that she was fighting.

Perhaps it would help them understand the gravity of the situation.

He couldn't seem to take his eyes off it, so she cautiously kept explaining. "I came face to face with Malaphar just a short time ago."

"*Armoras.* The *Chaosbringer*, my kind call him."

"Yes. An accurate name, I'm discovering."

He didn't reply, but he was watching her carefully now, his lips drawn in an even line.

"I don't know the extent of his plans," Cas said, "but I know that he is responsible for the Fading Sickness that has ravaged Kethra's human population over the past decades, and that he has been growing increasingly angry with the people of this empire."

"So what is your plan regarding him, precisely?"

His suddenly intense, almost-serious gaze made her less sure of the plan she had been rehearsing in her mind.

"Don't be coy about things now," he said. "My advisors are going to want to know why I made guests out of our prisoners, why I should trust Laurent, and why I have brought *you* into my own private office." He placed his glass upon the windowsill, got to his feet, and stepped closer to her. Too close, almost. He lifted a lock of her hair and twisted it between his fingers. The sweet-smelling alcohol on his breath was potent. "Tell me why I would put *any* faith in you as a ruler? Enough faith to align myself with you, no less?"

Cas lifted her chin and forced confidence into her reply. "We drove Varen's forces out of Sadira just days ago. People rallied to that cause, and more are joining our side every day. And my plan, my *hope,* is that our entire, fractured empire might be put back together in time to stand against whatever the Dark God unleashes upon it."

"That is quite the lofty goal," he remarked, walking back to his chair and sinking down into it.

"So you see why I need help. And any other knowledge you have of those gods. More about that sacred place on the north shore, perhaps, or—"

"That place is not meant for humans, whether they've tangled themselves up with gods or not."

"Then help me stand against my brother before he makes a bigger, more divided mess of our world."

"I'm not interested in more wars with more human rulers."

"You will not be able to remain neutral."

"I assure you I will."

"I think you're making a mistake."

"Laurent warned me you were relentless." He laughed, and he closed his eyes as he leaned his head back against his chair. "He was right."

She bristled at his laughter. "If Malaphar decides to make his final move against us, then your battles with the Queens of Ethswen won't matter. Your desire for seclusion and peace for your kind won't matter. *Nothing* else will matter."

"It is foolishness for us to even talk of this." An edge had crept into his tone for the first time. "Even if you vanquish your brother, what does it matter? You cannot fight a war against the gods too."

"I already am." Her voice was quiet, steely with a

resolve that had been forged by her growing frustration with the conversation.

He glanced over at her, and his eyebrows arched at the defiant glare she was giving him.

They stared at one another for several long, tense moments, until finally he sighed. "Do you know, when my father passed, for a fraction of a moment I was... happy. Glad to have a chance to rule with a kinder, more delicate hand than he had. Turns out this is a terrible, impossible job. I'm not enjoying any of this at all, just between you and me."

As though you're the only one not enjoying himself, Cas thought bitterly.

"Have a drink, my young Queen." He poured two more of those drinks and offered one to her. "It's been a long day for both of us, it seems."

"I'm not thirsty."

"A cake, perhaps?"

"No thank you."

"How about a capsule of kimaris root powder, then? It is a powerful, pleasant aphrodisiac, if you didn't know." He gave her a rakish smile. "And I can also arrange for a companion for you to share that pleasantness with, if you'd care for such a thing. Or multiple companions, if that's more your thing. We have some very talented and enthusiastic servants to choose from."

"I'm fine."

He made a face. "You're no fun."

"I hardly think this evening calls for *fun*, given everything we've just discussed."

He was undeterred. He drank without her, chugging it in one long gulp, and then plopped the empty goblet onto the windowsill, right next to the one from earlier. "Uncalled-for fun happens to be my favorite kind of fun," he informed her.

Cas opened her mouth to fire out a retort, but the sound of someone climbing the steps reached them before she could.

Laurent appeared in the landing a moment later, and Alder looked so relieved Cas thought he might actually collapse from the sudden dispersal of tension.

"Ah, good," the Prince said, sweeping across the room and clapping Laurent on the back. "I was hoping you'd be back soon."

Cas pursed her lips. She wasn't finished with him, but now she was reminded of the conversation she needed to have with Laurent—about all of the *details* he had failed to mention.

The Prince flashed her another one of those rakish smiles. "I sent for your other friends as well, and they should be around here momentarily. In the meantime, why don't you two talk while I gather us something to eat?" he suggested cheerfully.

He was gone before either of them could argue against it.

He seemed to be an expert at disappearing whenever the conversation at hand became too difficult.

Cas took a deep breath. Then another. Finally, she collected herself enough to look Laurent in the eyes and somewhat calmly say, "Your brother? *Really?*"

"Half-brother," Laurent corrected.

"Why in the world would you keep that from us?"

"It's complicated."

"Obviously. But that isn't an excuse. What *isn't* complicated for us these days?"

He sighed, walked over and settled down into the same seat his half-brother had recently vacated. "I can explain."

"You'd better. The others are going to be furious. Nessa might get violent, and I'm not sure I want to protect you from her at this point."

He grimaced, likely remembering the last time Nessa had gotten violent with him. It had involved a stolen piece of cake, a wayward fork, and a stabbing that Nessa still claimed had been accidental. It was the day they *all* had learned that one did not steal sweets from Nessa unless they were feeling very lucky.

"I wasn't planning on revealing my identity beyond the fact that I have blood ties to this realm," he said. "I knew my father was King Theren, but I don't believe he would have recognized me. I didn't *want* him to know who I was. It probably would not have gone over in our favor. But his son has a reputation for being more level-headed and approachable, so when I realized he was going to be the new king...I saw a way for us to get closer to the ones now in charge of this realm, and so I decided to take it. Especially since the alternative was not looking good. I believe the future Queen of this realm would have already had us before a firing squad if I hadn't revealed myself."

I suspect she still might want to do that, Cas thought. But she didn't mention this; she could sense cracks forming in Laurent's usual armor, and despite her lingering irritation with him, concern gnawed itself into her heart and kept her quiet.

"I didn't want this reunion," he continued. "Would you want a reunion with Anric de Solasen if he were still alive, with everything you know about him?"

She sat down in the chair beside him. Considered the question, and she tried to picture herself having an actual conversation—perhaps even a relationship—with that man who had sired her into this life.

She couldn't do it.

Finally, she said, "No. I guess not."

"Theren was not known to be a good person. I was better off not being tied to him, if I could help it."

"...Family ties can be messy," she admitted.

"Yes. And I don't *need* any family in this place, despite what Nessa and you and anyone else might have been hoping for on my behalf."

"You don't need any family?"

"It's just that I...I mean to say, I already have..."

Cas propped her chin on her fist and eyed him more closely. "Have what?"

He looked like he was scowling as he turned away.

She suspected he was hurting deeper than he let on —all these encounters with the Prince and the rest of this realm had to have stirred up unpleasant memories. And it was all too much hurt and mess to sort through before the Prince returned with dinner, so she decided to try and lighten the mood instead. "Admit that we're your family," she said, "and I will forgive your little lie of omission because that's something a family member would do."

He rolled his eyes. "Gods, you're worse than Nessa."

"Admit that we're family, or I am going to tell her that you admitted to it anyway—that you gave me a lovely, heartfelt speech about your undying love for all of us, and how you couldn't survive without our companionship. And then we'll throw you a party and everything when this is over."

He pinched the bridge of his nose. "A party?"

"I'm going to bake you an official welcome-to-the-family cake."

"This situation is serious, Casia."

"I know. And so are my baking abilities."

He lifted his eyes to hers, his expression perfectly impassive. But he couldn't hold on to that stony look; it eventually gave way to a sigh, and then a slight smile.

"Fine. I will admit that, *yes,* sometimes I wonder what my life might have been like had I not...joined you all."

"Less harrowing and more predictable, almost certainly."

This finally drew an earnest laugh out of him. "And yet, I don't think I would have been better off."

"So, you're glad you have us?"

"Yes."

She grinned triumphantly. He scowled at her again, and her gaze shifted to the windowsill beside him, to the two goblets Alder had guzzled. "Your *actual* brother is kind of a drunken idiot, by the way."

"Half-brother."

"Right. And you two are definitely...*different*, let's say."

They shared another quiet laugh.

"Also? I think his wife might try to murder me if I don't sleep with at least one eye open."

Laurent stretched his legs out in front of him and rolled the tension from his neck. "Not exactly the valiant knights we were hoping would come to our rescue, eh?"

Cas sank more deeply into her own chair, her gaze sliding out of focus as she replayed her conversations with the Prince in her mind. "He didn't completely throw us out of here, though. Maybe there's still a chance of getting through to him."

"Ever the optimist."

"It's gotten harder lately," she said. "But I'm trying."

"I'm glad."

"You are?"

"Yes. Because it means I can keep being a cynic, and we'll simply balance each other out."

She smiled at this, and they sat in an almost relaxed silence for several minutes until they heard voices down below—a whole crowd of people, it sounded like. After listening for a moment, Cas thought she recognized several of those voices.

She was down the stairs in an instant, Laurent following closely behind.

Relief flooded her as she took in the sight of the crowd that included all her friends and allies, safe and gathered and waiting. She moved silently toward them, too overwhelmed by that relief to speak as she embraced Nessa, Rhea, and Zev in turn. They were all *safe*.

For the moment, at least.

She turned to Elander last. He held her longer than any of the others, and his hand stayed lightly braced against her side as he finally leaned away and nodded toward the group of elves standing nearby. They were circled around Lady Sarith, giving her their full attention. A few of them looked as though they might have been too terrified to *not* give her their full attention. Prince Alder stood off to the side of their circle, having a private conversation with an elderly-looking elf whose clothing and plentiful weaponry made Cas think he was a guard of some kind.

"You've made new friends, it seems," Elander said, quietly.

"Yes." Her gaze fixed on Sarith. And as the elven lady barked out orders regarding the palace's new *guests*, a foreboding feeling slithered through her, lifting the little hairs on her skin. "But perhaps some new enemies too," she muttered.

CHAPTER 19

THE NEXT MORNING, CAS WAS AWAKENED BY THE SLAMMING OF a fist upon her guest room door.

She rolled out of her sinfully soft bed and stumbled across the room, bleary-eyed and cursing. When she flung open the door, Prince Alder stood on the other side of it. His smile was bright.

"I have something I wanted to discuss with you," he informed her.

She blinked. Glanced over her shoulder and narrowed her eyes toward one of the windows. The sunlight streaming through it was weak, still shrouded and bound by the last threads of night. "Now?"

"Come along, come along," he said, already down the hall and nearly out of sight.

"Give me a moment," Cas yawned.

She walked back to the bed and started to dig

through one of her bags, searching for clean clothing—only to pause as it suddenly occurred to her that she was alone. The sheets still held the outline of Elander's body and his cold winter scent, but he was gone, and she didn't know where to. She had apparently been asleep when he left.

She'd actually been *asleep*.

And she was tired now, and weak with what felt suspiciously like hunger.

Was it because of the strange air in this realm? It dulled her divine magic, and apparently her other divine tendencies as well. Elander had seemed restless last night too. Was he succumbing to the same things?

Where did he go?

There was no time to find out, or to even give it more thought, because Alder was suddenly back at her door. He pounded on it even harder on it this time.

"I'm *coming*," Cas growled, yanking her clothes on and twisting her hair into a messy knot on top of her head.

She caught up to him and followed at a slight distance, studying the paths they took, making notes about how to find her way through the labyrinth-like halls...just in case she needed to make a quick escape.

She was met with a mixture of expressions as she passed the various palace dwellers. Some gave her the same bright greeting their Prince had. Others seemed to be following his wife's lead, instead, and they regarded her with what— at best—seemed like suspicion.

"I found it very peculiar yesterday," said Alder as they walked, "that you were able to summon that Storm magic in the garden. Nobody is able to use such purely divine magic in this realm."

Cas didn't reply. That moment in the garden felt like a fluke—she hadn't been able to replicate it since—and she was trying not to think about how quickly and utterly this place seemed to be smothering her powers. It was a relief to not have to endure the full force of those different powers battling for dominance inside of her... and yet more strange and disconcerting than she thought it would be, to not be able to easily summon either of those kinds of magic.

"And it was Sun-linked magic, at that," Alder went on. "So, there's something else to you aside from that mark of the Dark God that you wear so brazenly."

"We didn't have a chance to finish our conversation last night," she pointed out. "I was going to explain all of that to you."

"I'm sure. But you don't have to tell me anything." He tilted his head toward her, looking very obviously pleased with himself.

"Because you already got somebody else to talk?" she guessed.

"I had a long conversation with Laurent. A lovely bonding experience for the two of us." That bright smile of his wilted a bit. "I'm quite certain he hated every second of it."

Cas was quite certain he was right, but she only shrugged. "Maybe."

"And he was very stubborn with his words."

"Of all your current guests," said Cas with a yawn, "he's the one you're least likely to get information out of."

"Noted." They had reached the bottom of a winding tower staircase. It was not unlike the one that led up to the Prince's observatory—except this one was far less inviting and so dark that Cas could not see beyond the fifth step.

Alder placed his hand against a panel on the wall, and a trail of torches ignited, illuminating the way up.

Cas's gaze lingered for a moment on the receptacle of light closest to her. The flames that danced within that iron vessel were clearly not natural; there was magic in this realm, even if it wasn't of the purely divine sort. She wondered at the depths of it. Every day, the sea of things to learn about all of these different magics seemed more vast—which was both terrifying and awe-inducing.

"But Laurent was the one that was awake last night," continued the Prince, "and so he was the one I spoke with. And luckily, I can be very persuasive. Particularly when I have the help of the aleberry we drank."

"You got him to drink?"

"All it takes is one sip of that warm, potent nectar, and the rest goes down alarmingly easy."

It wasn't like Laurent to give in to even *one* sip. She wondered if maybe he wanted to connect with this half-brother of his more than he'd claimed.

"So he told you my story, did he?" she prompted.

"Much of it. The most interesting parts—such as those about a certain trinket that once belonged to a certain upper-goddess. One that has guided you, lent you its powers, and which you've had in your actual possession until only recently..."

"The Heart of the Sun."

"Yes." They reached a wooden door at the top of the staircase, and he opened it and ushered her inside. "Which is why I had the idea to show you something this morning." He ignited more torches with a touch of his hand against the wall, and Cas felt her mouth falling open as light spilled over the space before her.

Mosaics covered the walls, wrapping the room in a dizzying display of color.

There had to have been tens of thousands of tiny pieces of glass, each one a small yet significant piece of the countless stories being told by these mosaics. The ceiling soared high above them, so far away that the torches at the door were barely bright enough to allow Cas to see them; she could only just make out the shine of skylights. The panes were covered now—something resting over them on the outside—but she suspected they created an even more dazzling show of colors whenever they were opened.

"My kind have a story regarding the origin of that Heart. I thought you might like to hear it." He still stood in the doorway, watching her as she studied the art on the walls. His face had taken on an almost solemn appearance—a look that suggested the conversation was heading toward larger, darker things.

That combination of fear and awe overtook Cas once more, making her hesitate, but she eventually managed a slow nod.

He worked one of the torches free of its holder and carried it deeper inside. He searched the walls for a moment, sweeping firelight over the tiled images, before stepping closer to a section where the chips of glass formed a swirling ball of golden light.

He ran his fingers over the creatures emerging from that light—all manner of people and beasts—then tapped the center of the light itself and said, "This is the creation. The moment when, after the Stone God shaped the world, the Goddess of the Sun filled it with life."

"And then the Rook God filled that life with knowledge," Cas recited, her eyes already jumping to the image next to that creation one. The glass panels here put together a vision of a person huddled in a cave. A towering figure stood on the outside of that cave, pulling shadows away from it—or pushing those shadows *into* it, maybe. It depended on the angle she looked at it from.

"Eventually, yes," said the Prince. "All of the upper-gods worked in tandem in the beginning; the one that humans know as *Solatis* is the one who convinced the now-called Rook God to give my ancestors an intelligence that nearly matched the gods' own. Because of this, the elves walked on almost even footing with the upper-gods."

"But that didn't last."

"Correct. However, even though that first experiment failed, the Rook God was eventually persuaded to try again, to grant *humans* a gift of knowledge as well—though a less substantial one than the one he gave my ancestors. He was not known as the Rook God in the beginning, but the God of Shades. So called because he was the counter to the Sun Goddess's beautiful but blinding light of creation. He created shades of grey in the minds of the non-divine beings. Because, as I'm sure you're aware, knowledge—and what is right and wrong—is rarely black or white."

Cas's gaze settled for a moment on a picture of the upper-god trio that was centered in the wall to her right. *Shade, Stone, Sun.* They looked imposing even on this small-scale—even contained within the pieces of mosaic.

"What does this have to do with the Heart?" she asked.

"As their created world grew more complicated, the battles between the Sun and the Shade grew more fierce." He pointed to a scene sparkling higher up, where the two deities were engaged in one such battle. Their wings were flared, their swords of light and darkness crossed, while a crowd of monsters and winged soldiers in white armor watched from below.

Cas couldn't take her eyes off those soldiers.

"Those are the Vitala," Alder told her. "A small army of Solatis's most loyal creatures—divine beings that preceded the Marr that we have today. There are twelve of them in most stories, and these twelve faced off with the worst of the monsters the Dark God had tamed to do his bidding in a series of legendary battles—battles that eventually came to a crescendo along those very shores we were discussing last night."

"What happened to them?" Cas asked, running her fingers over those white-clad warriors.

"The twelve were lost. The blood of those guardians of light, her most loyal children, stained the sand and the rocks, and it is said that one of the rocks transformed into the Heart. Supposedly, the scattered power of those warriors seeped into this Heart, like the blood seeped into the rocks, and it was trapped there. Long before it found its way to you, Solatis carried it with her, and as centuries passed, it absorbed more and more of her power—the Heart *consumed* that power, just as a real heart is consumed by grief. As the divine courts rose and fell, and changed, it was common knowledge among all of them that this object existed. Because Solatis never put it to rest. She never secured it back into the true fabric of her being.

"For another age, the Dark and Light deities went about their business with few altercations. But it was only a matter of time before the Dark God grew restless and decided to restart their war. He knew of the Heart's existence, too, and he came to steal it." The Prince paused, and his gaze flickered back to Cas. "But he didn't have to steal it."

"Why not?"

"Because she freely gave it to him."

"Why would she do that?"

"I don't know the real reason," said Alder. "No one does. But after he'd taken it, he supposedly tried to use it to give life to some of his monsters that had been lost in that final, catastrophic battle at Dawnskeep—monsters that Solatis had refused to bring back."

"But it didn't work?"

"No. The Heart cracked in his hands instead. The magic leaked out, the old story goes—it dripped down from the lower heavens and stained the mortal sky; the eternal impression of this is supposedly what causes the display of bright white lights that you sometimes see if you look to the north on summer nights. Although that last part is a little farfetched, admittedly."

It *all* would have seemed farfetched to Cas just

weeks ago. But after coming face-to-face with so many gods and monsters, there was very little she wouldn't believe in at this point.

"So what happened to the magic that was released?"

He shrugged. "Lost to the wind and aether, according to some. Or bound into souls that were reborn as lesser beings, according to others. There is a young Prince of the elven realm of Lightwyn, in the Belaric Empire, who swears he is one of these reborn warriors of light. One of the kings in the Sundolian Empire to the south of us also claims to be one of Solatis's lost children, but there is never any real *evidence* of such claims. Plenty carry her mark these days, but none truly wield her power. And certainly not as much power as the Vitala did." He arched a brow. "Unless, of course, they once possessed that Heart that carried the Vitala's power."

"...A Heart that apparently didn't lose *all* of that power whenever the Rook God stole it and mishandled it," Cas thought aloud.

"So it would seem, if all that Laurent told me about your abilities, your rebirth, and everything else is true."

Cas almost wished she could pretend it wasn't. But they were past that now, she supposed. So she said nothing; she simply kept quiet and tried to make sense of all of these strange new stories.

"That Heart may have been unusable to the Dark God in its pure form," said Alder, "but if its power really did bring you back, if you truly *do* carry some of it inside of you..."

"Then it seems he wants to wield it through me," Cas said, quietly.

"So you are not a fool after all. You understand what is at hand."

She nodded.

"You have gotten yourself tangled up in a feud that is far bigger than yourself. And despite carrying her power, the Sun Goddess has not come to your rescue, has she?" His tone was grim.

Cas frowned. He was trying to intimidate her into walking away from all of this, wasn't he? Just as his wife had tried to stop her from attending that meeting last night.

"She has forsaken you, left you at the mercy of that Dark God that hunts you."

"Or perhaps she intends for me to fight him myself," Cas challenged.

"Do you honestly want to retread the steps of the ones who fought under her banner in the past? The Vitala carried more power than you do now, almost certainly, and they *still* died a bloody death."

Cas lifted her chin, refusing to let her fear show. "What is your point, Prince Alder?"

He exhaled a slow breath. "What hope do you honestly have of fixing things?" he asked. "Even if you managed to get every single person in this empire on your side, it still would not be enough to overcome that god who has cursed you with his mark."

She fought the urge to reach for that mark.

"What hope," he repeated, "could you honestly be carrying with you?"

Her eyes lifted once more to the image of Solatis brandishing her sword against the Dark God.

She kept staring at it, even as the Prince moved toward the door. It was clear that he thought he had made his point. That they were finished with this conversation—perhaps with *all* conversations between them.

But Cas could not let it end this way.

"I am carrying very little," she said.

He stopped walking. A quiet noise of exasperation escaped him, and after a moment of debating with himself, he turned back to face her.

"Almost none at this point, actually."

He canted his head. "Then why are you here? Why are you risking yourself and trying to gain allies against your brother? Even if you survive him, you won't *triumph* at that point. You have too many wars that you are trying to win, Casia Greythorne. And I don't think there are enough allies in the collective empires to see you through to victory."

This very thought had occurred to her countless times, of course. She had survived it in the past by keeping quiet and still until the waves of doubt washed over her. So that was what she did now.

"I have connections in more distant lands," said Alder, stepping closer to her once more. "If you wanted to hide, I could arrange it. I've thought of escaping myself, honestly. Maybe we spare ourselves and leave this empire to whatever fate the gods have decided for it. You could live a little longer, at least. Something worth thinking about."

"I am not hiding. And I am not going to leave you alone until you agree to help me."

"Relentless indeed," he muttered.

"Yes. I am."

"Or perhaps *foolish* is the better word."

She had been called a fool so many times by this point that the word simply hit and bounced off of her.

She closed her eyes for a moment and breathed in one last deep, steadying breath.

"I had a lot of hope in the beginning of this," she told him. "Too much, maybe, but if I had not had that *foolish* amount of hope, I probably wouldn't be here. I never would have started trying to do...well, any of these things. And now I've come too far to stop."

"Too far?" He scoffed. "You can always turn around. You could simply let all these things go."

She shook her head, digging her fingernails into her palms as she tried to keep calm.

There was no letting this go.

"I am tired of people suffering," she said, quietly. "I am tired of my friends being in danger constantly, but there is no peace without some sacrifice. No end to that suffering if we don't *work* to end it. So no, I am not going to turn around, and I am not going to stop hoping."

He sighed.

A powerful feeling sparked in her chest—that exact, defiant, foolish hope that she was so desperately trying to make him understand. "Don't you know what it feels like? To hope for something so badly that it keeps pulling you along, even when you can barely stand up?"

His gaze locked with hers, and his lips parted thoughtfully, and for a fraction of a moment she thought she saw recognition lighting in his eyes. That maybe he *did* know about that dogged hope she spoke of.

She held her breath, bracing for a breakthrough.

Even the tiniest of understandings between them would have kept her going in that moment, if only—

"No. I don't," he said, handing her the torch. "Now, if you'll excuse me, I need to go drink away this conversation."

And then he walked away, leaving her to study the glass-covered walls and make sense of them on her own.

CHAPTER 20

FOUR MORE DAYS PASSED IN THE RELATIVE CALM AND SAFETY OF Briarfell's expansive halls.

For four days, Cas continued to try and convince Prince Alder to swear allegiance and pledge help—*any* help—to her various causes.

For four days, he denied her.

After each denial, he changed the subject and summoned servants to bring him wine.

The more she pestered him, she noticed, the more he drank.

He was more forthcoming with his stories and such after he'd been drinking, however; so at least she was accomplishing her goal of gathering knowledge from this realm.

Still, by the fifth day, she was beginning to lose heart. The stories were not enough. She had promised

Soryn she would secure allies here. And though she and the future king were kindling something akin to friendship, he had still given no signs that this friendship would extend to her on any of the various battlefields that loomed ahead of her.

Tonight, he had insisted on a banquet to celebrate that newfound friendship of theirs. *A waste of time and resources*, Lady Sarith had declared it, at which point he had insisted on making it an even *grander* celebration, complete with copious amounts of drinking and dancing, and then Cas had promptly made herself scarce before Lady Sarith could make a target out of her.

But tonight, there would be no hiding. She would confront Alder one last time. She would force him to either make a final declaration about whether or not he would aid her...or to kick her out of his realm.

One way or another, this part of their journey ended tonight.

She had only a few hours left to prepare herself for that confrontation. At the moment, she walked alongside Laurent, and together they wound their way through the shaded paths that wrapped around the palace. Massive trees dipped over their route, their supple branches heavy with white flowers. A stream bubbled nearby, just out of sight, hidden by the lush vegetation that also camouflaged all manner of twittering birds and chirping insects.

It would have been an exceptionally peaceful walk, if their topics of discussion had been less...*stressful*.

The sound of a laughter-filled conversation interrupted them and drew their gazes toward the banks of the stream. Cas recognized one of the voices in this conversation, even without being able to see his face—Zev's. The other voices belonged to various elven women. A quick peek through the trees found few familiar faces; these were different from the women Cas had seen him with yesterday evening, she was fairly certain. And the evening before *that* too.

"Alder is a generous host," Laurent said, drily, as he kept walking. "Or a generous *enabler*, rather. It's only been five days, and I'd bet a fair amount of coin that Zev has slept with half of the Morethian Court."

"He told me he was gathering information from them."

Laurent huffed.

Cas understood the sentiment. "I just hope he's being...smart," she said.

Laurent glanced back and gave her that familiar look of his—the one that told her such hope was likely a waste of energy.

She sighed before catching up with him. "I'm going to end up an aunt to a dozen half-elven children, aren't I?"

Laurent chuckled at her comment, even as concern

knitted his brows together. "Perhaps we can rein him in before he does too much damage."

"And before the gene pool of Moreth is irreversibly changed."

"I'll talk to him later."

"Then again, we may be banished from this realm by this time tomorrow, and it won't matter."

"None of that cynical talk, now," said Laurent, cutting her a sidelong look. "You sound like me."

"Ah. I forgot we had to stay balanced."

"Keep up, Greythorne."

She grinned, and they walked on in companionable silence. Soon they were strolling along a steep stone path, one that rose up into a bridge over an expansive flower garden. She spotted Lady Sarith down below, stalking through those flowers. Several servants flanked her, their arms laden with baskets.

Cas instinctively moved to the opposite side of the bridge, to where Sarith hopefully couldn't see her. Not because she was afraid of her, but because she knew that not all battles were worth fighting. She needed to focus on her battles with the Prince

But she kept drifting close enough to steal glances at that lady anyway. Her mind was stuck on what she'd said minutes earlier; she had been joking about the possibility of more half-elven children, but it brought questions to mind—about Laurent's family, and about the way family houses worked in this realm in general.

"It's unfortunate that Lady Sarith doesn't seem to get along with the prince very well, isn't it?" she said, once the lady in question had moved out of sight.

"Unfortunate?"

"I mean, perhaps I'm wrong. I don't know her well enough to say, I guess."

"I don't think you're wrong." Laurent shrugged. "But she's simply a noble with a role to play, that's all."

"Yes. And that makes me feel kind of...sad on her behalf."

"I doubt she would want your sympathy. And I also doubt they married for love in the first place." They had reached the end of the bridge, which had brought them to a large wooden door with elaborate, swirling patterns carved into its face. Laurent held it open for her. "My father didn't either, as I understand it. Hence why he came looking for companionship in the village where my mother lived. Not that this excuses anything he did, but..." He trailed off, and though Cas was curious about the other things he might have learned about his father while staying here, she didn't ask. It was still clearly a sore subject for him.

"And as for Lady Sarith," he continued, "she is of the Mistwilde Realm, not Moreth."

"A marriage for political reasons?"

"Exactly. There are only two real clans of elves remaining in this empire, and their numbers are dwindling at an alarming rate—which makes it all the more imperative for the two realms to cooperate. So it goes."

Simply a noble with a role to play.

It seemed that everywhere she looked, this was the case. With Soryn. With Alder. With his wife. And Cas herself was tied a crown that she still did not particularly want. So she understood what such an obligation felt like, and she *did* feel sympathy toward Sarith—even if she would never dare say this to the noblewoman's face.

When she and Laurent parted ways a short time later, Cas was left pondering all these things, and that odd sadness persisted. Her quest to relieve it brought her to one of the many studies scattered about—to the one that overlooked a wide part of the stream that encircled the palace. On the far wall was a row of tall glass windows that allowed for a brilliant view of the grey-blue water and the flowering trees surrounding it.

She found Elander here, as she'd assumed she would; this had become his favorite haunt over these past days. He was relaxing in an exceptionally large and squishy-looking chair by that wall of windows, a book propped open in his lap.

She leaned over the back of the chair and kissed him —first his temple, then his cheek, and then she took hold of his chin and tilted his face up so she could press her lips more completely against his.

"What was that for?" he asked as she pulled away.

"Nothing. I just missed you."

His lips quirked. "You saw me at lunch. An hour or two ago, at most."

She shrugged, and she slipped around the chair to sit on the arm of it. "What are you reading?"

His hand came to rest on her hip, steadying her on her perch. He offered his book to her—though, upon closer inspection, it wasn't so much a *book* as a file full of scraps of parchment that looked as if they'd been torn from several different sources.

"It's a collection of everything the keeper of records could find regarding Dawnskeep, the monument within it, and the sacred shores you told me about the other night," he explained. "I was trying to pinpoint the location of it all. Most stories state that the monument was originally on the shore itself, but the sea has changed with each passing age, so newer accounts say it's now on an island by itself, though you can still technically reach it when the tides shift just right."

"Technically?"

"Well, there's that overwhelming concentration of Sun magic that pushes everyone and everything away."

She frowned at the reminder of this particular challenge they faced. "Do you think the Storm Goddess, or any of her court, would know more about getting into this place?"

"It's possible." He mirrored her frown. "I still haven't heard from them, however."

She tucked the papers in her hands back into an orderly stack, placed it all on a small table beside the chair, and then laid her hand over the one that Elander had against her hip. "I want to go find that place for myself," she told him. "Alder claims it is useless to go there now, that Solatis hasn't walked there in ages, and that there's little chance we'll even be able to approach it, as we established. But..."

"Terrible odds have never stopped you before?"

"Exactly. I think it would be worth a try. I wonder if the essence of Solatis that covers that place might help the Sun magic inside of *me* overpower the darkness, the way you talked about beings of the same divine court lending strength to one another. Or perhaps I can catch her attention there, if nothing else."

"Maybe."

He didn't look convinced—particularly about that last part. But she had latched on to the idea, and now she couldn't let it go.

That upper-goddess might have been the only chance they had at winning their war against Malaphar. If there was *any* chance of drawing her attention, of summoning her help...

"When we leave here, we'll go to those sacred shores together," she said decisively.

He agreed to this—though he was studying her closely, a slight frown on his lips, clearly reading the other parts of this plan that she hadn't spoken aloud. "You suspect we'll be leaving quickly, I take it."

She fidgeted with the hand he had against her, tracing and tapping the spaces between his knuckles. "*Hopefully* with a new ally in place. One that can help keep my brother and his followers under control while we take care of that business in Dawnskeep, and then whatever divine business comes after it. But... I am going to finish things here tonight, one way or the other."

Elander lifted his brows, urging her to continue.

She took a deep breath. "And also...yes. There's a chance we'll have to make a quick exit."

He nodded, and the beginning of a smile curved his lips as he slipped his fingers through hers and gave her hand a little squeeze. "I'll make sure my bags are packed."

CHAPTER 21

WHEN SHE RETURNED TO HER ROOM LATER THAT AFTERNOON, A trio of servants awaited her, all of them gathered around a dress that was hanging over the door of one of the room's three wardrobes.

"A gift from Prince Alder," one of the servants said as Cas approached, "for you to wear to tonight's festivities."

Cas stepped closer to admire it. The silky fabric begged to be felt, and yet it seemed too beautiful to touch without cleaning her hands first. It was a lovely shade of purple, almost blue in the places where the afternoon sunlight didn't hit it. The bottom half was swirled with gold, wrapped in a dazzling pattern that reminded her of scattered starlight. The longer she stared at it, the more convinced she became that it wasn't simply her eyes playing tricks on her; those golden threads were actually shimmering as though they possessed a bit of dancing stardust, and she found herself wondering again about the different types of elven magic.

"It's...glowing," she said.

"Yes."

"Is it enchanted?"

One of the servants giggled. The third servant shushed her, and then offered an explanation. "Lanilisk thread. The shimmering effect comes from crushed lani flowers—from the petal dust that those threads are rubbed with. This dust reacts to intense heat, which we applied just before you arrived. It likely won't last through the night, but it will be a radiant display before it fades away. *You* will be radiant, my lady."

Cas felt a blush creeping along the back of her neck.

"And, if you don't mind my saying so, we could make you even more radiant."

Cas lifted her gaze to the woman's hawkish face.

"A bit of rouge and powder, perhaps. And your hair could also use..." She eyed the messy bun that Cas had wrestled her grey locks into, and she plastered on a smile. "Attention," she concluded.

Cas glanced at the mirror attached to the side of the wardrobe. She couldn't argue against the need for that attention, and she was, as a general rule, hopeless with matters of hair. But she had seen these servants with Lady Sarith far too often. She didn't trust them.

So she lied.

"My friends are much more adept at beauty matters than I am," she told them, "and they will be in here in a moment to help me prepare—and we would prefer privacy, thank you."

The woman's plastered-on smile faltered a bit at this, but after a brief standoff, she bowed and led the other servants away.

To cover up her lie, Cas actually *did* send word for Nessa and Rhea to join her in her chambers—she was glad for the company anyway, and Nessa was only too happy to have a chance to primp and polish herself and everyone else. Rhea was less enthusiastic about the idea, but Nessa eventually won her over as well.

While Nessa worked Rhea's dark hair into an intricate, braided crown, Silverfoot napped on a nearby chair, and Cas worked to tame her own hair into smooth waves. She preferred the practical bun—particularly if things went poorly tonight, and they had to make a quick escape—but she had to admit it didn't suit such an extravagant dress.

Once she was satisfied with her hair, she put on that dress. It was somewhat loose, but the ties in the back were easy enough to adjust. The strapless bodice draped elegantly from her shoulders. The material was unimaginably soft, and it rested so easily against her that it felt like a second skin. She was inspired enough by the look and feel of it that she decided to take that servant's suggestion and apply a bit of powder and rouge, and even kohl around her eyes; she couldn't remember the last time she'd done such things. But it was satisfying. Like transforming into somebody else—somebody who was less apprehensive about what awaited her this evening.

When she turned around, Nessa let out a low whistle.

"Stop it," Cas laughed.

Rhea's expression was, as per usual, more serious. "Laurent told me you planned to corner Prince Alder tonight."

"Yes." Cas picked up her skirts and turned back to her reflection, hoping she'd moved quickly enough that they hadn't seen her uncertainty.

Nessa was at her side a moment later, wrapping herself around her arm, and admiring their reflections more closely. "Nothing like a gorgeous dress to inspire courage, right?" she asked, cheerfully.

"I suppose," said Cas.

"You look beautiful."

"So do both of you."

And they did; they had changed, too, and Nessa looked stunning in a dress of ivory that accentuated her curves, while Rhea was a vision in a delicate gown of scarlet that flared gracefully around her at her slightest movement.

Nessa let go of Cas, folded her arms across the

beaded and sparkling top of her dress, and leaned back against the chair Silverfoot was still napping in. "I wonder if Lady Sarith knows that her husband gifted you such a pretty dress?"

"He had to gift us something, didn't he?" said Cas. "It isn't as though I had room to pack ballroom clothes in my saddlebags. And there are nobles from Mistwilde here tonight. I'm sure he just wants to make sure we don't embarrass him."

"That isn't just any old dress, though," said Nessa, her smile sly.

"Well, I don't plan on bringing it up either way," Cas said. "Actually, I'm going to try and avoid talking to Lady Sarith at all this evening."

"A good plan," said Rhea.

Cas looked toward the door, making sure it was tightly shut before she quietly continued. "I've been trying to pay attention to who looks to Sarith, and who looks to Alder, over these past few days. There's a definite division among this court, isn't there? And if I *do* manage to get the Prince to agree to help me, then I suspect that is only going to make that division worse. So be on guard tonight. Be careful of what you eat and drink."

The other two nodded in agreement.

"And I need you two to keep track of Lady Sarith while I focus on her husband."

"We need a signal," Nessa suggested. "So if she

starts making you nervous, you can just give me the sign, and I'll swoop in and stab her with my hairpin." She slammed her fist against her palm for emphasis, making Silverfoot pop upright with a tiny yelp.

Rhea snorted. "And then what would you do?"

"I don't know. I haven't gotten that far. But it wouldn't be the first time we had to make up a plan on the fly, right?"

Nessa's grin was infectious, and Cas couldn't help but return it, even as she shook her head and said, "Let's try to avoid stabbing *anyone* tonight, with hairpins or otherwise, if at all possible."

Nessa shrugged, her attention now on Silverfoot and the little bowtie she was fashioning for him out of the ribbons she hadn't used in her own hair. The fox was not a particularly willing model; he kept trying to eat the ribbons, and batting at the unraveling fabric with his paws. But Nessa was stubborn, and she eventually succeeded in her task.

"So handsome," she cooed, to which Silverfoot responded with a sneeze.

"And that means we're all ready, I suppose," said Rhea, opening her arms so the tiny creature could leap into them.

They left the room and walked together through the halls until they came to the door that led outside, over a bridge, and into the banquet hall. It was the same bridge that Cas had crossed with Laurent earlier. Silverfoot walked along its stone railing, and as they approached the center of it, he stopped and let out a soft whine. Cas glanced below. It wasn't Lady Sarith who caught her eye this time, but Laurent; he was standing alone in the gardens, a contemplative look on his face.

"Zev was trying to talk him up when I last saw them," said Rhea, softly. "Part of the reason Alder invited those nobles from Mistwilde was because he intends to introduce his brother to them. I don't think Laurent is particularly excited about being introduced as such—he's probably considering skipping the whole affair."

"I'll go talk to him," said Nessa, and she was off without a second thought.

Rhea excused herself as well, needing to return to her room for something before continuing on to the banquet, and so Cas stood alone on that bridge for a moment. She watched as Nessa approached Laurent and put her hand on his arm.

In the gathering dusk, the Feather-kind symbol on Nessa's wrist was easy to see, even though its glow was subdued and pulsing unsteadily. Her magic couldn't have been having much of an effect. It had always proved less efficient on Laurent than it would have been on a full-blooded human, and the airs of this realm were smothering that magic as much as they were smothering Cas and Elander's.

And yet, after a minute of listening to Nessa talk,

Laurent seemed more relaxed. Cas suspected it had less to do with Nessa's divine power, and more to do with the way she was smiling and still holding onto his arm. There was powerful magic in such things—not divine, perhaps, but close enough.

Through whatever magic she had, she eventually managed to coax Laurent into walking with her, and the two of them went together into the banquet hall.

Cas closed her eyes and breathed in deep, bowing her head, preparing to walk into that hall herself.

"Excuse me, have you seen my friend Casia?"

She turned and found Zev approaching her, and she gave him a questioning look.

"Oh gods, that *is* you," he said. "I had no idea you were capable of looking so pretty. It must be that old elven magic at work."

She gave him a saccharine smile as she looked him over. He wore well-tailored pants, polished boots, and several pieces of jewelry that he may or may not have stolen. His hair was neatly brushed for once, and the jade color of his shirt made the swirls of green in his eyes seem startlingly bright.

He looked very handsome, really.

But there was no chance in any hell she was going to tell *him* that.

"Yes," she said instead, "but it seems that no amount of magic, elven or otherwise, can help *your* looks. What a shame."

He smiled at the insult and offered his arm. "Let me escort you in. Maybe your good looks will somehow rub off and improve mine."

"I am not a miracle worker, Zev."

"Just humor me."

Her own smile brightened, and she took his arm and strolled alongside him, trying to focus on the solidness of that arm instead of the knots in her stomach.

Inside, the party was just beginning. Elegantly dressed guests filed in from every door and greeted one another, and a gentle hum of conversation, punctuated by occasional flurries of laughter, grew steadily louder. There was soft music playing in the background, coming from a string ensemble that she couldn't see. The air was warm and even more heavily spiced than usual, and within minutes it was making Cas feel entirely too relaxed.

Not good.

She needed to stay focused.

She gave her head a little shake, and she forced herself to take extensive notes of her surroundings. The exits. The faces, both familiar and not. The clothing that looked as if it might be able to hide weapons, and any other potential threats. She spotted Lady Sarith sitting on a plush sofa against the edge of the room, surrounded by servants and admirers, a crystal goblet clasped in her fingers.

The Prince was nowhere in sight.

Cas tensed as Lady Sarith's eyes briefly darted toward her.

Zev kept her moving, steering her toward another familiar face; Elander was standing near one of the balconies, chatting with a guard.

They stopped talking as Cas and Zev approached, and Elander's gaze slid over Cas. "Hello," he said, a corner of his mouth lifting.

The rest of the room briefly melted away as her eyes locked with his. "Hi."

"You look..." He took a moment to settle on a word. "Breathtaking."

"You don't look too bad yourself," she informed him.

A gross understatement, of course. He was the most eye-catching thing in a room full of beautiful, eye-catching things. Casual, yet polished, with the sleeves of his dress jacket rolled up to reveal his muscular fore-arms. The waves of his hair were loose, framing his strong jaw, and she had to resist the urge to press her hand to that jaw, to wrap her fingers through that hair and pull him in to kiss her.

Zev cleared his throat, as if to remind them there were others still standing there, and Cas stopped staring at Elander and went back to searching for Alder.

"I wish I could stay over here, but..." She finally spotted the elf Prince. He was surrounded by a group on the other side of the room, busy regaling them with an amusing story of some kind, judging by the smiles on every face.

Elander followed her gaze. "But duty calls?"

"Exactly."

"I'll be close by if you need me." He tucked a few strands of hair behind her ear. "Good luck."

"Thank you. I believe I'm going to need it."

His gaze slid over her body, drinking her in one last time before she left. "For what it's worth, I don't think *I* could say no to anything you asked me while wearing that dress."

She smirked; she couldn't help it. "I'll keep that in mind for later."

He looked as though he was at a loss for words—a rare occurrence with him. She turned away before he could reply. Flirting with him was much more enjoyable than politics, but she had a job to do tonight, and she was determined to stay focused on it.

She crossed the room alone, her gaze narrowed on the Prince. People stepped aside as she strode toward them. Heads turned to follow her movements. She felt each gaze like fingers raking upon her back. She thought she understood why people were staring. Why they whispered. Because she was a human amongst elves, and because most of them, by this point, knew of her interesting, budding relationship with the soon-to-be King of Moreth.

But then she caught her reflection in a nearby

window, and she saw the way her dress shimmered with that special thread, the way it had wrapped her entire body in a subtle golden glow that warmed her skin and highlighted her pale hair...and she began to suspect there was another reason for the stares.

Because she looked just as that servant had predicted she would. *Radiant.*

The rest of the room was melting away again. Except she was not melting into Elander's gaze, this time, but into a far darker place. She was an island unto herself, surrounded by too many faces that were watching her too closely, each one of them a possible enemy. She felt the thrum of anxiety rising through her, threatening to send her thoughts spinning away from her.

Stay, she commanded herself, digging her fingernails into her palms.

She couldn't turn around now.

She kept moving, kept dragging her nails across her skin and counting. A scrape of skin for every step, and then she was upon her target, suddenly, and all those steps she'd taken to him were a blur. She managed a deep breath. To still her hands. And then, a relatively calm greeting. "Good evening, Prince Alder."

His mouth had been opened, prepared to continue whatever amusing story he'd started for his crowd, but he slowly closed it as he turned to meet her.

"Ah. Good evening, Casia." Her name rolled off his lips, made smoother by the copious amounts of alcohol she suspected he'd already consumed. He took her hand and kissed it. "I don't believe I've introduced you to the head general of my army. This is Kolvar Aendryr." He indicated an elf with grizzled hair and eyes the same strange, coppery shade as his own. General Kolvar gave a little bow. "And this is Lord Taron Kallas, from the Court of Mistwilde," he added, nodding to a tall male with a boyish face and a jagged scar running up his throat. "Lady Sarith's cousin."

Cas greeted them both, along with a dozen others that Prince Alder quickly rattled off names and facts for. Several of these others did not seem to speak the common tongue as fluently as the prince, so their greetings consisted mostly of smiles and nods.

The prince finally finished his flurry of introductions and turned his attention fully to her. "Now, was there something you needed from me, Casia?"

"A great many things."

His brows rose. "Oh?"

"That is, there are plenty of things we have left to discuss," said Cas pointedly. "And I was hoping we might do so before dinner."

He gave her his usual debonair smile. "Yes—I was afraid you were going to say something like that."

She worked her mouth into a friendly enough smile in return, but her gaze turned hard and insistent.

He considered her for a moment, until suddenly he looked as though he was holding in a sigh. His gaze tilted toward the group watching them. "I need a moment, my friends. Dinner will be served within the hour. In the meantime, enjoy yourselves!"

After a brief moment of confusion, that group scattered, chattering softly amongst themselves and casting a few curious looks back at the prince.

"You know," he said, "if word gets out that I am letting you boss me around, I'll be ruined."

"I'm confident you'll survive any falls you might take." Cas's eyes followed General Kolvar as he made his way to the same guard Elander had been speaking with earlier. "That general of yours..." she began after a moment of thought "...how many does he command, precisely?"

"Casia, my dear little Queen, are you still going on about that, even now? Do you ever stop working and just *enjoy* yourself? This is a party, you know. Have I not made that obvious enough?" He looked genuinely concerned about the possibility of that last part, and he plucked a drink from a passing servant's tray and offered it to her—as if to remedy things.

Cas took the drink but didn't sip from it. "Are we celebrating our friendship or not?" She gestured to the splendor surrounding them.

"We are."

"Then perhaps we should more fully discuss how we plan to help one another. As *friends*. This all seems a little premature, otherwise."

"A friendship with you comes with rather stringent conditions, doesn't it?"

"I've been upfront about that from the beginning, I believe."

And she felt she had to be upfront with him now, too, or else risk letting him escape her again.

"Straight for the jugular tonight, eh?" he mused. "Though I suppose I should have expected that by now."

"I've found it to be an effective way to end problems in the past."

"True enough." He laughed. "But what say you put down your knives and dance with me instead? We can discuss things to the pulse of music. That sounds more enjoyable, somehow."

"You overestimate my dancing ability if you think it will be enjoyable."

His laughter was even louder this time. But she could sense a growing trepidation in between the peals of that laughter; he was still considering making a quick exit, wasn't he?

She placed her drink on a nearby table, and then she took his hand and guided it to her waist before he could escape.

He took hold of her other hand, and together they waltzed their way toward the center of the room, drawing eyes and parting crowds as they went. Cas was acutely aware of all of the gazes on them, but she kept her own gaze locked on Prince Alder and the careless smile he wore.

"I've concluded that you are not going to drop your conditions for our friendship, no matter how many times I deny them," he said, a touch sardonically.

"Relentless," she reminded him.

He didn't need to know that she actually planned to give up if tonight proved fruitless.

"Have you given any more consideration to running away with me?" he asked.

"No."

"I could hide you well."

"The Dark God would find me."

"If and when that time came, you could simply...*end* things"

"Kill myself, you mean? How honorable."

"*Noblesmor*. A noble death. My kind do it when their long lives are approaching the point of discomfort."

"If I *did* go, the ascension mark that Malaphar cursed me with would transfer to someone else, and then the mess would only continue." She set her jaw. "This is my war, Prince Alder. I've accepted that, along with all of its *discomforts*."

He glanced toward a servant who was edging closer to them with a tray of drinks. "You didn't drink the wine I gave you earlier. Would you like another glass? Something different?"

"No, thank you."

"You wound me with your constant refusal of my hospitality, you know."

His grin suggested he wasn't wounded at all. All the same, she didn't want to seem unnecessarily combative, and so she decided to be truthful. "I've noticed a large number of food and drink in this realm that I don't recognize. And I mean no offense, but I've seen some of them having disturbing effects on the ones consuming them, so..."

His grin only widened. "Most of it's harmless. We just like to have fun, that's all." He guided her toward one of the counters running along the sides of the room, and he slowed their dance so that he could point out specific bottles of various colored liquids. "That particular drink, for example, is made with abseth berries, grown only in the northern foothills of the Bloodstone Mountains, and it will change your voice temporarily. Have you ever wished you could sing? Because there's your opportunity, if so. We make another elixir from those same berries that can briefly change one's appearance, not unlike the divine magic of the Mimic spirit. They say that spirit still moves over those hills on particularly dark nights, and thus the plants there are coated in its magic."

She looked over that counter, studying the seemingly endless array of refreshments and wondering what sort of distorted, minor magics they all contained.

Even now, Cas thought, the elves were still trying to

scrape magic away from the divine beings—while tampering with and trying to force their own control over it. She'd always heard that the elves were the ones who had first created the contraband magic crystals she'd made use of in the past, and this seemed like further evidence that those stories were true.

"And the seeds on the table over there?" continued the prince. "A single bite of them makes one feel as if they are flying, I've heard it claimed, though I've never tried it myself. But the night is young—maybe the two of us could experiment."

She shook her head. "I'm fine with just dancing, thank you."

"Very well then." He returned to that dancing with renewed vigor, twirling her out and then back to him in time with the music. His eyes followed the movement of her dress for a moment—those shimmers of gold that seemed to spill from it—before lifting back to meet her gaze.

The ensemble ended one song and then began another, this one louder and more jovial than the last. The wine flowed more and more freely. The scent of food being laid upon tables permeated the air. The conversations around those tables grew increasingly boisterous, and Cas felt as if the evening was already beginning to slip away from her.

She kept her gaze steady with Prince Alder's, trying to think of how to get the conversation back to where she needed it to go, but he spoke again before she could. "You're thinking about another way to try and wrestle an army out of me, aren't you?"

"Maybe," she admitted.

"Can I ask you something unrelated to all of that war nonsense?"

She stiffened but forced a nod. "Of course."

"You know my brother very well, I've gathered."

This was not the topic she expected.

"We...we've lived and worked together for several years now," she said. "And yes, we're close. He's my older brother, essentially."

He inhaled a bit oddly at the word *brother*.

He didn't speak for a long time after that, but she thought she could read the silence. She knew that look he wore, because she knew the feeling behind it. It was the look of the lost, of one whose family had been uprooted—or perhaps whose roots had never really taken in the first place.

She got the sense, as she had before, that he had lived a very lonely life in these halls—even *before* his father had died. Seeing Laurent probably made it seem all the lonelier. What would it have been like if they had grown up as true siblings?

Or if he had gotten as lucky as she had, and found his own family?

"I just wondered if he had mentioned anything to you about..." His eyes looked upward and slid out of focus, and he seemed to be speaking as much to the ceiling as to her as he said, "Well, *me*."

Cas's heart clenched in a way that made her briefly forget her mission. "He's not always forthcoming with his thoughts," she told him.

The Prince nodded, as if he'd expected this answer.

"But I think he's glad to have met you," she added.

He eyed her as though he thought she might be lying, but he eventually gave her a thankful smile anyway. "He's lucky to have a friend like you. I'm glad he has a family outside of the disastrous one he technically belongs to."

"You're his family too," she insisted.

He lifted one shoulder and let it drop. "I'd like for him to think so."

It was a low strike, perhaps, but she couldn't stop herself. "Help him, then. He's my ally, and so he needs your help as much as I do."

He inhaled deeply. But the wall between them seemed to have cracked, revealing an opening large enough for her to work her way through, and so she kept going. "I won't ask you anymore after tonight. If you won't help us, then I will have to move on—along with Laurent and all my other allies." The room seemed to tip and sway around her as she held her breath, awaiting his reply.

Please, just say yes.

But all he said, after a long, heavy pause, was, "Well, it's been lovely having you all as guests."

Her heart sank.

He had actually proven more stubborn than herself.

She had failed.

"And you look beautiful tonight, by the way," he added. "The dress suits you as well as I expected it would."

The compliment felt more like an insult; she didn't care about looking beautiful. There was no dress that could have made her feel better about this defeat.

She was numb, unable to reply. Despite the apparently insurmountable differences between them, he seemed very close all of a sudden. Too close.

She suddenly became very aware of Lady Sarith glaring at her from the other side of the room.

Cas narrowed her eyes, and she fought to keep her voice steady. "Your wife looks eager to dance with you, my Prince."

"Doubtful." His smile had taken on a forlorn quality. "But I suppose I should ask her to do me the honor, all the same."

She nodded. It was all she could manage with the taste of defeat souring her mouth. She started to pull away, but he held her arm more tightly.

"One last question." He hesitated.

She waited.

"Were you being honest, when you said my brother was glad to have met me?"

She could have just told him *no*. There was a bitter side of her that *wanted* to do this, to crush that faint hope in his expression as thoroughly as he'd just crushed hers.

But instead, she canted her head so that she couldn't see Lady Sarith's face, and she said, "Yes. He revealed his true identity because he wanted to meet you. And because he believed you might be a better person than your father—that you might help us." She shrugged. "That was what he told me, anyway."

"A better person?" He gave a short, almost savage little laugh. "Why would he believe that? Why would *any* of you believe that?"

"I can't speak for Laurent. But as for myself... This world is a dark place, Prince Alder. And I have been hurt more often than many." Her gaze swept over the room, avoiding Lady Sarith and catching briefly on each of her friends in turn. "But I've also been *helped* by a lot of people. So I keep looking for helpers."

He slowly released his hold on her.

"And if you will not be one of them," she added, "then I will simply move on and keep looking for others —because I know they are out there."

He said nothing to this.

She excused herself with a slight bow of her head and turned away.

Zev and Nessa were standing nearby, and she made it halfway to the comfort of them before the Prince called her name. She stopped, but she kept her back to him, even as she heard him stepping closer to her. She had lost the battle. He wouldn't see the frustration spreading across her face, at least.

He drew close enough to speak in a low voice that only she could hear. "I will have General Kolvar draw up a preliminary agreement of alliance," he said. "I have five thousand at my command, to answer your question from before. Even more than that, if I call on the King and Queen of Mistwilde to honor the ancient bonds of our respective courts—and I believe they will. And whatever we can do to help you, we will do it."

She turned back to him, almost certain he was making a joke, expecting to see him laughing at her.

But his face was as serious as she'd ever seen it.

"I still believe it is pointless," he said. "Foolish. But if the world is to descend into chaos, then I believe I would like to descend with you."

She couldn't reply; she wasn't sure what to say.

"I do hope you'll stay here for a few more days, as there are still a great manner of details to work out, and I would prefer we do this face-to-face."

"I...yes. Of course. Thank you."

"Very good, then. Enjoy the rest of the evening." He bent at the waist, rose slowly, and then crossed the room to his wife.

Cas stood, rooted to the spot, while her mind and her heart raced, unable to settle on any single thought or emotion. She had gotten precisely what she had come for, and yet...

It was like so many of their victories lately—they all seemed to come with a caveat.

As she watched the soon-to-be King of Moreth lead his wife onto the dance floor, her earlier conversation with Nessa and Rhea resurfaced in her mind.

The division among this court was real, and it was dangerous, and the ones who had been gathered around Sarith earlier were not watching their future King and Queen dance, she noticed.

Most of them were glaring at her.

CHAPTER 22

THE DARKNESS OF NIGHT HAD SETTLED ENTIRELY, AND CAS HAD been sitting on a bench in the courtyard for so long that she was starting to lose the feeling in her lower body.

She should have been inside. Should have been mingling with the nobles and the soldiers who might ultimately answer to her. But she had hit her limit. It was frustrating, this need to escape. Better than hyperventilating in front of the prince who had just sworn his allegiance to her, but still...

It felt like she was constantly trying to keep all of these powerful allies and enemies from figuring her out —from realizing she was in over her head—and it was exhausting, and she just wanted to be alone.

And for the better part of the last hour, she had been.

It couldn't last forever, of course. She eventually heard the sound of boots upon the gravel path behind her. She didn't have to take her eyes off the flowers at her feet to know it was Elander approaching; she recognized his energy, even in its subdued state.

"You found me," she said.

"I always do, don't I?"

She tucked her hands under her arms to hide their shaking.

"Are you okay?"

She tilted her face toward him. "Yes. It was just...it was too crowded inside. Too many faces, too many complicated things. I needed to be alone for a little while. It was getting hard to breathe."

He nodded, glancing back toward the door, looking hesitant.

Quietly, she said, "You can stay, if you want."

He sat down. He stayed silent, patient, while she found her calm and centered herself within it. It took a long time, but he didn't rush her back. He simply waited there beside her.

"Prince Alder has agreed to ally his army with Sadira's," she finally told him. "And he thinks the rulers of Mistwilde will join the cause as well."

Elander looked almost as shocked as she'd felt when the Prince had called after her on the dance floor. "That's excellent news," he said.

"I still don't quite believe it."

His gaze was full of admiration. "Have I ever told you that I think you would make an extraordinary queen?"

She blushed. "Maybe. But I feel like I'm faking it at the moment. Like I've tripped and stumbled into somebody else's life." He scoffed at this, but she continued. "And it's still just beginning, isn't it?" She clenched the edges of the bench as she bowed her head and tried again to find balance. "I don't know. It feels like nothing I do is ever enough. I have thousands more soldiers for my army now, but to what end? These past days have felt so...detached from everything outside of this realm —so much so that I'd almost forgotten about some of the things we're facing.

"Once we leave this place, it will be back to those things, back to the problem of...*us*, for example." Her hand traced the mark on her face as her gaze fell over the one he carried on his own skin. "All of the solutions we have for *that* problem are mere theories, still, and I just..." She bent and picked several of the flowers at her feet. She needed something to do with her hands.

"Let's not think about all of those things just yet," he suggested, voice soft with concern.

"I can't *not* think about them, Elander."

He slipped an arm around her waist and pulled her closer to him, but then he fell silent again.

She laid her head on his chest. Closed her eyes. Listened to the music drifting over from the party that felt miles away now, and she picked at the flowers in her hands, ripping off their petals, one by one, until she was left with only naked stems. She crushed those stems in her fist. A shudder of anxiety tried to sway her body, but she steadied herself through it. Mostly.

"Tell me what you need right now," Elander said, his fingers stroking her arm, leaving a trail of raised bumps behind. "Not when we leave this place. Not tomorrow, not the next day—just now."

"I can't even think of an answer to that. I'm too stressed to think clearly."

A pause, and then, "Would you like me to help you destress?"

She lifted her head from his shoulder and found him watching her with a look that was still concerned...but also amused—likely at the blush she felt warming her face.

"By *dancing*, I meant." He got to his feet, took her hand, and pulled her to him. "A proven mood booster, you know."

"Horizontal dancing, I assume?" A hint of hope had snuck into her voice.

"That's one way to do it," he said, smiling.

"Just one of many."

"I know lots of others."

Desire stirred deep in her belly. It distracted her from everything else, if only for a moment. "And now I'm intrigued about those others."

His smile quirked as he held more tightly to her hand and led her away from the bench.

The music drifting from inside had grown softer; it

sounded as though the dancing had given way to the feasting. Cas suspected she might be summoned any minute to return to that feast, and the thought was still...paralyzing.

Elander drew her closer to him, as though he could sense these thoughts. They moved together in a slow, mesmerizing sort of sway over the cobblestone and dirt paths. After a moment he pressed one hand against the small of her back, and he guided her even closer to him. Close enough that he could tilt his head down and sweep his lips over hers.

"I don't even like dancing," she murmured, as his lips trailed away from hers.

"I don't either," he said, spinning her in a slow circle before pulling her back against his chest, facing away from him. His arm settled around her waist, and his chin came to rest on her shoulder as he said, "And yet, suddenly I feel like I could do it all night long."

"Me too." She relaxed more fully into him, enjoying the feel of his strong arms, of his skin warming against hers. She tilted her face toward the sky. She felt him following her gaze, and they stared together at an orange moon half-hidden by clouds.

Others came and went around them, on the bridge above them, in and out of the party. She paid them little mind. Elander's hands were both against her waist, now. Occasionally, they slid lower, tracing along the curves and dips of her hips and thighs before returning to their place against her stomach. His face nuzzled into her hair, kissing the soft waves of it one moment, simply breathing her in during the next.

After a few minutes, he moved his mouth to her ear and whispered, "I don't think this counts as dancing."

"Nonsense. This is the most enjoyable dance I've had tonight."

"Really? You looked like you were enjoying yourself with the Prince earlier." His tone was teasing, yet something else lurked just beneath the surface of his words. Something darker.

Her skin tingled, and heat shot through her. She wanted to draw that darkness out to play.

Perhaps *that* was what she needed tonight.

She pushed the curves of her body more firmly into his, and he responded by sliding a hand below her waist once more, tracing circles on her inner thighs through the silky fabric of her dress.

"Were you jealous?" she asked him.

He laughed. "Just disappointed I had to wait. Though I can't exactly blame Prince Alder for wanting you to himself."

"No?"

"No." He twisted her around so they were facing each other again, and his gaze caressed her body as he said, "I told you this before, but I'll say it again—you're looking especially breathtaking tonight."

"Yes, the Prince said the same thing."

He rolled his eyes. "Should I be worried about his obvious interest in you?"

"Maybe." She shrugged, and lifted her gaze to a nearby balcony, to where a young elf was enjoying a drink while he stared at the clouds that were glowing, edged in moonlight. "I do have a thing for pointed ears."

"You're actually *trying* to make me jealous, aren't you?"

She grinned. "Is it working?"

He returned her grin, but like his quiet voice, there was a hint of something dark about it. Something rough and...*untamed*. He took a fistful of her dress in his grip and pulled her toward him, jerking swiftly enough that she nearly lost her balance. "Is this the part where I get all dominant and possessive?" He nodded toward the ivy-wrapped table next to the bench they'd been sitting on earlier. "Shall I throw you onto that table over there and stake my claim on you?"

"Sounds good so far."

His nose bumped hers. His breath fell over her lips, warm and laced with the sweetness of the wine he'd been drinking. It smelled good. *He* smelled good, as he always did—like cedar and winter and other dark, wild things. "Be careful what you wish for," he warned.

He backed her toward that table.

She moved with him, step for step, until they were mere inches from the ivy-covered stone. Then she stood on her tiptoes and pressed her lips to his. Distracted him long enough to turn him around and press *him* to the table.

"I think I'm safe at the moment," she taunted, slowly dragging her mouth away from his. "Considering we have an audience." She nodded toward that elf on the balcony, who had just been joined by a companion.

"You think that makes you safe, do you?"

She cut her gaze back to Elander and found him staring at her, only her, as if he hadn't even registered the existence of those balcony dwellers—or any of the other countless beings who sounded close by.

"You don't think I would take you right here in the middle of this garden?"

"Right in front of them?" She laughed—though that intense way he was looking at her made it come out more breathy and faint than she'd meant for it to.

He finally glanced toward the audience in question, and his lips curved with a much more obvious, wicked intent than before. Then his eyes were back on hers, his gaze smoldering, as he said, "I promise you I will. And I will stare them down the entire time I'm inside of you. Them and whoever else cares to watch."

She swallowed, searching for words.

Nothing came to her.

He kissed her speechless lips, let his mouth hover over them as he whispered, "You're so beautiful when you blush like that."

She blushed even more deeply.

He took her chin between his fingers and lifted her gaze to his. "Don't tempt me if you don't want me to act on it, Thorn. You look too good in that dress, and I only have so much self-control." He sat on the edge of the table and pulled her into his lap. His hands pushed the skirts of her dress up, eventually finding skin. "Jealous," he scoffed in between trailing kisses along the hollow of her throat. "As though I have any reason to be."

"My, aren't we confident?"

"Yes. I am."

She started to reply, but whatever she'd been trying to say was lost as he raked his fingers along the inside of her thigh and her mind went momentarily, blissfully blank.

"But you can go ahead and get up, if you'd like." She didn't move, which made him smile as he added, "You don't want to get up, though, because you were hoping I'd reach higher, weren't you?"

She wrapped her arms around his neck, steadying herself as a wave of pleasure nearly overtook her. "Maybe I was."

His eyes darkened further at the words. But rather than reaching higher, he lifted his knee and slid her more completely into his lap. He kept his leg lifted against her, so there was hardness pressing upon her backside, while a different, throbbing hardness met her front. It felt unbearably good, even with the layers of clothing still between them. His hands moved to her hips, gripped them tightly, and he pulled her more fully against him.

Her head fell back, and she stopped herself from letting out a sigh of pleasure—only because she heard footsteps approaching. She started to twist toward that sound, but Elander caught the side of her face and pulled her attention back to him.

"We can go somewhere else," he told her.

"Oh, you'll settle for someplace more private after all?"

He smirked. "I don't need to throw you onto this table and claim you here, unless you want me to." His thumb traced her lips, parted them. "Because before I am finished with you tonight, there will be no doubts about whether or not you're mine. This entire realm will hear the evidence of it, whether we're behind closed doors or not. I am going to make certain of that."

Her heart pounded, and her breaths were rapid, shallow. Speech seemed impossible. But she knew what she wanted to say—that she wanted him alone. Wanted to test that *behind closed doors* claim.

She climbed out of his lap, and then she was moving, pulling him after her. The room they'd been sharing was just around the corner. They reached it in a blur of heat, of stolen kisses, of hands fumbling and pulling at clothing.

An instant after she closed the door behind them, he had her backed against it.

His mouth overtook hers while his fingers fought with the ties along the back of her dress. The top fastenings were undone quickly, enough that the bodice slipped down, along with the stays beneath it, pushing her breasts up and free of their satin cage. He met them eagerly, caressing the curves and trailing fingers over the newly exposed, velvety peaks, leaving those peaks stiff and ready for his mouth to claim.

Her hands slid beneath his clothing, tracing the hard lines of his stomach, pushing the fabric up until he paused long enough to slip free of both his coat and shirt. He tossed them aside before turning his attention once more to the ties of her dress.

He moved more slowly this time, savoring every new inch of skin he revealed. Her dress eventually pooled into a still-shimmering pile at her feet. Everything underneath it joined a moment later, until she was laid bare before him, a pale silhouette against the dark wooden door. He leaned away from her, then, just far enough that he could study the entirety of her through eyes that were dark and burning with desire.

"Breathtaking," he said.

"You've already mentioned that. Twice."

His lips were curving into a smile as he pressed them to hers. "Just in case you'd forgotten."

He took her hand and pulled her to the sofa that stood nearby.

He laid her down upon it.

And then he was kneeling before her, his hand sliding around to the small of her back, pulling her forward to meet his mouth. Her back arched at the first breath that fell, warm and heavy, against her sensitive folds. His tongue traced the same nerve endings that breath had brought to life, and a soft whimper escaped her.

His tongue pushed inside her in response to that sound, and she writhed against the velvet cushions until he gripped both of her legs and held her still.

He seemed determined to make good on his promise to let the entire realm know what was happening inside this room, and soon the sounds that were finding their way out of her mouth were no longer...soft.

They weren't even entirely *human*.

She raked her hands through his hair as he continued to wield his tongue against her. She didn't want him to stop. But she needed control, or else he was going to finish her off, and she was not ready to be finished with him.

Her hands pushed him back just enough to give her leverage to sit up. He didn't miss a beat; he simply shifted to trailing his lips and tongue across her stomach, her breasts, her throat.

She tightened the grip she still had in his hair, pulled his mouth to hers as she stumbled the rest of the way upright, and she kissed him as fiercely as he'd been pleasuring her just moments ago. She lost herself in that fierceness, in the feeling of his tongue dancing with hers. Her teeth caught his lip. She bit gently upon it, earning a moan that sent shivers coursing through her.

Her hands grew restless. She moved them to the belt of his pants, undid it, continued stripping him down until the full, erect length of him sprang free.

Her fingers caressed that impressive length. His mouth pressed against her neck. The deep sounds of his pleasure rumbled over her skin, and suddenly, she needed more—more than his touch, his lips, more than his arousal throbbing against her palm. She needed to feel that throbbing *inside* of her.

She brought her mouth closer to his ear. Hesitated for a moment, her lips brushing his earlobe, her lungs inhaling that intoxicating wintry scent that clung to his hair, and then she whispered, "I believe *this* is the part where you get all dominant and possessive."

"No table to throw you onto in here," he replied in between rasping breaths. He drew back so he could see her, his eyes burning with thoughts that she could only guess at. "But you looked so pretty against that door a few minutes ago..."

She was back against that door a moment later, pressed so quickly and roughly into the wood that it took her breath away.

He didn't wait for her to catch it.

He lifted one of her legs, angling her hips so they were better aligned. His gaze took hers again, held it as he guided the tip of his erection to her entrance. "It's not a table," he said, glancing at that door, "but it will suffice."

The slickness of their combined arousal helped him slide easily into her, and then he picked her up just as effortlessly, wrapping her legs around him and pinning her between himself and the door.

Despite all of the times she had seen his strength in action, she was always newly surprised when he used it against her like this. He held her there as if she weighed nothing at all. One of his hands braced against the doorframe, while the other cradled one of her legs and helped her balance. Her arms linked around his neck. His hips moved in a deliberate rhythm against her, gentle at first—until a harder thrust made her cry out, which only urged him deeper. Faster. It rattled the door. It rattled her bones, her senses, her every remaining tether to anything outside of him. She might have thought to be quieter—to be embarrassed by the amount of noise they were making—if she could have managed to think about such things.

But all she could think about was how deeply he was pushing inside of her. Physically. Mentally. So completely, so relentlessly, that there was no end or beginning to her or to him in that moment—there was only *them*.

In time, his breaths grew more ragged. His thrusting faster, more desperate. He was nearing an end, and Cas's eyes had been closed, but they fluttered open now because she wanted to see his face. To catch that brief moment when he looked vulnerable, when all the darkness and tension he carried...*released*. When he let it go and simply collapsed against her and took those few rare, peaceful breaths. She craved that moment as much as she craved her own release.

The hand he had braced against the doorframe moved, slipping between her legs instead. He was still inside of her, but he'd slowed his pace. His fingers were doing more of the work now, tapping and rubbing circles against her sex, making her body writhe in a way that was increasingly out of her control. It seemed he intended to make her finish first, as usual. She'd once asked him why he insisted on this, and he'd laughed and said, "Because I'm a gentleman."

She'd playfully accused him of being overly competitive, of turning everything between them into a determined battle of wills.

"That too," he'd admitted.

Tonight she would be *more* determined, she decided.

Her arms lowered from their place around his neck, and her fingers dug into his backside, gripping tighter, pulling him deeper inside of her. She rolled her hips until he could no longer resist rising to match her rhythm. And once she had him caught up in that rhythm, it was only a matter of time.

She felt his muscles clenching beneath her touch.

He cursed, buried his head into the curve of her shoulder, and she won the battle this time—though his victory was not far behind.

And if there was anybody left in this wing of the palace who did not know what was happening in that room...

Well, they knew it now.

His hands dug deep into the backs of her thighs, and he pulled her completely flush against him, held her there until he had fully emptied himself into her, until her own tremors of release had finished and every breath and thought briefly left her body.

He kissed her gently, slowly, until she came back to him. Then he took a step away from the door, his arms still wrapped tightly around her, securing her quivering body against him.

He carried her to the bed and collapsed on to it with her. Only then did they separate. He didn't go far, stretching out beside her and pulling the covers up over her still-shivering body. His eyes closed. His fingers traced a path up and down her arm while his breathing became slower and slower.

Somewhere far off in the distance, a banquet was still going on. Outside of this sheltered realm, wars were building, blood was very likely spilling, and the list of the impossible things they faced was growing.

But here in the quiet, in the stillness between his breaths, she felt warm. Hopeful. She curled closer to him, and he whispered something into that stillness, something that sounded like..."*Mine*." But it was not that same playful, flirting tone he'd used earlier. It was not part of a game, but of something altogether different.

It was a vow.

She was his. He was hers.

And in that moment, it felt as if not even the upper-gods could tear them apart.

————————

THE NEXT MORNING, Cas woke up alone.

A cold panic sliced through her, but it didn't last long before the door to the bedroom opened, and Elander stepped inside.

"There you are." She tried to sound normal, as if she hadn't just immediately thought of a hundred different worst-case scenarios at the sight of his empty spot on the bed.

He nodded, but otherwise didn't greet her, clearly distracted by something.

She stood slowly, wrapping a sheet around her naked body like a dress. "Is everything okay?"

His distracted gaze finally focused on her. "We're going to be here for a few days more, correct?"

"That was the plan, yes. There are still a lot of details about our alliance that we need to sort out."

The frown he was wearing deepened.

"Why do you ask?"

"It's been nearly a week since I sent Caden to Stormhaven."

She settled back on the edge of the bed, clutching the sheet to her chest. Had it really been that long since they entered this realm?

"Maybe it's nothing," he continued, "but...he should have reported back by now. So this morning, I went to speak with some of the guards who man the realm's main gates. I wanted to see if they might have accidentally turned him away, despite Prince Alder's orders. But they claim there's been no sign of him. And I've been trying, but I can't feel his energy either."

"Probably because of the suppressive air of this place."

He hesitated. "Probably."

"Maybe...maybe you need to get out of here and see if that's the case," she said quietly.

"It shouldn't take long," he said. "I should be able to sense his location once I'm outside of this realm, and then it will just be a matter of getting to that location and back."

She nodded, even as her heart clenched at the thought of the wars that awaited them outside of this realm—of him going out there and facing them without her, if only for a brief moment. Even though she'd suggested it, she didn't like the idea of it. At all.

But she also found it worrisome that Caden hadn't made his way back to them. They were counting on the goddesses of the Sun Court and what they could do regarding Solatis, as well, and she knew it was past time to check on the status of all these things.

So she didn't stop Elander as he prepared to leave.

"Promise me you'll stay out of trouble while I'm gone," he said, readjusting his belt and the sheath clipped to it, and then switching out the knife in that sheath for a different one from his bags.

She managed a small smile. "When have you ever known me to get in any sort of trouble?"

He didn't return her smile. "I mean it. You're safer here than outside, I believe, but I don't trust everyone in this place, and I know you don't, either."

"I trust Prince Alder, and he seems to have things under control," she said—mostly in an attempt to alleviate the concern that was so obvious on his face.

"Let's hope it stays that way."

The air was too tense, too heavy, too far removed from the bliss of last night. So she jokingly said, "Just be aware that I might have to sleep with him to see if I can secure more soldiers for our army."

His hand slipped against the knife he was securing, and he lifted a deadpan gaze to her.

She shrugged. "A mission is a mission."

"Keep teasing me, Thorn."

She grinned. "And?"

"And you'll pay for it when I get back."

The sly curve of his lips told her she would probably enjoy whatever punishment he had in mind.

But she stopped her teasing for the moment and turned serious once again. She tried to keep her voice from shaking as she said, "Promise me you *will* come back."

He fixed his full attention on her once more. He closed the space between them, and his hand reached up and brushed the mark on her cheek. His eyes closed, concentrating, and after a moment, Cas felt his familiar magic—subdued by this realm, but still strong—pulsing between them like a shared heartbeat.

"Do you feel that?" he asked.

She nodded.

"I've always felt drawn to your energy. It's even stronger now. Stronger than anything I ever felt toward Caden or any of the other members of my divine court. A silver lining of this curse trying to work its way between us, I think. We are connected by that magic that's been transferring between us, for better or worse. And I have to think that it will lead us back to one another, no matter what happens."

She inhaled deeply, breathing in his comforting scent, letting that belief wash over and sink into her. "Nowhere you can go that I can't find you."

He smiled and kissed her cheek before wrapping her in one last embrace. "Exactly," he said.

CHAPTER 23

As soon as Elander stepped through the last of the gates surrounding Moreth, the air immediately felt thinner, and it became easier to breathe.

He glanced back one last time. A trio of guards stood before the tall gate of twisted iron. A bridge lay beyond that, stretching over a grey river and into the main grounds of Briarfell. The way to that bridge would open only for ones of certain elvish blood, but Prince Alder had assured Elander—and those three guards had reiterated—that he would be welcomed back in when he returned, as would Caden. And he wouldn't be gone long.

The others would be fine without him for a little while.

She would be fine.

Steadying himself, he turned and walked into the

trees before him. He hiked for nearly two miles before he felt the grip of elven magic truly loosening.

After checking his surroundings for any potential threats, he knelt in the shade of a particularly large willow tree. He bowed his head, concentrating. His fingers traced through the dirt, which briefly lit with a pale blue light that took the same shape as the Death mark on his wrist. That light was there one moment, gone the next...not deep enough or powerful enough to leave the lasting impact he needed it to.

He refocused and tried again.

This time he managed a brighter mark—one that still eventually faded, but which glowed back to life as soon as he inwardly flexed his hold on his power.

As the mark pulsed, he stayed crouched over that stamp of his magic, holding in a sigh. This trick used to be so *easy*. An afterthought. Now it took all his concentration, and it was...exhausting.

Was this a new, permanent low point of his fading powers?

Or just the lingering side effect of these past days he'd spent inside of Moreth?

Whatever the reason, at least he had accomplished this first part of his plan—which meant he could now get back to this spot quickly—so he stood, and he turned his attention to his next task: Finding out where to go from here. Yet another thing that used to be easy, back when he and Caden were at their full power, and thus their connection was equally powerful.

This time, when he reached out into the void of space between them, it was a long time before anything reached back.

When it finally did, it was faint, very faint—that flickering of energy that told him his once-servant was still alive and on the move. He closed his eyes as he took in that energy, and an image came into view, filtering through the darkness: Caden was standing on a hill, overlooking a sacred ground covered with flowering white trees.

In the center of these trees was a stone pavilion with a towering black obelisk on each corner. Between the obelisks were shallow, rectangular pools of grey water, and beyond it all was a mountain, jutting up in a sudden, dramatic fashion that didn't look at all natural —because it wasn't. It wasn't a true mountain at all, but a tangible manifestation of the Rook God's power, placed there to continuously feed this location with dark energy.

Elander knew this place well, even after all the things that had ravaged his mind and memory.

It had once been an important part of his obligations as the God of Death, and he had been to it often; this was the gateway to Bethoras—one of their world's three hells. And there was enough residual Death magic lingering there that traveling to it would be almost as easy as traveling to Oblivion.

But why would Caden be there now?

Only one way to find out.

He braced himself for traveling.

The familiar hitch in his chest told him he had successfully taken hold of the energy surrounding Bethoras, and a moment later, he was lifted off his feet and yanked forward, passing quickly through the quiet darkness of the space between.

The sound of birds squawking and scattering announced his arrival. Hot, humid air sank over him, and he opened his eyes and found the crumbling edge of the pavilion beneath his boots. He kept his chin tucked toward his chest for a moment, fighting off a wave of exhaustion and dizziness.

Slowly lifting his head, he glanced around, overwhelmed for a moment by a strange combination of nostalgia and trepidation.

It had been a very long time since he'd stepped foot here. He had been banned from all of these divine places as part of his punishment after his fall, and he had never really felt a desire to rebel against that ban before now.

His gaze lingered on the grey 'water' to his right. It wasn't truly water, but a strange, fluid, magical substance, and the 'pools' were portals that could take one into the depths below—if they possessed the right power, of course. Beneath those pools and the pavilion he stood upon was a vast network of stairs—of caves and cages that went deeper than any human could possibly comprehend. Bethoras held human souls, yes, but also the essence of all manner of beasts, and there were *also* things that were not truly associated with death, here—things like monsters that had been deemed unfit to roam free in any realm.

The garmora that had been set upon the city of Belwind months ago—the one he and Casia had slain—had been one such monster; the other two upper-gods had sought that creature's destruction, but the Dark God had chained it here instead. It had remained dormant for at least a century before he'd unleashed it.

Elander wasn't sure if he could still pass through the pools and get to the world below, given the state he was in, but part of him wanted to, to check and see if any *other* monsters were missing from their cages.

Before he could move either way, he heard footsteps behind him, and he turned to see Caden approaching.

Caden didn't look at all surprised by Elander's sudden appearance. "I wondered how long it would be before you got impatient and came looking for me," he said.

Elander frowned. "Why are you here? This place is dangerous—you shouldn't have come here alone." That divine energy that shrouded this place *also* meant it would be an easy spot for Malaphar or any of his other servants to appear without warning.

"I wasn't planning on being here long," Caden said. "And I was headed for Moreth immediately after, ready to give my report. But this will save me the time of having to repeat whatever they have to say, I suppose."

"They?"

"I'm not here alone." Caden pointed to a woman who had just stepped out of the shadow of one of the pillars surrounding them—Nephele.

And Inya was right behind her, though Elander almost didn't recognize the Moon Goddess at first; the usual freckles and various symbols that glowed upon her dark skin were merely blotches of discolored skin at the moment, and her hair was a dull shade of white, rather than the stunning silver it had been during their last meeting. She might have passed for an unremarkable human if not for her disturbingly pale eyes—which was important, as the occasional human still happened upon this place. Not as many as in years past, but Elander still vaguely recalled a time when the nearby villages would leave offerings at the base of the false mountain. They built pyres in the pavilion too, where they would burn messages for their deceased loved ones and for the god and spirits who tended to the lost.

"Hello, Death," Nephele said as she approached. "You look a bit...anxious. Does this not feel like a homecoming for you?"

"One I would rather have skipped," he replied.

"Well, we aren't enjoying our visit either, for what

it's worth." She looked toward Inya, who had gone back to the pillar. The other goddess was now stepping in and out of the shadow of the towering obelisk, examining her hands in both the sunlight and shadows.

"What is she doing?"

Nephele exhaled a slow, slightly flustered breath. "It's been a while since she took a more human-like form. She keeps getting distracted by it; it's apparently very strange to her to not have glowing skin."

He watched as Inya picked at one of those muted swirls on her skin, as though that might make it glow again.

"Speaking of strange things," Nephele said, beckoning him as she turned and started toward the false mountain, "follow me. There's something you need to see."

Elander was eager to finish whatever business needed taken care of here—and to then get as far away from this place as possible—so he complied without any more questions.

They walked a winding path away from the pools and pavilion, Caden trailing behind them. Inya joined them as they passed. Nephele's fingers kept absently brushing over her skin, same as her fellow goddess; she was just more subtle about it. This empire and its lack of divine magic made it difficult for them to appear even in a subdued form, and all of the magical energy that *was* present in this particular location was derived from

Malaphar—which meant these two goddesses of the Sun Court were as out of their element as they could possibly be.

But whatever discomfort she felt, the Goddess of Storms kept a steady pace through it. She was almost to the base of the mountain when she veered off toward a rocky escarpment and started to pick her way down it. At the bottom of this slope was her apparent destination —a large pit that appeared bottomless. The air above it swirled occasionally with a foreboding, shadowy energy.

Elander crouched beside the edge of this abyss and cautiously peered down.

An enormous amount of that shadowy energy washed up and over him, the likes of which he hadn't felt since his last encounter with the Rook God. He fought off a shiver as he sensed Nephele drawing closer.

"What do you make of this?" she asked.

He couldn't answer right away; he was too busy staring.

Because in the center of the crater, something was suddenly moving—a tumbling mass of faint, golden light. One without definite shape or size, but which carried a definite energy that separated it from the other energy around it. It pulsed beneath the shadowy veil that covered the crater—bright one moment, squeezed back into darkness by invisible chains in the next.

Without any further comment, Nephele reached out her hand, and with obvious effort, she pushed through the dark magic drenching the air and summoned a few bolts of her own magic. Lightning struck the space above the chasm. Those chains that had been invisible became more obvious, now, revealed as the lightning sparked and died against them.

The mass of golden light tumbled more violently. A bit more brightly. It seemed to be trying to rise up to meet Nephele's power, and as Elander stared, he would have sworn he saw a clear figure emerging amongst the tumultuous energy for a brief moment...only to be pushed back down an instant later.

He glanced up at Nephele, his eyes demanding an explanation.

"We did as you suggested," she said. "A gathering of our divine court, that is. And once the four of us were together, we tried to summon the attention of the Sun Goddess...only to be met with silence. But we *did* experience a strange surge of power."

The Moon Goddess came to stand on his other side, and she elaborated, her airy voice trembling slightly: "Faint, yet unmistakable once we truly focused our collective energy on it. So we followed it, and it led us to..." She seemed too overcome to finish, suddenly.

"This," Nephele finished for her.

Elander straightened back to his full height and took a wary step backward. "Yes, but what *is* this?"

"We still aren't entirely sure. But it resembles the same shadowy bindings you once maintained around troublesome monsters, doesn't it? Does it feel the same, too?"

It did, now that he focused on it.

But that was not a *monster* he'd seen a moment ago.

The dark skin swirled with distinctive gold patterns, the dark waves of hair, a glimpse of white wings...this was the form that Solatis had often taken when she walked among the mortal realms. He was almost certain of it.

"So the goddess is not simply sleeping, but trapped?" wondered Caden.

"Trapped?" The word felt foreign on Elander's tongue. Strange and...*impossible*. "By who?"

"Who do you think?" asked Nephele.

He had a guess, of course, but it seemed equally impossible. "How could Malaphar have done this? He doesn't hold this kind of power over her."

"That is the question we've been wrestling with," said Inya.

"And we've come to suspect that *you* might be partly responsible," said Nephele. "Think about it... do you really believe it was all your own doing, lasting this long after you crossed Malaphar? He isn't known for his patience, even toward his once-favored servants like you. But he has yet to kill you. Maybe because he *couldn't*." Elander shook his head, but she continued anyway. "You told me that the Heart of the Sun activated for you in Oblivion, driving him away when he should have ended you then and there."

"Yes, but—"

"And you *also* told me that Casia's magic did not surface until she met you."

He stared at her, still trying to come up with an argument, but unable to do so.

"Solatis could have taken that magic you stole back, presumably. But she didn't. Instead, she guided Casia back into this world and left that magic inside of her— perhaps even amplified it—to help protect her for some reason. And maybe she granted some magic and protection to you too." Her gaze shifted to the ball of golden light, which had grown fainter. Her tone became strangely detached, as if guarding against sorrow, as she added, "Whatever Solatis gave, whatever she did, I suspect it left her drained enough that the Dark God was able to trap her here. This is how he's been causing so much havoc as of late—the Fading Sickness, monsters like the garmora, and who knows what else. Most of that started soon after you stole from the Sun Goddess, didn't it?"

"It's been decades since that happened," he said. "How did you not realize she was here before now?"

Nephele pursed her lips.

Inya tilted her face toward him. "Have you fallen so far that you truly forget what time is like for the divine?

This may have been escalating for decades, but that is the blink of an eye to us."

"It's been decades since you've been to this gateway yourself," Caden quietly pointed out.

"And the Moraki have been known to disappear for longer stretches," added Nephele. "They come and go as they please—and why would we have assumed *this* was the reason for her absence? It isn't like this sort of complication happens every age. Or in *any* age before this one, to my knowledge."

Unprecedented.

That was the word he'd said to Casia, and it came to mind now, bringing a sinking, gut-wrenching feeling with it. There was no map to fixing any of this. It was fully uncharted territory.

The four of them stood in the middle of that strange territory for a long moment, each lost in their troubled thoughts until Caden finally interrupted the silence. "So if something happens to Casia and the magic she carries..." he began, uncertainly.

"Like death, or her fully ascending into the Dark God's control?" Nephele suggested.

"...Then whatever part of Solatis's power resides in her will be permanently out of the Sun Goddess's reach?"

"Yes. That's what I fear." Nephele's eyes glazed over, briefly lost in thought once more before she added, "This is probably the *real* reason he wanted to get his hands on Casia. He is trying to do away with the one being who has kept him in control all of these years by killing off whatever parts of her power he can. Or pulling it into his control... by getting a carrier of this power to make a stupid bargain with him." She cut her eyes toward Elander. "I honestly don't know why Solatis would choose to give you two fools *any* magic."

"You also gave Casia magic," Elander reminded her. "And you're currently helping fool number two."

"Against my better judgment," she mumbled.

"The goddess has a reason, I'm certain," Inya insisted. "Maybe she believes Casia is meant for greatness? She does have a history of empowering humans."

That last part was true enough. It was Solatis who had convinced the Rook God to bless humankind with knowledge. Solatis who had convinced the other divine beings to bless mortals with magic, even after the mistakes they'd made with the elves, and Solatis who had stayed close to those mortals for far longer than the other two Moraki had.

But Nephele's lip was curled in distaste. She was more fond of humans than most of the other Marr, even now, but perhaps not fond enough to believe that one of them might be worth such trust and sacrifice from her upper-goddess.

"We can ask her why she did it whenever we wake her up and free her," suggested Caden.

"If we can, certainly," said Nephele. "The question is

how to do that. We've been trying to pool our magic, to send it toward her and draw a response, but the air here is stifling it." She reached into the inner pocket of the long coat she wore and pulled out a small object—the Heart of the Sun itself. "And this has shown no signs of life, either," she said, offering it to Elander.

They were all silent for several more contemplative moments. Elander turned the Heart over and around in his hands. Nephele's comment regarding the stifling air made him think about his conversation with Casia yesterday, about that sacred spot near the northern shore and her theory that it might help the full power of her Sun magic surface.

He explained this theory, and when he'd finished, Nephele and Caden wore identical, skeptical looks.

But hope flickered briefly on Inya's face. "If Casia could fully awaken the Sun magic that is dormant inside of her, it might be enough to do what we cannot. Particularly if our court can keep directing power toward Solatis as well."

"Or that part of her power could be forever diluted," said Nephele, "now that it's within Casia—too diluted to ever be truly recovered. And so we could all be doomed."

Elander shot her a look.

"Sorry. That's me being unhelpful again, isn't it?" Her apology rang hollow, as they typically did—if she bothered with them at all. "What a mess we have." She folded her arms across her chest and went back to staring at that faint, trapped light below them.

"We need to hope that Casia can be the missing piece," said the Moon Goddess.

"There are far worse things we could be putting our hope in," Elander said.

Nephele sniffed at this. "I think you might be biased."

The two of them exchanged another tense glare, prompting Caden to clear his throat and redirect the conversation. "Are you ready for some more worrisome news?"

Elander wasn't, but he nodded for him to continue anyway.

"Varen is not in Ciridan. He was reported to be leading his troops back to that capital city, but he never arrived there."

"Then where is he?" demanded Elander.

"I haven't been able to get an exact location. I've spoken to various witnesses, and stolen what information I could with my magic, but I haven't been able to pinpoint a definite spot. But he's somewhere near Malgraves as best I can tell. Which is, as our bad luck would have it, very close to those northern shores. If he catches wind of our plan to go to Dawnskeep...well, that's another possible wrinkle to that plan."

Elander breathed out a curse. "We need to get back to Moreth with this information."

Caden nodded, already heading back up the hill, away from the pit and the overwhelming, chaotic energy it was giving off. Inya followed him, but Elander hesitated, staring into that chaotic chasm for another moment.

"You're weaker than you were the last time we met, Kerse," Nephele said, quiet enough for only him to hear. "I can sense it. And your servant told me what's happening with that bargain Casia made."

"And?"

"And yet you stay by her side and let her drain you. What are you going to do if she takes every last drop of magic from you? How do you plan to keep fighting if that happens?"

"With a sword," he replied. "I'm quite good with those, in case you'd forgotten."

"A lot of good you'll be with one if you're *dead.*"

"We don't know exactly what will happen. The rise and fall of a Marr has never happened like this before, has it? Maybe we'll get lucky."

Nephele appeared deeply unimpressed by this answer. "You're an idiot," she said.

"Yes, I think you've mentioned that before. Many times, actually."

"And yet it doesn't seem to be sinking in. She is not worth such reckless—"

"*Enough,*" he snarled.

Nephele's irritation flared, and with it came sparks

of her magic. But those flashes of lightning were quickly smothered by the Dark power hovering around them.

That darkness continued to build, drawing around Elander, pushing away the weariness he felt from his earlier travels. The goddess took a step back. She was the stronger, divine one between them, perhaps, but this was not her territory.

"I don't care if you call me an idiot," he continued in a low, dangerous voice, "but if you say one more ill word against *her*, then you are going to see, firsthand, just how much power I still have."

Frustration sparked in her violet eyes, and her lips parted, prepared to fire back. But she ultimately held her tongue.

"I won't let her face this alone," he said. "And there is nothing you could say to change my mind about that. *Nothing*."

She closed her mouth and set her jaw.

He didn't wait around for her to unclench that jaw. He simply turned away and started up the hill. "We'll need to plan for that trip to Dawnskeep as though Varen intends to meet us there," he said as he reached Caden. "The more allies we can have close by and ready to protect Casia while she carries out her mission in that place, the better."

He glanced back, saw that Nephele's lips remained stubbornly pursed, and so he instead looked to Inya. "You'll be able to rally the rest of your court into directing their magic toward Solatis, as you suggested?"

"Perhaps. Though Cepheid has been...hesitant about getting involved thus far," she said.

Elander frowned, though this was not particularly surprising; the Star Goddess had a fickle nature. She was wildly unpredictable when it came to what she would and wouldn't do— particularly when it came to matters that concerned humans.

"And the Goddess of Sky?" he asked.

Nephele finally uncrossed her arms and rejoined the conversation. "Currently confronting the Fire God about his reckless attack on her haven," she said, nodding toward the Moon Goddess.

"She was not pleased to hear of his behavior," added Inya, looking vaguely amused.

Those two had a bit of history as he recalled. But like so many other things, the full details of that history were lost among the wreckage of his fall from divinity. The familiar ache of not being a true part of any realm, mortal or divine, washed through him. But he shook it off more quickly this time; he had too many other things to worry about.

"As for more allies to cover your charge into Dawnskeep," Nephele added, somewhat hesitantly, "I have followers I could send, I suppose. It will take time —maybe a plea to the Air spirit that serves Namu...but I can arrange for them to meet you in the north, one way or another."

"We can send word to Soryn too," Caden suggested. "She may have allies already close to there."

"The more, the better," Elander agreed.

"And I can send a guide," offered Inya, "to help Casia find her way through the power that veils that place."

Elander took a deep breath. "It's all settled then. We might actually have a chance to pull this off."

"A very small one," Nephele said, drily.

His gaze locked on hers, and her fierce expression softened. Just for an instant. Likely the closest she would come to admitting that she was concerned this might be the last plan they made together—the last goodbye said between them.

"Any followers you can send will be of great help to us," he told her. "So thank you."

She stiffened. Then nodded. A silent understanding seemed to pass between them, as it always—*eventually* —did.

They both knew that it was reckless, marching into this battle with his magic—his very *existence*—in such a state of flux. There were far too many ways things could end poorly for him.

And they both knew that he was going to march into that battle, anyway.

Caden was moving again, putting more space between himself and the crushing magical forces of this place, preparing to focus on traveling back to Moreth.

Elander started to follow him, but he paused as Nephele called out to him.

"I hope she's worth this chance of ruin."

He turned back to his old friend one last time. "And then some," he said.

AFTER WORKING through a few lingering details with the two goddesses, Elander pocketed the Heart of the Sun, caught up to Caden, and the two of them returned to the outskirts of the elven realm.

He wished he was returning with better news. Last night had been a hard-won victory, and they had scarcely had time to celebrate that new alliance with Moreth's army, or to even work out the details of said alliance, and now...this.

It was already a lot to ask of Casia, to fight her way into Dawnskeep and do what no other human had done before—try to break free of that ascension mark. And now she apparently needed to break Solatis's chains, too...*and* she might have to do it all with her brother snapping at her heels.

And what would become of the Sky Goddess's confrontation? Would there be fallout from that to deal with as well? His thoughts were suddenly filled with images of fire hounds and more beasts made of ice. His former court had countless other weapons at their disposal, he knew, and if the Court of the Sun could not keep them in check...

He felt sick at the thought.

All their wars were converging, building into a dangerous wave that was going to break over them as soon as they left the safety of Moreth behind.

"Ready to be the harbinger of doom?" Caden asked.

Elander huffed out a laugh. "I suppose I have enough experience at it." His laughter died abruptly as the gate and bridge to Moreth came into view.

It was shut, as expected, but the ones who were supposed to open it were nowhere to be seen.

An uneasy shiver went through him. "There should have been guards here to let us in."

Caden frowned. "Perhaps it's just an oversight? Have we arrived during a shift change?"

Elander shook his head. "Something feels wrong," he muttered, and though he knew it was pointless, he placed a hand against the gate's cold bars, and he tried to summon his magic—magic that could neutralize most things.

But it only darkened the air for a brief moment, and then it faded against the wall of elven power.

Cursing the elves and their backwards magic, he started to withdraw the knife strapped to his leg. The Death power it was infused with tingled to life at his touch, but Caden put a hand on his arm before he could strike at the gate's locks.

"That isn't going to do any good either," Caden said.

Elander knew he was right. It still took effort to remove his hand from the weapon, to resist the urge to start wildly stabbing at things. It wasn't like him to panic, but something about this just felt...*off.*

"Let's circle the grounds," said Caden. "Maybe there's another gate we can use." He moved off to the left.

Elander went the opposite direction, searching— hoping Caden was correct.

But there was nothing to the right except an impossibly high wall of polished white stone. It stretched on beyond what he could see, covered in vines that started to crawl and lash toward him whenever he got too close.

He backed away from the wall, and he paused and lifted his hand, studying the mark on his skin as he remembered the last conversation he'd had with Casia.

Nowhere you can go that I can't find you.

He tried summoning again, and this time he closed his eyes and focused, waiting to see if Casia's own Death power rose in response. Any magic between them would have been muted because of the damn elvish air, but it should have still been powerful enough for him to at least *sense* it. He would have settled for even a flicker of that energy. Just enough to know she was still *alive.*

But minutes passed, and nothing came.

"Found the guards," Caden called a moment later. His voice sounded oddly hollow.

A cold sweat washed over Elander as he turned and raced to Caden's side.

And there they were.

One, two, three guards, all of them dead, their limp bodies all impaled upon separate trees.

CHAPTER 24

ELANDER HAD BEEN GONE FOR TWO DAYS, AND CAS WAS beginning to worry.

"Lady Casia?"

She gave her head a little shake, refocusing on the elven man standing before her—General Kolvar—who had spent most of the morning assaulting her with questions and thinly-veiled criticism. Prince Alder trusted this man immensely, but he had warned Cas that the general could be extremely cold and unapologetically blunt.

So far, that description was proving accurate.

And he already seemed to be losing his patience with her, and perhaps doubting his Prince's decision to support her in the first place.

"The northern shores?" he prompted in his gruff voice.

She met his hard gaze and managed to hold it. "Yes. That will be our next target; Prince Alder told me you had several soldiers that were more familiar with the area, and that they might be able to guide us into that territory."

He nodded. "We'll need plenty of help covering our descent into such a place. How many shall we aim for?"

How did one plan for a possibly deadly trek into the unknown? She felt like she should know that by now. But she didn't. She didn't hesitate in her answer, however, because she didn't want him to *realize* that she didn't know. "A hundred strong, at least."

If he disagreed with the number, he gave no indication of it. He simply nodded again, and then he turned to the elven woman beside him and gave her a quick series of commands in the language of their realm.

As he did, a sudden tingling across Cas's skin threatened to once again steal her focus.

This kept happening—little bits of energy shooting through her, drawing chill bumps along her skin—and this was why she was growing increasingly worried and distracted.

It felt like Death magic.

Like the subtle but powerful waves of cold she felt whenever Elander was nearby. But he *wasn't* nearby as far as anyone knew. And every time she tried to grab his energy more tightly, that sensation of him slipped from her grasp, leaving her feeling ever more hollow and confused in its absence.

General Kolvar's attention had shifted back to her.

She took a deep breath. "Unless there's anything else you need from me, General..."

"Not at the moment," he replied tersely. His gaze remained hard and unflinching. Still sizing her up. She should have stayed longer and tried to make a more imposing impression, maybe...

But they had been at this for *hours* now, and she was tired. She needed to breathe fresh air—to see faces that were friendlier than the general's—so she excused herself and went to seek those things.

After a meandering walk, she found what she was looking for in a courtyard adjacent to one of Prince Alder's many offices; Nessa, Rhea, and Zev were sitting on a group of benches gathered around a bubbling fountain, enjoying their lunch. Silverfoot was perched on the edge of the fountain, snapping at the bugs skimming across the rippling surface of the water.

The Prince was in that adjacent office—the door was made up of glass panels, so Cas could see that he was deep in conversation with Laurent. Their words were muffled by the glass, but judging by Laurent's unusually animated movements, it looked as if they might have been on the verge of an argument.

She watched them for a moment, until Laurent appeared to grow calmer, and then she greeted her other friends and slumped down onto the bench next to Nessa.

She'd meant to speak beyond that greeting. But her gaze caught on the fountain's centerpiece—a tree of white stone, with water flowing from its various branches—and her attention stayed there. It was mesmerizing, and somehow comforting, watching the unnaturally blue water pouring out in an endless loop.

"You okay?" Nessa asked, nudging her.

"Fine." Cas sat up a little straighter. "Why?"

"Because you look like you're thinking of drowning yourself in the fountain."

"It's because she's gone almost an entire two *days* without her lover," Zev teased. "Poor, pathetic thing."

Cas's reply was flat. "I can survive without him for more than two days." Zev kept grinning like a fool at her, so she narrowed her eyes and added, "Which, incidentally, is much longer than *you* seem to be able to go without sticking it in one of the ladies of this court. So honestly, who's the pathetic one here?"

He arched a brow. "Nothing pathetic about what I was sticking in those ladies, I assure you."

Nessa groaned.

Rhea got to her feet. "And with that," she said, "I'm excusing myself from this conversation. I need to go check on the messages we sent to Soryn, anyway. We should have replies by now." She clicked her tongue, and Silverfoot—who was halfway in the fountain at this point—crawled out of the water, bounded to her side, and gave his fur a quick shake. His glowing eyes fixed on each of their group in turn, and Rhea added, "In the meantime, the three of you make sure you *behave*."

"I always do," Zev told her, which drew a laugh from Nessa and a sigh from both Rhea and Cas.

It wasn't long after his sister left that Zev started to grow visibly restless and announced his own departure.

"Off to invade the bedrooms of more unsuspecting ladies of the court?" Nessa guessed.

He stood and stretched lazily, like a cat shaking loose after a nap in the sun. "If they're lucky," he said with a wink.

Once the two of them were alone, Nessa turned to Cas with a wistful smile. "At what point do we stage an intervention for our wayward brother?"

Cas started to answer, to tell her that Laurent had already attempted this with no luck—but she was interrupted by the voice of Prince Alder. It was once again rising to a level that sounded unmistakably hostile.

She and Nessa exchanged a concerned look.

"Wonder what they're arguing about?"

"No idea," Cas replied. She tried to shrug it off, but it was so...strange to see the two of them going at it like this. It wasn't like Laurent to raise his voice, and it didn't *seem* like the Prince she'd gotten to know over this past week, either.

She wanted to get close enough to hear, but it would have been difficult to do it discreetly.

"How'd it go with General Kolvar?" Nessa asked. "It seemed like he was being difficult; I started to rescue you several times, but Rhea insisted I let you be."

Cas managed a small smile. "He isn't that bad. But I'm not sure I've made the greatest impression on him."

Nessa waved this assessment away. "You're too hard on yourself."

Cas hesitated, unsure if she wanted to tell this next part. She wanted to believe it was nothing to worry about, but... "I keep getting distracted by little flares of magic too," she said as she picked at a few chips of loose stone on the bench.

"Magic?"

"Elander's," she clarified. "It's as though he's close, but the air in this realm is making it hard to tell *how* close."

Nessa's eyebrows drew together, and a frown threatened to drag down the corners of her lips. "The air in this place is definitely strange. Maybe you could ask the Prince about it?"

"Maybe."

"Once they're done arguing," she added, glancing worriedly over her shoulder at the sound of another shout.

They sat in silence for a moment, listening to more

of those muffled shouts, until uneasiness brought Cas to her feet.

She strolled down one of the nearby paths, pacing between the tree-shaped fountain and a second, dragon-shaped one. She hugged her arms against herself and drummed her fingers upon her elbow, counting each tap. When that didn't help settle her queasy stomach, she closed her eyes and tilted her head back in thought for a moment.

She had just decided to go intervene in Laurent's argument when Nessa suddenly called over to her in a dazed, uncertain little voice.

"He has a sword in his hand."

"What?"

"Why is he..." Nessa trailed off with a gasp.

Cas strode toward her with quick steps, followed her horrified gaze—

Her eyes found Laurent just as he lifted his sword and plunged it into the Prince's neck.

CHAPTER 25

CAS WAS TOO STUNNED TO MOVE AT FIRST.

But Nessa was already stumbling—and then sprinting—for the door.

Cas broke from her stupor, caught her before her fumbling hands could wrench that door open, and pulled her back into the courtyard.

The inner doors of the office flew open. Guards poured in. They quickly surrounded Laurent. He didn't put up a fight—it would have been pointless, given the number that swarmed him.

Cas kept her arms wrapped tightly around Nessa, kept Nessa's face firmly buried against her so that she couldn't lift it up and see the horror unfolding before them.

Nessa fought her for a moment, until shock overcame her and she simply crumpled against Cas's chest, her hands clenched tightly in Cas's shirt to keep herself from slumping all the way to the ground.

So she didn't see the way the guards roughly took hold of Laurent, or the way one of those guards whipped something from the bag at his side and slammed it over Laurent's mouth—something that immediately caused Laurent's head to loll lifelessly about.

She didn't see the unnatural sprawl of Prince Alder's body either, or the crimson spraying from his neck and pooling around him, or the sword that fell from Laurent's suddenly limp hand and clattered against the bloody floor, or the way the guards callously dragged Laurent's body from the room.

"Breathe," Cas whispered, as much to herself as Nessa. "Deep breaths."

One of the guards turned his gaze on them, and Cas suddenly couldn't follow her own advice.

Her head told her to run.

Her heart told her to do whatever it took to chase Laurent down, to fight her way to his side. She couldn't just leave him at the mercy of those guards.

And where would they run, anyway?

How would they get out of this?

"Stay behind me," she quietly ordered Nessa. Then she was moving numbly forward, her hands lifted in a gesture of peace. She had no real plan beyond stalling for time so she could *think* of a plan.

But as she crossed the threshold into the Prince's

office, another woman was entering from the other side, and at the sight of her all of Cas's thoughts crashed to a stop.

Lady Sarith.

She froze in the doorway as her gaze fell upon the fallen Prince.

One of the guards bowed his head and said something in the Morethian language. Sarith's breath hitched, and she braced her hand against the doorframe, steadying herself for several long, tense breaths. Then she slowly knelt and picked up the sword that was coated in her husband's blood.

The tip of it was against Cas's throat a moment later.

Everything around Cas seemed to stop, and then to disappear—all save for that sword at her throat and Lady Sarith and her bulging, fury-filled eyes.

"Tell me why he did it," said the lady in a trembling voice.

But Cas couldn't, because she didn't *know*.

"TELL ME!"

Cas reflexively staggered backward at the booming command, and Lady Sarith followed like a wolf closing in on a kill. The sword dug into the hollow of Cas's throat, and the pressure made her reply come out in a cough. "I—I don't know why he did it!"

Lady Sarith's eyes were still wide, more white than green. The blade shook in her hands. She took a deep breath and seethed out more commands, this time for her guards. "Round up her companions. Take them all to the *proper* dungeons this time. Except for this one." She threw the blade to the ground, not even blinking as the metal clanged against the tiled floor, and never once taking her glare from Cas. "I want to talk to her in private."

It grew so silent that Cas could hear the beat of her own heart, drowned out only occasionally by Nessa's shallow, frightened breaths.

Lady Sarith dropped to her husband's side. Her shaking hand reached toward his neck. The skirts of her dress smeared blood over the white tiles.

Then the entire room seemed to be converging on Cas at once, a blur of guards twisting her arms behind her back, holding them there until someone strode into the room carrying shackles to properly bind her with.

They took Nessa in the next instant. A hand went over her mouth—one apparently holding the same toxic substance they'd used against Laurent, because she immediately began to cough and sputter. Her chin tipped heavily toward her chest. As she slipped from consciousness, their eyes briefly met, and Cas tried to call out to her. To tell her they would be okay, that things would not end here.

But there was no time.

They were pulled in separate directions, and Cas's shout died a painful death in her throat.

. . .

THEY TOOK her to a small room on the highest floor.

Her hands were bound behind a chair. It faced a desk littered with papers, and behind that, a blank wall. The walls were blank and painted a dark shade of grey that made the low lighting of the room feel even more oppressive.

They left her alone in that near-darkness for what felt like hours.

Finally, the door behind her creaked open.

Lady Sarith strode in, her boots making loud *clicks* upon the floor.

The door stayed open, allowing a few weak rays of light to shine in from the hallway. Cas kept her eyes on one of these rays, but she could hear what sounded like at least two guards hovering, shuffling into place by that door behind her.

Lady Sarith settled down at the desk. Her husband's blood had stained most of her dress, and her hands were still splattered with drops of it.

She didn't speak.

The silence stretched, heavy and ominous, until Cas couldn't take it anymore. "I don't know what happened," she whispered. "I didn't—"

"Be quiet." Lady Sarith's eyes were no longer wild. They were glazed over and disturbingly... *empty*. She still looked as though she intended to kill something; she was just going to be quieter about doing it.

Cas subtly searched the room for weapons, for exits,

for a sign of Sarith's weaknesses—for *anything* she could use to her advantage. Her heart was aching. Her mind, a disaster. She could hardly begin to process all that had happened. She only knew she couldn't die here, no matter how badly she might have wanted to. Dying would have been easier.

But she had to come up with a plan.

At least several minutes passed before Lady Sarith finally broke the silence, her voice chillingly calm. "What a messy means to an end *that* turned out to be."

Cas jerked her gaze back to her, and she found her studying a bit of blood on one of her nails, frowning as though that spot of congealed gore was the worst thing to have happened today.

A means to an end?

A series of terrifying possibilities flickered through Cas's thoughts. Her heart raced faster. And though she hadn't successfully controlled *any* of her magic since entering this realm, desperation suddenly made her want to try again.

The hair on her arms began to lift as she concentrated on the Storm power sleeping inside of her. The air wavered. Brightened a bit, maybe.

"Oh, I wouldn't do that," Sarith warned.

The sound of swords being unsheathed rang through the room.

"Not unless you think your suppressed magic can be quicker than my guards."

Cas took a deep breath.

Could it be quicker?

She doubted it; just her brief hesitation had been enough to stifle what she'd started to summon.

While Sarith spoke Morethian to those guards in a low voice, Cas went back to darting her eyes around the space, searching for another way out of this latest mess.

She glimpsed a stretch of flat roof through the room's only window, and she was in the middle of testing the shackles around her wrists and crafting an— admittedly reckless—escape attempt when her gaze fell on a stack of letters on a corner shelf.

They were too far away to read, but they caught her attention because they all shared the same handwriting, the same parchment type, the same color wax seal... She narrowed her eyes on the letter closest to her. A ribbon of light from the hallway fell on it just so, illuminating the bottom and allowing her to see what was stamped there.

It was a black tiger, rearing on its hind legs with its jaws opened and its claws swiping.

The symbol of the House of Solasen.

Of her brother.

And suddenly the day's events began to make a terrifying kind of sense.

"Nosy, aren't we?" mused Lady Sarith.

Fury briefly burned away Cas's fear, and it made her voice bolder than before. "What is going on?"

"I would think it was obvious enough," said the elven lady as she stood, walked over and picked up those letters, and then plunked them into a drawer of the desk.

"What did he promise you in exchange for me?"

She laughed, but otherwise didn't reply.

"It must not have been a very impressive deal if you don't want to tell me about it," Cas goaded.

A muscle in Lady Sarith's jaw twitched. It was only another moment before pride pushed a response out of her. "It was simple enough. If I could imprison you here —isolate you from your followers, trap you in a place where you and your magic could not interfere with his plans—then he would help me deal with those annoying Queens of Ethswen. Help us reclaim the lands and resources that their kingdom stole from us, and then some."

"He's lying."

"Yes, my husband said the same thing. Then you came along, and all of a sudden he decided he wanted to ally with a Solasen after all—and the weaker one at that. And look where *that* got him."

Cas briefly closed her eyes, steadying herself as images of Prince Alder's partially-decapitated head flooded her mind. "So, because of some strange, misplaced jealousy toward me, you decided to—"

Lady Sarith closed the space between them so

swiftly that it made Cas recoil, sending her chair teetering dangerously onto its back legs.

"Let me make one thing perfectly clear," Lady Sarith said, putting her boot onto the chair and slamming it back to the floor. "If I'd cared about my husband's various *affections*, then I probably would have taken offense to the myriad of women he paraded in and out of our so-called sacred bed. But I didn't. I took offense to his *weakness*."

Cas's lungs felt painfully tight as she tried to force air into them.

"For my entire childhood, I watched the lands and power of my people dwindle," said Lady Sarith as she took a step back. "My father was a Lord of Mistwilde, you know —and he was very close to their sorry excuse for a king. I grew up in the palace, and so I had an up-close view of the failings of that king. I lived through sieges and helped see off countless armies that returned to us in pieces—if they came back at all. Do you know how many vigils I attended as a child? How many dead faces I've seen? Dead faces that eventually included my father and brothers. And then I was married off into this family, in this new realm, and I learned quickly that my father-in-law cared more about throwing lavish parties and sleeping around than he did about securing his realm's future. So I swore to myself that *I* would secure it—whatever it took—lest Moreth end up in the same sorry state as my home."

A chill wound through Cas as she thought about King Theren's sudden, unexpected death.

Had Lady Sarith had something to do with it?

Had Varen bribed her into doing that too?

"Alder was just as useless as his father. And he was afraid to align himself with someone so powerful and ruthless as Varen," Sarith continued. "But a touch of ruthlessness is needed in this chaotic world, I think. And luckily for this realm, I can be that hard-hearted leader that my husband so *tragically* could not. I had hoped it wouldn't come to all of this. But he made a mistake, siding with you. I only did what was necessary to correct that mistake. And I will *continue* to do whatever it takes to secure things."

"Including killing anyone who disagrees with you?"

She put a hand over her heart. "*I* didn't kill my husband. His angry little brother did."

The gravity of the situation settled fully over Cas once more, and her voice cracked a bit as she said, "You had *something* to do with it."

"You think so? Or perhaps you simply don't know Laurent as well as you thought you did."

Cas refused to even acknowledge the possibility of this.

"The roots of this court run twisted and deep," said Sarith. "And Laurent is a product of this court, even though he tried to escape from it. He had demons you don't know about. Ones you couldn't possibly understand."

"*Liar*," Cas snarled.

She smirked. "Even if I *was* lying, it wouldn't matter. Your friend killed our King before he even had a chance to put on the crown. The evidence is overwhelmingly against him, and no one here is going to believe otherwise. No one here is going to help you."

Cas tried again to loosen the bindings against her wrists, but it was useless.

She sat up straighter in her chair and lifted her chin as Lady Sarith once again drew uncomfortably close.

"Which means that you're mine to do whatever I wish with," she said, in a voice that made Cas's pulse race to a dangerous, dizzying speed. "And something tells me that the nastier I treat you, the more favor I can gain with Varen. Wouldn't you agree?"

Cas didn't reply.

Sarith tilted her head to the side, studying her. "He'll be sending a messenger to check on my end of our deal soon, I suspect. So let's make sure you look the part of a tortured prisoner, shall we?"

She struck with no more warning than that, slapping hard across Cas's jaw.

Cas's teeth caught her tongue. Blood filled her mouth. She spat at Sarith's feet, showering her boots with flecks of red-tinged spit.

With a furious snap of her fingers, Sarith summoned

the guards from the door. She ordered something in the Moreth language, and a moment later, the chain between Cas's shackles was being loosened. The guards worked together, yanking her hands away from her back and instead fastening them together in front of her.

"Stand up," Sarith ordered.

Cas stood, working the pain from her jaw and subtly testing the strength of her newly arranged bindings.

One of the guards disappeared into the hallway for a moment, only to quickly return with a bundle of cloths which he handed to Lady Sarith—who took one and immediately flung it at Cas.

"Clean up the mess you made," she snapped.

Cas inhaled deeply. She moved to comply only because those two guards were still extremely close, and both had a tight, ready grip on their swords—and she still refused to die here, no matter how bleak things looked.

Lady Sarith sneered down at her as she worked. "This seems a more fitting vocation than a queen, or a war hero, or whatever it was you were aspiring to be."

Cas kept scrubbing, fighting the urge to see if she could send a bolt of lightning shooting up the leg attached to the boot she was cleaning.

"You know," said Sarith after a minute, "I rather like the idea of you being my little servant. Varen wanted you alive for some reason—and I was debating following through on that—but this could be a nice compromise, I suppose."

Almost every muscle in Cas's body recoiled at this idea. *Almost.* But she held her tongue.

Because that disgusting idea also felt like an opportunity.

Something strange had happened in that office between Laurent and his brother. She had no proof that Laurent had somehow been framed, but she felt it in her heart. And if Lady Sarith locked her away with the rest of her friends, she would not be able to find the proof she needed. But servants could move more freely than prisoners.

So it was only a matter of seizing the opportunity.

"I would rather be dead than serve you," said Cas in a quiet, seething voice.

Predictably, Lady Sarith's eyes lit up at this. "Well that settles it then." Her gaze fell to Cas's clenched hands. "Keep the rag. And you can start your service to me by cleaning up the blood your friend spilled."

No part of Cas wanted to enter that room.

But her plan was off to a promising start, and there could be no hesitation now.

One of the guards grabbed her arm and jerked her into motion. She resisted just enough to keep her ruse believable, and then she bowed her head, feigning defeat, as she was led from the room and marched back downstairs.

Her skin tingled as they approached the scene of the Prince's murder. Not as strongly as when she'd encountered the dead or dying outside of this realm, but enough to remind her that the Dark God's power still lurked inside of her, waiting for its opportunity to rise once more.

She pushed it down as best she could, focusing instead on studying her surroundings.

Prince Alder's body had, mercifully, been taken elsewhere. There were three other servants already working on cleaning the space, flittering about like nervous little birds collecting things for their nests. General Kolvar stood in the doorway leading out to the courtyard, his stern face looking even more grim than usual.

"They missed a few spots," grunted one of Cas's escorts, jerking her around and pointing her toward a section of red-smeared floor.

They had missed *several* spots.

Cas was provided with a bucket, which she took and filled in the fountain outside. She struggled to heave it out and carry it, given that her hands were still loosely bound in front of her. But she managed, all while under the silent, watchful gaze of the guards and General Kolvar.

As she knelt before the largest of the blood trails, she imagined herself someplace far, far away. Back in the house in Faircliff with its treehouse, perhaps—or in any of the other places she and her found family had called *home*.

She would get through this the same way she had gotten through everything else before now.

She went to work.

She counted each swipe of her rag. Up to ten, and then back down. Up and back, up and back in a soothing rhythm, grounding herself in the feel of the smooth, predictable motions.

This kept her calm for several minutes, until, without warning, the scene from earlier was playing through her mind with brutal clarity—the sword, the shouting, the awful, contorted shape of Prince Alder's fallen body...

Her fingers clenched the rag in her hand, squeezing pink-tinted water back onto the floor. All she could think about was Laurent. Where had they hauled him off to? Was he even still alive?

And what about the rest of her friends?

What in the hells happened here?

She felt a strange flicker in her temple, as if in response to her question.

She paused, staring at the stained rag.

A possibility occurred to her.

She took a deep breath, and slowly, tentatively, reached for a glob of blood next to her knee. Ran her finger over it.

Another quick throb in her temple, and this time it

was accompanied by images of the room flashing through her mind—but they were not her own memories, as before. They were from different angles, and they weren't clear, as if the scene playing out was underwater, wobbling and shifting as she watched.

Another tap against another speckle of blood, and she saw Laurent's face.

She realized what was happening, and her hand slipped against the wet marble, nearly causing her to lose her balance.

Death magic.

If not for the oppressive elven power surrounding her, she suspected she would have been flooded with visions of Prince Alder's last moments, as seen through his own eyes.

But maybe if she could concentrate, she could still see enough to answer some of the questions she had?

She wiggled the tension from her fingers and prepared to try again.

"Why did you stop?" came a low voice.

A woman was standing against the wall, watching her. Her bony face and long golden braid were vaguely familiar; she was one of the ladies of the court that Cas had often seen at Sarith's side.

How long had she been standing there?

What had she witnessed?

The others in the room froze as she sauntered toward Cas. As she crouched purposefully in front of her.

Her dark eyes shimmered with something akin to eagerness, as if she had only been waiting for this opportunity to berate. To punish. Cas thought of how often this woman—and all the other members of Lady Sarith's personal entourage—had stared daggers at her as she had maneuvered and bargained her way through this realm, and her chest tightened.

The woman hooked a finger under Cas's chin and lifted it. "I told my lady I would help keep an eye on you," she said. "She'll want a report of everything you've done. So, I'll ask you again. *Why did you stop?*"

Cas was still dizzy from the unintentional use of her magic, and she couldn't think of a lie quick enough.

This woman did not slap her as Lady Sarith had.

Her fist was closed as it collided with Cas's face, and the force behind the swing was enough to send Cas tumbling. With her hands bound, Cas couldn't catch herself properly, and her head slammed into the marble, leaving her even more dizzy than before. She blinked, trying to bring the room back into focus.

General Kolvar still stood in the doorway.

He looked away when a second blow fell—clearly disgusted—but he did nothing to stop it.

The elven woman grabbed a handful of Cas's hair and yanked her up, high enough to look her in the eyes. "Get back to work," she said, before dropping her back to the floor.

Pain blossomed through Cas's face. Anxiety wrapped

an oppressive hold around her lungs and stomach. Her eyes darted wildly around the room, searching for...

She didn't know.

General Kolvar still had his back to her. All the other beings within the room seemed equally determined not to look at her, and as dark spots danced in her vision, Lady Sarith's cold declaration whispered through her thoughts. *No one here is going to help you.*

And she feared it might be true.

CHAPTER 26

SEVERAL HOURS AND BEATINGS LATER, THE BLOOD WAS WIPED away, the office cleaned—along with several other rooms around it—and Lady Sarith ran out of tasks for Cas to do for the moment, so she sent her to the dungeons to wait for another summons.

It was not meant as a kindness, Cas knew. But the quiet and the dark of this lower level was a marginal deterrent to the throbbing pain in her head, for which she was grateful—even more so when she realized Nessa and Rhea were in the cell next to her, and that Zev was leaning against the back wall of her own enclosure.

Zev quickly got to his feet and wrapped her in an embrace. It was strong enough to hurt her battered body and make her head pound all the more painfully, but she didn't pull away. They stayed entangled in one another for at least a full minute, until he finally stepped back. His gaze fell on her swollen eye and lips.

"Cas, your face—"

"I'm fine."

He took several deep breaths, clearly fighting to hold back his anger.

"It could have been a lot worse," she said, moving away before he could inspect her more closely. She moved carefully through the near-darkness, seeking the rest of her friends.

Nessa was mostly unharmed, only a small cut under her eye and a lingering grogginess from whatever they'd drugged her with. Vertical bars separated them, but Cas was able to get her fingers through and squeeze Nessa's hand, and then Rhea's too, as Rhea felt her way over to them.

Rhea was fine physically. But Silverfoot was missing. She'd spent the past hours trying to connect to the magical link they shared without any success. Without his eyes, and with no more light than what a few torches in the hall outside were giving off, she was essentially blind—and clearly rattled by it.

It was so unusual to see her rattled that it threatened to make Cas even more anxious than she already was.

Nessa informed her that the Sadiran soldiers who had accompanied them into this realm had been marched past just recently, taken deeper into the dungeons. After a moment of watching for guards, Cas chanced a soft shout toward those soldiers, and they replied—so that was more of her allies accounted for.

Laurent, however, was nowhere to be seen.

She settled down onto the cold floor. For several minutes, she sat there in a half-daze, tapping her fingers, sorting through her thoughts, and waiting to make sure the guards were not hovering nearby and trying to eavesdrop.

"I don't think that was Laurent who killed Prince Alder."

Nessa had curled herself into a miserable ball, but now she lifted her head toward Cas, wearing a confused but cautiously hopeful look on her face.

"I was cleaning up the Prince's blood, and I...I think the Death magic inside of me reacted to it," Cas explained. "Elander used to read the dead for the royal family in Ciridan. They called him the Death Speaker, remember?"

Rhea nodded slowly. Nessa continued to look hopeful. And Zev was listening, at least, though he offered no comment from his place against the wall.

"I didn't get the details. I wasn't able to focus because I had guards and members of Lady Sarith's court breathing down my neck, but I could sense something of those last moments that Alder spent alive, and it was like...like a realization he was having. I don't know what that realization was exactly. But I have a plan to get the rest of the details."

Zev gave her a dubious look.

"I mean, well, I *sort of* have a plan."

A slight grin started to spread across his face. Cas knew that look well; it was the one he always got when he was thinking of a joke that was in no way appropriate for the seriousness of a given situation.

"Why are you smiling?"

"No reason. I was just thinking that 'She Sort of Had a Plan' will make a great epitaph on your imminent gravestone. And I volunteer to give your eulogy too—I already have the first line."

"Which is what?"

"*Casia died doing what she loved most...trying to carry out a half-assed plan.*"

"There's no way in the three hells I'd let you give my eulogy," Cas told him. "I don't want it to be filled with random tangents and awful, inappropriate jokes."

"You'll be dead, so how exactly are you going to stop me from giving it?"

"You do realize that if *I* die here, you will probably not be far behind?"

"Can we please stop being so morbid?" Nessa asked.

"I second that motion," said Rhea.

Zev shrugged. "What? I just think it's smart to start planning for these funerals—because at the rate we're going, there are a lot in our future."

Nessa made a soft noise of despair.

"Don't listen to him," Rhea said. "We'll be fine. If we could just *focus*, perhaps?"

Cas nodded. "So...Prince Alder's body is on display in the throne room—there's some sort of Morethian funeral rite that requires this, and Lady Sarith is apparently following through with the tradition."

"Probably to keep his supporters from giving her trouble," said Rhea.

"Probably," Cas agreed. "Anyway, I suspect his entire being might be easier to read than a few drops of dried blood. I just need to get to that body, and to be better prepared to try and use magic this time."

"The same magic that's so far proven particularly unreliable in this realm?" Zev asked.

Cas shot him a look.

"I'm just saying."

"I'm open to better ideas," she said.

"I've got nothing."

"Right—I generally assume that at this point, which is why I just proceed with my own half-assed ideas. Saves time."

"That's fair," he said with a shrug.

Their eyes met. He grinned at her, and they dissolved into quiet, nervous laughter until a wave of emotion—some strange mixture of fear and resolve—overcame Cas and stifled that laughter.

She took a deep breath. "So now I suppose there's nothing to do but wait."

HOURS LATER, while the others slept fitfully around her, Cas sat watching the dark hallway that stretched away from her cell.

She didn't move as a door creaked open in the distance, spilling light toward her. She hardly breathed as footsteps closed in. She didn't want to wake her friends, to alarm them—especially Nessa, who had cried herself to sleep.

She got to her feet and went to meet two guards as they approached.

"Lady Sarith has need of her servant girl," said the guard carrying the keys.

She nodded, and she glanced back one last time just as Zev's eyes popped open. She warned him into silence and stillness with a look, and then she quietly went with the two men.

She could feel Zev watching her go, could almost sense him fighting the urge to try and chase after her. She didn't glance back. She didn't want to encourage him.

The guards led her to the same upper room as before; she was beginning to suspect that they were trying to see how tired they could make her by marching her repeatedly up and down the stairs.

Lady Sarith was already in the room this time, bent over the desk and writing something that was already several pieces of parchment long.

A letter to Varen?

Cas decided not to ask.

"I heard you were dawdling earlier," said Lady Sarith, sparing her the briefest of glances. "And then it occurred to me that we didn't have a chance to discuss my full terms and expectations for you, did we?"

Cas heard movement behind her—what sounded like someone being forcefully carried through the door. She started to turn to see who it was, but one of her guards grabbed her face and forced her to look forward.

"Eyes on the lady when she's speaking," he growled.

"So, I thought I should make things more clear," Lady Sarith continued, not bothering to glance at Cas this time. "Lest you forget who you now serve, and what the consequences for insubordination will be."

More movement behind her, and then the source of it finally appeared. An elven woman wielding a broad sword came first, followed by two guards with a young man secured between them.

Cas's breath caught as her gaze fell on the man's familiar face.

Jeras. That was his name. Soryn had introduced him as one of her most faithful soldiers. And he had served Cas just as faithfully—he had been the first to volunteer to continue on to Moreth with her, and he had already committed to marching onward to the northern shores with her. He had a family in Olan, she knew, but she realized then that there were too many things she *didn't* know about this man who had risked everything to follow her. Things she would never learn.

His death was swift.

The sword plunged into his chest, and the elven woman twisted it in so deeply, so viciously, that Cas was surprised to not see Jeras's heart caught and speared onto the blade when she finally withdrew it.

Cas dropped to one knee. Her stomach roiled, her face flushed with sweat, and all her focus shifted to trying not to vomit. She winced at the sound of Jeras's body slumping down and thudding against the floor.

"Now, you have...ten or so allies in the holds below, I believe?" asked Sarith. "And I could choose any one of them at any moment, should you test my patience. The only *difficult* thing, at least for me, will be deciding who's next."

The thought of anyone else suffering this fate was the only thing that could have driven Cas to speak in that moment. She swallowed the bile burning in the back of her throat, and she said, "Choice won't be necessary. I...I won't test your patience."

"Good. Now get up."

She rose on shaky legs, trying to keep her gaze straight ahead, staring but unseeing. But even as she tried to blur her surroundings, the blood on the floor remained bright and clear as it seeped toward her.

She was still dangerously close to being sick.

"The halls will be filled with people by this evening, here to pay their respects. I can't have you causing me any extra trouble."

Here to pay their respects...

Cas's heart pounded harder as she remembered her plan—the funeral rites would be a chance to get close to the prince's body.

And no matter how sick she felt, she couldn't waver from that plan.

Her voice was quietly numb, a perfect imitation of a broken servant, as she asked, "Shall I help prepare the throne room for more visitors?"

Lady Sarith placed her letter and quill aside and got to her feet. The guards holding Cas gripped her more tightly, forcing her to stand up straighter, as their matriarch stepped toward them.

Lady Sarith grabbed Cas's face between her elegant fingers, tilting it this way and that, inspecting the bruises that the lady of her court had left. A pleased smile stretched across her own face as she did. Cas could only imagine what sort of twisted thoughts were behind that smile.

"Won't that be terribly uncomfortable for you?" It wasn't a question so much as a gleeful declaration, one that perfectly matched her unnerving expression.

Cas lowered her head. It *would* be terribly uncomfortable for her, but she assumed this would be the very thing that made Lady Sarith agree to it.

And it was.

"Yes," said the lady after a moment of thought. "I think there are still a few demeaning tasks for you to see to in that room." She ordered the guards to see this plan through, and then she went back to her desk without another glance at Cas or the bleeding body between them.

CHAPTER 27

An extravagant display awaited Cas in the throne room.

The thrones themselves were hidden from view by a newly placed platform, one that was draped in the Moreth royal colors of navy and silver, with stairs that led up to Prince Alder's body. The room itself was surrounded by a courtyard and extensive gardens on three sides, and normally it was open to that greenery outside, but now white cloths had been hung over the exits. The slight breeze pushed those cloths about. With the falling twilight casting a purplish glow through them, they made Cas think of restless spirits.

All around the Prince's still body were evenly-spaced torches, illuminating offerings—everything from food, to books, to works of art—all meant to recapture *his* restless spirit.

The elves of Moreth believed that their souls could

return to the mortal realm if they chose to. The preferable choice, according to some, because they could no longer enter any of the heavens. But sometimes souls drifted toward those heavens anyway, and then they were lost after being turned away. The torches were meant to guide them back to the mortal realm; the offerings were meant to convince them to stay.

Cas had been given orders to set the tables along the room with plenty of wine, and to arrange all of the offerings to the Prince in a pleasing manner.

Lady Sarith had not specified what she meant by *pleasing*.

But Cas suspected that whatever she did would be wrong, and would then be used as an excuse to punish her, so she didn't dwell on it. All she cared about was using it as an opportunity to get close to the Prince's body.

The room was thinly populated for the moment. There were only a few servants, and a handful of guards —one of whom was General Kolvar. She subtly tried to catch his attention, just to see if she could. But he kept averting his eyes, same as he'd done in the office earlier. She suspected her bruised, swollen face made him uncomfortable.

Most of the room's inhabitants were keeping their distance from the platform. Someone occasionally arrived with more offerings, but they left them at the tables by the main door, expecting Cas or one of the other servants to carry them to the prince's side.

She waited for a lull in these deliveries, and then she gathered up one of those offerings—a basket of some sort of cloyingly sweet-smelling fruit—and started what felt like a very long walk to the platform.

Her muscles threatened to seize up as she drew closer to it, but she pushed through. She paused, foot on the bottom step, and she bowed her head. Partly because she was trying to collect herself and her magic, but also because of a sudden, heavy surge of guilt that settled over her.

It was impossible not to think about what Prince Alder's fate might have been if she hadn't entered his realm. If she had not talked him into swearing his allegiance to her, he might still be alive.

As would Jeras, and countless other soldiers who had fought alongside her.

How many more would her wars claim?

Would this bloodshed and violence be worth it in the end?

She'd been holding her breath, she realized. She let it shudder out of her. *Keep breathing,* she commanded herself. *Keep moving.* She couldn't know the ending unless she kept moving.

She repeated those words over and over to herself as she placed her basket down and reached out her hand.

Her fingers shook as they brushed over the prince's pale arm.

His skin was warmer than she expected, and not as stiff as she thought it should have been; she wondered if it was some sort of elven magic at work. They'd certainly done something—magical or otherwise—to hide the horrifying wounds his neck had sustained. Aside from being more pale than usual, he looked almost...*alive*.

It unsettled her, and this unease was all she felt at first. No matter how hard she concentrated, her magic would not rise, and she neither felt nor saw anything of Prince Alder's last moments.

A door opened somewhere behind her. She fought the urge to jump. Every tiny sound seemed like a sign of oncoming disaster to her anxious mind.

Keep breathing.

She pretended to rearrange some of the offerings on the platform for several minutes, all while trying to settle her nerves and solidify her magic.

Then she tried again.

And again.

On her fourth try, as her hand covered Prince Alder's, it finally happened—the familiar sensation of Death magic swelled inside of her. It took an agonizingly long time to build up; she could feel the airs of this realm attempting to weave through it, to pry it apart before she could do anything with it.

She closed her eyes, trying harder to concentrate.

She imagined herself and the Prince as beings that were separate from this realm and its oppressive air. She thought of a cocoon of Death magic wrapping around them, molding against her until its pulsing power was beating in time with her own heart. Sounds and images began to seep into her mind with each pulse. A confusing barrage of whispers, a rapid succession of faces and places...

Too much to sort through.

It felt remarkably like the beginning of a panic attack, and that was perhaps the only reason she managed to breathe through it and stay focused—because she was experienced at such things.

When she opened her eyes, it wasn't the throne room she saw before her.

A room flooded with sunlight. A door made of glass panels. A courtyard, a desk littered with the beginnings of letters and contracts. And then a voice, Prince Alder's own voice—

"Who are you?"

A being stood before him, half elf, half human, all rage in his eyes. Laurent. Those eyes were reminiscent of their father's. So stern, so cold, so familiar...

But an unsettling feeling had blossomed in Prince Alder's chest. Something that told him those eyes were playing a trick.

"Where is my brother?" he asked.

That trick before him smiled and reached for the sword at

his hip.

Cas heard footsteps—in the present, not stifled by the heavy cocoon of her magic—and she again yanked her hand away from Prince Alder. Dizziness flooded her as her connection to her magic snapped. She started to reach for something, anything to catch herself.

Someone else was already reaching for her.

A hand closed around her arm and jerked her away from the steps—another one of Lady Sarith's close confidantes. Her poison-green eyes raked over Cas's face, hesitating for a frighteningly long time on the Dark God's mark.

Was that mark reacting in some way, announcing the fact that she'd been using magic?

"You have tables to set, servant girl," the elven woman finally sneered.

Cas didn't argue.

She hurried away, and she quickly lost herself in the repetitive movements of setting out wine glass after wine glass. Her thoughts went round and round, trying to decipher what she'd seen.

It seemed she hadn't been mistaken about what she'd felt while cleaning up that blood earlier; something was off about the *Laurent* that had drawn that blood.

It was not unusual for a person to disguise themselves in this empire—she had used plenty of Mimic-kind crystals in the past to change her own appearance.

And those crystals were a corrupted form of divine magic that some legends linked to the elves, so perhaps such things could fare better than true magic in this realm?

Then again, she hadn't seen any of those crystals here. And if there was a supplier of such things in this place—or a hidden stash of them anywhere—she suspected Zev would have sniffed them out within days of their arrival; he had a talent for finding corrupt and questionable things.

But hadn't Alder mentioned something with power similar to the Mimic spirit's magic? A type of fruit, harvested in the foothills of the Bloodstone Mountains...

The word came to her after a moment of thought —*abseth berries*. He'd offered her one just the other night at the banquet. It was one of the things his kind had *fun* with.

Her skin prickled, and a cold sweat swept over her as she realized she was inching closer to the truth. It was a victory, and yet...

She was uncertain of what to *do* with that truth while she was surrounded by enemies, with all her most trusted allies either missing or locked away. And it was only a matter of time before Lady Sarith's mood changed, and then she herself would be tossed back into prison.

She needed help from *outside* of that prison.

Her gaze drifted toward Prince Alder, and her heart

squeezed painfully as she remembered more of that conversation they'd had the night of the banquet.

I keep looking for helpers, she'd told him.

There had to be more within this palace. Lady Sarith might have claimed otherwise, but Cas refused to believe her.

She needed to find some way of writing a note that she could discreetly slip to someone. It would be safer than trying to talk in a palace full of beings with above-average senses.

She went back to keeping her head down and arranging wine glasses, doing her best not to attract attention while she silently plotted out a way to send a message.

There were more offerings being brought in every few minutes, many of them being placed on those tables near the room's main entrance. Cas slowly made her way toward those tables, drawing close enough that she could peruse their contents with some measure of subtlety.

What could she use?

More guards seemed to be arriving along with those offerings. Her heart skipped faster, wondering if she was the reason for it. That elven woman had seen her lingering over Prince Alder for too long, hadn't she? She had let her go, but had summoned more guards to keep a closer eye on her, and now...

Cas forced her attention back to the tables.

What the hell could she use?

The pair of guards closest to her looked away for a moment, and she made her move. She carefully picked up one of the books from the offering table and pretended to be looking it over. And though it pained her to do it, she quietly pulled one of its loosely-bound pages free, folded it, and slipped it into her pants pocket. She also took a handful of dark purple berries from a nearby bowl, and then she picked up that entire bowl, carried it to the Prince's platform, and placed it among the other offerings.

She kept moving after this, back to the business of arranging wine and other refreshments. She went to a table in the back corner of the room.

After waiting to make sure no guards followed her, she pulled out the book page and one of the berries. She popped the flesh of the berry and smeared its juice over the page, testing it. It was messy, but dark enough to be seen over the existing type.

After casting a few wary glances around her, she scribbled three lines:

> *killer disguised*
> *abseth berries?*
> *real laurent...?*

She waited for her makeshift ink to seep fully into the page, and then she slid the note back into her pocket. As she turned away from the table, her eyes scanned the room, searching for one of those helpers that she so desperately wanted to believe existed.

And her gaze eventually landed, once more, on a familiar face.

General Kolvar.

He seemed to be following her everywhere she went today. He had yet to get involved, to intervene with any of her punishments, but she had not forgotten how disgusted he'd looked when he'd turned away in the office earlier. Nor had she forgotten the way Prince Alder had spoken so highly of him.

Admittedly, it wasn't much to go on. A lot had changed over the past day. And if she got this wrong, if word got back to Lady Sarith about what she was doing...

She could picture the consequences entirely too clearly. Each of her friends with a sword impaling them. Like Jeras. Like Asra. Like—

Gods.

She could barely breathe, suddenly.

"Servant girl," came the sickly-sweet voice of that woman who had grabbed her earlier. "Lady Sarith would like to see you in her office."

Dread clenched Cas's stomach. "Coming," she called, somewhat hoarsely.

She had to make a decision.

She pulled the note she'd written from her pocket

and slipped it into her sleeve instead. As she walked through the main doors, past the general and two guards he was quietly chatting with, she tripped.

The conversation stopped as she hit the floor. She landed awkwardly on her elbow, and pain rung through her arm, causing her to let out a hiss that wasn't entirely an act.

One of the guards laughed.

General Kolvar made no sound.

As Cas lay there, clutching her throbbing elbow, he simply stared at her. His gaze bordered on cruel. For a moment she thought she might have misjudged him. Terribly.

But then he reached out his hand and helped her up.

She pressed the crumpled page into his palm before striding quickly away.

CHAPTER 28

Two more days passed.

General Kolvar did not return her message, and she hardly saw him—nothing more than an occasional, distant glimpse—as she went about trying to survive the cruelties and intricacies of her indentured servitude.

She made it through the days with relatively few altercations, largely because Lady Sarith was otherwise occupied with securing her hold on the court. She was slowly convincing more and more people that she was the only one fit to rule the realm—not a terribly difficult task, considering one of Theren's sons was dead and the other was allegedly a murderer. Cas had heard several people already referring to her as *Queen* Sarith, and each time she heard that title being thrown about, it felt like someone jerking a knife over the thin threads of her hope, fraying them a little more.

She was still holding on to those threads, but now she was constantly anticipating their complete breakage and waiting for the fall that would follow.

As that second day drew close to an end, she was ordered to a large sitting room and instructed to scrub the floors.

Two of Sarith's inner circle watched her work, sitting upon velvet sofas and drinking from delicate cups while they chatted in their native language. Judging by the occasional snorts of laughter and haughty glances thrown in her direction, Cas assumed they were mostly discussing her.

She ignored them as best she could.

She was sneaking a glance at her reflection in the window, trying to check on the healing progress of the bruises on her face, when she caught sight of General Kolvar entering the room.

He strode directly toward her.

She kept scrubbing the floor, doing her best to look inconspicuous.

He paused and gave a slight bow to the ladies of Sarith's court before jerking his head toward Cas. "Two of the stablehands have fallen ill," he said, "and the stalls they should have been tending to are overrun. Lady Sarith thought this one might be good at shoveling shit."

One of the women on the sofa snickered. The other one looked mildly suspicious, but she eventually gave a single, curt nod.

Cas rose slowly to her feet, and the general grabbed her roughly by the elbow and dragged her out of the room.

She struggled to keep up with his long strides as they wound their way through the halls, eventually exiting through a set of double doors and into an expansive garden. The cool evening air prickled her skin. They passed the same area that she and Elander had danced in, and her chest felt as though it might cave in. It had been only days since she'd seen him, but it felt like another lifetime.

Another thread of her hope frayed and snapped.

Finally, they reached a relatively secluded corner of the gardens, at which point Kolvar stopped jerking her about. He shoved her toward a tall hedge—practically *into* that hedge. Then he glanced over his shoulder several times, and he looked back to her and said, "He lives."

She was too shocked—and overwhelmed with relief—to reply right away.

"He's been locked in a section of the palace that we haven't used in years. He didn't even know his brother was dead."

Cas's words trembled slightly as she finally managed to speak. "Can we get to him? What about—"

"I can't take you to him now. It's too dangerous. But I just wanted you to know."

He started to turn and walk away, but Cas caught his arm and held him still.

"You helped me," she said.

He pulled out of her grasp and averted his gaze. "I sought the truth alongside you, nothing more. What you do with it is up to you."

His voice was as cold as ever, but Cas was convinced that she had not been wrong about his loyalty to his dead Prince. Which, by extension, seemed to mean he might be loyal to *her*. "I saw you look away when that woman was beating me in the office the other day," she said.

He didn't reply.

"You don't agree with what Lady Sarith is doing."

"There are lots in this court who don't. Plenty are suspicious. I imagine there are some dark days ahead for this realm."

Cas decided to take another chance on him. "Then let's leave this place. Together. Help me and my friends escape, along with whoever else doesn't want to call Sarith *Queen*."

He shook his head. "It's all Lady Sarith's underlings surrounding the grounds now. They patrol the woods and the cities beyond too. The guards that refused to keep you and your friends hostage here—Prince Alder's loyalists—are all dead. No one is getting inside or outside of this realm without a battle that will likely turn into a massacre."

"How many of those loyalists to Alder remain?"

He hesitated.

"Is it enough to have *any* chance of overpowering Lady Sarith and her followers—assuming we were to properly coordinate such a move?"

"Not everyone who disagrees with her will be ready to—"

"*Is it enough?*"

He threw an alarmed look over his shoulder, scanning for anyone who might have overheard them.

Cas lowered her voice but kept up her questioning. "If you stay here, what do you think is going to happen? If Lady Sarith does not kill you herself, I promise that her alliance with my brother will still end very poorly for you. *Dark days ahead* will prove an understatement."

He started to shake his head, but stopped, clearly at a loss for how to reply.

"Escape with me," she pressed. "Pick up your sword and fight. For the sake of your fallen Prince, if nothing else. He told me he trusted you more than any other being in this realm. And he trusted *me*—even without seeing the full extent of my power. If you can get me out of this realm, I will *show* you that power. And they won't be able to stop us at that point."

His eyes truly locked on hers for perhaps the first time. Crickets chirped, a cold breeze tossed her hair about, and the night seemed to grow rapidly darker and more hopeless as she waited for him to speak.

Finally, he sighed and said, "I can't guarantee much help with the escape. Plenty disagree with Lady Sarith—and even more suspect her—but they're also afraid of her. I won't put a number on how many will be willing to fight. I can't speak for them."

"Then at least speak for yourself," she challenged. "Are you with me or not?"

Before he could reply, a series of terrifying sounds reached them—swishing dresses and clinking boots, and an angry conversation, led by a voice that Cas immediately recognized.

Lady Sarith.

She stormed into sight a few seconds later, followed by the women who had been watching Cas in the sitting room. A third person had joined them as well—the one who had left the bruises on Cas's face.

"Servant girl," Lady Sarith barked.

Cas gave General Kolvar one last pleading look, and then she stepped away from him and bowed her head as Sarith approached her.

"Leave us," Sarith growled at the general.

The general didn't hesitate. Not because he didn't want to, Cas chose to believe, but because he was smart enough not to show any more signs of their potential alliance.

Though there was a good chance it wouldn't matter.

Lady Sarith was staring after him, looking suspicious, and Cas felt briefly paralyzed as she wondered if she had just condemned another person to death.

Once he was out of sight, Lady Sarith spoke in a quiet, clenched voice. "Why were you talking to General Kolvar?"

"He was informing me of a group of stables that needed cleaning. He requested that I help him with this."

"Is that so?"

"Yes."

"Another question, then." She stepped closer, and Cas fought the urge to back away. "Some of my closest advisors tell me you've been acting...suspiciously. Talking to people you have no business talking to. Sneaking about in ways you shouldn't be. Taking advantage of my so very *kind* decision to let you serve me, in other words."

"I haven't done anything wrong."

Lady Sarith summoned her three followers to her side with a subtle wave of her hand, her eyes still on Cas. "You accused me of being a liar the other day, didn't you?"

Cas decided it was safer not to answer this.

"Well, you weren't wrong." Sarith cocked her head to the side, studying her. "But, you know, the thing about habitual liars...is that they're usually good at spotting *other* habitual liars."

Along the edges of her vision, Cas saw the woman

who had bruised her face pushing aside the coat she wore, revealing a sheath at her hip. It held a strange weapon; it had a hilt like a sword, but when she withdrew it, it had a flexible, whip-like attachment instead of a solid blade. At the end of that whip was a small, shiny metal barb.

Prince Alder had mentioned such a weapon in one of his rambling stories. It was one that the warriors of the Mistwilde Realm were known for using. She couldn't remember the name of it.

She could barely remember anything in that moment, aside from how hard this woman had hit her the other day.

"Now, tell me again what you two were talking about," said Lady Sarith.

Cas swallowed hard. If she told the truth, General Kolvar would suffer for it, and any chance of him being able to help her would be gone.

She lifted her gaze to Lady Sarith. "I already told you what we were talking about."

They locked eyes for a long, tense moment, until Sarith said, "Nalia."

The women holding the strange weapon stepped forward.

"Liars should be punished, shouldn't they?" asked Sarith.

Nalia accepted this with a slight bow of her head, and then she lifted the weapon and prepared to strike.

Lady Sarith stopped her with a raised hand. "Now, remember what I said the other day about you disobeying me?" she asked Cas. "And about how *difficult* it would be for me to choose which one of your allies I wanted to kill next?"

Cas stared at a flowering tree behind Lady Sarith, willing her eyes to unfocus, trying to take herself away from the moment.

"I've thought of a better idea," said Lady Sarith. "I'll let *you* choose. And, in exchange, I won't punish you for your behavior. At least not tonight."

Cas did not have to ask what the price would be for refusing to choose.

She already knew.

But that didn't stop her from quietly saying, "I won't do it."

Lady Sarith smiled knowingly, as though this was the response she'd expected. "Very well then," she said, stepping out of Nalia's way.

The first strike fell upon Cas's chest, carving an excruciating path across it. A second lash quickly followed, crossing the path the first had made. Then a third. A fourth. The metal barb ripped cloth and skin alike. Blood ran in winding streams beneath her shirt, dripped between her breasts, pooled in her navel, and her balance swayed as black dots danced in her vision.

"Don't kill her," said Sarith, sounding almost bored.

Nalia agreed, and the next command came from her. "Hold out your arms."

Cas refused.

It was foolish, but she didn't care.

She wouldn't give them any more satisfaction than she had to.

But her refusal again didn't matter; the other two members of Sarith's court stepped forward, and each took one of her arms and held them open to embrace her punishment.

Nalia struck hard and fast, over and over. The whip wrapped around one arm and then the other, and the barb dug in—and then violently back out. She kept going until the sleeves of Cas's shirt were mere tatters, until the path beneath her had turned from solid grey to soaked red stone.

"Enough," Lady Sarith finally said, just as the whip wrapped around Cas's left wrist.

Nalia ripped the barb away one last time, taking a large piece of Cas's skin with it.

And as blood trickled toward her fingertips, Cas felt the last shreds of her resolve trickling away with it.

Those black dots in her vision swarmed, blinding her completely, and she fell face first toward the ground.

WHEN CAS's vision came back, a flood of confusion came with it.

She was no longer in the gardens. She was moving, but her legs were not. She was being held up by two men, who were dragging her down a set of stairs, bumping her against the steps with little regard for her injuries.

They carried her half-conscious body into the depths of the palace and dumped her, wordlessly, back into her prison cell.

Zev took one look at the blood covering her, and then he was racing toward the bars of that cell, flinging himself against them. The guards simply secured the lock and started to walk away, but he continued to shout after them, demanding they come back.

They kept walking.

Zev's demands turned to insults—an impressive barrage of them in the common tongues of both Sundolia and Kethra, as well as some new curses that Cas was fairly certain he'd learned during their stay in this realm. There was fire dancing off a few of his fingertips. More faint than normal, but still alarmingly bright —just bright enough to draw more trouble.

Nessa and Rhea both jumped to their feet and hissed at him to stop.

He ignored them and kept shouting

Cas thought she might faint again from the effort of moving. But through her blurry vision, she saw one of the guards stop. He turned, starting to withdraw his weapon, and panic launched her to her feet. She dove at

Zev, wrapping herself around his waist and throwing all her weight backwards, dragging him down with her.

"What the *hell*—"

"Let them be," she growled.

He shrugged her off, but she got a hand wrapped in the front of his coat and yanked him back to face her. It was the last show of violence that sent him over the edge. He pushed with the same force she'd pulled with, and then they were tumbling across the floor, clawing and swinging at each other.

Rhea screamed at them to stop, but they ignored her. They were children again—orphans on the floor of their house full of stolen things, hurting and confused and aimless in their fury.

The scuffle lasted only a few moments—just until Zev managed to pin her beneath him, and their gazes locked long enough that he came to his senses. He started to lean away from her, but she grabbed him and held him still.

"I've watched two people die over the past few days," she said in a seething voice, "and I *won't* watch the same thing happen to you."

Behind her, the guards were still watching. One of them was laughing. The sound threatened to ignite the fury inside of her all over again, but she didn't take her gaze from Zev's.

Finally, she heard the sound of the guards walking away.

Zev's eyes turned to follow them.

"Let. Them. *Be*," Cas repeated.

He slowly turned his gaze back to her. "If they come for you again," he said, still heaving for breath, "I am going to kill them. I won't need divine fire to do it. I will rip them apart with my bare hands. And if I die in the process, then so be it—as long as I take a few of those fuckers with me on my way out."

And with that, he stood and walked over to the corner of their cramped cell, bowed his head, and closed his eyes.

———

THEY DIDN'T COME for her again.

Not that evening, not during the night, not the next morning.

Rhea was marking the time as best as she could guess it, dragging a chip of stone across the wall and announcing each hour. She'd made it to seventeen so far.

Cas laid completely still on the hard floor. At some point, Zev had draped his coat over her, trying to stop her shivering. She curled more tightly beneath it as she listened for Rhea's next scrape.

Eighteen.

Cas counted up to eighteen and then back down, tapping each number into a worn groove on the floor

426

beside her. And she might have stayed in that same place for the next eighteen hours, tapping and drifting into a state of protective paralysis, if she hadn't heard Nessa sniffle. Her stomach twisted at the sound.

She was out of strength, out of determination—out everything, really. But for Nessa's sake, she sat up. She slipped Zev's coat on so that it covered her tattered, bloody sleeves, and she crawled over to the bars that separated her and Nessa.

"Hey," she said.

Nessa sat up and rubbed at her face, trying to erase the evidence of whatever tears might have fallen.

"Help me stay calm."

Nessa stared at her. "I can't."

"Yes, you can."

"The elven magic is too suffocating. I tried—"

"Try harder," Cas snapped, fiercely enough that it left Nessa too shocked to argue—which was precisely what she'd been trying to do, because it made Nessa's focus shift from fear to movement.

Cas put her hand up to the bars.

Nessa did the same, and after several slow, shaking inhales and exhales, the feather-shaped mark on her skin flickered. It was soft, yet bright in the darkness, and it faded quickly. The air around them stayed cold and heavy. Cas acted as though she felt lighter anyway, rolling the tension from her shoulders and sitting up as straight as she could.

Nessa mirrored that posture, and it helped her concentration—the magic flowing from her grew more powerful. Still not enough to make Cas's nerves truly settle, the way this Feather magic usually did, but at least it was a distraction for both of them.

After a few minutes of this exercise, Nessa's breathing was no longer shaky, and the tears that had been shimmering in her eyes were gone.

"We're going to make it to the other side of this, okay?" said Cas.

Nessa nodded, and they laid down, facing each other, holding hands through those bars between them.

More time passed—so much time that Rhea finally abandoned her counting, slumped against the wall, and went to sleep.

Cas had nearly drifted off again herself when all of a sudden she heard a commotion from somewhere in the palace above. She sat up, blinking heavily. Zev was standing at the door of their prison, his gaze fixed on the faint light by the staircase at the end of the hall.

"Something is going on upstairs," he said.

They listened together. She tensed every time the noise drew closer to their prison. If Lady Sarith was rampaging up there, the chances of that fury being turned on her were very high, Cas suspected.

But though the noise did not settle, no one came to take her, nor any of her friends.

No one came at all. Not to bring food, or water, or punishment.

At least another hour passed.

And then another.

"Are they just going to leave us down here and starve us to death?" Nessa wondered.

"No," Cas said, getting to her feet and walking over to the cell's door. "We're not going to let that happen." Her hands moved up and down the bars beside that door, gauging their thickness. She started to ask Zev if he thought he could manage enough magic to soften the metal, when Rhea suddenly stood up and walked toward them as if in a trance. Her eyes were gently closed, fluttering beneath the lids, and her lips were slightly parted.

It was the look she normally took on whenever she was trying to concentrate on something that Silverfoot was sending her.

"What is it?" Zev asked.

She opened her eyes, and Cas thought she saw the faintest trace of a hopeful smile cross her friend's face. "Help is coming."

There was a loud crash against the door at the top of the stairs, and a moment later, the door swung open. Several figures rushed onto the landing. They were obscured at first by the light behind them, but as Cas squinted toward that light, she spotted a streak of silver and black shooting out of it.

A fox.

Laurent followed an instant later, with General Kolvar and two other grim-faced soldiers close behind him. The arms of all of them were full of weapons—including Nessa's bow and Rhea's staff. The general held the keys to the prison doors as well, and without so much as a greeting he got to work opening those doors.

Cas's gaze caught on Laurent's as she stepped toward freedom. A thousand questions sprang to mind, but she couldn't get any of them out.

"Time to go," he said, pressing a sword into her hands.

CHAPTER 29

ALL OF THEIR ALLIES WERE FREED AND ARMED WITHIN minutes, and together they raced for the stairs.

As they burst into the room at the top, they were met almost immediately with a wave of equally armed soldiers.

Three soldiers rushed toward Cas. The first one was stopped by an arrow, swift and perfectly placed above the leather collar that protected his throat. Nessa's work, Cas assumed—though she didn't have time to look, as the other two soldiers were upon her.

Laurent took one of these, grabbing his shoulder and slamming him into the wall, then following it up by plunging his sword into the man's stomach.

Cas handled the last of them, ducking his swing before slicing at his thigh, aiming for the vulnerable artery within it. The others were engaged in similar battles nearby, and the floor was soon slick with blood and littered with fallen bodies.

Every room revealed more bodies—fallen and otherwise. It might have turned overwhelming very quickly, but the feel of a sword in her hand had done wonders for Cas's exhausted body and mind. That, and the familiar feel of fighting alongside her friends.

How many times had they fought their way out of trouble, back-to-back, just like this?

It was the one thing that *hadn't* changed over these hellish last months, and it lifted her heart and pushed her onward.

Rhea's staff swept out first in every room. The elven air seemed to have little effect on the staff's power—it emitted more than enough to throw most of their opponents off guard, giving them a preemptive advantage in every battle they entered. A wall of fire preceded them into each of these battles, and as it died down enough to reveal their singed and startled enemies, Cas and the others charged forward through the smoke and ash, their swords swinging.

They burned and carved their way away from the prison, room by room.

Finally, they came to a clear stretch of hallway, where they slowed their pace long enough to sort through the rest of their plan.

"We have horses readied and waiting," said General Kolvar as he herded them forward, "and my soldiers have been doing their best to clear a path to them. We'll need to make for the woods, to the path that leads around to the back of the stables. The more direct route is overrun with fighting at the moment."

He guided them out of the palace and across the yard, over a small bridge, and into the trees.

It wasn't a proper forest—Cas could see the lights of the city of Galizar clearly on the other side—but it was thick enough to muffle the sounds of battle and make her feel oddly removed from what was happening in the palace.

The path they ran along was ill-used, overrun with wayward branches and creeping brambles that clawed and caught at their hair and clothing. But it was mostly empty of other people, and after a few minutes of running and pushing through, the back of the stables came into view.

The sound of a fight breaking out behind her drew Cas to a stop. She twisted around to see that she had somehow outran most of the others, and now it sounded as though they were in trouble.

Someone leapt onto the path in front of her in the next instant.

She staggered back quickly enough to lift her sword and block his blade, but her foot caught a root as she did, sending her stumbling down into an awkward crouch.

She caught her balance and looked up just in time to

catch a glint of steel in the moonlight. Her sword came up again, barely catching her attacker's, and she was shoved down into an even more uncomfortable position.

Her balance was nearly lost when an arrow sank into her attacker's right eye. The man fell back, howling like mad, and Cas scrambled away.

Nessa appeared on the path behind her, her gaze hard and unyielding as she nocked another arrow. She started to aim it at the man, but she hesitated at the sight of him dropping to his knees and rolling about.

Laurent arrived and finished the job, putting the man out of his misery with a quick swipe to the throat before picking up Nessa's bloody arrow and offering it back to her.

"Thanks," Cas told them both, averting her gaze from the dead man and his blood-drenched face.

The others caught up a moment later—Zev was bleeding heavily from his shoulder, but he insisted they keep running, and no one argued.

A full-scale battle was raging in front of the stables. Cas caught only a glimpse of it before being ushered around to the back, where the promised horses were waiting.

They wasted no time being picky about mounts.

Cas hoisted herself onto the back of a silver-grey beast with wild eyes; he looked ready to run. That made two of them. There was another sword and scabbard hanging from his saddle, so she tossed her other one aside before taking up the reins.

"More help is waiting at the edge of Galizar," said General Kolvar as he swung onto his own horse. He led it in circles, settling it, while the rest of their allies scrambled into saddles.

Then he rocketed off toward the gates. Cas and the others followed, the sounds of swords colliding and the screams of the dying growing increasingly quieter behind them.

As they barreled through the last of the gates being held open for them, Cas thought she heard what sounded like a scream borne of fury, not from a fear of dying—an awful, shrill sound that turned her stomach.

She had no way of knowing who had bellowed it out, of course.

But something told her that Lady Sarith still lived.

Regret stabbed through her, but what could they do but keep going?

They reached the edge of the city of Galizar within minutes. Once there, she drew her horse sharply to a stop, because the sight before her took her breath away.

She had asked General Kolvar for a hundred soldiers to escort her to the northern shores, and there were at least as many awaiting her here, holding the gates open for the last stretch of their escape. There may have been more—she didn't pause to count them.

She urged her horse back into a gallop and raced

through those soldiers, and they fell into ordered ranks and followed her into the barren lands that surrounded the realm of Moreth.

They rode for several miles, and soon Cas could feel the air beginning to shift. To thin. The oppressive hold over her magic grew weaker, and her body shivered with waking power.

They came to a riverbed that was all but dried up, its muddy water almost indistinguishable from the grey dirt around it.

General Kolvar ordered their company to halt just long enough to readjust their tack and allow their horses a quick drink. There was a brief discussion of what route to take to the northern shores, and while arguments about the matter carried on, Cas left her horse to drink and went to each of her friends, checking on them.

She found Rhea and Nessa tending to Zev's shoulder, which thankfully wasn't as badly injured as all the blood suggested.

After leaving them, she finally had a moment to wrap her arms around Laurent. She tried several times to speak, to tell him she was sorry about his brother, about *everything*. But it was just as before—her mouth was too dry and her heart too overwhelmed to allow her to speak.

He found his voice first. "So much for the happy family reunion, hm?"

She managed a small, choked little laugh before she embraced him again.

When she pulled away this time, he was frowning at something behind her.

"Company," she heard General Kolvar mutter.

She turned, and she saw a group of riders in the distance, throwing up dust as they raced toward them.

"And who knows how many more could be following," added the general. "We're better off trying to outpace them rather than fighting."

Cas started to agree, but something gave her pause. Her magic was continuing to unfurl inside of her. It was pushing through her, pounding against her veins like a war drum trying to convince her to fight instead of flee.

She pushed it down, climbed once more onto her horse's back, and rode on.

The magic persisted.

The bindings around it continued to loosen as she rode away from Moreth, and all the different shades of it seemed to be trying to leap to freedom at once, eager to show themselves after a week of suppression.

She slowed to a trot, trying to catch the breath those surges of magic had stolen away.

She looked over her shoulder and narrowed her gaze on those riders, who were still pursuing her and her company.

Lightning would be swift.

Too swift, maybe; it wouldn't make them suffer the

way they had made her and her friends suffer. The other option...

No.

It was too dangerous. She'd sworn she wouldn't use her other magic. She knew the consequences of using it, had spent the past week reciting those consequences to herself. The small amount she'd used to read the dead Prince's memories was nothing compared to what it would take to make their pursuers suffer the way she wanted them to.

She knew this.

But every drop of blood that had been spilled over these past days was suddenly bursting brightly into her memory. Every new scar on her skin burned. And suddenly she heard a dark voice in her thoughts—one that didn't sound like her own.

They want to bring death to you and your friends.

Show them what death truly looks like.

You could kill them all with only a bit of concentration.

She guided her horse in an about-face, just in time to see that group of riders rising over a hill, close and clear enough to count now. There were ten of them, and a second line was emerging further back, blurry but materializing quickly against the bleak landscape.

Someone behind her shouted her name, shouted for her to hurry up. To keep moving. Most of her party had already raced into a dip in the land ahead of her. They were out of sight.

She stood alone.

She felt cold all over, inside and out. Cold and convinced that their pursuers didn't deserve to live. Not after what they had put her and her friends through.

Her horse trembled beneath her. Pinned its ears back. She gripped the reins more tightly and sank into the saddle. The space around her began to darken. Her horse stomped its hooves. Cas closed her eyes—

A hand closed over hers and yanked her back to her senses.

Zev.

"What the hell are you doing?" he demanded.

"Nothing," she said, jerking her horse away from his. "Nothing, I—I'm fine."

He glared at her, obviously not convinced that she was *fine* at all.

She managed to tamp her magic back down for the moment, but she still wasn't *fine*. Because now that they were outside of Moreth, all her questions rose up and assaulted her just as mercilessly as that magic had, and she suddenly felt as if she was going to be sick.

What happened to the alliance she'd struck with the elves now? Would Mistwilde still support Prince Alder's agreement, now that he was gone? What about Moreth's army? The ones who didn't support their new *Queen*, but who weren't traveling with Cas now?

Did Lady Sarith know of her plans to go to the northern shore?

Where was Elander? And what would become of them, now that they were out in the open air once more?

This last question made her the sickest. She had been outside of the suppressive magic of the elven realm for mere minutes, and already she was struggling. It almost felt like the time her Dark power had spent being crushed down in that realm had only made it stronger. *Angrier.*

That couldn't bode well for their future.

Laurent and General Kolvar had followed Zev to her side. The general gave Cas a long, wary look as he reached them, and he said, "It's a day and a half's ride to the spot on the northern shores that you need to reach. And not an easy one at that. Let's save our strength as much as we can."

Cas nodded numbly.

He turned and rode on without further comment.

Laurent and Zev each gave her one last concerned look before turning away.

She followed them, lagging behind, the weight of all of those questions making her feel heavy and sluggish.

The Dark God's mark tingled and made her scalp itch, and the magic he promised called out to her once more. Softer now, but still there. Still trying to climb out of her.

She knew she couldn't use it.

But it was getting harder and harder to push it back down.

CHAPTER 30

ELANDER'S EYES SHOT OPEN AS A PANG OF FAMILIAR ENERGY
raced through him.

He had been leaning against a tree, silently focusing
on that similar energy that he and Casia shared, sending
bursts of it out every now and then—like flares to lead
her back to him.

This was the first time in days that he'd felt anything
in return.

He rose slowly as that feeling shivered through him,
his eyes scanning the encampment for any new arrivals
that he might have missed.

It was a bustling camp before him, full of evidence of
his work over these past days.

After the gates surrounding Moreth had proven
impenetrable, he'd decided to keep moving, and he'd
started the preparations for their mission into

Dawnskeep. He'd gotten word to Soryn and her allies, as planned, and he'd called once more on his divine allies as well, asking them to send their promised help sooner rather than later. That help had been trickling in, collecting here, and now they were nearly two hundred strong—with still more promised from the goddesses.

This place they were gathered in was Stonebarrow, a fortress once used by the Grand Army as a lookout and first line of defense against Kethra's enemies across the Glashtyn Sea. Elander was familiar with it from his time spent in the service of Varen and the King-Emperor before him. He knew it hadn't been used in decades, and he had suspected, correctly, that he would find it empty —albeit in a state of ill repair. The three stone towers that had once cut imposing silhouettes on separate hilltops were now partially crumbling from disuse, as were the walls that surrounded their yards. Weeds and clutches of ivy had overtaken most of the standing structures, and the crisscrossing, once well-marked paths between those structures were nearly invisible now.

It was not the shining fortress it had once been, but it would do for a few days—long enough to serve as a base while they carried out their business at Dawnskeep.

As he moved toward the edge of Stonebarrow's grounds, he again focused on pushing a flare of his magic outward, and then he waited for a response.

He felt it, just as before—a response of that same magic, but with an undercurrent of a different, lighter energy. Both Shade and Sun...

Casia.

He saddled a horse and quickly gathered a small party to ride out with him.

After a mile or so, they finally spotted movement.

A scattered group of people and horses was making its way across the plains ahead of them. He squinted into the setting sunlight, and one of the women at the head of this group began to take shape. Casia's grey hair stood out and made her easy to see, even with the sun's low position backlighting and blurring her. More familiar faces surrounded her; it seemed that most of the ones who had trekked into Moreth with her had also trekked out with her.

He breathed a sigh of relief and kicked his horse into a gallop.

Casia was on foot, as were most of her companions, and she was leading a horse that looked to be on the verge of collapse. *All* of them—human and beast alike—looked to be staggering in on their last scraps of faith and vigor.

But they were alive.

She was alive.

She stopped as her weary gaze caught sight of him. He leapt from the saddle and ran the rest of the way, sweeping her into his arms as soon as he reached her.

Her hands clenched into his shirt. Her grip felt alarmingly weak. Her chest heaved with silent cries, but there were no tears on her face when he pulled away—a sign of what appeared to be dehydration setting in.

He leaned back and started to look her over, inspecting for damage. He didn't get beyond her face, beyond the skin around her eye that was a mottled shade of purple.

It wasn't a shadow as he'd first thought. Nor was it that symbol of the Dark God's curse spreading further across her face.

It was a bruise.

Violent heat unfurled in his chest. His hand lifted, carefully pushed the loose strands of her hair away from that bruise. She winced even at the gentle touch, and his vision blurred slightly.

"What the hell happened to you?" he asked in a low voice.

"Later," she insisted. Throwing a glance over her shoulder, she added, "Some of them are in much worse shape than me."

His skin was still hot, his blood pounding in his ears. But he nodded. "We have healers that can help them back at our fortress."

Her tired eyes brightened a bit at the word *fortress*.

"Come on—we can talk about it on the way there." He helped her onto his horse's back before swinging up behind her. They set off at a slow pace, and her own horse and the rest of her followers trudged dutifully behind them.

They were silent for the first several minutes. Her eyes were closed, and all of her focus seemed to be on remaining upright. He kept an arm around her waist, steadying her against him.

"Where were you?" she asked suddenly, quietly.

The question had been gentle, not an accusation of any kind, but guilt still tore through him at the sound of it. "I went back to Moreth," he told her, "but the way in was shut."

"The guards were dead, weren't they?" She seemed to be thinking out loud, the words slurring and tumbling out of her.

"Yes. But I tried to get in without their magic, over and over—I swear I tried."

She shifted against him. Her balance swayed a bit. He wrapped his arm more tightly around her, and her hand came to rest on the one he had against her waist.

"I couldn't get in, but I couldn't simply sit still," he told her. "We'd agreed to go to the northern shores next, right? So, I prepared accordingly. Because I've learned by this point that you always make it to where you plan to go, one way or another."

Her head tilted toward him at that last sentence, leaned into his chest, and he thought he saw the corner of her lips lift. Barely a hint of a smile, but it made the guilt clenching his stomach loosen a little.

The three hilltops with their neglected towers soon came into view. Elander slowed to a stop, waiting for the rest of their party to catch up, and Casia lifted her head. "This is Stonebarrow, isn't it?" she asked. "Prince Alder mentioned it when we were discussing Dawnskeep and the rest of the northern shores."

"Yes."

Her eyes widened a bit as she took in the bustling crowd moving about in the shadows of those towers. "And all of these people..."

"Are here to help us," he confirmed. "Since I couldn't get to you in Moreth, I thought I'd make up for it by meeting you here with a gift."

"A gift?" She laughed. "You got me an army."

"Just a small one." He lifted that hand she had against his and kissed it. "Sorry I didn't wrap it."

She smiled in earnest at this before taking a deep, bracing breath.

"Most of these soldiers were sent by Soryn," he continued, "but there are several expert magic wielders from one of Nephele's temples as well. And the Moon Goddess should be sending aid, too—a guide to help you find your way through the magic that surrounds Dawnskeep."

"You've been busy," she commented.

"As have you." He glanced behind them and saw that the last of her party was finally catching up. "We should get everyone settled in and tend to the wounded."

She agreed, and she inhaled one more deep breath before she slipped from his horse's back, took the lead of her own horse, and headed down the gently sloping hill into the heart of the camp.

Though she was among the wounded, she refused to take care of herself until all of her fellow travelers were seen to. And even then, she insisted on working—introducing herself to their newest allies and discussing preliminary plans with them—while she rehydrated, and she shooed away any healer that got too close and started inquiring about any of her injuries.

She was wearing Zev's coat, Elander noticed, and every now and then he caught a glimpse of the shirt beneath it—one of the cuffs appeared to be stained with blood.

Concern ate a deep pit into his stomach, but she refused to talk about what had happened. She just kept moving through the camp, focused on the mission before them.

When he finally managed to pry her away from that camp and its business, he brought her to the room he'd stayed in the past few nights. It was located within the most intact of the three towers, in a quiet corner tucked away from the surrounding noise. It was not exactly the picture of comfort, but he'd procured plenty of blankets to make a soft bed on the wooden floor. The fireplace was in good shape, too, and it quickly warmed the space once he got a blaze going in it.

He left her in this room to rest while he went back to the camp. He checked in with several scouts he'd sent out earlier, and also with a group of Storm-kind who had gone to investigate the nearby shores. He purposefully took his time as he did these things, hoping that Casia actually *would* rest if he stayed away long enough.

While he was away from her, he also spoke privately with Laurent and Zev, and from them he extracted and pieced together details about what had happened in Moreth. About Prince Alder's death, about the elven woman now calling herself Queen, and what she'd done to Casia.

And at this point, he briefly considered making a quick trip back to that elven realm and setting it all on fire. Impenetrable gates or not, he would find a way to burn it *all* down.

He decided against it only because they had so many other problems to focus on at the moment.

When he finally returned to Casia, she wasn't resting.

She had taken off her bloodstained clothes. Her feet were bare, her hair was loose, and for the moment she wore only a long shirt—the one he'd been wearing himself, yesterday—draped over her like a dress. She was digging through a satchel full of clothing and other supplies that had just been left for her, her eyes glazed over in thought. After a moment she pulled a fresh change of clothing from that bag and turned around. She looked a bit startled at the sight of him.

"Unnecessary," he informed her, leaning against the doorframe.

"Pardon?"

His eyes darted to the clothing in her hands, and then over the stolen shirt she was currently wearing. "I like what you have on."

"Won't make a very good impression when I'm outside trying to give orders, I'm afraid."

"It's made a good impression on *me*."

She laughed softly at this, and so he kept teasing her —just for the chance, any chance, that he might hear that laugh again.

"Either way," he said, strolling closer, "it seems like a lot of work to put all of those clothes on just to take them off again once we're alone."

"There you go again with that entirely-too-confident attitude. One day it's going to get you into trouble."

Her eyes locked with his, and he felt that familiar sensation of his heart lifting, threatening to run away with him. He breathed a soft sigh and kissed her forehead. "I think I'm already in trouble," he told her, resting his chin on top of her hair.

As she wrapped her arms around him, he eyed the bags behind her—not just the bag that had been left for her, but his own belongings and weapons that were resting against the far wall. It looked like she had been rearranging all of these items. Organizing them, perhaps to distract her from her anxious thoughts. From those things she wasn't telling him. He knew most of what those things were, now. But he still didn't know how to broach the subject...or if he even should.

"You didn't rest much while I was gone, did you?" he asked.

"I was...distracted."

He frowned.

"And now I'm much more interested in washing away these past few days," she gathered the clean clothes to her chest and fixed him with a pointed look. "I suspect this fortress doesn't have hot water?"

"Afraid not."

"Did I see a creek on the way in? That will do."

He didn't want to argue after everything she had been through, so he let the issue of rest go for the time being, and he led her to a secluded stretch of that nearby creek.

He stood guard while she bathed, sitting on the rocky bank, his body tense and eyes narrowing toward every strange sound. The sun had set. The air was rapidly cooling around them; she had to be freezing in that water. And yet she took her time in it.

But then, a lot had happened that needed to be washed off, he supposed.

He tried not to think about all that had happened.

It was a useless exercise, however, and concern soon

brought him closer to the creek's edge. He let his attention drift toward her, let it linger just long enough to make sure she was all right. He didn't mean to stare. But as her shoulders rose above the surface of the water, he caught a glimpse of scars that hadn't been there before —a whole collection of them running down to her wrists, raised slashes of pink and red shining angrily in the moonlight.

He'd known they would be there.

It didn't make them any easier to look at.

Her back was to him, but she must have felt him staring because she tilted her face toward where he stood. "Such discipline up to this point," she mused. "I was expecting you to join me well before now."

His gaze slipped over the curve of her back, down to her hips that rose just above the concealing dark water. The thought of joining her was tempting, but he shook his head. "The last time you were wading around in water like this, I nearly lost you to that monster made of ice. I thought it would be wise to be more on guard this time." He hesitated. "But I couldn't help but get distracted by your...skin."

She turned her face back to the opposite shoreline.

"I spoke with your friends. They told me what happened."

"So we don't need to talk about it then, do we?" she asked quietly.

He took a deep breath. "No. I guess we don't."

She waded into a deeper section of water, until everything below her head was obscured by the cold water, while Elander sat down among the rocks once more. He rested his elbows on his knees, leaned forward, and went back to scanning the space for threats. He didn't speak of her scars again. They didn't speak at all for the remainder of her bath, even as she swam closer and nodded toward the pile of clothes and the blanket folded next to him.

He grabbed the blanket and held it open for her to step into. He pulled it around her shoulders, and he couldn't seem to make himself let go after that. He clenched the ends of the blanket in his fist and drew her closer to him.

She shivered. His hands moved over her body, pressing the woolen cloth to her damp skin, rubbing warmth into it as best he could. She kept her eyes on his face as he worked, her lips softly parted. She didn't back away even after her shivering had ceased.

He cleared his throat. It was a strange combination of feelings fighting for dominance inside of him.

Her latest scars worried him. Angered him. *Gutted* him.

But they did nothing to lessen the attraction he felt toward her.

"You should put your clothes on before you catch your death in this cold air," he said.

"Pretty sure I already caught my death," she replied,

slipping her hand out of the blanket so she could poke him in the chest.

His expression was somewhere between a grin and a grimace. "I love it when you attempt to be funny."

"I *am* funny, and you know it."

He started to reply, and then promptly forgot what he was going to say. He studied her for a moment instead, a bemused smile on his face. It was an impressive defense mechanism, her ability to make jokes even as she stood there, shivering and covered in scars—and on the eve of what could very well prove to be an impossible mission. And it made no sense to laugh after everything that had happened to her over these past weeks, but she still did it.

It made no sense to want to kiss her as badly as he did in that moment either. But he still wanted to. He wanted to do *more* than just kiss her, and to hell with everything else.

She seemed to be able to sense that last thought, because the hand she'd freed from the blanket moved to his chest. Her fingers splayed over it, playing at the collar of his shirt.

His gaze strayed to the drops of water still clinging to her throat. Images of her rain-slicked skin in the moonlight flashed in his mind, and he thought about other...dampness. About how wet the space between her thighs likely was. And of all the ways he could make it wetter. Now was not the time, but there were certain parts of him that didn't give a damn.

Her hand slipped away from his collar and traveled down over his chest, and then lower, teasing across his stomach before she hooked her fingers into his belt.

Voices rose nearby, reminding them that they were just around the corner from a camp full of people— people who were probably wondering where they were —and her hand stopped its wandering.

Her eyes closed for a moment, and then she quietly said, "We have a lot left to plan and figure out. We should probably..." She trailed off, reluctantly, and he leaned down and captured her lips in a slow kiss.

"Finish this later," he supplied, his voice dark and filled with promises that he had every intention of keeping.

CHAPTER 31

AFTER SHE'D DRESSED AND OTHERWISE MADE HERSELF—TO USE her word—*presentable*, they walked toward the camp together. They gathered all of their most trusted allies, and Elander filled them in all at once on the things he'd discovered while they were apart. About what he'd seen at Bethoras, about what he'd witnessed during an earlier visit he'd taken to the northern shore, and what information the follow-up scouts he'd sent to that shore had come back with.

After he'd finished, their small council sat with grim expressions around a low fire, contemplating the details of their next move.

"The tides will be lowest just after daybreak, and the island that contains the monument we're targeting is easily accessible at that point," Nessa began.

"Except it's not really accessible at all, right?" Zev asked, frowning.

"*I* couldn't access it," Elander replied. "But I got close. And Casia should be able to get closer because of her magic."

There was a strange mist shrouding that tiny island. Yesterday, he had walked across the path that the low tide revealed, trying to get a better look. As expected, he'd sensed an overwhelming amount of magic that was Sun-derived, and he *thought* he'd seen the stone faces of statues through that tumbling mist. According to the research he'd done regarding Dawnskeep, the twelve different statues represented the *Vitala*—those ancient warriors who once fought on Solatis's behalf.

He hadn't been able to push through the clouds and reach them, or the island they stood on. The Storm-kind soldiers he'd sent for a follow-up exploration had not been successful, either—but they had managed to get closer than he had.

And Casia's magic was stronger than theirs, so she would be able to get even closer, he reasoned.

"Hopefully that power that's overwhelming everyone is a sign that we're in the right place, at least," said Rhea.

Elander nodded. "And the Moon Goddess swore a guide to our cause," he reminded them. "I presume whomever—or whatever—she sends will be able to aid Casia as well."

General Kolvar started to comment on this several times, only to shake his head and go back to silent contemplation. It seemed like he still had not fully accepted the extent to which they were all interacting with the divine.

"So we have to wait until the tides shift, and until that guide shows up?" asked Zev,

"We need time to set a perimeter anyway," said Laurent. "We should have enough bodies to create blockades on all the major routes that lead toward that stretch of the shores. Maybe not indefinitely, but long enough to let Casia do what she needs to do."

"And Varen?" asked Rhea.

"Last sighted just north of Grayedge," Caden replied. "Presumably on his way to or from business in Malgraves. We have a chain of scouts watching the routes between here and there, keeping us informed."

"So we have plenty of bodies to give us the time and protection that Casia will need," said Zev, "but do we have a backup plan for what happens if things in Dawnskeep go poorly? You know, if our beloved Goddess of Life decides she'd rather just keep sleeping? Or if..." He trailed off. Looking uncomfortable—which seemed like a rare emotion for him.

Elander had given the Heart of the Sun back to Casia before this meeting, and she had been quiet for most of the past hour, studying it as she listened to everyone else speak.

But now she closed it in her fist, and her eyes lifted to Zev. "If I can't access enough Sun magic to summon her, you mean? If the Dark magic inside of me overwhelms it?"

Zev's gaze held hers for a long moment before his chest rose and fell with a deep sigh. "Yes. That."

The entire group was watching Casia now, expressions ranging from uncertainty to grim resolve, but she kept her eyes on Zev.

"No," she said, "I can't think of a plan beyond not failing. So I guess I'm simply going to have to *not fail*." She gave a confident smile that likely would have fooled everyone except the ones present, who knew her too well to be tricked by it.

No one disagreed with her, however, and no one tried to stop her as she excused herself and headed up the hill toward the towers.

Elander watched her go with a worried frown on his face—a look that was mirrored by almost everyone else in the circle.

They all went back to their silent contemplation for a while, until General Kolvar got to his feet and said, "It seems to me that all *we* can control is how much support we give her. I don't trust that Varen isn't planning to sneak his way up here. I also wouldn't be surprised if Lady Sarith sent more trouble. She knew too much of Casia's talks with the Prince, and so she probably knew about Casia's plans to come here. Honestly, the list of people and things that could interfere with our operation is long. We should focus on setting up our protections, as Laurent said."

The rest of the group agreed, and they moved on to doing precisely this.

Elander spent the next hours poring over maps with the leaders among the camp. Identifying possible routes and weak points. Dividing soldiers into regiments and giving them assignments. Checking weapons, supplies, horses, and everything else he could think of.

When it was all finally taken care of, he turned from the camp with a weary sigh and walked the same winding path that Casia had taken earlier.

He found her sitting cross-legged among a pile of blankets in their room, the Heart of the Sun in one hand, tiny bolts of lightning dancing upon the other.

"Sorry I left," she said without looking up from her magic. "I know there were still plans that needed to be made."

"It's fine. Kolvar and I managed. We're the more experienced with that sort of thing, anyway." He walked over and settled down beside her. "Besides, you have other things to focus on. Like breaking free of one god and summoning another."

"Yes." Her concentration broke, and the lightning vanished as she huffed out a humorless laugh. "Just the small matter of those things."

He let out an unamused laugh of his own, and then

they fell silent. Only the crackling of the fire interrupted that silence, and the quiet felt strange after the commotion of arranging things in the camp below.

"So," he began after a moment, "we have several hours until those things begin in earnest, it seems."

"You're going to suggest that I use those hours to rest, aren't you?"

"Would it make any difference if I did?"

"No," she replied, her concentration already back on her magic. She was drawing another bolt upon her palm, swirling it into existence with precise twists of her wrist.

He watched her work. He couldn't help but notice the way the white branches of lightning illuminated the bruise on her face. And from that bruise, his gaze automatically swept over her arms, which were fully covered, and then to her chest, where the unbuttoned top of her shirt revealed a patch of scarred skin. He was faster about looking away from those scars this time, but she still sensed him doing it.

"I know what you're thinking," she said.

"Do you?"

"You're upset with yourself for not being there to stop it."

He stood, suddenly restless. He moved to the fireplace and added another log to it, even though the flames were already eye-wateringly bright.

She continued dancing that lightning across her

palm, making it leap from the Heart of the Sun and then back again. "My scars aren't yours to bear, you know."

"Maybe not." He picked up the metal poker and stabbed at the burning wood, sending showers of glowing embers into the air. As he watched one flutter down and die against the hearth, he thought again of that elven realm and its so-called queen, all gone up in flames. "And yet every time I look at them," he said, more to himself than her, "it feels like someone is taking a knife to my own skin."

"We had to go our separate ways," she insisted. "If you hadn't left, we wouldn't have half of that army outside. We wouldn't have all the information you've gathered about Solatis and her apparent imprisonment. *Too many wars*, as Prince Alder told me." Her breath hitched. Remembering what had happened to the Prince, Elander assumed. She quickly shook her head, as if annoyed at herself for letting her mind stray to such memories. "We can't fight all of them without making a few hard choices. You did the right thing. You believed I could fight my way out of Moreth. And you were right."

He *did* believe in her; he hadn't been lying when he'd told her he knew she would make it to this place, one way or another.

But he still didn't feel right about any of it.

He hated that he hadn't been there to stop those scars. Hated that his magic was no longer capable of leveling entire realms. Hated that he would have to rely on a sword to protect her, and that a sword might not be enough.

From god, to king's captain, to...

To what? He wasn't even sure what he was now. He knew that he would have given anything to keep her safe—but the problem was that this form he was in was failing him a little more each day, and he was running out of things to give.

Where would they be this time tomorrow?

A thousand answers sprang to mind at this question. Most of them were not good. All the horrifying possibilities ran relentless, exhausting circles around his mind, but when Casia tilted her face toward him and asked, "What are you thinking about now?"

All he said was, "You."

She stopped summoning her magic, pocketed the Heart of the Sun, and moved to his side. "Is that really all?"

He couldn't fool her anymore, could he?

"Mostly you," he said. "But also tomorrow. And after that...about what I am going to do to that bitch of an elven Queen if I ever have the pleasure of seeing her again."

"It involves a sword, I presume?"

"If she's lucky."

"Lucky?"

"And I don't have the patience on that day to derive a more drawn-out, torturous method."

Casia's eyes slid out of focus, and she was quiet for a long time before she swallowed hard and said, "Either way, you'll have to beat me to her."

Her eyes stayed distant. Her breathing had turned shallow and slow. It felt like she was drifting away from him, so he took one of her clenched hands and gently pried it open, slipped his fingers through hers, and used his thumb to tap a stable rhythm against her knuckle. After a few minutes of this, Casia's lips were silently moving, counting each tap, and she gave his hand a little squeeze.

"We don't have to talk about Moreth anymore," he said. "But at least let me look more closely at those scars. Do you still have that balm the Healing Goddess gave you?"

It took only a moment of searching. She'd escaped Moreth with only one of the bags that she'd entered that realm with—but they were lucky, for once, because it was the bag that held the balm in question.

She handed it over to him and then took off her coat and the long-sleeved tunic she wore, leaving nothing on except a thin camisole.

He willed himself to focus on the task at hand, and not on the way that sheer garment left almost nothing to his imagination.

She was silent as he worked his hands in gentle, methodical paths over her battered skin. He could feel the magic tingling in that balm he was spreading. It made the scars flare to what looked like a painful shade of red, but she remained perfectly still—at least until his fingers brushed over a particularly deep wound on her right shoulder, at which point she sucked in a sharp breath.

He hesitated.

She shook her head and urged him to keep going. "It just burns a bit," she said.

His fingers clenched more tightly around the jar in his hand. "All the more reason to go back and set that elven realm on fire once we're done with our business here," he muttered. "A burn for a burn."

"If you set fire to everyone that wants to cause me harm, you'd be burning most of the world down."

"Still tempting."

"We're trying to save the world, not burn it down."

"Oh, is that what we're doing?" he teased. "I keep forgetting."

She softly punched his arm, and he smiled, glad to see a bit of a playful spark back in her eyes, even if it didn't last long.

Her expression turned serious again as she studied the balm he held, and she asked, "Would they fight with us, if it comes down to it? The Healing Goddess and the rest of her court, I mean."

He didn't answer. He'd been wondering the same thing.

"Zev was right earlier," she said, shaking her head. "We're probably going to need a backup plan."

"Not necessarily."

She hugged her arms tightly around herself. She didn't speak, but he could read the question in her eyes easily enough.

What happens if I fail?

He wished there was something he could say to take away her fear, but he could think of nothing in that moment. Truth be told, he was afraid too—he was just good at hiding it. And he wasn't only afraid of her failing, but of all the things that could happen if she *succeeded* too, or if she managed something in between. This was powerful magic they were dealing with. Unpredictable things they were trying to summon.

Casia didn't seem eager to continue their conversation—neither was he. They could talk in endless circles about these things, but what would it solve?

He instead worked on rearranging the pile of blankets, dragging them toward the wall and closer to the fireplace. Then he leaned against that wall and motioned for her to join him.

She slid between his knees and rested her back against his chest, tilting her head toward the fire and watching the embers dance. He wrapped one hand around her waist, and he used his other to knead the tension from her back and neck, carefully avoiding the tender cuts and bruises.

It took time, but eventually she relaxed fully against him, and her eyes grew heavy. She slipped in and out of awareness—not quite asleep, but something like rest, at least. He kept absently massaging little circles against her warm skin. Some of the more shallow scars on that skin had already started to fade thanks to the goddess's ointment, which gave him some measure of peace— enough that he found himself slipping off to sleep as well.

It wasn't long, though, before he sensed an emptiness where she should have been, and it startled him back awake.

She was only inches away, staring into the fire. Her eyes were still full of questions when she glanced back at him. Questions that neither of them wanted to ask.

They didn't ask them.

He drew her back to him and kissed her. Slowly. He didn't want to rush through it. He didn't know how long it would be before they were back together like this, and it made each of her breaths feel sacred as they spilled over his skin, made every soft sound she made into something he wanted to pause and memorize so he could play it back when he needed it.

She brushed her hand along the stubble of his jaw. "It's later," she pointed out, reminding him of that promise he'd made beside the creek.

"So it is," he replied, a corner of his mouth lifting.

She leaned close, brought her lips a breath away

from his own. "What are you thinking about?" she asked, again.

"You," he answered again. He mirrored her reaching hand, trailing his fingers across her cheek. Then he swept those fingers lower, caught a strap of the thin top she wore and slowly pulled it down, exposing her breast.

"Only me this time?" she whispered.

"Only you this time," he said. "And every inch of you that I want to touch." He pulled his fingers over her stomach, slipping them beneath the band of her leggings and toward the warmth between her thighs. "Every inch I want to kiss." He captured the tip of her breast in his mouth, rolled it between his teeth until it grew stiff for him. "And to taste." He cupped that hand he had against her center, and used his thumb to stroke the sensitive, swollen bud of it. A small gasp escaped her, and the desire that lit in her eyes sent a shiver of dark, fiery need curling through him.

"Only you," he repeated.

"Good." She twisted her fingers into the front of his shirt. "Because I need you to do me a favor," she said, pulling his lips toward hers, "and help me forget about everything outside of this room for a little while."

CHAPTER 32

As her tongue pushed its way into his mouth, one of his fingers pushed its way inside of her, drawing a gasp in response. Her thighs clenched around his hand, and her hips rocked, trying to urge him deeper. He answered by curling his finger against her inner walls—only to withdraw it slowly, smiling at the soft noise of protest she made.

He pulled his shirt over his head and tossed it aside. He rose onto one knee and started to undo his belt, intending to slip out of the rest of his clothing. But she moved with him, pressed her hands against his bare stomach, and pushed him the rest of the way upright—and then back against the wall.

He let out a low laugh, caught off guard by the aggressiveness of it. "Feeling a bit controlling tonight, are we?"

"I seem to recall you telling me you weren't against the idea of me being in control."

The velvet tone of her voice sent a shock of arousal through him. "Not against it at all."

She continued the job of undressing him, her hands moving deftly to undo his belt and stripping everything down with it, allowing his erection to spring free. She lifted onto her toes and pressed her lips to his once more. Her hand moved over that erection as she kissed him, and it pulsed at her touch. His stomach clenched and his knees buckled. He sank back against the wall, digging a hand into the small of her back, dragging her with him.

His fingers slipped lower, cupping the back of her thigh and lifting her higher so he could attack her more ruthlessly with his tongue, plunging it deeper into her mouth, intertwining it with hers until he drew a moan from her.

She took a step back.

Her gaze lifted to his, full of heat and intent.

Every muscle in his body tensed in anticipation as she knelt before him—as she wrapped her fingers once more around his hard shaft and brought it toward her mouth.

She focused on just the tip at first, tracing slow, mesmerizing circles with her tongue while her hand moved up and down the full length. His eyes lifted toward the ceiling, and he breathed out a curse as her lips closed over that tip and slid down, up, and then further down—

He raked a hand through her hair, taking a tight grip on her head and holding her still as he rocked his hips and pushed deeper into her throat, and he held her in place until she gasped for air.

She leaned back but stayed on her knees, gazing up at him, eyes heavy with lust, mouth parted and glistening from his seed. Her tongue slipped out and along her lips.

Another curse fell from his mouth.

She repeated the act, the beginning of a smirk crossing those lips as she licked them this time.

He gripped her beneath the chin and pulled her up to him, roughly claiming her mouth with his own. "You have my attention," he rasped.

"And control?"

"For now." His lips grazed hers as he whispered the words, and her body quivered against him. "So what would you like me to do to you, hm?"

Her eyes darted toward a nearby chair, betraying her thoughts before she could speak. He grabbed the chair and shoved its back against the wall—she was going to need a more stable platform to balance against before he was done with her.

He closed the space between them and slipped a hand beneath her camisole, urging it upward.

She stripped it the rest of the way off.

The remainder of her clothing followed, and his breath caught as he drank in the fullness of her body. He would never get tired of the sight of her standing before him like this, exposed and expectant, her soft skin pebbling, her eyes burning into his.

He glanced toward the chair.

She didn't move toward it right away, but stepped closer to him instead, that rebellious little smirk back on her face. Teasing him again.

"If I didn't know any better," he said, darkly, "I would say you're testing me and *my* control."

Her fingers splayed across his chest, tracing circles before trailing lower. "When have I *ever* tested you and your control?"

He caught her fingers. Twisted her around and then pulled her to his chest. The heat from her skin seared into his, and it was precisely the sort of *test* he'd been talking about. And he had a feeling he was going to fail this particular trial.

He massaged her swollen breasts with one hand, while the other slid between her thighs and rubbed until she was moving, pushing against him without restraint. Until she seemed to let that desire for control slip away in favor of a desire for pleasure.

Make me forget, she'd said.

And that was what he was going to do.

He guided her toward that chair.

"Bend over it," he commanded.

She didn't hesitate this time. He grazed his fingers along the curve of her back as she went down, pushing her more completely against the chair's bottom. He admired the view for a moment before slipping his palm against her warm center and jerking her hips higher.

Her legs stretched apart, inviting him in. He guided the tip of his arousal over her, teasing and tapping until she was slick and ready to take the fullness of him in, and then he entered her, letting out a shuddering breath as he did.

That feeling from earlier struck him again—he wanted to take this slower. To move in an easier rhythm than the wars they were facing and savor every tremble that traveled through her, every clench of her desire. Every slow thrust, every deliberate move he made, felt like an act of rebellion against that ever-present feeling of time running out for them.

But it couldn't last forever, and after a few minutes her hips were moving with increased fervor, begging him faster.

He caught one of her wrists and then the other, and he pulled her toward him, arching her back as he thrusted deeper. The first of those deep thrusts caused her to cry out, a beautiful sound that made his body shiver and his breath catch. He latched his mouth onto the side of her neck, stifling his own cry, and he continued to thrust, harder and deeper.

He soon felt her building toward an end, her legs

quivering and threatening to give way beneath the waves of release.

He lifted her away from the chair and carried her to the blankets by the fire. Laid her down on her back, so that he could see her face. There was no more talk of control, no more teasing—only a single, essential thought: He needed to be inside of her, to bring her to that place where nothing existed outside of the two of them.

He drove into her once more, and he pounded until her fists clenched in the blankets and her head tipped back and her lips opened in a soft little 'o'.

The sound of her release sent him roaring toward his own. His mouth came down upon hers, and he pushed deeper and held there until every last drop of himself was hers, until the tension in both of their bodies shuddered away, and they drifted into that peaceful emptiness of *after*.

His arms were braced on either side of her, shaking slightly. He held himself over top of her for several moments, his forehead pressed to hers, his eyes closed, their bodies still joined and throbbing in the same rhythm.

Finally, he withdrew. He gathered her in his arms and leaned against the wall as he'd done earlier, holding her tight against him and resting his head upon hers.

"You're terrible at ceding control," she murmured after a minute.

He laughed, the sound soft and muffled by her hair. "I'll work on it." He kissed her temple, and then added, "If you could work on not being so tempting, so that I wouldn't feel the need to have my way with you so often, that would help."

"I'll see what I can do," she yawned, burrowing into his chest and closing her eyes.

A half-hour passed. The fire was dying, taking its warmth with it. There was more wood on the hearth, but he didn't want to move. Casia's eyes were closed, the stiffness finally gone from her muscles, and he didn't want to disturb her.

He reached for one of the blankets and pulled it more completely around her. And as he held her against him, his conversation with Nephele played through his mind again.

I hope she's worth the chance of ruin.

What the Goddess of Storms did not realize—or perhaps chose to ignore—was that he had already been walking a road to ruin for most of his existence. He had seen too much darkness. Killed too many who may or may not have deserved it. Stolen too much. Rebelled too often, and yet not often enough.

And he'd left more chaos and destruction in his wake than he cared to think about.

So no, Casia would not be the thing that ruined him.

If anything, she was the one who had pulled him back from the edge.

She curled closer to him. He smoothed her hair from her face. His fingers accidentally brushed over the mark his former master had left, and Death magic flared, soft but certain, between them.

More of the chaos and destruction he had helped cause.

He pulled his hand away from her, closing it into a fist. He couldn't tell who that magic had originated from. And he didn't know how this connection—this latest chapter in their strange story—would end. He still didn't see a way that it could end happily for *both* of them.

But he had promised to stand side-by-side with her no matter what, and so as long as his heart was still beating, that was what he would do.

He wrapped his arms around her once more. "I love you," he whispered, even though he was certain she was too asleep to hear it, "and whatever comes next, don't forget that."

CHAPTER 33

UNDER A DEEP BLUE, PRE-DAWN SKY, THE CAMP WAS BEGINNING to stir back to life.

Cas walked the edge of it, keeping to the shadows and avoiding eye contact with anyone who passed too close to her.

She'd had that dream again. The one with the cold, the emptiness, the great black void that threatened to swallow her up. It seemed to linger on the edge of her vision even now, that void—black fingers closing in, tunneling her sight and making it impossible to focus on anything that wasn't directly in front of her.

And the mark the Rook God had given her...oh, how it *ached*.

It had ached worse when she'd first woken up. Throbbed with the same sort of pain that had overtaken her after she'd accidentally seized and channeled

Elander's magic while fighting the Ice Goddess's monster.

Elander had been asleep when she left. It was unlike him to not wake soon after she did. He could always sense her moving about the room, no matter how quiet she tried to be. She wondered if she had been inadvertently siphoning power from him even as they slept.

They were supposed to face things side-by-side.

But how could they do that if she was a danger to his very existence?

It was the same question that had haunted her for weeks. And today would bring answers. She was determined to make that so. But she was also terrified of what some of those answers would be.

Someone coughed close by—too close. Cas wrapped her coat more tightly around herself, lowered her gaze, and hurried on. The air tingled with trepidation, with sounds that made all the little hairs on her body stand on end. The rattling of weapons and armor, the nickering of horses, the steady drum of orders being recited. The various regiments were already starting to move out, it seemed, off to create their blockades. To buy her time, to protect her so that she could focus on what she needed to do.

She made her way to the section of creek she'd bathed in last night. Knelt beside it. Splashed several handfuls of icy water onto her face. Stared at her reflection—at that mark on her cheek, which now appeared to be glowing around the edges.

She was bristling all over with Death energy.

And somehow, she had to make it *stop*.

Today was about Dawnskeep, and summoning the Sun Goddess and appealing to her for help. Or, at the very least, it was about waking the full extent of that goddess's power within her. *Lightness*, not darkness. If she could just focus on that light...

She had managed it last night, when she'd slipped away, alone, to the tower. She'd been overwhelmed then, and she'd felt the darkness catching a foothold and preparing to overtake her. She'd sat in the room of that tower and focused on pushing down the dark until lightning rose from her palm.

She gritted her teeth and tried to do the same thing now.

But it wouldn't come. She kept trying, but every spark flickered out almost immediately, and every failure threatened to trigger that panic she'd been fighting against since waking up.

You can't panic.

She didn't have the time or energy to spare for that.

The camp was growing too busy, full of too many other potential triggers, so she crept back up to the tower room.

Elander was finally awake, pulling on the last of his clothes as she stepped inside.

She managed a *hello* that she thought had sounded perfectly normal, but she could feel the immediate shift in his demeanor, from sleepy to concerned, even though he kept his voice casual as he asked, "Where'd you go?"

"Nowhere." She started to sort through the weapons piled next to the fireplace, to select the knives she would carry into Dawnskeep. She didn't suspect she would need weapons if all went according to plan— but she felt better if she was carrying them. She kept her back to Elander as she added, "For a walk, that's all."

His reply was soft. "Casia."

"Just a bad morning," she said. "I'll be fine in a moment." She focused on wrapping a belt around her waist, clipping a sheath to it, and then kneeling and securing a second sheath at her ankle.

Elander's eyes were full of concern when she finally looked toward him.

And for some reason, it was that look that served as the final trigger.

She didn't want him to be concerned about her. She wanted to be *fine in a moment*, as she'd said. To have the courage, the focus, to take care of the things she needed to take care of. Like the heroes in stories who seemed to have an endless supply of both of those things. *They* did not hide in towers when battle plans were being made, and they did not have minds that went around and around in circles like hers was doing now, obsessively trying to destroy her as surely as any of her many, many other enemies were.

She was still kneeling on the floor, she realized, and now she felt too heavy to stand up.

"I just...I feel like I can't afford bad mornings anymore. Or bad *moments*, even. But they still come. Sometimes they just hit and I..." She lifted one of her hands from the floor. Watched it shake before her. Clenched it, unclenched, clenched it again, trying to make it stop. She wanted so badly to make it *stop*.

But she couldn't.

Her voice trembled almost as badly as her hand as she said, "How am I going to be everything that I need to be if I can't get rid of moments like this? They're going to find me out, Elander. They are going to see *this*—" she held up her shaking hand, and she had to grit her teeth together for a moment to keep from crying out in frustration "—and they are going to know I can't do what I need to do. I can't fake it all the time. I feel like I'm fighting my mind along with everything else, and it's worse than all of the monsters hunting us. There are people outside of these walls who think I'm going to be a queen. Gods, I *told* them that I was going to be queen, a leader that they could follow, a summoner of gods and —" Her words choked to a stop.

She was out of breath.

She felt like she was drowning. Her eyes darted around the room, desperately seeking...something.

Anything to grab onto. She could see Elander, but he was blurry, far away on a shore she couldn't seem to make herself swim back to.

He came out to meet her instead, and he sat beside her, but she still couldn't make herself reach for him.

She clutched a hand into her hair instead, squeezed until it pulled. Until it hurt. "You're thinking I've lost my mind, aren't you?"

He was quiet for another moment, his eyes on their feet. "I think," he said, slowly, "that nobody has to be okay all of the time. Not even queens."

She sucked in a deep breath. Held it. Tried to let it out slowly. "And what about potential saviors of the world?"

His head tilted toward her. "Not them either."

"But it would be helpful if I could be okay on *this* particular day, right?" she asked wryly.

He took her hand, gently pulled it away from her hair, and held it still. "I'd be lying if I said otherwise."

She sucked in another deep breath. Closed her eyes. Let that breath shudder out of her.

"But you don't have to do it alone," said Elander. "Side-by-side, remember? That's what we promised back in Kosrith."

"Yes, but that's part of the problem." She stared at one of the scars on her arm until her vision slid out of focus once more. "Because the pull of that Dark power we share is getting stronger."

He worked his fingers into the spaces between hers.

"I didn't think I was going to make it out of Moreth," she said quietly. "And once I *was* out, it all hit at once. That Death magic was in control of me, and not the other way around. I wasn't thinking about the consequences of it. I just wanted to make the ones following us out of that realm pay. It almost...consumed me. And that feeling keeps coming back."

His thumb traced up and down her skin, while his brow creased in thought. "We just have to stay focused on today."

Her hand shook in his.

"We're going to Dawnskeep, and once there, the energy that surrounds that place will push the darkness down. You'll be able to focus on summoning that Goddess of Life, and she can fix this. All of this."

"I can't stop running through worst-case scenarios in my head. If anything happens to you, to Zev, to Nessa —to *any* of them—then I am going to lose this battle. I am going to give into that darkness, and I'm afraid that no amount of power from the Sun Goddess will stop me."

"Nothing is going to happen to—"

"Don't."

He inhaled and released a slow breath.

"You can't promise that. So don't."

He didn't argue.

"Part of me thinks you should go," she said. "That it

would be safer. Just in case things go poorly today, and I *do* lose control again, like I did that night at the river."

"You know I'm not going anywhere."

She bowed her head, frustrated, because she did know that. And she also knew she needed him to stay.

"It's normal, you know," he told her, "that growing lack of control. It's part of ascension—and the Dark God is particularly merciless in his grip."

She managed another deep breath. "*You* fought that grip, though."

"...Eventually." There was a knock at the door before he could elaborate. He rose to his feet and moved to answer it.

Cas could not take her eyes off him. "How?" she asked. "You denied that control even *after* you had fully ascended as his servant. But *how*?"

He stopped. Turned around and studied her for a moment, and then took a few steps back and offered his hand. "I got lucky," he replied.

She gave him a curious look as he helped her to her feet.

"I found something that pulled me back," he said with a shrug.

Another knock, and this time he hesitated before heading to answer it. "Whatever that is about, I can deal with it," he said, glancing toward the door. "And I'll see you outside in a few moments."

She nodded.

He left.

After several minutes and several more deep breaths, she successfully managed to slow her racing thoughts to a more manageable rate.

She picked up the Heart of the Sun from its resting place by the fire, slipped it into an inner pocket of her jacket, and then walked back to the pile of weapons and supplies she'd been sorting through. She secured the last of her knives. Took the sword she planned to carry, and she withdrew it from its scabbard for just a moment, just long enough to catch a glimpse of her face in its polished blade—a glimpse of that dark, feathered mark stretching across her skin.

After today, that mark would be gone.

One way or another.

ONCE OUTSIDE, she quickly spotted Elander; he stood with Caden and General Kolvar, speaking with one of the scouts who had been sent to patrol the area north of Grayedge where Varen had most recently been spotted.

The scout briefly lowered his head as she approached. He looked exceptionally young. And nervous. He stuttered and shook through most of the report he was giving, but he eventually gave it clearly enough: He'd spotted Varen and his traveling party moving closer to Malgraves, rather than away from it like they'd hoped. Which meant he was now further north than they would have liked—but still a good way's off.

So they had *some* time to work with, at least.

She had her own regiment to work with as well; after dismissing the scout, General Kolvar led them to the group that had been chosen to accompany her to Dawnskeep.

They had decided to build this group out of magic wielders who all ultimately derived their power from the Sun Goddess, in hopes that their pooled magical energy might help Cas with her summoning task.

Two dozen Storm-kind were among them, all lined in orderly rows and all baring the symbol of the goddess they served. A few looked vaguely familiar; Cas thought they had been among the servants that had walked the halls of Nephele's mortal-side haven. The horses they held on to wore the same armor—special protective coverings to guard against electricity—that Cas had seen once before, when they had rented beasts to cross the Cobos Desert in Sundolia.

Behind these horses and their riders were at least twenty more riders, most of them Sky-kind. All of them wore the royal insignia of Sadira— a combination of the Sky Goddess's wind and clouds with a sword wrapped within them.

"The guide that the Moon Goddess was going to send..." Cas began, her eyes scanning her group for the one thing that seemed to be missing.

Elander frowned. "Late, I'm afraid."

"But Varen has drawn closer," General Kolvar reminded them, "and I don't think it would be wise to wait another day before we try to put *something* into motion. If our plan doesn't work, then we'll need time to come up with a different one. Guide or no guide, you should get moving."

Uneasiness curled in the pit of her stomach, but Cas agreed with him. "We'll proceed as planned."

Laurent approached soon after she'd made this decision, bringing news of more decisions that he and the others had been busy making.

"Zev and I will lead a company to block any trouble that may come from the roads to the east, and we'll be close by in case you run into any unexpected problems at the shores," he told her. "Rhea and Nessa will stay at camp and keep things organized and prepared here, and Silver will go with you so you can keep a link to this base, and they can watch over you and send more aid if need be."

Their gazes met and held as he awaited her reply.

Cas was slow to answer. She was only just allowing herself to accept the fact that he was *alive*, and that they'd actually made it to this next part of their mission. She'd been so certain she'd lost him in Moreth—and in the Cobos Desert weeks before that—and it was becoming a reflex now, the way her heart squeezed every time they started to part ways...even if only for a little while.

There was no such thing as *business as usual* between her and her friends anymore.

But she still tried to act as if that was exactly what this all was, and she nodded. "I'll see you on the other side."

He surprised her by wrapping her in an embrace. "You can do this," he told her as he pulled away. "If the goddess will answer *anybody's* call, it will be yours."

She hoped with everything in her that he was right.

Zev appeared a moment later and pulled her into a second hug, and he was followed quickly by Rhea and Nessa. More encouraging words and too-brief goodbyes passed in a blur, and then suddenly she was on the back of her horse, Silverfoot sharing her saddle, heading north with her small army. Elander had one last brief discussion with Caden before he joined her, and after that, Cas didn't look back.

It was only a five-mile ride to the edge of the sea, but the landscape changed dramatically over that relatively short distance.

As she cantered alongside Elander, her eyes were constantly darting from one side to the other, trying to take in everything. She remembered Prince Alder's stories about these northern shores—about how the magic that emanated from them had created fertile stretches of land

487

all around. Now she saw the true evidence of this; the grass they moved through was a brilliant shade of green, swept through with white flowers, and so thick that they occasionally had to stop and cut their way through it. Cas would have sworn that grass started to shift and grow back as soon as it was severed.

Directly ahead was a forest full of the tallest trees she had ever seen, its lush canopy of leaves gleaming in the waning moonlight. Rocky outcroppings and cliffs rose to the left of this forest, half-hidden by vegetation that seemed to be growing out of every crevice.

Elander and several of their Storm-kind followers had taken this same path when they came to scope out the shores in the days prior, so they led the way into those trees ahead without hesitation.

It was almost completely dark within the cover of the forest. The Storm-kind summoned bolts of lightning and worked them into makeshift lanterns that floated alongside them. Cas did the same—partly because she wanted to be able to see, and partly to prove to herself that she could summon and control that lightning. It was easier with the other Storm magic already hovering around her, as she'd expected it might be. And it seemed to grow even less demanding on her as they traveled closer to the sea—toward the energy she could already feel radiating from it.

The orbs of electricity drew moths toward them and stirred all manner of things in the shadows; she heard birds fluttering awake, small animals panting and scurrying, frogs croaking and splashing into the streams and pools of silver-blue water that seemed to be everywhere she looked.

The air felt thick on her tongue. It reminded her a bit of the Wild In-Between that separated the Kethran and Sundolian Empires—too much magic confined into too little space. Except it was all magic that complimented each other—all derived from the Sun Goddess—and so it wasn't nearly as disorienting or unsettling as that wild place. It was the opposite, really. It was a relief, because it was already pushing the darker shades of her magic down, just as Elander had said it would.

Something like hope was rising in her, lighting her from inside as surely as those orbs of Storm magic were lighting up their path.

Silverfoot growled suddenly. His fur bristled and his tail fluffed as he placed a paw on the saddle's horn and leaned forward.

Cas followed his line of sight, drawing her horse slowly to a stop.

Elander glanced back. He started to speak, but then fell silent in concentration. He sensed it, too.

Something was moving among the tree branches.

A shadowy figure encircled them, leaping gracefully from one branch to another until it was directly beside Cas's horse. It paused. Hooked its long arms around a white limb, lowered itself down, and peered back at her.

And she was certain of it, then—she *knew* those lanky limbs, that deer-like face, those glowing white eyes.

Because they had met months ago, in a forest not unlike this one.

"The Mist spirit?"

Elander released a slow, relieved breath, and he nodded. "He serves Inya," he reminded her. "So there's your guide after all. Let's hope he's not feeling as mischievous as he usually is."

The spirit let go of the branch and fell toward the earth. He swirled into tendrils of blue smoke and disappeared before hitting the ground, mildly spooking a few of the horses as he went.

Even though he had a reputation as a troublemaker, he'd seen Cas safely through that last forest they'd met in—so his appearance didn't deflate that cautious hope that had started to blossom inside of her.

She could hear the sea crashing in the distance. And she didn't know how this would all end, but she had powerful allies, at least. She wasn't alone.

She could do this.

That newly-strengthened resolve that lasted for approximately half a mile, until they left the sanctuary of towering trees and started on a downward trek toward that sea—and then she saw something that made her heart drop into her stomach.

A group of riders stood on the shoreline, most of them wearing the regalia of her brother's Grand Army, and several wielding banners that featured the black tiger of the House of Solasen.

And though she was still too far away to see him clearly, she was almost certain that the man waiting at the front of this group was Varen himself.

"Of course," Elander muttered.

She thought of that scout giving his report back at their fortress. Of how nervous he'd looked when telling them about Varen's whereabouts. She'd suspected it had been because he was young and frightened, but maybe it was because of something else. Maybe...

"The scout lied," she whispered.

"Why would he lie?"

She scanned that group below them, focusing on a different flag that fluttered in the breeze alongside those black-tiger banners—silver and blue flags. The colors of Moreth. Elander followed her gaze, and realization registered in his eyes a moment later. His jaw clenched. "Another case of a stolen identity?"

"Seems like it. Whether by magic, or questionable elven tricks, or otherwise."

"So what's become of our actual scout? Of *all* the scouts we sent toward Grayedge?"

Cas didn't want to guess.

She also didn't want to think about all of the other messengers that had been coming in and out of their camp. All the moving pieces, all the work they'd done to arrange things and make this mission as foolproof as possible...Was *any* of the information they were working off of accurate? What had become of the other groups they'd sent to secure other places?

Her horse shuddered beneath her, flicked his ears, and tried to turn back toward that forest they'd just passed through.

She twisted them around and saw more enemy riders heading toward them, already close enough to block off any mad dash that she and her allies might try to make back to their fortress.

Her heart thundered in her chest.

Were they completely surrounded?

Silverfoot pawed at her hand. His eyes were aglow with his magic, burning brightly in the twilight.

Running her fingers through his soft fur helped anchor her back in the moment. "This is why we brought Silver with us," she said, as calmly as she could manage. "Rhea will see what's happening, and she'll pass the message on to the ones at camp, and backup will be here soon. We have plenty of bodies to fight. The others just need to readjust and reassign them."

Elander agreed, though the corners of his mouth fell as he looked toward the sea.

The sun was rising over that sea, and Cas could see the path of stone and sand sparkling in the low tide, leading out to a series of small islands. A haze of magic surrounded them.

"My plan hasn't changed," she said quietly. "I can

feel the power of this place, and you were right—it's pushing the dark magic inside of me down. If I can just get to that path through the sea and into Dawnskeep, Varen won't be able to follow me through that veil of magic that surrounds it, right? He won't be able to stop me."

"No," Elander said. "He won't."

"And then you just need to hold on until reinforcements arrive, or until I manage to accomplish what we came here for, and..." She trailed off, her chest suddenly too tight to allow her to breathe. It was that look he was giving her. The admiration in it, the concern, the hope, the everything, *everything* that she was so afraid to lose.

I found something that pulled me back, he'd told her earlier.

He'd meant her.

And she had him to pull *her* back—him, and all her other friends who were counting on her to succeed. To come back with help, whether in the form of her fully awakened magic, or the Sun Goddess herself.

She would not fail them.

She managed to release a slow breath, and that steely resolve from earlier came back and settled over her.

Elander's mouth edged up in a half smile, as if he could sense that resolve. "We've been in worse situations," he said with a shrug.

She mirrored that crooked smile. "I'm fairly certain this doesn't even rank in the top five."

His amusement faded as he turned and raced his horse up and down the lines of their followers, giving orders. Then he was back to her, giving her one last long, meaningful look.

"Side-by-side?" he asked.

She nodded, and together they descended.

CHAPTER 34

"GREETINGS, SISTER," VAREN CALLED AS SHE APPROACHED.

She didn't bother with a greeting herself. "I warned you to stay out of my way, didn't I?"

He glanced around at his fellow riders, as though he thought she might be talking to someone else. "Am I in your way?"

"I have business off these shores that doesn't concern you," she said. "Let me pass."

"I didn't hear you say *please*."

The air around her was full of subtle crackles of power—the Storm-kind were not even visibly working to summon it; the energy of this sacred place was pulling it out. A twist of electricity sparked inside of Cas as well, eager and ready to rise alongside the rest of that power, but she pushed it down for the moment, trying to stay focused.

"I'm not here to fight you," she called.

He shrugged. "Likewise. I didn't actually come to the north to deal with *you*. I was on business in Malgraves." He looked to one of the riders on his left—an elven woman wearing a sapphire headpiece that shimmered as it caught a piece of the rising sun. "But then I got word from Queen Sarith that you were making yourself a nuisance again. That you had made a mess of the accommodations I so lovingly tried to arrange for you in Moreth. You keep insisting on breaking free from me, on meddling with magic and making yourself more danger-ous, and what am I supposed to do? Let that go unchecked? That's how you get tyrants, you know."

"And you can only have one of those in the family at any given time, I suppose," Elander remarked, deadpan.

Varen's gaze slid over him. Lingered for a moment on the Death mark on Elander's hand. Then it jumped to all of the Storm-kind and Sky-kind who were assembled beside him and Cas. "Yes," he finally replied. "Otherwise it gets too complicated."

He looked back to her, and even though Cas was used to that cold, empty stare of his, it still made the hairs on the back of her neck prickle.

"Let me pass," she said again.

He held up a finger as though overtaken by a sudden idea. "How about this," he said. "I'll make the same offer I made back in Kosrith. Let's sit down and talk about that magic you and your friends possess, and how you can use it to help me in my noble endeavors, and then perhaps we can stop with these little scuffles."

She didn't reply. She had been done trying to negotiate with him when she was in Kosrith, and nothing had changed since then.

Her head tilted toward Elander.

"Be quick," he said under his breath—the last words they exchanged before everything sprang into motion.

He signaled. A line of the Storm-kind raced forward, darting between their group and Varen's and summoning their magic as they went. A deluge of lightning danced toward their enemies, pushing them back.

Once more space was established between the two groups, the Sky-kind rushed in and started to weave a wall of magic, holding that space. Cas hesitated only a moment to see their success. Their side was outnumbered, but the energy of these shores was clearly turning their magic into an even bigger advantage than it normally would have been.

With her route now guarded, she leapt from her horse and thumped it hard on the hindquarters, sending it galloping back up the hillside and away from the battlefield. Then she turned and sprinted for the edge of the sea, for the exposed path of rock and silt that was glowing a molten orange in the dawn's light.

That elven woman who'd been beside Varen had somehow wiggled past the barriers of magic. She raced toward Cas with her sword drawn.

Cas let the eager lightning inside of her burst free.

It sought the elven woman with vicious, deadly speed. Its strike was so powerful within the airs of these shores that it nearly made Cas lose her balance.

She could sense the elf's passing almost instantly. Her Death abilities were still there, just buried—and she might have panicked at the way that magic had abruptly resurfaced...if it hadn't felt so *good*.

It briefly satisfied her itch for revenge, killing one of Sarith's followers, and the Dark magic inside of her grabbed hold of that feeling and nearly used it to climb to the surface.

She shook it off, turned back to the sea, and ran faster.

The shallow water was shockingly cold; she could feel it even through her thick boots. It was made bearable only by the warmth of her Sun-derived magic, reacting to the warmth of the magic in the air—a reaction that grew even more pronounced as she drew nearer to the veil of magic that separated Dawnskeep from the shores it faced.

That veil...Elander had gotten close to it, and their Storm-kind allies had gotten even closer, but what if she couldn't get close *enough?* What if she couldn't get through it?

She didn't stop running mainly because she didn't have any other plan at this point.

And luckily, she had only an instant for doubt to truly sink in, and then she was on the other side.

The change around her was immediate. It was like stepping into an entirely different world—one far removed from the shores behind her, even though she could still see a hazy image of those shores. There were no sounds, save for her own breathing. Not from the battle waging behind her, not from the water shifting over the rocky, shell-scattered path below her.

She jogged onward. And onward, and onward until finally she saw a small island ahead of her, a bright light in its center and at least a dozen statues encircling it.

A shiver washed from her scalp down to the tips of her toes.

But the tide was not in her favor as she'd expected it to be—there was a very large expanse of water between her and that island.

She had just started to brace herself for a very cold swim when suddenly she heard a sound like raindrops falling through leaves. Fog appeared above the water, and it quickly twisted into a familiar shape.

The Mist spirit, here to guide her.

"Hello, old friend," she said, her voice slightly hushed, overtaken by the same awe that had struck her when she'd seen this spirit for the first time.

He floated above the water for a moment before lowering onto the surface of it. Wherever his mist-shrouded feet fell upon that water, stones appeared. He ran in a circle before her, creating more of them, until she got the idea—and the courage—to step forward onto one of those stones.

Then he turned and bounded away, leaving a trail for her to follow.

The stones disappeared almost as quickly as they came, so there was no time to second guess the path she was being led on. If she stopped, she feared she would sink.

The spirit bounded toward the island. His body shifted and changed as he went, stretching out and becoming more beast-like. He was swift—a blur against the gray water—and Cas kept waiting for the moment when her legs would get too tired to keep up with him.

It never came.

The energy of this place seemed to fuel her body as much as her magic. They reached the island in moments, and her feet fell upon solid, sandy ground once more—and then she was immediately faced with another dubious surface; the only solid part of the island, it turned out, was the ring around its edges, upon which those twelve statues of the Vitala stood. The center was a pool of silver liquid that offered a star-tlingly clear reflection of everything above it—too clear to be natural. She wasn't even certain it was water.

The Mist spirit made no path against this surface. He simply dove into it, and then reemerged twenty feet ahead, slinking up onto the one solid place within the center of the island—a small platform with a statue of the Sun Goddess. The goddess's palms were cupped together and lifted up to the sky; they were the origin of that bright light Cas had seen earlier.

She hesitated on the edge, peering down. She could only see her own reflection. She couldn't see anything below or even guess at how deep it might have gone.

But when she tested it with a light, tapping step, she found that it splashed like water, and it barely covered the sole of her boot. She took a few more cautious steps. The water never splashed higher than her ankles. It was still unnerving; she felt as if that mirrored surface could be concealing drop-offs, and that one wrong step would send her plummeting down into a cold abyss.

But the lesser-spirit was sitting beside the goddess, watching expectantly, and he had not led her astray thus far.

So she kept moving.

She made it all the way to that center platform without sinking.

The goddess's entire statue was imposing, but Cas's gaze caught on those upturned palms and the light coming from them, and she couldn't look away. They made *Dawnskeep* seem an appropriate name for this place; they looked as though they were collecting the emerging sunlight, while the statues surrounding the island looked ready to protect that light at any cost.

She hadn't known precisely what to expect once she

arrived in this place, or how to proceed once here, but now an idea came to her.

She took the Heart of the Sun from her pocket. Walked up to the goddess, and she placed that stolen treasure within her cupped palms. A shiver of power seemed to race through her as the Heart settled into the stone. Her imagination, maybe, but she still clung to it, hoping...

The Mist spirit watched her curiously as she backed away and sat down before the goddess.

She bowed her head and focused on channeling her magic. Lightning rose around her easily enough. But she also thought of the other times she'd used power derived from Solatis—of the power the Moon Goddess had given her to open paths, of the Sky magic she had used to protect herself and her brother as children, and of all the other strange things that had seemed to be without explanation or purpose until now.

She felt herself slipping out of awareness of her surroundings, and into a place that felt expansive and eternal. The goddesses of the Sun Court were directing magic toward their master too; she could feel it. And there were those Storm and Sky-kind close by on the shore, fighting with her. All this magic... She felt connected to *all* of it. She just had to keep that connection, to keep directing it toward the hands of that goddess before her.

She wasn't sure how much time was passing.

But then a sudden wave of exhaustion overtook her, and her hold on her magic released with a jarring snap.

She'd hoped for some sign of progress following the release. But the only change she felt was the wakening warmth of the sun. Her head lifted and she saw that sun rising, red and blinding, behind the goddess. The color almost made the statue seem more alive, and Cas almost dared to hope as she rose to her feet and lifted her gaze.

But no—only stone eyes looked back at her.

She felt utterly and hopelessly alone.

"Please," she heard herself whisper. "*Help.*"

Her gaze trailed away from the goddess, away from the blinding light behind her and the warriors surrounding her, and she fixated on her own reflection instead. On the marks and bruises on her face. On the memories of what had *caused* those bruises.

And suddenly she felt it—the same energy that had overtaken her after she'd killed that elf woman. The cold, distinct energy of a life slipping away.

People were dying on the other side of the quiet she sat within, and she could sense it. Too many people. But she had no way of knowing *who*.

Not as long as she was here, focusing on what was beginning to feel like a waste of her time.

Fear took her in a merciless embrace. And she would have sworn that she heard the sounds of battle emerging through the crack in her concentration— which only made it *harder* to concentrate.

She turned frantically back to the goddess's statue. Her heart clenched like a fist, furious and tight. She couldn't believe that such a powerful deity might truly be chained, and so the only explanation she was willing to believe in that moment was that Solatis *had* forsaken them. She would not fight for them.

"Why won't you *help*?" she pleaded.

The Heart still rested, dull and useless, in those upturned palms.

Cas snatched it away from the goddess, and she very nearly flung it at one of the solemn-faced warriors surrounding them. The only thing that stopped her were more ribbons of cold energy, those telltale signs of fading lives— so many at once that it nearly brought her to her knees.

So many were dying.

And the goddess slept on.

Hadn't they sacrificed enough? Hadn't *she* sacrificed enough? Her body ached. Her skin was covered in scars. Her magic itself had nearly torn her apart, over and over again, and it felt powerful enough in that moment to shatter the entire island that she stood upon. It would have taken little more than a snap of her fingers. So why wasn't it *enough*?

The Heart shook in her hands. She tried to calm herself down. She needed more time to figure this out.

But she wasn't going to get it.

She was no longer in a quiet, separate world. Reality

was bleeding into it. It was not her imagination—she could hear the clash of steel and the cries of the battle nearby. Panic spiked through her.

"I need to go back."

She spun around, searching for that spirit that had led her to this pointless place.

He was gone.

"No! I need to go back!"

He didn't reappear.

But suddenly she turned, took a step, and the island and all of its contents—all of the statues and the strange, silver water—were gone. She was standing on an empty sandbar. Directly in front of her was that natural path made by the low tides, ready for her to walk upon it once more.

How?

It had to have been a trick. She had raced across the water, followed those stones the spirit had left for her....

But trick or not, the path before her was rapidly washing away as daybreak arrived, so she didn't waste any more time.

She ran until she came again to the veil of magic that separated Dawnskeep from that battle on the shores. No one seemed to notice her, so she stared for a moment, alone and shaking, and tried to get her bearings.

Varen's army seemed to have multiplied.

Her own had as well, but not by nearly as many. She spotted a man that she thought looked like Laurent.

Puffs of smoke and fire that could have been Zev. But it was hard to tell anything for certain from this distance, and with so much chaos between them.

Closer to where she stood, she spotted Elander, a whirlwind of blades cutting down body after body. Seeing him alive alleviated the panic in her somewhat— until she caught a glimpse of the man a short distance away from him, cutting through an equally impressive number of bodies.

Varen.

She slipped the Heart of the Sun back into her pocket. She would have thrown it into the sea if not for the way it made her think of Asra. Sentimental value. That was clearly the only power it held, now.

Which meant she would have to rely on her own power.

So be it.

Suddenly she didn't care about that Sun Goddess who had forsaken her. Didn't need her help. Didn't *want* her help.

Because she was perfectly capable of using her sword.

And now she would use it to end her brother's reign of terror on her own, once and for all.

CHAPTER 35

SHE STEPPED BACK THROUGH THE VEIL AND STRODE TOWARD the shore. Her gaze leveled on Varen. She bellowed out his name.

He turned. Caught sight of her and smiled.

Then she was running again, hand on the knife at her thigh.

Her recklessly quick approach seemed to catch him off guard. He turned to face her more fully, and he started to change his stance, to lift and ready his sword —but he was too slow to manage a swing.

The magic of these shores was still feeding into Cas's strength and stamina, it seemed; she moved so quickly it surprised even her. She whipped the knife free and stabbed for his stomach.

He managed to twist aside, and she caught his hip instead.

As he danced back and away, she sensed another body approaching. She spun around and stabbed at this one too, moving even faster than before. She managed a better-targeted strike, and the knife sank into her attacker's belly. She shoved it deeper, then aimed a kick into his groin and put him on the ground.

She abandoned her knife to his stomach, and she withdrew her sword as she spun back toward her brother.

He swung immediately for her.

She met his blade with enough force to knock him aside, but he only laughed, regained his balance, and swung harder. She fended him off, bounced back, and readjusted her grip.

"I thought for sure you'd run away," he said.

She didn't reply with words—only with a sweeping strike toward his chest. He deflected. Another swing from him, another parry from her. Over and over in an exhausting, seemingly endless dance. She was good, but so was he. They traded blows at equal rates until he somehow managed to back her toward an outcropping of rocks without her realizing it, and then suddenly they were no longer on even footing.

She stopped backing into the rocks and set her feet as best she could in the limited space.

He feinted. She flinched—just barely, just enough to give him time to follow-up with a true swipe that came too fast for her to properly block. His blade caught her sword arm and ripped through, leaving a line of fiery agony in its wake.

She managed to hold tight to her weapon, but the pain briefly disoriented her. She stumbled, hit a bit of shifting stone, and went down hard on one knee. Blood wound its way down her arm, collecting between her palm and the grip of her sword.

"Your technique is sloppy. Not at all like a queen's," Varen informed her, stalking closer. "You'll have to work on that if you intend to...what was it you said you were going to do?" His sword caught her beneath the chin, lifted it, poked deeper into her throat. "Rip the crown from my head? If you want to—"

She grabbed a loose rock and flung it, striking him in the eye.

He stopped talking. As he reached for his face, she rolled away, braced a boot against a sturdier bit of rock, and then launched herself at him.

It was *sloppy*, maybe, but her sword managed to catch the hand he had against his eye, and part of the face beneath it. She pressed in and tore through.

He responded with an adrenaline-fueled cry, spinning after her and slamming his sword into hers.

Her hand was already slick with too much blood. The shockingly powerful swing was enough to make her precarious hold on her weapon slip further. He saw that weakness, and the hilt of his sword came down hard against her shoulder a moment later, jarring her and knocking her blade the rest of the way free. As it clattered to the ground, he brought his fist up into her stomach.

She staggered back.

He wasted no time with words. He was all rage, now, his face covered in blood, one of his eyes swollen shut. He swung for her chest. She barely managed to dodge it. The movement itself was enough to cause a fresh surge of pain through her bleeding arm—one so excruciating that it took away her breath.

It was the last strike she could handle.

The space around them began to darken.

There were Storm-kind battling nearby. Sparks of their magic filled the air all around...until suddenly they *didn't*. Because a cold magic was rising around Cas, draining it. Draining *all* of the Sun-derived magic that drenched these shores.

Maybe the lighter magic had never really been there at all; it had only been a trick of the Mist spirit—of the divine beings he served—trying to make Cas believe that she had help. That there was *hope* here.

And now it was all leaving her, just as the upper-goddess had left them all, alone and covered in blood in the middle of another battle she couldn't win.

But the darkness surrounding her now was not a *trick*. It was solid, and it could protect her. It could do *more* than protect.

Varen had started to back away from her.

Like a rat fleeing for higher ground.

Her earlier assessment held true.

She wasn't going to let him escape this time. She couldn't seem to make herself move after him—her magic was too heavy, too tightly wrapped around her—but she didn't need to move.

She felt the threads of Varen's life from where she stood. Of *all* the lives around her. She reached out a hand and bent her fingers, imagining herself pulling those threads taut. Snapping them. And then she found that she could move after all. She only needed to let that magic pull her, guide her. Every drop of blood that dripped from her arm to the ground was like a torch in the darkness she'd summoned, urging her to keep moving into that darkness—

"Casia!" It was Elander's voice, somehow rising above the roaring in her ears.

She ignored it.

"STOP!"

She didn't *stop* so much as stumble as someone grabbed her and she tried—unsuccessfully—to rip free of them. She ended up hanging awkwardly in the air, her feet just barely skimming the ground.

Elander had an arm hooked around her waist, she realized.

"*Stop,*" he repeated.

She stopped.

The space lightened.

Allies and foes alike were strewn across the ground around her. Her blood curdled. Had she...?

Elander let her go, and she landed in a crouch, hissing at the pain that shot through her injured arm as she put weight on it. She rose carefully, searching her surroundings. Her brother had escaped her reckless display of magic. He was standing perhaps thirty feet away, watching her.

She started to search the dead around her, frantically trying to see who she *had* killed, but Elander clutched her face and held it still, forcing her to look at only him. There was blood on his hand. She didn't know who it belonged to. It was warm. Fresh. His arm was shaking a bit, the divine mark on his skin pulsing and fading, pulsing and fading...

Because she had ripped more of his power away from him, hadn't she?

"I'm sorry," she whispered.

"It's fine."

"You're—"

"I'm fine." He abruptly let go of her and threw her behind him, stepping to meet a blade as it swung toward them. He engaged in a brief battle with the woman holding that blade, ended her with a jab to the stomach, and then ripped his bloodied sword free and turned back to Cas and demanded, "What happened in Dawnskeep?"

The empty, stone-eyed gaze of Solatis flashed

through her mind, and the weight of all of her failures made Cas want to drop back to the ground.

Nothing about this was *fine*.

She swallowed hard. "I don't think the goddess is coming to save us."

He stared at her, his eyes full of more emotion than she'd ever seen in them. Mostly fear. For her, for them, for their world—for all these things they couldn't fix.

Another of their enemies descended, and Elander seemed to channel all of that fear into the swing of his sword. It was a brutally powerful swipe, enough to lift the enemy solider off his feet when their blades collided. The soldier never regained his footing. Elander brought his sword down upon his neck as he tried to, and the soldier fell to the ground, choking in a mouthful of his own blood.

She and Elander worked back-to-back after that, striking down attacker after attacker.

She fought because it was what she had always done.

But she no longer knew who, or what, she should be striking toward. What end she was fighting for.

And what did it matter, now?

Minutes later, she put her blade through yet another stomach—she'd lost count of what number this one was —and then the seemingly endless stream of enemies ceased long enough for her to catch her breath.

"There are too many," she whispered. She had

miscalculated. She had been so *certain* she had a chance of waking the goddess. Certain they had enough help to hold the shore while she figured things out... That was such a short time ago; how had it gone so wrong, so quickly? "This was a mistake. We should never have come here."

Elander didn't reply. His gaze was on the distant trees, from which more riders were emerging.

More reinforcements?

She took a few steps toward them with trancelike steps. They should have given her hope, maybe. But the sight only filled her with dread. Because with them came more collisions, more blood, more threads of life snapping. She hadn't been prepared for how overwhelming it would be, being able to feel those cold threads fraying all around her. How did Elander do it? How had he escaped this overwhelming cold, this darkness...this *hopelessness*?

So much death.

She was so, so tired of it.

"Look out!"

She twisted around. Brought her sword up without a second thought. Another strike, another parry, another kill. Still fighting, because it was reflex, because she had no choice but to keep fighting now.

But as her sword felled another target, she caught a glimpse of an archer taking aim at her.

Too late.

An arrow struck her arm, digging in at almost the same spot Varen's blade had cut through. She let her sword fall. She couldn't swing it anymore. She grabbed her arm and hugged it against her stomach, her fingers scraping over the arrowhead lodged into her skin, trying to assess the deepness, the damage.

She stumbled from the pain, nearly tripping over a dead body as she went, and her gaze briefly met Elander's. His eyes jumped to that arrow in her arm, and he yelled something—she didn't know what.

Everything had turned strangely quiet.

Strangely slow.

He was fighting his way toward her, but there were too many bodies between them, suddenly. And he was distracted, drained of his magic, looking only at her— he didn't see the enemy who had closed in on them once more.

Varen.

Another soldier darted into his path, and Elander handled him easily. But as his sword plunged into this second man's side, Varen's sword was just as swiftly rising behind him.

And then her brother's sword was falling, sinking in deep between Elander's shoulder blades.

CHAPTER 36

CAS'S HEART POUNDED IN HER EARS.

Then it stopped—she *swore* it had stopped—along with her breathing and everything else.

The strange silence was shattered by a scream. Cas didn't realize it was her own at first, not until a sharp pain in her throat strangled her back into silence.

Oh gods, the *silence*.

It felt like it would never end. And everything that happened next happened within that quiet, and it seemed to happen all at once—

She ran for Elander's side. The sky darkened, and that darkness fell around her, gathering so violently, so quickly, that she couldn't see through it. She just kept running, blindly. Cold sank into her. It was the most violent show of Death magic she'd ever felt, and she didn't know who that magic was coming from—

whether from herself, or Elander, or both of them—but Varen's body convulsed as he was overtaken by it, and then he was on the ground several feet away from Elander, not moving.

Neither of them moved.

Why hadn't Elander moved?

The darkness persisted. People had scattered in all directions. No one dared to approach Cas, which left her free to fall at Elander's side, to lift his head into her lap without interruption.

He wasn't breathing.

A realization that was made all the more horrifying because she didn't know what had finally *ended* that breath. The sword had struck deep, but that magic that had blackened the sky in response...

Had she done this?

"Talk to me," she begged.

No reply.

"*Look at me.*"

He didn't open his eyes.

"What are you doing?" she whispered. It was a strange question, the wrong question, but it was all she could think to say, and so she just kept repeating it, over and over and over. "*What are you doing?* You can't do this. We said side-by-side. *Side-by-side.* I can't—"

She choked.

She didn't know what to do.

What to say.

How to breathe.

How to move.

The world was still moving, churning around her. She held him more tightly, the way she always did when her world began to spin, but this time it didn't make that spinning stop.

"Nowhere you can go." Her words were growing more desperate, more rasped, more slurred—though in her head she could hear them perfectly in his voice. "There's nowhere you can go...nowhere... *You can't go*."

He was already gone.

She knew it, because they shared the same magic, and so she could feel the last of that energy leaving him, the last of his power seeping into her instead. She desperately wanted to reject it. To give it back.

Would that have stopped this?

She would have given it all back, and then some. He could go back to being a god, he could ascend, he could leave her behind, so long as he didn't leave *everything* behind.

"Not like this," she said, her voice breaking.

But it was already happening. The mark on his wrist was fading away. And the place where the Dark God had struck her was burning. *She* was burning. All of her was twisting, writhing within some sort of divine, invisible fire, and something new and terrifying was being forged within that inferno.

She curled into herself, and she sat within the flames

for what felt like hours until, finally, the burning stopped.

She lifted her head.

Her eyes fixed on the spot where her brother had been. He was gone. She didn't have to look far to find him—one of his soldiers was carrying him away from her. She didn't know if he was alive or dead. She couldn't focus well enough to pick apart the different strands of energy, the different life-forces around her. There was too much death to sort through.

So much death.

She stood slowly, flexing her blood-coated fingers.

The sky was suddenly, completely black once more.

She took a few steps in the direction her brother had been carried in. She could almost hear Elander's voice in her head, telling her to stop.

But he was not there to pull her back this time. There would be no pulling her back. She would rise up, fully grasp that power that had shifted from his body to hers, and now she would finally have the sort of magic that could keep her from hurting like this, ever again.

Almost as soon as she thought this, she heard a shrill sound, echoing high above her—the call of a rook bird.

The upper-god himself, come to claim her completely this time?

Good, she thought. *Let's be done with it.*

But when she lifted her gaze to search the skies for that god, it caught instead on the distant shoreline—on a show of fire flaring amongst the battle taking place there. Still divine in origin, she believed, but different from the flames that had been burning so fiercely through herself.

She couldn't see clearly enough to know where that fire was coming from.

But she thought of Zev, and of Rhea wielding her staff, and of *all* of her friends, somewhere off in the distance. Still fighting. Still trying to make it to the other side of this, just as they always did.

She heard another cry above her, but she didn't look up this time.

Because she could have killed every single person between here and that shoreline, she knew. The dark magic inside of her was eager to do it. But she wasn't sure she could keep herself from accidentally killing her friends. And either way, it would not bring Elander back. Death magic could not give life. It could not bring *anybody* back.

So she stopped searching the skies, and she turned and stumbled once more to Elander's side, and she fell to her knees beside him.

Another plea shuddered out of her. "Live. Please, please *live.*"

It occurred to her then that they hadn't even had a chance to say goodbye. To say *anything* at the end. He'd been gone before she could reach him.

She collapsed the rest of the way to the ground,

curled up beside him, took his cold, bloodstained hand in hers. "I don't want this Death magic. I don't want *any* magic. I just want you to stay. I just want you to live."

The sky above them was still dark.

But as that plea played over and over in her mind— *live, live, live*—something in the pocket of her coat began to radiate warmth. She reached into it and withdrew the Heart of the Sun. Cracks had formed across its face.

"Broken," she muttered.

Just like everything else.

But as she stared at it, she thought she saw light seeping out of the cracks. She held it more tightly, desperate for more of the warmth it was giving off.

Then its face shattered completely, and suddenly she was drowning in brilliant, blinding light.

CHAPTER 37

As the waves of light overtook her, Cas closed her eyes.

She had a vision.

A perfectly clear vision of a woman waking up. Of a face lifting to the sky. An unfurling of wings. A body twisting, rising up as chains fell away from it.

Her eyes blinked open. She was still in the middle of the battlefield she thought she'd left behind. But now it was bathed in bright white light, and nobody seemed to be moving except for her.

Trying in vain to shield her eyes from the brightness, Cas rose to her feet and started to walk.

She didn't know where she was going. And it was disorienting to be the only thing moving. She kept thinking she heard footsteps, heartbeats, gentle breaths...but no. Everything had stopped.

She was dead, she was almost certain of it.

She had often wondered how souls navigated to their respective afterlives without the God of Death to aid them, and now she knew—a bright path, endless and quiet, and she had to walk it alone.

Alone.

Not side-by-side, as they'd promised.

She walked that bright path for so long that she began to forget about the hurt, the blood, the darkness of that battlefield she'd left behind. She was still walking through that field, but everything was hazy, and the bodies—the ones frozen in both life and death poses —were growing more scattered.

She spotted movement just ahead of her.

She should have been wary, but she didn't have the strength left to be anything. She didn't have enough energy to make herself turn around, even; it was easier to just continue walking. So that was what she did. She saw a grey, spindly tree on a hilltop, and she kept moving until she reached it.

A woman was standing beneath this tree—the same one Cas had seen in her vision.

Solatis.

She seemed strangely human, dressed in simple, gold-accented armor, and without the wings that had accompanied her in that vision. Her dark skin shimmered as if she was standing in a patch of sunlight— except the haze of this place was blocking the true sun, as far as Cas could tell. Her hair seemed cast in that same unexplainable glow. It fell in thick waves, nearly down to her waist. Her golden eyes were kind as she watched Cas approaching her. She didn't speak. But she did breathe a small sigh, as though she had been waiting for a very long time—like a worried mother who had been hoping against hope that her runaway child might still come home.

There were a hundred different things Cas wanted to ask this goddess, but only one question made it out of her mouth. "Am I dead?"

The question seemed to amuse the goddess. "No. Not quite."

Cas looked back toward the battlefield. "Then why has everything stopped?"

"It hasn't for them."

Cas felt a spark of true emotion for the first time since entering this warm, foggy place. "If my friends are still fighting, then I...I need to go back to them."

"Soon," the goddess told her.

Soon.

"Why didn't *you* come sooner?" Cas demanded.

"I couldn't."

She wasn't satisfied by this answer, and her anger must have been obvious, because the goddess shook her head. "It will all make sense before the end." Then she turned and started to walk away.

Cas followed, her anger still building, and all of her many questions fighting for precedence in her tired mind, until she finally settled on one: "Could you not have sent more help?"

The goddess didn't reply.

"I *begged* you. I know you must have heard me. You must have seen what I was going through."

"I've seen many wars. And I've sent what help— what warriors—I could over time."

Cas pictured those stone sentinels that had surrounded Dawnskeep. "Warriors like the Vitala, for example?"

She nodded.

Cas clenched her fists. "Yes, but we need help *now*. Something else, something stronger— those warriors all perished a long time ago."

"All, save for one."

"Save for one?"

"You knew him quite intimately."

"I..." Cas froze. Her scalp tingled as a realization slowly settled over her. It seemed impossible, and yet...

She didn't have to speak her thoughts; the goddess clearly already knew them, judging by the slightly sad smile spreading across her face. "He was the God of Death when you met him," she said, "but he was a warrior of mine long before that."

Cas tried to think, to sort through the memories that were suddenly all rushing into her mind at once.

The first time her magic had manifested—when she had protected her brother as a child—Elander had been there. Months ago, when her magic had roared to life for the first time in forever—Elander had been there. And, even more recently, he'd managed to use the waning power in the Heart of the Sun to drive away the Dark God in Oblivion...

He had been the God of Death, and yet, now that she thought about it, his connection to the Sun was glaringly obvious.

"Malaphar and I have been playing a deadly game for a very long time now," said the goddess. "And I'm afraid I'm running out of ideas. Out of power. Out of warriors to send."

Cas could not stop thinking about those warriors. "So Elander..."

"Malaphar destroyed the others, as you said. Elander alone survived. And what the Dark God could not destroy... he eventually managed to corrupt. He offered Elander a place at his side as his servant—a power beyond what I could give him. And Elander took it. I could do nothing after that ascension. And within the cage of that new power, he forgot me. He forgot *himself*. Until..."

She trailed off, and she was quiet for a long time.

Cas finally glanced over at her, and she realized that the goddess was staring at the broken Heart in her hands. "He stole this from you, right?"

Her smile was slight. "He *thinks* he stole it. But it was freely given. I knew he was coming. I knew what he sought. I knew who had sent him, and for what purpose. And the Dark God had a very tight grip on him, but in that moment, I also saw a chance to sever that hold. *You.* Because I expected he would give that stolen piece to you rather than that god he served—and I was right."

Cas ran her thumb along the cracks in the Heart, feeling lightheaded.

"And just so you know," continued the goddess, "he was the one that brought you back into this world, not I. Though he never realized it, he used the power I'd given him—one that was locked in that Heart, and that had been lost to him for a very long time. His desire to save you is what unlocked it, I believe, and that is what set the two of you on the winding path you've taken to... well, *here.*"

A path that ultimately ended in his destruction.

And now she couldn't save him, it seemed.

"So, I was just a human..."

"Yes."

"Who happened to fall in love with him."

"Not happenstance. *Choice.* That is the important thing. And the choice to love—to hope—in spite of the chaos and the darkness is no small thing."

Cas shook her head, still unwilling to believe that there wasn't more to it than that. She *needed* there to be more. In the legends she'd heard throughout her life, people always spoke of the Chosen Ones. Great heroes and heroines destined from birth to do great things.

But now it seemed that she was nobody special really.

She was not a Chosen One.

She was just a person who had made choices. Some of them terrible. Some of them good. Some that seemed small and insignificant at the time. So many that *anybody* could have made.

So where did that leave her now?

Useless and without any real power to fix things.

"And, just as importantly," the goddess continued, "the one you chose...chose you back. He chose you over the darkness, and my fellow upper-god *still* has not figured out why. It baffles him—that one he'd given so much power to could so recklessly deny him. But power isn't everything."

"I wanted to choose darkness," Cas said. "I wanted that same power." She hesitated. But something about the knowing light in the goddess's eyes made her feel as though she couldn't get away with anything other than the truth, so she said, "I *still* want it, because I hate how useless I feel right now."

"Yes. But you won't give in to that desire."

"How can you be sure?"

She studied Cas for a long moment. And then she reached out a hand and brushed it across her cheek. Warmth blossomed at the touch.

"This mark would have caused most to ascend into his control a long time ago," the goddess told her. "His magic is stronger than mine, and yet, you held on to what light you'd been given. It was enough to keep the darkness at bay."

"It doesn't matter if *I* held on or not," Cas argued, weakly. "I've accomplished *nothing*. Everything in our world is still broken. Or breaking."

Including me.

Though she didn't say this last part out loud, the goddess answered her as though she had. "There is nothing so very wrong with breaking, so long as you put yourself back together in a better way." She took the Heart from Cas's hands, ran her fingers over it, and Cas watched as those cracks filled with golden currents of magic. "And either way," she added, "broken souls can still be bright lights."

Cas stared at the light in between those fissures, unable to come up with a response.

"Also? You have not fully ascended, so I believe I can give you *something* that you seek at least." She reached again for that mark, and Cas braced herself for something similar to that burning she'd felt on the battlefield earlier.

And it *was* hot, but it was also quick—a cleansing rain of fire rather than a punishing inferno—and then it felt as though a literal weight had been pulled from her body...because it *had*.

She watched as that weight drifted into the air

between them, a tangle of shadows that the Sun Goddess held afloat without any obvious effort.

She should have been relieved. But all Cas could think about was what happened next. She gingerly touched her cheek and asked, "It's fully withdrawn?"

"Yes."

The goddess had made removing it look so easy—which only made Cas angry again. Because it was over and done, just like that, but it all felt too late. "It's gone, but Elander is still..."

"Yes. That. It had to happen, I'm afraid." Solatis frowned. "Death was the only way he could be free of that servitude he agreed to—everything else was only a temporary solution. His death also released the extra power I gave to protect him after that *thieving* incident all those years ago. Power that I needed so that I could break free and come to you like this—another necessary thing."

Cas stared at that tumbling ball of shadows, still desperately hoping there was something the goddess could do. Something she wasn't telling her. "Can't that divine energy be given back to him somehow?"

Solatis shook her head.

"But without it, he's..."

The goddess inhaled slowly, as if bracing herself. It seemed like a very odd—very human—gesture from this being as old as the world itself. "The God of Death is gone. Truly fallen this time. A new one will rise soon. My counterpart already has another vessel chosen, I suspect. Deep down I'm sure he already knew he couldn't take you, so he will have made a second plan. But he does love his twisted games and prolonged suffering."

"And you honestly can't fight him anymore?"

"I'll do what I can. But he is far more powerful than I am, now—he has already slain the third of our order, and that being was even stronger than I."

Cas did not think she had the energy left to be surprised or alarmed by anything else, but this made every nerve in her body flare back to life. "The third upper-god, you mean?"

"Yes. For ages, we kept the Dark God in control, Belegor and I. But now the Stone God is gone, and what remains of my own power is not enough to do the job alone."

"Most humans believe that third god simply...left us."

She shook her head. "He didn't leave. He was slain, and Malaphar continues to try and do the same to me. He hasn't managed it, obviously. Not yet. Perhaps because of the very thing we've already discussed—as long as my light, my power, is scattered and given to others, he will have a difficult time extinguishing it completely. It is both my weakness and my strength... such is the nature of these things."

"Is there any hope of stopping him?" There were still

a hundred other questions she'd wanted to ask, but suddenly this felt like the only one that mattered.

The goddess took a long time answering it.

"I won't lie to you," she finally said. "It would take an alliance of divine beings and mortals unlike anything the realms have ever known, along with several other equally improbable things. And even then, it might not be enough. This might be the way your world ends. Yours and others—I don't honestly know the extent of what he has planned."

Cas clutched a hand over her face and bowed her head.

And of all the things she could have done in that moment, she almost... laughed.

Because it was too much. It was too hard, too impossible, too unfair, after everything she had already been through. *Choice*, the goddess had said. *That is the important thing*.

What were the chances that her choices would bring her to a place such as this? It was such terrible luck that she almost *had* to laugh, or else she was going to start weeping.

But she didn't laugh.

More surprisingly, she didn't weep, either.

The seconds ticked by, and she simply stood among the waves of fear and uncertainty, just as she'd always managed to, one way or another.

And then it came to her—she knew what she had to say. "It can't end this way."

When she looked up a moment later, the goddess was smiling at her. "I agree."

Cas took a deep breath. "What can I do?"

"Shadows are falling," said Solatis, "and it is too late to stop them from coming now. But perhaps you can still drive them out."

She turned to where that ball of darkness she'd extracted was tumbling. She closed her eyes. It took no more movement than this to fill the space around them with the same blinding light that had heralded Cas's arrival to this place.

The sphere of shadows pulled that light in, and the two energies fought wildly for a moment, twisting together and pulling back apart, over and over, until Cas thought she saw something taking shape in the center of them.

The goddess reached into that churning mass of magic and pulled out a sword.

It was one of the most beautiful weapons Cas had ever seen. Its hilt was white and gold, its blade etched with the main symbols of the Sun Court. There was a circular opening in the pommel, and Cas watched as Solatis took the Heart that she'd repaired and placed it inside that opening. With a quick wave of her hand, a few more golden threads of her magic appeared and sealed the empty spaces, and the two weapons became one singular piece. She reached back into the mass of feuding energies and pulled out a scabbard—equally beautiful, white and polished and etched with golden symbols that matched the ones on the sword itself. She offered them both to Cas.

"Shadowslayer," the goddess told her as she took them.

The sword was impossibly light, and the instant Cas's hand wrapped around its grip, the symbols etched upon the blade began to glow with a faint white light.

"Hold tightly to it," the goddess commanded, "because it's time to go back."

CHAPTER 38

As she pulled the sword in close, light flooded over her once more, and Cas returned to a blood-soaked battlefield and a chorus of screams—mere feet away from where she'd left it all.

Elander's body was gone.

Most of her army was gone, it seemed, and the ones that remained were *trying* to flee. She spotted Laurent in the distance, shouting and trying to organize a chaotic retreat. Nessa was beside him, and she appeared to be using her magic to try and calm horses and people alike.

She searched and searched for Zev, for Rhea, for General Kolvar, for other faces she might recognize, other things to pull her back and keep her legs from buckling underneath her—but she didn't find them.

Soldiers on both sides rushed past her as though

they couldn't see her. Several even ran *into* her, but they didn't seem to feel it, and neither did she. So she walked back over the battlefield with relatively calm steps, a ghost among the dead and the dying, trying to figure out a way to keep living.

As she walked, she kept searching for her allies.

Her search ended on the same hill she'd stood upon with Elander earlier. The memory of his voice, of his promise of *side-by-side*, echoed painfully through her thoughts. She wanted to look away from that spot where he'd made that promise. But she couldn't.

Because up on that hill, a dark cloud was billowing.

Her brother was crouched in the center of it, and a black bird soared around his bowed head.

The air was chokingly thick with power. It was so cold she almost couldn't breathe. That shadowy cloud soon engulfed her brother entirely, and the frigid, unstable power in the air grew more and more unbearable as the seconds passed. She realized what was happening, but it was too late to stop the shadows from coming, just as Solatis had said it would be.

But perhaps you can still drive them out.

Those shadows were growing to an unimaginable size. And then they began to shift and take on a more terrifying shape. Like Elander used to shift into that wolf that had once haunted her dreams—except it was not a wolf now, but a tiger-like beast with glowing blue eyes.

She watched, horrified, as this new beast took its

first steps. As it opened its mouth and a dark wind roared out, flattening small trees and leaching the life and color from every blade of grass on the hillside.

That initial wave knocked her to the ground, along with everyone around her.

Another roar of wind, stronger than the first, followed immediately after.

She scrambled for a nearby tree and dove behind it. The second wind wrapped around the trunk and turned it to an ashen shade, peeling the bark as it went. That trunk took the brunt of the attack, but some of the wind still wrapped around and brushed over Cas's skin. Her body shivered with the familiar, empty cold of it. Her muscles tingled as the magic drained them, and she slumped down against the dying tree, gritting her teeth against the pain.

The wind finally settled, and she glanced at the people around her who had tried to dodge that dark breeze with varying levels of success. The magic had left behind countless shocked faces and dead bodies the same shade as the dying tree creaking behind her.

Screams and cries for mercy filled the air.

Between the building chaos and the grey haze that was settling over them, she could no longer tell who was a friend and who was a foe. She doubted her brother could either—she also doubted that he cared.

They were all going to die here if she didn't do something.

The scabbard and sword that Solatis had given her were resting on the ground a few feet away, dropped there when she'd been knocked off her feet. The blade's symbols were unlit, and the whole thing suddenly seemed much less impressive in the bleakness of this real, war-torn world.

Cas stared at it, her lungs heaving for breath. It was so quiet within the fog of the Death God's magic that each of those sharp breaths seemed to echo.

She crawled to the sword.

Picked it up.

Got to her feet.

Everyone else who had managed to stand was running the other way. She was a laughable sight—a lone figure walking toward a raging god. Toward disaster. And it felt as if she had nothing left to give, like suffering one more tragedy might erase her from the world entirely.

She walked forward anyway.

Through swirling magic and dust. Through the pain stabbing and burning through her muscles. In spite of the tears that blurred her eyes and the sorrow that clenched her heart into a fist so tight it made it feel like it had stopped beating. Every pained step brought back every doubt she'd had on this journey thus far. Every loss, every mistake, every question that had been asked by ally and enemy alike.

Why?

Why do you keep fighting?

What hope could you honestly be carrying with you?

She had no hope left, really.

But she had a sword, and so she held tightly to that, just as the goddess had commanded her to do.

The Death beast had opened its jaws, preparing another of those roaring winds, she suspected. But it paused as she approached. It lowered its head, its blue eyes staring directly at her. Her brother was in there, somewhere—and she briefly wondered if he could recognize her anymore, from this close up. If he would ever recognize her again.

His mouth opened.

She gripped the handle of her sword more tightly.

The symbols on the blade ignited.

She swept up as the god bit down, and light swept up with her swing, filling that shadowy mouth just before it closed over her. The beast staggered back, and its jaws snapped shut, extinguishing the light she'd summoned.

Again, came a soft voice in her mind.

She swung again.

Again, again, again, until the air between them was full of too much bright, blinding magic for even the God of Death to extinguish it completely.

And swing by swing, she managed to push the beast back.

But to where?

Her arms already ached. The sword seemed to be pulling its light directly from her—from some deep reserve of power she had only just uncovered—and she could feel that power fading a little more with every swing.

One last time, she told herself, over and over again. *One last time, and maybe that will be enough.*

She lost track of how many *last times* she went through.

Then she stumbled.

Her body simply...gave up. Her muscles seized. Remnants of her summoned light floated around her, just barely penetrating the fog left behind by the Death beast's magic, lighting it up just enough that she could see that shadowy beast within it, stalking back toward her.

She tried to raise her sword. But there was more magic leaking from the god's bared teeth, and it was drifting over her, numbing her. She was fading into a cold, dark place that she didn't want to return from. Her grip on her sword slipped, and a thought wound tightly around her mind.

This is how I'm going to die.

She was certain of it.

Until a sudden warmth overtook her.

An arm wrapped around her waist. A hand closed around her grip on her sword, steadying her, anchoring her as what felt like the final wisps of her magic, of her strength, tried to slip away.

And a voice whispered, not in her mind, but directly into her ear, pulling her back to the moment. "Stay with me, Thorn."

Her body still wanted to collapse, but she couldn't—Elander's hold on her was too strong.

And with him by her side, she managed to finish lifting her sword.

One last time.

She swung into the shadows, and she wasn't certain *what* Elander did in the next instant—but the combined force of their attack was so bright that she had to close her eyes for several moments afterwards.

Her ears were ringing. Her body humming. Muscles twitching, threatening to collapse once more under the impossible powers all around her. But she could still sense the moment the Death God's energy started to flicker away.

A minute later, he was gone.

For the moment, at least.

She stumbled back. Started to fall. Stopped, and felt herself being lifted, instead, and then cradled against Elander's chest and carried away from all of that impossible, exhausting power.

She looked up.

The last thing she saw before she closed her eyes was

his face, peering down at her, and she would have sworn there were wings flaring out behind him—but not the black, clawed appendages of that upper-god he had once served. These were golden and brilliant and bright.

Like the sun.

CHAPTER 39

CAS SLEPT FOR ALMOST THREE DAYS.

She drifted occasionally into awareness whenever she heard the door to her room open, whenever she sensed someone moving through it. But she didn't recognize faces. She didn't understand voices. She didn't *want* to recognize or understand these things.

She just wanted to keep going back to sleep.

By the end of that third day, she was marginally better, and the faces that checked in on her started to take on meaning in the haze of her battered mind.

One by one, they came back to her—Zev, Laurent, Nessa, Rhea. It still felt like a dream every time she saw them. Not nightmares for once, but actual dreams that she wanted to stay in.

It was cold when she finally woke up and *stayed*

awake. She was in her tower room at Stonebarrow, she realized, and the fire in it had nearly gone out.

She moved numbly to the stack of wood on the hearth, and she tossed a piece into the fire. She was stoking that fire to life when there came a soft knock, and she hoarsely called for whoever it was to come in.

The door opened, and Elander stepped inside.

He looked precisely like he always had. No wings, no armor—no other signs of his ancient warrior status. There was a new glow about his skin, perhaps; like that sun-touched warmth that had surrounded Solatis. But otherwise, he was just...him.

And yet she felt like she was seeing him for the very first time—and just as it had that very first time, her heart skipped several beats as their eyes met.

He threw a quick glance toward the fire; he'd been coming to check on it, she suspected. Seeing the job already done, he came over and sat down on her bed. He took her hand. His thumb traced over her knuckles. He started to speak several times, only to stop and settle for simply staring at her instead.

She was too overwhelmed to speak, too, so they just sat there and held on to each other for several minutes, until she finally found her voice. "You carried me away from Varen."

"Yes."

"I thought I'd imagined you."

He shook his head, a trace of a smile on his lips. "Turns out I'm still not quite finished with you yet."

Cas sucked in a deep breath, trying to focus on his smile. Here. He was here. He was okay. *They* were okay. "You're one of the Vitala."

His brow furrowed, and he was silent for a long moment before he said, "I have a lot of things to figure out, but...yes."

She nodded. She tried not to be terrified of what else they had to figure out, of what other strange things they could possibly uncover. And she tried not to think about all that had already happened, and all that she might *never* understand or make peace with.

She'd seen him die.

Now he was back.

But if these past months had taught her anything, it was that such things did not come without consequences.

Still, the fact that he was *here*... That was all that mattered now. Because it meant they could keep trying to make sense of it all together.

And they had a lot of things to make sense of, so she didn't waste any more time in bed. With a bit of help, she managed to dress, to clean herself up, and then to walk outside.

All of her friends were waiting around a campfire in the tower yard—seemingly for her, though none of them outright said it.

Her restlessness had not settled, so she walked deeper into the camp. They all followed, filling her in on what she'd missed while she was asleep.

The fortress of Stonebarrow was as intact as before, but eerily empty.

General Kolvar had taken a group and headed east, off on a mission to speak with some old acquaintances in Mistwilde.

Caden was missing, and his absence filled Cas's mind with still more questions: What became of a middle-god's servants once that god had fallen? Were Caden and Tara simply gone, now? Or something worse?

As for everyone else...some had gone back to their home cities, to their usual posts. Some were lost. Some were retiring to their bedrolls as the sun sank below the horizon. It felt very strange to move through it all in the wake of what had happened. It was so *quiet*. If no one had told Cas about the number they'd lost, she could have gone on believing that most of her camp was still here, and that they were simply asleep.

That they would all wake up tomorrow, and carry on as usual, as if nothing had changed.

But she knew that *everything* had changed, and her heart ached when she started to think about what those changes might mean.

"So," Rhea began, as if reading her thoughts, "Varen is the new God of Death."

"Wonder if that will cause any problems for us?"

said Zev—and though Cas could tell he'd been trying to make a joke, for once his tone was entirely serious. Afraid, even.

That same gravely serious feeling was evident on the face of each of her friends.

"He wanted to eradicate divine magic at the start of all this, and now he is the very *embodiment* of divine magic," said Nessa. "I don't get it."

Cas thought of the last real conversation she'd had with him—that day in Kosrith. Of how he'd spoken of his childhood, and the ones who had constantly tried to take his crown. Of the spark of desperation she'd seen, however briefly, in his eyes. And the cold resolve in his voice...

"He craves power above all else," she said quietly. She had told them this before. She hadn't really *believed* in it quite as much then as she did now.

And she never would have guessed that his craving would lead to *this*.

"He and the Dark God have that in common," Elander added. "I wouldn't be surprised to learn that said god paid him a visit over these past weeks. Maybe it was no coincidence that we all ended up on these northern shores together."

Perhaps it was the conversation she'd had with Solatis, but nothing felt like a coincidence to Cas anymore.

"So, what now?" Laurent wondered.

The group of them fell into a tense discussion about the matter. Cas watched them silently for a few minutes, playing through that conversation with the Sun Goddess in her mind.

There was one part that kept repeating itself, over and over—

Choice. That is the important thing.

She was not here by chance, but by choice.

And now she would make another one.

"We'll ride for Ciridan," she said, drawing the hum of anxious conversation around her to a stop.

"Ciridan?"

"We are going to need to work harder to form an alliance of our mortal kingdoms—and that will be easier to do from a throne. Varen's throne just happens to be vacated now. So I'll start there. The people under his rule will be looking for someone to follow." She lifted her eyes to the distant cliffs, to that last sliver of sunlight slipping behind them. "They will follow me."

A small crowd had drifted toward them, eager to be part of the discussion. They watched and listened to Cas's declarations with a mixture of interest and doubt.

In the past, she might have withered under those doubtful looks.

But now, as she stood in the quiet wreckage of her latest battles, she was steeled by a sudden, fierce thought. It didn't matter how she had arrived here. It didn't matter what had already happened, either. All that mattered was what she *chose* to become from it.

And she was about to become a Queen.

AFTERWORD

Thank you for reading! If you enjoyed this book, please consider taking a moment to leave a review to help other readers find and enjoy it :) After you've done that, I hope you'll grab book four in the series, *A Crown of the Gods*!

Also, if you want to connect further, see behind-the-scenes stuff, get the first look at covers, teasers, character art etc... or just come yell at me for my cliffhanger endings, then you can do all that in my V.I.P. Reader's Group on Facebook!

S. M. Gaither is the author of multiple bestselling romantic epic fantasy books. And while she's happiest writing stories filled with magic and spice, she's also done everything from working on a chicken farm to running a small business, with a lot of really odd jobs in between. She currently makes her home in the beautiful foothills of North Carolina with her husband, their daughter and one very spoiled dog. You can visit her online at www.smgaitherbooks.com